Imperial Legionary

Decline and Fall of the
Galactic Empire

Book 7

Andrew Moriarty

Copyright © 2025 Andrew Moriarty
All rights reserved.
Version 1.00

ISBN: 978-1-956556-28-5

This is a work of fiction.

Names, characters, businesses, places, events and incidents are either the products of the author's imagination or used in a fictitious manner. Any resemblance to actual persons, living or dead, or actual events is purely coincidental.

Special thanks to my dedicated team of beta readers – A J, Adam G, Aleeta, Alex, Barbara M, Bryan, Christopher G, Daniel C, Danny H, Dave M#1, Dave W, David H, David M#2, Djuro D, Elizabeth S, Greg D, Haydn H, James A, Jim C, John E, John S, Jolayne W, Justin H, Keith C, Kent P, Lorna R, Mark H, Michael G, Michael R, Nathan T, Penny L, Peter B, Ralph J, Ryan P, Scott, Skip C, Susan G, Tigui, Vince, and to my editor Beth Lynne.

Chapter 1

"Just once, I'd like to land without puking." Dena held the bag in her hand as the Heart's Desire rocked sideways. "Do you know how many pairs of pants I've ruined?"

"Aim better." Ana gripped the wall beam in the lounge, and cycled through the planetary display. "And practice."

"How do I practice puking?"

"Drink a lot of water and I'll punch you in the stomach."

"Is there any problem that you don't immediately try to solve with violence?"

"Not that I can think of, no." Ana twisted a knob to focus the telescope on the landing complex below. Their converted freighter, *Heart's Desire,* was making a low altitude pass over planet Kraz-1D's starport, checking for Naval or Militia units, and any defenses they could see. Tribune Devin, or the Rebel Tribune, as he was now called, had diverted the *Heart's Desire* on a scouting run to the Imperial Fleet Base at New Malaya in the Sarawak Sector. Dirk, Ana, and crew were to spy out intervening systems for Imperial presence.

Dena vomited into the bag. The acid smell mixed with the week's worth of ships smells—ammonia from the recycling system and ozone from the water crackers. "How am I supposed to update the landing checklist if I'm puking?"

"We'll land whether Pilot follows the checklist or not. Only question is what sort of shape we'll be in if we miss something off the checklist. Fancy getting smashed to bits because our punk engineer forgot to lower the landing legs?"

Dena cursed the centurion, the *Heart's Desire*, and the universe, then brought the landing

Imperial Legionary

checklist up on her comm, and called the engineer.

Ana tapped his own comm unit. "Scruggs, have you been scanning for radio sources?"

Scruggs replied from the control room. "Yes, Centurion. I'm scanning for radio sources. And infrared. And beacons. And visual anomalies. And running it through the database. And I'm recording everything as well. Plus, I'm reviewing the footage in real time, and I'm forwarding anything I find unusual to the crew for review."

She's catching on. But she still needs more responsibility. "What are the rules for who gets what?"

"Gavin gets anything that looks industrial because he's an engineer. Pilot Dirk gets anything Imperial or starship related, Dena gets animals or trees. You get anything that looks like ground forces or army. Lee gets a copy of it all. Stand by."

Dena turned from her screen and spat in her bag. "Nothing to complain about there, is there. Very on top of her job, Baby Marine is. I'm really looking forward to the day that the newly promoted Imperial Lieutenant Scruggs starts giving her grumpy old former trainer orders."

Ana ignored her. "Lee doesn't need to be bothered with everything. Why give her extra data?"

"Because she's so smart," Dena said.

"Not that smart. Not smarter than me."

"Old Man," Dena said. "Trust me. People do not look at you and say 'Hmm. That guy in the armored skinsuit carrying all those weapons, he looks pretty smart. They think, hmm, that guy likes to shoot people for fun."

"Appearances can be deceiving."

"But are they?"

"No." Ana shook his head. "No, they are not. Shooting people is fun."

The *Heart's Desire* cut power, and Dena and Ana automatically grabbed handholds. Dirk, the pilot, pivoted the ship thirty degrees right, then fired the main engines. They held tight as the ship rocked.

Ana slapped the intercom. "Scruggs, ask that idiot Navy Pilot why he has to yaw like a drunken tabbo."

"I'm right here, Centurion." Dirk's voice came up on the channel. "You can insult me to my face if you want. Or my radio face. Or my voice. If you want."

"I do want. You fly like a drunken tabbo. Why now? What was wrong with our old approach?"

"Check the screen."

Ana and Dena swiveled to the screen. Scattered clouds foretold storms moving in from the west, but the screen showed a dozen streets lined with prefab metal buildings—a standard colony town—on a level plain, surrounded by farmland. A river meandered through the frame. Between the town and river, three blackened landing pads surrounded a cluster of warehouses. The main road ran through the town, between the pads, past the warehouses, and ended at a pier on the river.

"Looks like a spaceport to me, Navy." Ana zoomed in. "Three landing pads—primitive, baked dirt not concrete. Connections to land and water transport. I don't see any hangars. Just some warehouses and a walled storage yard. Wait." Ana zoomed in on the storage yard. "That's not good."

Dena craned her head to get a better view. "What's not good? What are they storing?"

"Missiles. That's not a storage yard, that's a missile battery. A full six-pack. And it's moving. It's tracking us." Ana slapped the intercom. "Contact. Pilot, sub-orbital missile battery tracking us. Abort fly-past before we come into range."

"Centurion," Lee's voice interrupted. "How

confident are you about that missile battery?"

"Confidence is high ma'am."

"Ma'am?" Dena gaped at Ana. "Are you drunk? Something's wrong. You're being respectful."

"I fall back on military courtesies when I'm stressed. Those are anti-starship missiles. Pilot, abort now. We're nearly in their range envelope. If we get closer, and they start up their tracking radar…"

BONG. BONG. BONG. The *Heart's Desire* was a freighter, not a warship. Lots of military equipment had been bolted on, including a temperamental laser. It had neither the electricity, computing power, nor sturdiness to be a real fighting ship. But it did have defensive electronics, like infrared and radio detectors, and a military-level radar detector.

Which had just alerted them that a targeting radar had locked on.

Ana and Dena slammed into their restraints. They weren't proper acceleration couches, so Ana's arm smacked onto the table. Pain flared. *Sprained my wrist. Again.*

Dena cursed but didn't let go. This wasn't the first time the crew had to flee a more powerful opponent, and she was used to hanging on as they dashed to safety.

The main drive cut out. Dirk fired the thrusters in two different combinations for three seconds. The ship corkscrewed down and left. Ana cradled his injured wrist on his lap, and Dena cursed again.

"Well, that's interesting," Ana said. "Nothing in the database about that type of weaponry being located here. They've gunned up since—Vampire! Vampire!" A light plume flashed on the display screen. "Fast mover coming at us."

"Hang on," Dirk said. The ship darted down. Ana and Dena lifted on their restraints, then slammed right. Dena dropped her bag and cursed. The bag splatted into the ceiling as Dirk threw them into a dive.

Dirk came over the speaker. "I can't climb out of this. I'm dropping. Everyone hang tight."

"Up," Ana said. "Seize the high ground."

The extra G force squashed Dirk's reply. "Can't. Dropping."

This time, Ana cursed as Dirk fired the thrusters, pivoted the ship stern first, and fired the engines to drop them lower.

Ana couldn't change the display controls with the acceleration pinning him in his seat. The town flashed by in the view, then farmland, then low hills. The ship jerked to the side, and the flare of a rocket motor appeared on the display as the missile overflew them. Dirk threw the ship into a left turn, and leveled. The vomit bag dropped from the ceiling and slapped onto the floor.

Mountains filled the display.

"We're going to crash!" Dena yelled. "Tell him to pull up."

"Nope. Missile will catch us." Ana watched the screen. "If he can get us low into that ground clutter, we're safe."

Dirk flipped the *Heart's Desire* between two hills, then into a valley. The valley ended at sheer rock face, stretching up and filling the screen.

"Don't you see that rock cliff thing, you crazy old man? He's going to kill us."

"Space is dangerous," Ana said."

"We're not in space." Dena slapped the intercom. "Pull up."

Lee came over the radio. "Not now, friend Dena. Pilot, there's the lake. We have enough space."

"Where's the missile?" Dirk said.

"Behind us."

"Dirk," Dena yelled.

"Shut up," Ana said. "Pilot has this. Any second, he'll drop us."

"Drop us into—yaaauggh."

The *Heart's Desire* flipped onto her back and fired her main engine. The ship shook violently, spattering vomit in all directions. Ana and Dena got a clear view of the pursuing missile weaving to follow. The ship dropped lower. A ridge popped up behind them. Then the main engine cut, and they floated into their restraints. The ship pitched back, righting itself. A grey-red granite cliff filled the view screen. They dropped, then bounced. The lounge cabinets flapped open. Stored food trays tumbled in all directions. Outside, superheated water flashed to steam, blocking the camera.

Dena and Ana jerked in their restraints. Then the ship shuddered and pitched almost to a stop, but continued to roll until it stopped with a bump.

Dirk's voice came over the intercom. "Turn everything off, full ecom. Gavin, cut all the power. Everyone sit tight."

The lights darkened. The fans spun down. After two seconds, the screen died. Even the emergency lights shut off. The ship was dark and dead quiet.

Dena took three deep breaths, then wiped a spot of vomit off her collar. "That was close."

Ana agreed. "Closer than I thought."

BOOM. An explosion, but far away.

"Holy crap, Old Man. That missile could have killed us."

"Would have for sure if they'd fired sooner, or fired a pair. They're programmed to work together. Avoiding one would have brought us into the other. They should have fired two."

"Why didn't they?"

"Money." Ana wiped his forehead. "You're going to clean all of this up."

"What do you mean 'money'?"

"Missiles are expensive. And hard to find. Once you fire one, it's gone. They don't want to blow us up, they want us to go away. Getting radar lock solves that problem. That was a warning."

"Some warning. Why not use the radio?"

"You can ask them, if you want," Ana said. "I'm sure they're sending a party after us."

"Party or no party, I need to get outside for a minute. I hate these landings."

"People out there are trying to kill us."

"Not close by. People have tried to kill us before and we're still here. I'm going outside to check things out," Dena said. "Anyway, they won't know where we've landed."

"Good for you, Nature Girl." Ana laughed. "Hope they don't notice the burning fireball streaking across the sky, or the jet of the main engines firing, and perhaps they won't notice the multiple sonic booms banging across the hills. That's your plan?"

"Yep." Dena unhooked her restraint belt. "Planets are big, some grumpy old guy once said to me. And you told me they don't have orbital scanners or anything fancy, just regular colony sensors. Weather and all that. So unless they've got somebody with a radio and sensor binoculars sitting in those hills watching us this second, as soon as we dropped below the horizon, we were invisible. They'll never find the ship. We can hike into town and check things out." Dena stuck her tongue out at Ana. "Bite me."

Ana glared at her. "They can put up planes. Or even spaceships like this one. You notice that we have sensors."

"The same grumpy old guy also told me sensors and planes are expensive. You think that people who have their own surface-to-space missiles won't worry that other people have them? If I was in charge down there, I'd hesitate before I sent an expensive plane or spaceship out hunting for somebody with their own weapons. Especially since I've irritated them a tiny bit." Dena held her thumb and forefinger an inch apart. "Even just a little bit by shooting an orbital missile at them. They might decide to return the favor."

Ana glared some more. "Surface-to-air."

"What?"

"Surface-to-air. Those were short-range missiles. They can't reach orbit."

"But they can still knock us down."

"Oh yes." Ana drummed his fingers on the table. "You raise an interesting point. I need to look at those pictures again." He brought the scan of the town back up and zoomed in. "Those are surface-to-air, not orbital missiles. And they're actual missiles, not counter missiles."

"So?"

"They can knock us down when we're landing. But if we made a high altitude, high speed pass, we would have laughed at them. Too high, too far. They're only good at stopping ships that are landing. We could get up high and drop rocks on them. They can't intercept the rocks. And they can't get at us in orbit. So if we were a real military ship, we could bombard the town and then take it over, nothing they could do."

"Is that bad?"

"No, but it's unusual."

The internal lights came back on, and Dirk's voice came over the intercom. "Sorry for the rough landing. Had to avoid instant death and all that."

"Nice of him to apologize this time."

"Navy is an Imperial Dork," Ana said. "But I do appreciate a pilot who maneuvers first and warns afterwards. Especially when explosions are involved."

"In other news," Dirk said over the intercom, "Lee found us this lake in some woods two days' hike from the city. We're hiding here, after we do some camouflage."

"For how long?" Ana yelled.

"That's up for discussion," Dirk said. "But I can't lift with those missiles there."

Scruggs's voice came up on the radio. "I got a good look at their launcher, Centurion. A couple grenades should take care of them. If we can get in close, we can clear the way."

"Outstanding," Ana said. "Now I have to walk for two days."

"Better than walking for three days," Dena said. "And shows what you know. Two days' hike is perfect. Not close enough that people can cut trees or hunt animals and make it back to their bed each night. This far from town, people will only go there if there's something important like a mine or a special type of hunting. Chances are nobody is out here. If we hide the ship even a little bit, they'll never find us."

"That makes sense," Ana said. "You continue to amaze me with your practical wilderness knowledge."

"A compliment. Are you sure you're not sick?"

"It's just such a contrast with your usual thoughtless man-crazy actions the rest of the time."

"And now you sound like the old you. I was worried there for a moment. Hey, Old Man?"

"What now, Nature Girl?"

"You said they didn't have space sensors and all that? To see us in orbit before we flew over them."

"Weather satellites, some commo stuff. Nothing special. Nothing that would let them know we were here."

"Would they have seen us coming down from

far away? Before they put that radar on us, I mean?"

Ana looked at Dena. "What are you asking?"

"Seems like that radar picked us up pretty quickly."

"It's automated. Computers."

"So you put a radar-equipped missile battery right next to your spaceport, and set it to automatically shoot down any ships that try to land? Doesn't that defeat the purpose of this whole space 'port' thing? You want ships to land, right?"

"Yes. Yes." Ana flipped the display back on, then overlaid their landing path. "And Navy did his usual barrel in and smack into the ground as fast as we can. They might not have had time."

"You told me that the Navy trains pilots that way. Get down fast, get down low, so that they minimize the number of chances for somebody to shoot at you, like when you're hunting Draper's raccoons and you sneak from tree to tree."

"I don't know what a Draper's raccoon is, but sure."

"Big, angry predators. A hundred kilos or more. Teeth, claws, bad attitude. They'll eat anything, and they're not afraid of humans. Only way to kill them is get in close, and do it quickly before they figure out what's going on."

"Another exciting discussion of the natural world with you. So much useful information."

Dena rolled her eyes. "If they couldn't detect us because nobody was watching the sensors, and that gun wasn't automated, how did they track us so quickly?"

Ana bit his lip, then hit the intercom button. "Scruggs?"

"I'll be back in three minutes, Centurion. I've almost got a plan for hiking into town. Can we wait to discuss it then?"

"Yes. Yes. Did anyone else scan us on the way down?"

"That missile battery—"

"Other than them? Any other radio sources?"

"Two more towns show on the maps, but both still anti-spinward of us. They wouldn't be in range yet."

"Understood. We'll talk in a minute, out."

Ana killed the connection and stared at the screen.

Dena grabbed another bag and sopped up some vomit. "What do you think, Centurion? They had somebody on watch, didn't they? Waiting for ships landing?"

"Yes." Ana nodded. "Somebody fired up that radar as soon as we got in range, and were ready to take a shot at us. It wasn't automated. There were people involved."

"Takes a lot of effort to keep trained people watching scopes on a minor colony like this."

"Especially since they'd have to be right at the battery to control it. I didn't see remote sensors or control stations."

"Wonder who they were waiting for?"

"Don't know. But somebody scary." Ana frowned. "Somebody scary enough that they pointed big missiles at them. That's who we're up against. We need to find out if they're coming back."

Chapter 2

"Two hundred meters and closing." Rudnar, the acting helmsman, said. "Two hundred—strike that. Four hundred meters and closing. Fueling party reports ready." She placed a camera shot from the fueling hatch on the main display. Four skinsuited figures held oversized wrenches and pry bars, and white lights flashed in the distance.

"Which is it, helm?" Prefect Lionel, Battleship *Canopus*'s commander, asked. "Two hundred or four hundred?"

"Now one-ninety, Prefect. It was four hundred before. What?" Rudnar tapped her screen. "It says four hundred twenty now."

"Check your numbers." Lionel brought up the nearspace display. *I put the entire bridge crew on this. Can't they even refuel a ship between them?* "It can't be both." *Canopus* and escorts were conducting deep-space operations, including formation flying and refueling. The icon for the *Canopus,* in the center of the screen, displayed vector and thrust settings. A blinking box highlighted the open fueling port on the tanker *Hydrogen Pride*, ahead of them. But the icon for the tanker flickered closer.

"It isn't. Back to one-fifty. Prefect, the range is moving back and forth."

"Alert!" Lukas, the sensor operator, said. "Proximity radar is offline. Automated pilot disengaged."

"What's the backup say, for Jove's sake."

"Backup says more than ten kilometers."

Lionel shook his head. "That can't be right."

"The sensors are offline sir."

"All stop," Lionel yelled. "Reverse thrust. Hold us steady."

"All engines stop." Rudnar hammered her

board. "Unable to hold steady. We are making way, Prefect. We're still closing at seven point two meters per second, relative to the last position of *Hydrogen Pride*."

"*Hydrogen Pride* says loss of our telemetry. They're sheering off, spinward and north."

"Pitch south and pulse the main drive, now," Lionel ordered.

Rudnar's hands were already flying. "South and main. Hold for maneuvering."

Lionel lifted in his seat as the battleship's bow thrusters pitched it down, and he continued floating as he waited for *Canopus* to come on the new heading.

"And... pulse. Now."

Nothing happened.

"Pulsing." Rudnar tapped another button. Then another.

"Helm, get us moving, we're going to—" Lionel slammed back into his seat. The main drive engaged for five seconds. Then they coasted. He floated as gravity dropped, then slammed back again, and a third time. The drive stuttered twice more, then Rudnar slapped her board, and the drive failed. "Sorry sir." She wiped sweat from her face. "Pulse command didn't work. I engaged the main drive at full for two seconds."

"Why didn't it fire?"

"Have to check the logs sir." Rudnar wiped her brow again. "Not sure what happened there."

"Me neither. Sensors?"

Lukas shook his head. "Proximity sensors still down sir. Failing self-tests. I need some engineering resources."

"Very well. Let's—"

"Tribune on the bridge!" shouted a voice from behind Lionel.

"As you were." Tribune Devin, the Lord Lyon,

Governor of the Verge sector, stormed into the bridge. His normally immaculate uniform was stained red. He returned the on-duty Marine's salute, and waved the other officers down. A third of the bridge crew were former *Pollux* crew. They didn't even look up from their screens at his arrival. The other two-thirds, the battleship's original Core-based crew, had all jumped up to attention when he arrived. "As you were. All of you. Stop this infernal nonsense. Keep your stations. Prefect."

"Tribune. How may I help you?"

Devin pointed to his chest. "Do you know what this is?"

"A full-bodied red, from the look of it. What do you think, Rudnar?"

Rudnar looked up from the helm and back at Devin. "Definitely full-bodied sir. Very dark color. Possibly a blend. What does it smell like?"

Lionel leaned over and sniffed. "Earthy. Like dirt. With notes of cherry."

"Perhaps Chateau Nettoyeur de Tapis sir? That's popular these days."

Devin furrowed his brow and sounded out the translation. "Chateau cleaner of carpets? Very funny. What's going on?"

"We're trying to fuel the ship."

"And did we succeed?"

"We did not. We had an unscheduled over-rapid aborted docking maneuver."

"What?"

"The sensors failed as the auto helm tried to bring us to zero-zero."

"Is that bad?"

"Yes. The auto helm disengaged completely, and the emergency backups, rather than canceling our current motion, just dropped off. Rudnar had to evade manually." He raised his voice. "Rudnar, well done."

"Sir." Rudnar nodded. "Helm is responding now. I can dock us manually if you want."

"We are not bringing a crippled battleship up next to a near fully loaded tanker manually. No matter how good our helmsman is." Lionel unbuckled. "Not to mention that our proximity radar is acting up. Rudnar, put us dead in space. Lukas, tell *Hydrogen Pride* to dock with us."

"Sir." Lukas turned to his board.

"Tribune, do you have another bottle of that carpet cleaner stuff?"

"Imin can find one. Why?"

"Let's have lunch. In your cabin. This is going to take some time."

Imin, Devin's steward, could of course find another bottle.

"What's the problem?" Devin straightened his new uniform and poured drinks for the three of them. "The crew?"

"Some of them." Lionel sniffed his wine. "Now when I smell this, I think of carpet cleaner. Where did Rudnar learn about wine?"

"Same place she learned Français, I suppose. The crew? Do you need more training? Or to get rid of some of them?"

"Can't. Too many should go, no replacements. We're short crew as it is."

"I shouldn't have sent the others home." After seizing the *Canopus* for the rebellion, Devin had sent those he considered unreliable away on a chartered freighter. He staffed the captured battleship with transfers from his former frigate, *Pollux*, reserve spacers who hated the current Chancellor, and all the crew he could convince that he was acting in the Emperor's name.

"If they wanted to, one well-placed saboteur could destroy the whole ship," Lionel agreed. "But they'd have to want to. And I'll tell you something about this group we have here. Excepting those who have been with us, most don't care who the emperor is. I've been talking to a lot of the officers that stayed behind. They're happy that the nobles are gone. Did you know that they beat the crew?"

"Beat them? Like in chess?"

"No, not chess. Physically hit them for not doing their duties."

"Beat them individually?" Devin's eyes widened. "Did it work?"

"Thinking of instituting that policy yourself?"

"I wouldn't mind collecting some data… no, never mind. Still, I shouldn't have emptied the crew positions like I did."

"Out of curiosity, why did you?"

"I felt that they were insufficiently committed to our cause, and that they didn't deserve to be led by such as myself."

"Wow!" Lionel chortled and slapped his arm. "That's great. Pompous, superior, and condescending, all at the same time. Did you learn that at school, or is it your natural arrogance?"

Devin puffed up his chest. "I remind you that I'm the Lord Lyon, Imperial Tribune, and governor—"

"Right now, you're just a rebel, like me." Lionel waved his hands. "And we rebels have to stick together, and tell each other the truth. You dumped the crew because you couldn't trust them, and you couldn't convince them to be reliable rebels."

Devin dropped the act. "They didn't want to join a crusade."

"Crusade? I thought you just wanted to make sure your sister was safe."

"I do."

"Really?" Lionel raised his eyebrows. "And

you're willing to split the Empire just for that?"

Devin sagged even lower. "I never should have let her marry that fool. I thought he was dumb as a bag of moon rocks."

"I've met the Empress. I don't think anybody 'lets' her do anything. She does what she wants."

"I knew better. You could trust the Emperor, but those around him, like the Chancellor, they're not… honorable people. I could have made a fuss, made my feelings clear."

"Why didn't you?"

Devin grimaced. "Being Empress was a big piece of prestige for the family, for me. I wanted the prestige of being the Empress's brother more than I worried about what she was giving up."

"You did the honorable thing."

"Look where it got me. On an ancient battleship on the edge of the Verge arguing with my former first officer about crew issues. Speaking of, can we trust the crew we have now?"

Lionel nodded. "For now. The officers that you kicked out were the pompous, arrogant noble types. You know, like you."

"Thanks for that frank assessment, Prefect."

"More than a few were drunks and losers. They hit up every minor infraction and used every punishment they could—leave stopped, pay garnished, busted people in rank. For anything."

"How does the crew feel now?"

"Relieved. But I have to tell you, Tribune. They're not exactly fired-up revolutionaries. More like beaten dogs who are happy that the beatings stopped. They're adequate, barely, but I'm not sure that they'll take on the Imperial Fleet for us."

"Then we have a problem. How do we get them to help us remove the Chancellor and return the Emperor to power?"

"Ignoring for the moment that you're more

interested in returning the Empress to power, I'd say we can count on inertia to keep us moving coreward. But we need a real win over Imperial forces, a real battle. To show them that we're legitimate. You'll be the new protector of the Empire. You know, the righteous fleet returns to chastise the false rulers."

"Meaning if we win a battle, we're the legitimate rulers, and if we lose, we're dirty rebels who deserve what we get."

"Figured it out in one."

"That's why I'm the Tribune and you're just a Prefect."

"I thought that was more of an accident of birth?"

"Birth and ability."

"I'll go with birth. Thank you, Imin." Devin's steward had returned with a tray of salted fish on crackers, and another bottle of wine. "That wine is marvelous."

"Thank you sirs." Imin poured. "Does the Tribune require anything else?"

"Any idea why the auto docking failed during fueling today, Imin?"

Imin set the bottle on the table. "That system has never worked, according to my knowledge sir. Or at least never been used."

"Battleships need fuel, Imin. They must have fueled at some point."

"Yes sir, but never approached the tanker. The tanker always came to them."

"That's ridiculous. How could they sustain any sort of operational tempo doing that?" Doctrine was that the tanker keeps constant velocity and other ships dock with them. Fleet tankers could service multiple ships at once. When done properly, a dozen corvettes, a half dozen destroyers and two or three cruisers could couple with a tanker, fuel up, and leave in the time that a single battleship fueled up.

"Understood sir. But I talked to the boys and girls in engineering. *Canopus* had never done concurrent fueling, only consecutive."

"But, what if there was a battle, or an incursion, or they had to go on a raid…" Devin looked at Lionel. "Surely…"

"Tribune," Lionel said. "I'm sure you're the only serving Senator who has ever been on a battle or a raid, and it's entirely possible that none of the crew on *Canopus* has ever done such a thing and doesn't understand why it's necessary."

"The last major war was before my time, true," Devin said. "But surely somebody…Imin."

Imin shrugged. "Some of the oldest chiefs, perhaps. But not the current crew. When I joined—many, many years ago—maybe half of the Navy was long-serving professionals. The rest were volunteers, getting their benefits. Now, half of the crew are 'transfers' or 're-assignments' That's a conscript in all but name, Tribune. And even the volunteers are… not particularly energetic."

Devin shook his head. "I had an idea, but not that it was this bad. Are you sure?"

"Imin," Lionel said. "What would happen if the Confeds or the Nats attacked? Would the troops fight?"

Imin nodded. "The Marines would."

"But what about the Navy?"

"Hard to tell who would fight, Prefect. It's been thirty years since the Core fleets and the main battle fleets have sailed. Nowadays, the crews sit in orbit and get harassed by their officers. The best ones leave for the merchants, and the remainder aren't exactly the cream of the crop."

Devin grimaced. "Which explains why we can't even dock with a tanker."

"Yes, Tribune." Imin nodded. "With your permission, I have meat pies to make."

"What type of meat?"

"It's a surprise, Tribune."

"Corpses of his enemies," Lionel muttered.

"Well, whatever you do, it will be wonderful. Thank you, Imin." Devin waited until Imin left, and poured himself another drink. "I thought things were bad, not that they were this bad. We need to save the Empire. Restore the old ways."

"Sounds like a good portion of the Empire doesn't want to be saved. Just left alone to rot."

"We're going to stop that," Devin said. "Restore things to their former glory."

"Goody." Lionel nodded. "Us and the crew of this ship. This single ship. This single old ship. We're going to beat the biggest empire history has seen."

Devin grimaced. "I can't leave my sister in the clutches of evil men."

"Well, you haven't heard from her in a while, so perhaps the clutches aren't what you think they are. I'm with you all the way. But ask yourself this. Is it worth destroying the Empire just to help your sister? And what happens then? You kill the Emperor? The Chancellor? What?"

"Should I stand aside while evil men destroy it, sister or not?"

"Lots of questions. Where are you going to find the answers?"

"In the Core." Devin drained his glass. "Train up the folks we have, Prefect. Build me a flotilla, take us into the Core to battle our enemies, and we'll get our answers."

"I'll do that." Lionel stood, leaving the rest of his wine untouched. "But one question."

"Yes?"

"What if you don't like the answers you get?

What then?"

Chapter 3

"Either we leave right now or we camouflage the ship while we wait." Ana hauled the netting out of the dorsal hatch. "There could have been a hundred sensors pointing at us when we overflew that town. And don't just stand there like the useless regal duke that you are. Help me with this net."

"I'm not a regal duke, just a regular one." Dirk helped Ana haul the net up onto the ship's upper hull. "How big is this thing?"

"Big enough to reach the ground on both sides of the ship, if you hang it from the hooks." The camouflage nets were Ana's new toy. He'd managed to finagle them off of the Tribune's old flagship, the *Pollux*, with the help of the Tribune's devious steward, Imin. "Drape them across the ship and it softens our straight lines and makes us blend in for visual search." The *Heart's Desire* was grounded on the shore of a clear mountain lake, on a beach next to a dense pine forest. "Weave in these colored plastic strips, and as much vegetation as we can grab. Make us look like trees. We need concealment."

Dirk sniffed. "Gonna make the whole ship smell like pine."

"What's wrong with smelling like pine?"

"I'm used to ship smells, is all." Dirk tied his net tighter. "Back in my Navy days, one trip, the captain over-loaded the life-support with sprayed lemon scent. Suffocating. Now I can't even drink lemonade without getting a headache. I'm wary of strange smells on a ship."

"I'll spray you with lubricating oil and spoiled food if you want."

"Centurion." Dirk pointed at the net. "Much as

I like concealment as a concept, this net only hides us from visual scans. What if they come out with infrared?"

"Concealment will extend our tactical flexibility and provide more options. More options and tactical flexibility will keep us alive in a crisis."

"If we're leaving right away, we don't need to do this."

"We don't appear to be leaving right away, do we, Navy?" *If we can even leave at all. That missile battery is more of a problem than everyone realizes.* "Stop being lazy, and fix your side. I'll help the others." Ana heaved the net over the side of the ship, and yelled directions to Scruggs and Dena waiting below.

"No, we don't," Dirk agreed. He pulled the last of his net clear of the hatch. "Can we stow these in external lockers next time?"

"If we want them to melt," Ana said. "Otherwise, we need them inside behind the magnetics. What's up, Navigator? Are we leaving?"

Lee had stuck her head out of the hatch. "The engineer is still working with his console. He says that he doesn't like some of the readings—something wrong with system pressurization." The engineering console had shut down and auto-restarted when the ship slammed into the rocky shore. When it came back up, Gavin confronted a sea of errors. "He says he wants to purge the whole system and reload all our tanks."

"Then we'll be here for days," Dirk said. "Stuck here while we refuel."

"Better stuck here refueling then stuck here shot into little pieces."

Dirk heaved his side of the net down. "I can beat that battery. Give me an hour to run a few checks, change our alignment, I can blast out of here with the main drive and they won't catch us."

"They won't catch us because we'll be smashed into one of those mountains over there." Ana gestured at the cliffs surrounding them. "I've been on this ship as long as you, and I know we launch horizontal, not vertical. We can't get the angle to clear those cliffs from down here."

"We go out the way we came in, through that notch." Dirk pointed north. "Get the thrusters fired up, circle a few times, then we'll have enough altitude to hit orbit."

"By flying over that Jove-damned battery."

"I can do it."

"In your previous life, you commanded an orbital landing detachment on an auxiliary cruiser, as I recall."

"Yes. So?"

"Let's say you had to stay behind while somebody else did this. Would you order one of your fresh-faced lieutenants to do this?"

Dirk frowned, then shook his head.

"Thought so. You can be as crazy as you want by yourself, but if you're going to be reckless with others' lives, we need to discuss this."

"You're afraid to die?"

Ana shook his head. "I don't see any downside to it, to be honest. Not for me."

"Really?"

"Really." Ana nodded. "Either we escape, and everything is fine, or we crash, and I'll have the satisfaction of seeing that smug Navy grin wiped off your face."

"If we crash, you won't survive either."

"Wasn't planning on it."

"Then how will you know the smug grin got wiped off my face?"

"Because I'll shoot you at the last second." Ana slapped the holstered revolver he always wore planet side. "The feeling of satisfaction will be brief, but it will be glorious."

After setting up the camouflage nets, they all met to discuss their issues. One of the fueling valves had cracked open during landing, and Gavin wasn't happy with the way things were mixed up. He wanted to stay grounded three shifts to drain and purge the fuel system. Dirk made his case for immediate departure, insisting they could do repairs in orbit. Ana had no opinion—he expected the specialists in engineering and flight to do their jobs. Scruggs would do what Ana said, and Dena didn't know enough to object. The surprising vote for staying was Lee.

"It bothers me that the defenses here are so strong," Lee said. "We're supposed to be helping the Tribune get good intel on what's going on here."

Ana made a rude gesture with his fingers. "This to the Tribune."

"She's right," Dirk said. "Those are mainline Imperial weapons, albeit less-effective export versions. Why are they here?"

"Only way to find out is to get a closer look at them," Lee said. "Or at least a closer look at their emissions."

"Can't we do that from the ship?"

"Could. Didn't. Too much going on at the time," Lee said.

Ana turned to Scruggs. "Sensors are your job, cadet."

"They're her job if she knows how to use them," Lee said. "I didn't show her the recording and analyzing sensors we use to determine what type of ships or weapons we're facing."

"How do we do that?" Dirk asked.

"We... I have an electronic signature database."

"You have an electronic signature database of

Imperial Weapons?" Dirk asked.

"Yes."

Dirk crossed his arms. "I didn't know that. Where did we get that?"

"We...I got it from the Tribune. Well, his steward, Imin, got them for me. Software upgrade mostly."

The whole crew now glared at Lee.

Dena grinned. "And you didn't tell us this."

"Devin insisted."

"Oh, *Devin* insisted. Not the *Tribune* insisted. Well, we can't disappoint *Devin*, can we."

"This is a military operation."

"When did you start calling him Devin instead of the Tribune?"

"We had some private discussions."

"Private? Well, well, well." Dena grinned. "He is a handsome man."

Scruggs interrupted. "Dena! Don't say that."

"Why not?"

"He's her priest. Or he was her priest. That's wrong."

"Maybe. Depends on the details of the religion. I remember that reverend—"

"Stop, Dena. That's so disgusting."

"It was. Want to hear all the details?"

The others started arguing. Dirk leaned closer. "Later. Tell me later. And tell me everything."

The squabble resolved quickly. Staying would get them a maintenance period, a full load of fuel, fun times in the woods, and intelligence the Tribune needed. Leaving right away would leave them confused, or dead, or both.

"Right, we need a plan." Ana nodded. "Cadet Scruggs, think you can handle this by yourself with the others?"

Scruggs grinned. "Yes, Centurion. I sure can. If

the pilot permits."

"Good. I'll stay here. The pilot and I can handle things, once we get a briefing from the engineer. I've purged a fuel system before, and I'm sure he has too. In fact, Dena made us a checklist for that. The rest of you should be able to head into town and get the info that Lee needs, the Tribune's intelligence. And of course neutralize any threats to us."

Dirk opened his mouth, looked at Ana, then shut it.

Ana nodded. "Outstanding. Finish lunch, check your gear, and we'll meet back here to finalize things."

The others nodded and went to their rooms to collect gear. Dirk faced Ana. "You want to tell me what you're playing? Ground combat is your job."

"She wants more responsibility. Let's see how she does without her superiors around. If I was there, I'd squelch any sort of initiative by my presence, and she's far too deferential to your rank."

"And the others?"

"She won't be dealing with engines, medical things, or computers, so Lee and Gavin's expertise will be void. And Dena knows how to not do stupid things in the woods. It's a good test. Putting her out there without easy access to her superiors will give her room to stretch."

"Who you testing? Her, or you?"

"When I find out, I'll let you know. Let's go haul some hoses out of storage." Ana grinned. "We've got a fuel system to purge."

Chapter 4

"Sorry, Rocky, I have to stay." Ana bent and petted Rocky's head. He and the others had gathered at the base of the *Heart's Desire*'s landing ramp. Scruggs, Dena, Gavin and Lee shouldered their packs. Rocky barked at Ana. He could tell the big man wasn't coming along, and it bothered him.

"It's okay, furry buddy." Ana ruffled Rocky's fur some more. "Need to keep somebody behind. That's my job. Make sure they have a ship to come back to. Guard things."

Rocky whined, but settled. He understood guard. The pack was going into the woods. Somebody had to stay and keep an eye on the den. The big man would take good care of it.

"Bye, Rocky." Dirk leaned down to pet him.

Rocky bared his teeth and growled. Dirk yanked his hand back.

"I love that dog," Ana said. "Report on the radio only if it's an emergency. They might not be able to break encryption, but they can detect transmissions."

"Understood, Centurion." Scruggs chambered a round in her rifle. "Let's move out." She led off into the woods. The database had no maps of the Planet Kraz-1D, and their flyover had allowed only limited charting. With no planetary network, there was no GPS. But it had a strong magnetic field. Dena's personal gear included a high tech miniature gyro-compass that could download declination from the ship's sensors. She'd loaded up the necessary corrections and showed them all how to convert a regular compass course to a true one. She insisted they all carry it, along with a knife, water, and basic survival supplies.

Dirk and Ana watched as their crew disappeared into the pine woods. Ana stepped to the rock beach, searched for a flat rock then skipped it onto the green-tinged lake they had landed on. Dirk had done a competent landing, screaming down over a hill, slapping onto the lake, and riding a wave of water up the rock beach into a field of low green bushes. *Heart's Desire* had stopped meters from the tree line. It had been the work of only a few hours to cut enough bushes and tree boughs to cover the nets and break up the color and the outline of the ship. Only a direct overflight at close range could detect them now.

"Want to tell me why you agreed to my suggestion to stay behind, Navy?" Ana asked. "Agreeing with me is not your usual mode."

"No. Want to tell me why you decided to stay behind, Centurion?"

"I told you. Last few planets, I've been the one to go out and survey things. It's Scruggs's turn. She needs experience."

Dirk walked to the edge of the lake and stretched to retrieve a rock. "This water is cold." He weighed the rock in his hand. "She has plenty of experience with woods and planets."

"Not with being in charge of a party."

"As much as anyone can be in charge of this group." Dirk sighed. "Orders are considered somewhat optional with everyone. How do you feel?"

"I feel fine. Why are you asking?"

"You still spend time each week in the med pod. Injuries still bothering you?"

Ana stomped into the lake, splashing water in all directions. When he was knee deep, he stuck his hand down and fished around for another rock. "None of your business."

"Or is it the cancer?"

"Still none of your business. And whatever shape I'm in, I can still slap your smug grin sideways if I need to. So buzz off. I'm going to enjoy my time in nature." *While I still can.*

"You sound like Dena," Dirk said.

Ana blinked. "I do, don't I. Damn that girl."

"Well, she'll be useful on this hike."

"Unlike you."

"No, I wouldn't be." Dirk selected another rock, and skipped it over the water. "Three, four. Should have picked a flatter one. I'm no good in the woods. I'm a pilot. An Imperial Noble. A decent ship commander. A reasonable Naval officer. I'm good at that. That's what the Tribune said, back at the fleet."

"Then why are you even here?" Ana skipped his rock. It sank at the first bounce. Dirk laughed. Ana cursed and fished in the water, looking for a better candidate. "You should be back there with the Tribune commanding a trash scow or something."

"As exciting as a trash command might be, I've been a pilot, never a commander. Not of a regular warship at least. I wasn't told explicitly what to do, but Tribune Devin suggested I stay with all of you. I think I'm here to keep an eye on you all. And specifically, keep an eye on Scruggs. Which is why I'm back here with the ship. If they get into trouble, we can come screaming in and rescue them."

"Scruggs doesn't need keeping eyes on, she's doing fine herself."

"I agree. Army-Scruggs is doing well. Even Command-Scruggs seems to be doing well. But I think he wants Industrialist-Scruggs at some point. Her family ties are going to be important the closer he gets to the Core. He's smart. Smarter than most nobles, and he thinks farther ahead. But he's been away from the Core, and from the Court, for a long time. I'll bet my next leave ticket he's worried about what he's hearing on the nobles and the

Empire. While he figures that out, he can trust me to keep an eye on you."

"So you're the Tribune's spy now, are you?"

"Better say I'm his interpreter. He wants to see what we come up with on this route. Want to bet he has somebody else checking things out? He'll get two reports and compare them."

"No bet here." Ana skipped another rock. It sank at the third bounce. "Never was good at this. Fine. You're here to keep an eye on us, especially Scruggs. And probably Lee, and then Gavin's a spy, of course."

"Yes."

"What's up with this planet? Why did they shoot us down? Shouldn't they have warned us before firing?"

"Do you care?"

"No. I don't care where we are. This is what I do these days."

"Travel the galaxy and shoot people?"

"Why, yes. That's what I do. That's what I've always done. And I'm good at it."

"Do you care who you shoot or why?"

"Too much work. Not my problem. I like this job. Three meals a day. Travel the Galaxy. Visit new exciting planets, meet interesting people. Then kill them."

"Not much of an ambition."

"I lost my ambition years ago. Then tried switching to just surviving."

"So now you just want to survive?"

"No. I gave that up too." Ana grabbed a rock with his left and tossed off-handed. This time, it skipped five times before sinking. "Look at that. I tried something new, and I learned something new. I'm better skipping with my left hand than my right."

"Not much of a skill, Centurion."

"It's new to me."

"Is that important?"

"When you stop learning new things, then it's time to go." Ana skipped another stone with his left hand. This time, it sank on the second bounce. "And eventually, everyone stops learning new things."

"But how do the people here live?" Scruggs asked. "I mean, what are their jobs? There isn't anything to do."

"It's a planet, there's lots to do." Dena shouldered her shotgun and hopped from one rock to the next. The group had started climbing the hill next to the ship, but thick underbrush had pushed them to a stream bed. Dark clouds dripped occasional rain, but they made good time in the stream, and were heading south, toward the city. "Especially if you want to eat."

"But how do they grow food without technology?" Scruggs had her rifle, and both she and Dena carried bundles of explosives.

"It's not as hard as it sounds, Sister Scruggs." Lee said. She and Gavin trailed behind. Gavin was weighed down with his shotgun, tools and electronic cracking equipment. Rocky roamed the woods beside them. In addition to food and camping supplies, Lee had her med kit, some sensors, and a revolver. "When the Empire designed the terraforming system, they put a great deal of planning into the ecosystems. Most of the plants here are edible. You can survive for a long time by foraging. And you can eat the animals too."

"And the fish. And the birds." Dena splashed across a stream and onto the far bank. "And everything. And if you want to grow grains or corn or anything that needs to be processed, the engineered seeds grow super well. They're designed to be pest resistant and disease free too. If eating is all you want to do, you're not likely to starve on an Empire-seeded planet."

"So everybody gets to eat," Scruggs said. "But what about technology? What about harvesting and processing?"

"You need a tractor or a plow to grow wheat. But you don't need a hydrogen-fueled tractor run by a fusion reactor. You can make do with steel blades pulled by oxen. You don't need super high technology."

"Steel is high technology," Scruggs said. "Can't cook it up in a campfire."

"Nope. But the Empire can make one main city. Give it a fusion reactor, or three. A library and a school with the latest gear. Then you get one iron ore mine, one coal mine, one micro-steel mill, and a tiny fabrication plant. Mine whatever else is common nearby. Import some copper and other metals. As long as you make all the bulky stuff on planet, you only need specialized parts brought in for everything else. You don't need much tech to build a bicycle, or a steam engine, not if you can make metals locally. Add a few imported radios, and you've got a productive economy. Planets tend to fluctuate up and down on tech, then settle on a big group of items that they make locally, with a small group of standard imports. Rockhaul, we imported solar panels for electricity, but we burned wood for heat and used water power for mills."

"Fascinating," Gavin said, stumbling along behind. "Great history and economics course. But I need a break. Let's stop."

Scruggs sat on a fallen log. "How do you know all this?" Scruggs said to Dena. "You're, well, you're…"

"Not too bright?" Dena laughed. "I'm not

stupid. I get bored easily. I learned it when I worked with an importer. Rockhaul only imported one type of vehicle battery, and there were only three types of electric motors used on the farms for the whole planet. We standardized the parts so the import company could load up on the most common types of spares. That made regular shipments easier."

"Wow." Gavin sat and wiped his brow. "I was glad I had my jacket earlier, but it's warmed up."

"You'll be cool soon enough." Dena pointed at the clouds. "Those clouds are getting thicker. Wind's picking up. I sense more rain."

"Probably," Gavin said. "Did you get an A+ in weather class too, Dena?"

"I passed school with full marks. All my classes except two. I nearly failed Standard, and I nearly failed basic physics."

Lee sat next to them and unwrapped a cold ration bar. "I didn't know you were that academic."

"I wasn't. I hated school. I never studied. I wanted to get out of there."

"How come you did so well in your other classes but you failed those two?" Scruggs asked.

"Standard, the teacher was female. And the physics teacher was my cousin."

"Sooooo…" Scruggs bit her lip. "Your cousin. I don't know how to say this."

"Yes, I slept with him. It was fun. And that meant I passed."

Gavin laughed. "Too bad your cousin wasn't more receptive to your charms. You could have gotten good marks there."

"Oh, he was receptive," Dena said. "I really, really failed physics badly. Nobody would believe that I got an A. Best he could do was give me bare pass, even after all my activities, as it were." She shrugged.

"You slept with your cousin?" Scruggs asked. "Just to pass a test?"

"Who wants to waste time studying?" Dena shrugged. "Besides, he wasn't just a cousin. He was a second cousin. Once removed." She tilted her head. "Least I didn't have to marry him. That's what his parents wanted."

They crested a hill. The rain increased as storm clouds blew in from the west. Another lake stretched in front, stopping at one of the cliffs surrounding the valley. A small river ran west through a gap in the hills. The rain dimpled the river's surface and made the rocks in the stream bed slick.

"We need to check direction," Scruggs said. "Dena, report."

Dena rolled her eyes but consulted her compass. "Yes, Cadet. Stay to the west of this stream, we can follow along that lake. There should be a low pass there."

"Everyone see where we're headed?"

They all grunted assent, and kept on walking. Lee and Gavin exchanged grins. They remembered their first time in charge as well. The woods opened up on the side of the lake. Clusters of tall trees with red and yellow leaves dotted the plain. Each cluster was thirty to forty trees, widely separated at ground level, but with the branches overlapping.

"These trees are huge." Gavin tapped the bark on one as they angled through the woods. "They must be a hundred feet high."

The cluster they were under had branches starting five feet off the ground, and then a new major limb every four or five feet.

"Are they sick?" Scruggs pointed at the nearest tree. "The leaves are all gone."

The far cluster had been stripped up to double or triple a person's height. The top three-quarters of the tree was covered in red and yellow leaves, but the bottom quarter was stripped bare. In some cases, the bark had been removed along with the leaves.

"Weird disease that cuts the bottom leaves off and leaves the rest," Gavin said.

"Bugs?" Scruggs asked. "Or pests or whatever? Dena, you're our tree expert. What's going on with them?"

Dena surveyed the other trees. "I don't know. It doesn't look like budworms. Fires? But there's not enough ground cover to burn up that far. And where did the burnt leaves go?"

"It's not dangerous, is it?" Lee asked.

"Don't know. It's strange. And at least it's open under the canopy. And not as slippery."

They continued to follow Dena's compass. Scruggs's plan was to hike as far as they could the first day and make a late camp. Next day, hike down to the edge of the settlements using the darkness to recon the town, and the missile battery. Then decide how to shut it down.

The rain showers continued and the wind increased. Dense clusters of trees alternated with open clearings. The trees protected them from the wind and rain, but every five minutes or so, they had to cross long narrow clearings empty of trees, lashed by the weather as they ran across.

"Why these weird empty spots?" Scruggs asked. "Why not continuous forest?"

"Not sure," Dena said. "Could be different soils, buried streams that pollute the soil, or even old roads that haven't been cleared."

"They do look kinda like roads," Gavin said. "The way they run off to the distance. But roads that haven't been used in a while."

"I thought there was nobody living out this far?"

"We didn't see any lights, any buildings, or detect any radio when we flew over," Lee said. "I checked the recordings after we landed. There were heat sources, lots of heat sources, but that could be animals. Could be people too, I suppose. But if there were people out here, why would the roads be abandoned?"

"Not sure." Dena stopped and pointed at the roots of one of the trees. "What's that?"

"Somebody dug the roots up," Gavin said. "See? All the dirt's been scraped away from the base of that tree." Somebody, or something, had uncovered all the tree's roots, leaving holes several feet deep under the bottom of the tree.

"Who in Jove's name digs up trees?" Lee asked.

"Or what," Scruggs asked. "Dena? Problem?"

Dena had slipped her shotgun off her back and now carried it in both hands. "No problem. Not yet."

"Is something dangerous?"

"Something likes to dig. And they dig deep into the dirt. That's not sand, that's clay."

Gavin shrugged. "So it's clay. So what?"

"Dig into clay, you need claws. Big ones. Anything that can dig that deep into clay can dig into people."

Nobody said anything, but Gavin cracked his shotgun open to check his shell, and Lee unstrapped her revolver holster. Scruggs slid the bolt of her rifle back a fingers width, checked her brass, and let it slide back.

"Can't remember whether you loaded your rifle, Baby Marine?" Dena asked.

"If there isn't a round chambered, it's just an awkward hammer," Scruggs said. "Best to check."

"Rocky," Dena said. "Go search. Sniff."

Rocky ran ahead, sniffing at bushes.

"Search? When did he learn that?" Lee asked.

"He gets bored in jump. I hide treats inside smelly things, then tell him to search."

"So he finds smelly things? That won't help us." Lee pointed at the ground. "Dirt, decaying leaves, flowers. All sorts of smelly things here."

"Not just smelly things," Dena said. "Smelly things in unusual places. Like I put Dirk's socks in engineering, and he sniffs them out. Or, conversely, I put a rag of lubricating oil in my quarters, or wipe something in the galley with the Old Man's brandy. It's not the fact that they are smelly that he hunts for, it's the fact that something smells different than everything near them."

"That's smart," Lee said. "Well done."

"Surprised you, didn't I?"

"Unlike some people, I don't think you're dumb. You're smarter than you look. You just like to hide it and surprise people."

Dena glared. "You think so?"

"I know so."

"If I'm so smart, or hiding being so smart, why not tell me before now?"

"Why ruin your fun?" Lee pointed. "Rocky stopped."

Rocky was digging under a bush. When the group approached, he slid out and barked. Dena got down on her knees and dug deeper.
"Something big here. A bone. A couple bones." She dug around until the end of a bone protruded. She yanked at it. "That's not coming out easily. Scruggs, give me a hand."

"It must be pretty big to be buried that deep." Scruggs set her rifle against a nearby tree and climbed down to help. Between the two of them, they twisted the bones out.

"Not as big as I thought." Dena inspected it.

"Just stuck under this dirt."

"This is a pain." Scruggs wiped her legs. "I'm all wet. And I'm getting my knees all dirty."

"You'll have to get used to that if you keep taking Dena's advice," Gavin said.

"Her advice? What do you mean?"

The three other crew members exchanged glances and grinned. "Well, Sister Scruggs, Lee said. "We'll get Pilot to explain that to you when we get back."

"I hate it when you all grin like that," Scruggs said. "I'm not twelve. Somebody just explain it to me."

Dena did.

"Ewww," Scruggs said.

"Now you sound like you're twelve." The two women dug near the hole.

"Here's another one." Scruggs grabbed a second bone and yanked it free. She held it next to Dena's bone. "Looks like they go together. And this one has marks."

"Those are teeth marks." Lee took the bones from Scruggs and held them to the light. "That's a radius, and this is an ulna. Arm bones. This is a grave."

Chapter 5

"Why so many graves here?" Scruggs asked the group. They had continued following the stream to the gap in the mountains. Rocky had dug up three more sets of bones. "Was it a graveyard?"

"Doesn't look like it." Gavin removed his hat and wiped his forehead. The showers had paused. Warming rays of sun peeked between the branches. "Graveyards, everybody is together in one spot. These are random, and hundreds of meters apart. And we don't know how old they are. Lee, any way to tell how long these graves have been here?"

"Sure," Lee said, picking her way from rock to rock along the riverbed. "With a laboratory and a whole bunch of testing equipment. Without it, old enough that all the flesh rotted off."

"Or was eaten." Some of the bones had bite marks on them.

"That could have been Rocky."

"Rocky's ten kilos, that's twenty-two pounds for you colonials," Lee said. "I doubt he could chew a bird bone to pieces, never mind a person. And we would have noticed him chowing down on a freshly made corpse."

"Still, it's strange," Gavin said. "These don't look like graves. More like somebody died and dropped there, and the local animals ate them."

"What local animals?" Lee asked "We haven't seen any."

"Somebody ate all those leaves," Dena said. "And dug up those roots. Somebody or some animal. And if you noticed, those graves were all near one of the dug up trees. We have to be careful."

"I hate planets," Lee said. "I want to stay on the ship. Why couldn't I stay on the ship?"

"Because we need a medic more than Dirk and the Old Man," Gavin said. "We've got to get in there and shut down that launcher. This is a military operation. Dena and Scruggs are the shooters, you're the medic."

"What are you?"

"I'm the mule." Gavin hefted his pack. It was bigger than any of the women's. "I carry stuff."

Lee hopped to a rock. "Too bad you couldn't carry an un-interceptable encrypted radio and we could ask Pilot if he knew anything about killer animals on this planet."

"Call him on the regular radio," Dena said.

"No." Scruggs shook her head. "If we use it, that town could intercept it Then they'll know we're here."

"We could still ask," Dena said. "They might not intercept us. Could be too lazy to snoop all the time."

"No."

"Scruggs, be reasonable. This whole no radio thing is a bit too much."

"I said no, and I meant no." Scruggs frowned. "End of discussion."

Dena glared.

Gavin smothered a grin. "The old man was right. He said anybody who can bring a missile battery online that fast must have some radio direction finding gear. That sort of stuff can be automated. And as far as the planetary databases, that type of thing is never up to date. That's the problem with planets. You never know what's out to kill you."

"Well, we could—hold up. What do you smell, boy?"

Rocky had frozen. He growled deeply, then cocked his head. His tail lashed once, twice as he sniffed the ground. He shook his head, whuffed, then loped into the trees.

"That's the third time in an hour he's done that," Gavin said. "He smells something. Dena, what does he smell?"

"How should I know? Another grave? It's not like I have some sort of psychic connection with him. He's a dog."

"He digs when he smells graves. Not growls. What should we do?"

"Dena, compass check, please," Scruggs said.

Dena glared again, then looked at her compass. She took a bearing on the sun, setting above where the river disappeared into a notch between two hills. "Over there. Look."

The plain surrounding the town was barely visible, and the sun glinted off metal or glass in the distance. "That's light reflecting off the town. We can see them. They can't see us yet."

Scruggs pointed ahead. "See that wide spot in the river below?" The river they had been following down from the mountain widened into something bigger than a stream but smaller than a lake. It twisted between hummocks, then disappeared between the lower hills. "Let's get there and camp. There's water, there's trees, and we're within one day of getting to the edge of town. And we should be sheltered from direct view."

They continued their downward trek, stopping once more at a growl from Rocky. Since leaving the upper hills, they hadn't found any more bones, but something continued to irritate him.

The planet's moons performed their complicated dance as the sun set. Stars appeared, and the remaining clouds formed a red band on the horizon. Rocky prowled around the group, and attacked and killed a snake he found.

"Poisonous?" Scruggs asked. "There weren't any in the database when we checked."

"Don't know," Dena said. "But Rocky thought so. I trust his nose better than our database."

Gavin unpacked his sensors and they all helped him set them up in a triangle several hundred meters on a side.

"Why so far apart?" Dena asked.

"We separate them as far as we can, but keep them in line of sight of each other. That way, they can exchange information on a secure link in real-time. We're making a giant virtual antenna. The bigger it is, the more the sensitivity. Let this run for an hour and process what it gets, we'll have a good idea what sort of electronics are emitting in the town."

"We can tell what type of missiles?"

"Maybe."

They slept in shifts in the twilight, inside the waterproof sleeping bags from the *Heart's Desire*'s stores.

Rocky woke them all in the middle of the night with long growls. He climbed out of where he was nestling with Lee and barked into the darkness.

"What is it, boy?" Scruggs was on watch. She cocked her shot gun and stared out into the gloom. There were plenty of bright stars, two small moons and some reflected lights from behind the mountains. It was light enough to see shapes, but too dark for colors.

"What is it, Scruggs?" Lee stopped beside her, pulling on her boots, the others following "Do you see anything"

"Rocky does, I don't, but I can't—wait. There. Behind those trees."

Shadows moved in the distance. Large shadows.

They all drew weapons and stood together, staring. Rocky stopped beside them, growling. He'd woken the pack, his job was done. Now the humans had to deal with the threat.

"What are they?" Lee asked.

"Can't tell," Scruggs said. "Like nothing I've seen before. They're all over the place."

"Tall." Gavin pointed. "Look, there."

They'd camped next to the tiny lake, on the slope of a hill, under a cluster of trees. Half of these trees still had their foliage, as did the clusters across the river. They'd wanted the extra shade to keep the inevitable drizzle off. They had a clear view of the far side of the river between two clusters of trees. Shadows moved against the backdrop, flowing out of the woods.

"See how far they reach up? They're twice, three times as tall as we are."

Scruggs dropped to one knee and sighted the approaching herd with her rifle.

"Scruggs, don't shoot them," Lee hissed. "They might get angry, and stampede, or attack us."

"I'm not shooting anything, yet," Scruggs said. "I'm trying to figure out how tall they are. They're as tall as the missing leaves. Those must be the animals that eat the trees."

"We're being attacked by twenty-foot-tall man-eating tabbos?" Gavin asked.

"Every animal isn't a tabbo. And nobody is attacking anybody."

"But they're moving toward us." Gavin pointed. The tall, skinny animals lumbered through the trees and splashed into the river. "Crossing the river."

"That river's deep," Lee said. "Six feet in the middle."

"Twenty-foot-tall animals, with six-foot-long legs. What are they, giants?"

"Giants don't eat leaves."

"Are they dangerous, is the question. Should we shoot?"

Scruggs wavered. What would the centurion do against an unknown threat? He'd shoot first at any known threat. But if they shoot, they might alert the town. And whatever they are, they don't appear threatening yet. There's no clear decision here.

"Scruggs." Dena had dug into her pack. "I've got the lantern light here. Should I turn it on?"

They'd slept without lights or fire, in case somebody in town did a nighttime flyover. They couldn't hide from infrared, but there were so many animals in the forest, sensors wouldn't be able to separate them out. Visible light, on the other hand, meant people.

"If they keep coming, we'll have to," Scruggs said. "However friendly they are, I don't want to get too close to them."

"If they're even friendly."

More animals splashed into the river. The darkness rippled like a forest of walking trees was stepping toward them.

"They're across," Gavin said. "And closing. Won't hurt to see what they are. Dena. Light them up."

"Not yet, not yet," Scruggs said. "We don't want to give ourselves away."

"They can see us already," Lee said. "They know we're here."

Scruggs grimaced. "Fine. But no shooting. Dena, turn on the lantern on low. Just enough to see, not enough that somebody in the town could see us."

Dena hit the switch. The lantern emitted a soft white glow, reflecting the pale faces of the group. She spun the rheostat on the bottom, and the light brightened, and the darkness receded.

The herd froze in the act of crossing the river. Eyes glinted impossibly high up – twenty feet off the ground. The animals were quadrupeds, with a horse-shaped lower body. A narrow head topped a ten-foot neck. The heads had all swiveled to stare at the light, long ears sticking out a foot on either side, and two bony protuberances on the skull above the eyebrows.

"Are those horns?"

"They have fur." Gavin pointed. "Mixed dark and light blotches. Like camouflage."

The animals' jaws worked. They chewed as they regarded the crew.

"They're like giant tall cows. Chewing. They look like herbivores," Lee said. "They must be what was chomping on the trees."

"Giraffes!" Dena grinned. "They're giraffes. I've read about them, but I never expected to see them."

"Are they dangerous?" Scruggs asked.

"Any animal is, if you frighten it," Dena said. "But they're not usually aggressive. If we sit still, they'll avoid us."

The herd had stopped and stared when the light came on. The light was bright, and out of place, but this herd of giraffes had seen humans with lights before. After their initial halt, they resumed their walk, cautiously stepping through the water, then veering away from the group. Some pulled mouthfuls of leaves from the trees to chew as they passed. Others contemplated the humans, while ruminating on the leaves they browsed on earlier.

It took half an hour for the herd to march by. Gavin lost count at two hundred, including several dozen cute juveniles. Rocky growled initially, but lay down after he was shushed.. Dena keep the light on so the herd wouldn't crush them.

After the last of the giraffes moved away, they killed the light and resumed their watches. One of the larger moons rose five hours later, giving enough light for them to wake up and continue their hike.

"We'll be in position to get direct eyes on the

spaceport in four or five hours." Scruggs walked down the hills. The forest was wide open under the trees, with plenty of space to spread out. "But we don't want to be seen. Dena, you can climb up one of these trees and get a view of the area."

"Why me?"

"You're the best tree climber."

"Because I'm from a planet? Lee's a pretty good climber. So are you, for that matter."

"Do you want Lee to climb up, then? Or me?"

"Nope. Just messing with you. I'll climb. I like climbing trees."

"Then why complain?"

"Keeps you on your toes, probationary lieutenant in the probationary rebel Imperial Navy."

"I'm not—never mind." Scruggs gave her a dirty look. "We need a route into town where we can get close to those missiles. Then we disable them somehow."

"And by disable, you mean, bomb, burn, wreck, destroy or explode?"

"Well." Scruggs dropped down into the riverbed. Rocky had gone ahead and was lapping up the cold water. "The centurion wasn't specific, but he said we had to guarantee that those missiles couldn't fire before calling the ship in."

"Fire and explosion it is." Dena bent down to refill her water canteen, and activated the built in ultraviolet sterilizer. "Sounds like fun." She took a swig. "Explosions are fun. I sound like the old man."

Gavin joined them and filled his own water bottle. "I've got some hacking gear here, and I'm willing to try shutting them down, but I can only shut down the targeting computer if I can get to it." He tore the top off a small packet of powder, and poured it into his bottle. "And we haven't found a planetary network."

"Not out here," Lee said. "But there's bound to be one at the starport, even if it's short range. If nothing else, they'll need it to check container stats, and shipping manifests and such like. What did you put in your water?"

Gavin held up some pre-made packets. "Basic powder. Mix it with water."

"All this fresh mountain water, and you mix that crap in with it?" Dena asked.

Gavin nodded. "I grew up with Basic. I'm used to it."

"But it tastes horrid," Dena said. "Like greasy old socks."

"Do you have any of the orange-lemon flavor?" Scruggs asked. "That's my favorite."

Dena groaned. "Space people. Never understand them."

Scruggs looked up at the lightening sky. "We're burning daylight. Move out." Scruggs picked up her rifle and led the way up the bank.

"Yes, Centurion," Dena said quietly, but she smiled when she said it. The others exchanged glances and grinned but followed in order.

Three hours later, they were deep enough in the hills that Scruggs decided they would get a good view of the town from up high. She and Dena both climbed to the top of a handy tree, while Lee and Gavin rested. Rocky wagged his tail and watched the climbers, ignoring another small herd of giraffes that sauntered by.

They'd seen three more herds since daybreak, and now they were part of the backdrop. They'd marveled at how the giraffes could turn their heads backwards and twist their necks, and how they used their long tongues to strip the leaves from trees.

"That's a cool pattern there." Dena pointed to

one of the animals walking below. "Her splotches are darker than normal. Good camouflage."

"Less animal, more spaceport." Scruggs pointed to the distance.

"Killjoy." Dena draped an arm around the trunk and leaned to see through the foliage. The branches were spaced close enough that climbing had been easy, and they were big enough to balance on without much difficulty. "One spaceport. Three dirt landing pads with earth berms. A little low to be that close together. Barely six feet, according to the sensor binocs. That doesn't seem high enough."

"Centurion said that big ships don't land here, so the berms don't have to be as large. Can you see the missiles?"

"I see a big rectangular box thing in the middle, with pointy things sticking out of it.. There's dirt piled around it on the ground, like the starship berms. There's a metal shed outside the berm with a truck parked next to it. The truck has a pole sticking up with a big square thing on the top."

"Centurion showed me the pictures. The big box thing is the missiles. The truck is the radar and the control console. The metal shed might have the control station, or the power connections."

"That makes sense. The shed is big enough that somebody could live in it. I can see red cables running from the truck into the wall of the shed. And there's a power line coming from the town on poles. It goes to the shed, not the truck."

"Must be from the mini-fusion plant in town." Scruggs climbed to the next branch down. "Centurion says we can either cut the power to the radars, or cut their connection to the control unit, or cut the control unit's connection to the missiles, or destroy the control unit."

"Lots of choices. But why not blow up the

missiles?"

"They're hard to destroy, and he said even if you don't set off the warheads, all that rocket fuel makes a big boom."

"Surprised that wasn't his suggestion. He likes big booms."

"Well, let's get moving." Scruggs climbed down another branch.

"Wait up, Baby Marine. Let's check the rest of the area." Dena swept the binoculars along the plain. "That's interesting. Oh, that's more interesting."

"What is?"

"There's no trees on the other side of the river."

"Why's that interesting?"

"Somebody cleaned them out and planted crops of some sort. Don't know why they didn't do it on this side of the river. It's flatter. And between the spaceport and the river is an airstrip. Grass, but still an airstrip. Flat, level, and mowed. There's a windsock on a pole too. Huh, there's a fence."

"What fence?" Scruggs stopped. "Where?"

"Come up and see. It's hard to explain."

The main river to the north of the town was too wide to cross without a boat. A wooden jetty stuck out into the river, and the road from town ran right out on it, built for docking and transferring cargo. The town sat south of the main river in the triangle made from the confluence with the junction of the mountain stream they followed. Dena counted over a hundred buildings, some substantial enough to have two or three stories. One was an Imperial colony administration building, another a fusion plant with attached switching station and power lines.

People walked the streets. Outside of the town were farm plots, growing grains or vegetables.

Tractors tilled the land, but one field had an ox team plowing. The plots were irregular sizes and shapes, with clusters of the trees spread around them, but all ended abruptly at a fence to the west.

The fence was above man-high, metal chain links, and ran in a straight line from the river bank to the north all the way to the stream on the south. It wasn't substantial enough to stop a vehicle, but it would stop animals. Even more interesting, it was a double fence, two parallel rows, with clear land in between. They climbed back down and briefed the others.

"That's weird," Lee said. "Why such an elaborate fence?"

"Don't know," Dena said. "There's plenty of good land outside it. Why constrain your growth that way?"

"Maybe to keep the giraffes from eating everything."

"Could be. But one person with a shotgun, or some sort of audio howler would do it." Seeing Scruggs's scrunched face, Dena explained that a howler was a noisemaker that scared animals away. "They come close and it plays growls from their natural enemies. They soon learn to stay away."

"That fence is a big deal. Expensive."

"So's a missile battery," Dena said. "Lots of money."

"What are they protecting? There's no gold mines or anything here, are there?"

"Not that I've heard of."

"Not too big. Should be easy to climb."

"Should be. But I see power lines running to it. Might be electrified."

"Stranger and stranger."

The stream arrowed northeast. The crew stayed on the south side well into the trees. They couldn't see the river or the nearby fence, but they could hear the water gushing.

"More foliage here," Dena said. Since he couldn't get lost if he followed the river, Gavin had gone ahead. To give him a break, she and Scruggs had split his loads of powerpacks, computers, and explosives between them. "Only maybe every tenth tree is stripped. The giraffes must not like it here."

"But more of those holes." Scruggs pointed. "Look at that tree. It's nearly toppled over. I've seen five in the last hour."

Rocky came over and sniffed. He spent a long time investigating before cocking a leg on it.

"Rocky doesn't like this type of tree," Scruggs said. "Neither do the diggers."

"This type? What do you mean?"

"There's at least two types. The ones that are dug up are all like this. Those ones have that long leaf. Not as many as the others. The others have those funny pointed leaves."

Dena ran her hands along the bark. "Rough, but not too bad. The leaves—this is a type of oak. Have you seen any acorns?"

"Acorns? Those little nut things?"

"Yes. Should be around here."

"Don't they spore or flower or something?"

"They should. We should see some of them. Shhh. Here comes Lee."

Lee jogged back from the woods ahead holding a finger to her lips. "Quiet. Gavin's found something. There's water lines ahead. But coming out of the trees."

"Water from trees?" Dena narrowed her eyes. "Like, catching drips from leaves?"

"Nope. Holes drilled into the trees."

"Drilled into the trees?"

"Like spouts, or hammered in, with hoses attached. You'll have to come up."

"Any people?"

"Nope." Lee had already turned and run back.

Scruggs and Dena stumbled up the hill. Gavin had overloaded their packs. His friendly, easy manner allowed them to forget he was a big man, nearly as big as the centurion. He hadn't made allowances for smaller frames.

They came over a ridge and found him standing next to a large tree with red-green leaves. It was shorter than the trees they had climbed earlier, but had the same funny-colored leaves. The slope was dotted with them. Every thirty or forty feet, a yellow plastic spout had been drilled into a tree. A short red connector dropped about two feet to a larger hose on the ground at a blue T-junction. The larger hose disappeared down to the river bed, connecting trees as they went by.

"This is the first human construction we've seen," Gavin said. "There aren't any people. No footprints either. I looked like you taught us, Scruggs."

Lee smothered a grin. Scruggs had given them all a class in finding footprints. Dena had sniggered through the whole thing.

"Doesn't mean much," Dena said. "The rain would have washed them away. How many are there?"

"Dozens," Gavin said. "Maybe hundreds. I can see seven of those hoses running uphill, and a half dozen connections just in view. If each one connects twenty or thirty trees, that's a lot. Look here." He held up one of the short connector hoses. A reddish sap dripped inside. "Whoever did this, the tree farmer or whoever, they screwed those metal taps into the trees, right through the bark into the wood. Then they attached these hoses, and collected the sap. Not sure why."

"Is it poison?" Scruggs asked. "Some sort of special poison tree?"

Imperial Legionary

"Noooooo." Dena twisted a hose. "I've seen pictures of this somewhere. Not on Rockhaul, but it's nagging at me."

"Why go to all this trouble to get tree sap?" Gavin said. "It's just sap. Why not cut down the trees and crush them?"

"Must be something special," Dena said. "And they must need the trees alive."

"But why? What is it?"

"I wonder…" Dena yanked the hose off the spigot. Sap dripped from the spigot. She bent over and sniffed it.

"Be careful, Dena." Lee said. "Don't get it on your hands. It might be a contact poison, or it might be some sort of drug, or—No! Don't!"

Dena stuck her hands under the spigot, and caught a drop. She held her hand up to her face, sniffed again, then licked her palm.

Lee gasped. "What is it? What's going on? Are you sick?"

Dena licked her palm again, then grabbed another drop.

"Is it poison?"

"Nope. Not poison. Even worse." Dena stuck her finger in her mouth and licked it clean. "Much worse. This isn't poison. It's maple syrup. We're in the middle of a secret maple syrup plantation." She licked it again. "And the maple syrup mafia kill strangers who find out their secrets. We need to look sharp."

Chapter 6

Franceska Monti, commander, under the emperor, or at least under Tribune Devin, of the Imperial Starship *Collingwood,* the finest corvette in the fleet, sat at her desk and cursed fate. Earlier, she'd been so angry, she'd even went so far as to look up the history of the word 'fate,' discovered it referenced strange Greek goddesses, and tried to pronounce them, in order, while she was cursing. Nothing was working properly on her ship, including her pronunciation. Her comm bonged. "Yes, Lieutenant Hooper, what is it?"

"Franky, how you doing?" Bronwin Hooper asked. She was Monti's first officer, longtime friend, and fellow Imperial Navy Volunteer reserve colleague. She was also nearly Monti's near physical twin, alike enough they had switched places in class or on dates a time or two, and shared Monti's thick Melbourne accent and casual mien.

"I told you not to call me Franky on duty."

"I'm off duty forty minutes ago. My watch is loooong over."

"What? Well, who's supposed to relieve you?"

"That would be one Franceska Monti, senior lieutenant."

"Oh, crap. Sorry, Bron. Doing the paperwork and I got stuck in it." Paperwork. I'm in the middle of a rebellion, and I'm doing paperwork.

"How's the fuel situation?"

Rather than answer, Monti sent a chart to Hooper's comm. "What do you think?"

Hooper whistled when she saw the numbers. "Holy hydrogen guzzling systems. That power consumption curve is way above specs. What's wrong with this ship?"

"We're old, we need more maintenance, we're driving things too hard. The crew sucks at maneuvers, which means we burn too much fuel, which means more frequent fuel stops—"

"I gotcha," Hooper interrupted. "More maneuvering to get said fuel, which means more fuel."

"Vicious cycle."

Tribune Devin had sent *Collingwood* to scout out the approaches to New Malaya, the biggest Naval base in the Sarawak sector, while he exercised his fleet. He'd shared his plans to sneak up and surprise the Imperial defense forces there, but he needed a warship-free path from his exercise area to the base.

"Want me to schedule more training maneuvers? Try to improve efficiency?"

"And burn more fuel and put more wear on the ship? No. Not until I get us more." Monti rubbed her forehead. She was stuck in a downward spiral of inefficiency, poor maintenance, and decrepit parts. *It's not my fault. Which makes me feel better, but doesn't help solve the problem.*

"Tell you what, we're drifting. How about I pull a double watch, if you don't mind me napping in the big chair."

"Somebody should be awake and looking at the board."

"Somebody should, and it's going to be either you or me. We're already running on nearly no sleep. Before we start making stupid decisions, no, strike that. Before we start making *more* stupid decisions or *stupider* decisions, let's see if we can get some rest up here. Besides, Silaski is up here, and that's supposed to be a good thing."

Silaski, their helmsman, was supposedly fully trained after eight years in the Navy. Monti found her one of the most incompetent ratings she'd ever come across. Bribing her way into her current position, paying off chiefs to certify her training, she'd advanced until she occupied an important spot on the ship with no idea how to do it. But she was willing to learn. Monti was suspicious, but not so suspicious that she didn't enjoy the extra four hours of sleep she got each time she 'supervised Silaski's watch-standing training.'

Totally against regulations, but as long as either she or Hooper were on the bridge, physically locked into their chairs, so they could react instantly to problems. *Put Silaski in charge. What could possibly go wrong? Or perhaps, what more could possibly go wrong?*

"What's she doing?"

"She's running sensor scans."

"Anything interesting?"

"Not really. We've got two Imperial freighters, and a system runabout."

"Sure it's a runabout?" Runabouts were big ships without jump drives, and without much in the way of cabins or accommodations.

"It's trundling along at a quarter G, and it's huge. Can't be anything but the ISS *Menard*. Flagship of Menard warehouse and shipping."

"Anything we need to check out?"

"Nope. You go back and enjoy your paperwork. But, ah, there is a Nat freighter in the system."

Monti whooshed a breath. "You had to save that for the end, didn't you?"

"That's because I love you. Don't want to ruin your day right away."

"Big one?"

"Big enough. More than twenty times our size."

"What's it doing?"

"Nothing. It's getting gas, out spinning around one of the gas giants."

"Any weapons?"

"Nothing visible in passive scan."

"What's it called?"

"It is the..." Hooper clicked through her screens. "*Peeter Strasser. Pieter Straser.* Don't know how that's pronounced. P-E-T-E-R S-T-R-A-S-S-E-R. General cargo, 240 containers, crew of 42."

"What are they doing out here?"

"Picking up fruit juice, seems like." System Cracodon had three agricultural planets with marginal atmosphere and marginal rain, but capable of growing crops. They'd formed some sort of loose confederation and exported fruits and juices to the rest of the Empire. The juices were well spoken of and often used to mix with the Basic that ships carried as emergency rations. "They responded to the automated hails, no worries on that. Their beacon gave us everything we needed, even gave us a manifest and a crew list, plus the clearance info when they crossed the border. They even checked in with customs."

"Interesting." Monti tapped her chin. Customs clearance had gone by the wayside in the last few months. Tribune Devin's incipient rebellion was causing some stress to the Imperial taxation infrastructure. Those tax agents that weren't directly under his immediate control had tended to either decamp with the local funds or simply lie low and hope the whole thing would pass over. "What are the other ships in the system carrying?"

"Fruit juice. Everybody's doing fruit juice."

"Big crew to carry fruit juice."

"Isn't it? And a long way from the border, and what Imperial company ships fruit juice on a Union of Nations hull?"

"Keep an eye on it. Tell Silaski to keep an eye on it."

"I get to stay up here?"

"Get your nap. I'll finish my paperwork and come up in a while."

Monti never did get her paperwork to balance.

No matter how she added things up or organized it, she was going to need to make at least one additional fuel stop. The Tribune had said no official contact with anyone while she scouted systems, and definitely no fueling up at official Imperial fueling stations.

Side jump. She brought up the sailing directions and found a nearby system, uninhabited and seldom visited, but had a gas giant. A hydrogen-rich gas giant. *Jump in, suck fuel. Treat it like an anchorage. Put one person on duty, everybody else sleeps a whole shift. Take a shift to run exercises, top up fuel again, and then continue scouting. Waste of time, but necessary.*

Monti set the jump parameters. She checked with Hooper. Hooper confirmed she was bored. Silaski confirmed that she had a course. And Hooper confirmed that she had taken Silaski's course and not only checked it, but double-checked it and triple-checked it, and then removed it from the computer and manually typed it in again. And then checked it again.

There had been an unfortunate mis-jump with one of Silaski's courses previously, so they were both a little wary of giving her unfettered navigation control.

"Hooper, what do you got?"

"Board is green. Engineering report's ready."

"Start the jump counter. Give me five minutes." Monti did her own checks while they sat and watched the green numbers on the screen in front of them count down.

"Jump space," Silaski announced. "All systems green."

"Very well," Monti said. "Set jump watches."
More time to do paperwork.

"Bron, what are we doing here?" Monti asked, a

few days later. The jump had been boring, the emergence unremarkable, and the gas giant bursting with elemental hydrogen for them to suck. They'd topped up and headed back to the jump limit.

Hooper had her own paperwork, mostly inventing excuses why their scratch crew performed so poorly. She blamed poor equipment, defective parts, limited supply, and when that didn't work, sunspots. "We're getting gas and then going back on our patrol. Tribune wants us to scout to see if he can sneak ships through here."

"Yeah, but you know we're in the Imperial Navy?"

"Pretty astute of you, Franky. I'm surprised at how clearly you see things. What gave it away? The uniforms? The salutes? Perhaps it was the armed starship that we've been dragging around with us?"

"No, I mean we're in the *Imperial* Navy. Why are we popping around for this rebel dude? We should have run off and, turned ourselves in to the nearest Imperial warship and said what he was doing back when this started."

"We probably should have, and we could have, but we didn't."

"Why didn't we do that?"

"Shhhhhsh." Hooper pointed forward. "Silaski, how's it look?"

The helmsman didn't look up from her board. "Counter is on. Stations nominal. I'm monitoring our course."

"Super! Good job Silaski." Hooper lowered her voice. "I don't know. Maybe it's the way that that Tribune guy talked. He's persuasive. Remember the dinner?"

Tribune Devin had invited both of them for a memorable dinner before they left on patrol. He'd provided Hooper and Monti with both a sumptuous meal, the best wine they'd ever tasted, and complete justification as to why it was necessary for them to return to the Core and take the Empire away from the evil men and women who now controlled it. Presentation, quality, and quantity of wine had made it seem like a great idea at the time. The next day, Monti wasn't so sure, both about the quantity of wine and whether it was a great idea. Her appreciation of the quality of wine remained intact.

"It was a great dinner. Were we sold a bill of goods?"

"Well, we've got to work for somebody. If we hadn't been working for the Empire, we'd have been working for some shipping line, plodding along. This way, we get to go where we want, see who we want, and be in charge. Jump in forty seconds."

"But what do you think…" Monti waved her hand at the bridge. "Of all this."

"I think we'll see what happens. Jump." The screen flashed green.

The next system looked similar to the others on the potential routes from where the Tribune's fleet was located toward the fleet base New Malaya.

New Malaya was in the Sarawak Sector, adjacent to the Core. Sarawak Sector was smaller than the Verge, but much larger than the Core. Trade paths crossed it, leading to the other great empires. And the closer they got to the busier systems, especially the cluster around the Naval base at New Malaya, the more the traffic would be expected to increase.

But seeing another Union of Nations freighter in the next system, again, was a surprise.

Hooper ordered the *Collingwood* to sailing stations—a level below general quarters— stations manned, but no need for closing up or sealing helmets. "Run the board for me, Lieutenant."

"Four Imperial freighters, nothing unusual in their beacons. One is an old friend from Krakatoa with a manifest of fruit juice, here to be transferred for almond milk."

"Almond milk is worth shipping across the Empire?"

"I'm not paying for it. This other Nat freighter, though. Interesting."

"Same one as before?"

"Nope, different beacon. This is the City of Strasbourg. Not Strassberg, spelled differently. According to the sailing directions, it's some sort of border thing. Some nationalistic argument they have with the Empire."

"Thanks for the geography lesson. Where is it?"

"It's out at the gas giant. Loading fuel."

"Cargo?"

"It doesn't say, specifically—mixed light industrial goods. Furniture. Power tools."

"Could hide anything in that."

"You could." Hooper switched the main screen to a telescopic view. "Here's something interesting. It's exactly the same size as the freighter from the last system. The fruit-freighter."

"Similar classes, right? Should be the same size."

"This one looks different. The visuals don't match, but the length overall does, and so does every other dimension I can measure."

"You measured everything last time?"

"I was bored. Check it out." Hooper put up two images on the screen. Both had been taken through the telescope, and from a long distance away. Both were clearly of different ships. Colors, logo, and some obvious sensor and docking extrusions.

Then she put a scale on both. "You notice that

nose to tail, the two ships are exactly the same length?"

Monti peered at her screen. "They're different classes. What's the chance of them being exactly the same length?"

"That's the question, isn't it?" Hooper highlighted a few details on the display. "There's an extra truss there, and it looks like this one is missing some containers."

"It may have offloaded them."

"But on this one, there's a void space, no container cradle. Easy to swap something in there. And look here." Hooper highlighted a point on one ship. "What about that?"

"Standard sensor array."

"Awful big for a standard sensor array," Hooper said.

Monti nodded. "Maybe they make them big in the Union of Nations."

"Maybe they do. But it could be a spy ship."

"Let's keep an eye on it. Silaski, keep an eye on that freighter."

Silaski looked up from her screen. She'd been reading checklists for firefighting equipment. "Yes ma'ams. What do you mean keep an eye on it?"

"If it does anything unusual that the other freighters aren't doing."

"You mean like sends its launch out to track the other ships in the system?"

"Sure, if it does that, let me know."

"Okay, Captain, I'm letting you know."

"What? Did it do that?"

Silaski laboriously paged through her screens. "See that beacon?"

"That's their shuttle." Monti expanded the screen display. "Shuttle's awful far away from its parent ship. It's in a different orbit. Why would you put your shuttle in a different orbit around a gas giant?"

"To shuttle to something," Hooper said. "That's why it's called a shuttle. Didn't they teach you that in captain's school?"

"Never went to captain's school. Is there even such a thing? But there's nothing to shuttle to."

"Tell you one thing, though. See how the orbit of the freighter is tilted? It's trying to hide behind that planet. The other ships in the system won't see it if they're in standard commercial orbits. Even if they do care to look."

"Silaski," Monti said. "Pitch north, climb at one G on the main drive. And remember to sound the warnings this time."

Silaski got the bonging alarms right, pivoted the ship, and started to climb over the ecliptic. Monti gave Silaski another 'attagirl' and settled back into her chair.

Hooper had already focused the available sensors. "Hello, Mr. Shuttle. How are you today? Interesting."

"Tell me."

"It's in an elliptical Molniya orbit. Once it goes up, I'll bet you it's able to get a sensor sweep, or at least a beacon reading, of all the ships in the system."

"Shuttles are too small to have a serious sensor suite," Monti argued.

"Shuttles are too small to *economically* have a serious sensor suite," Hooper said. "But if it was a military shuttle…"

The bridge was silent as she and Monti checked their readings.

"You think it's a spy ship?"

"I think there's a pretty good chance."

"Well, you know that the Nats are always keeping an eye on us."

"They're always keeping an eye on the Empire.

Here, there, everywhere. I'm just a little concerned that they're keeping an eye on us in this exact system, this exact place, this exact time. Right in the middle of a rebellion." Monti blanked her screen and sat back. "Right where we might be bringing a fleet through."

Chapter 7

"I call it Operation Pegasus," Devin said. He and Lionel had finished going over the daily fuel report and retired to his dining room. Imin had modified the dining room table so it could double as a pool table, and Devin had challenged Lionel to play a game.

"Operation Pegasus? We're dealing with winged horses?" Lionel took the cue that Devin offered him. "I've seen pictures of this. I poke those balls, right?"

"No, no, no." Devin shook his head. "You don't understand, Prefect. Pegasus is a symbol of rebirth. It's the fire that consumes and creates the new empire out of its ashes. And the proper word is 'strike' the balls."

Lionel hefted his cue. "Pardon me, Tribune. I know I'm a minor Prefect and all, using the wrong words and not knowing how to play pools. But isn't that a Phoenix, not a Pegasus?"

"A Phoenix? And it's pool, not pools."

"But there's more than one ball. Shouldn't it be plural? Pools?"

"It isn't. It's pool. Don't hold it like that, hold it like this." Devin demonstrated.

Lionel copied him, badly. "Fine, pool. But it should be Operation Phoenix, not Pegasus."

"You sure?"

"A hundred percent."

Devin drummed his fingers on the table then slapped his intercom. "Imin?"

"Tribune?" Imin said.

"Which is the symbol of rebirth, Pegasus or Phoenix?"

"Pegasus is a winged horse sir. Phoenix is the bird that burns up and then reconstitutes itself out of the ashes. It's the symbol of rebirth."

"I see."

"Would the Tribune like some wine delivered while he discusses it? I have a delightful Pinot Gris."

"Jove, I was sure….thank you. I mean, yes, that would be great. Uh..." Devin flicked the intercom off. "Right. Operation Phoenix, then."

"Bringing rebirth to the Empire. Good start on the planning, Tribune."

Devin held up his hand. "Be still. Here's my plan." He broke, and sank a solid-colored ball. "Once we've finished our exercises here, we will collect our fleet units together. We have battleships, we have heavy cruisers, we have frigates, we have corvettes. We will proceed to the Sarawak sector. We're going to attack the sector capital, New Malaya, and occupy the base and the main shipyards in a daring raid."

Lionel lifted a finger, but Devin waved him down. "Now I know what you're going to say, that these shipyards are not going to be undefended, but they're close enough to the Verge that we can access them quickly, and they're far enough from the Core that they won't be heavily garrisoned. And while we can expect to meet units of the Core fleets when they return to defend the situation, that won't be until after we seize the shipyards and their resources."

"I was going to say all that. And also, how do we get there?"

"These paths we've had Dirk and the corvettes scouting are going to give us a route to come into an attacking position. I expect the first reports soon. You, Prefect, are going to serve as my flag captain on board the *Canopus*. You'll be my tactical deputy. We will conduct a lightning raid. Blockade the shipyard and Naval base, seize the orbital infrastructure. And then we will send down

Santana's Marines to seize the base and any ships under construction. Once we have control, we can make good any shortages of supplies. And numerous ships are under construction there."

Lionel raised another finger. Again, Devin waved him down. "We'll seize the under-construction ships and use them to outfit our fleet, and then our next step will be to strike for the Core provinces."

Lionel held his cue. Devin waited. And waited. Finally, he asked, "Well? What do you think?"

"I can talk now?"

"Yes. What do you think about the plan?"

"I'm not at the plan yet. I would like to bring up a few points."

"Yes?"

"You do know that your flagship nearly rammed a destroyer yesterday."

"Yes, I heard. I also heard that it wasn't the helmsman's fault. It was a sensor failure. Make sure no blame should be attached to them."

"No blame is attached, Tribune. I think they did an excellent job under trying circumstances. However, the thing I'm concerned about is not the excellent job, it's the trying circumstances. If we're going into a battle and we suffer an engineering casualty, we won't be able to say that everyone did a good job, or even an excellent job, because we'll be blown into space dust."

"Well, yes, there is that." Devin potted another solid ball. "Two in a row. I'm on fire today."

"Second, our targeting is atrocious."

"Atrocious?"

"It sucks large tabbo—"

"I get the point. Anything else?"

"Other than engineering not able to give us full power when we need it, this beast maneuvers like a dropped rock, the crew is disgruntled, we've got pending life-support problems, and the aforementioned targeting, and a complete failure to achieve any of our training goals. Other than that, no, nothing right now. Not yet."

"Fine." Devin slapped his hands on the table, then stood and stalked to the sideboard to pour more wine. "Thanks for all of that. Have anything positive to tell me?"

"Yes." Lionel nodded. "Couple of things."

Devin turned. "Really? Good news?"

"Don't act so surprised. Did you know this is a battleship?"

"It did seem larger than anything I've been on before, yes. Stop being obtuse. You've told me it's old, slow, decrepit, undermanned and under-sensored. What's good?"

"The guns." Lionel stepped to the wall and brought up a schematic on the display board, then overlaid it with firing arcs. "They fire slowly, yes. But they're powerful, and we have lots of them. And the range—so much farther than any other ship I'm used to."

"Meaning?"

"No small ship can come within range of our guns and survive. Frigates, destroyers, cruisers, anything smaller than a heavy cruiser, maybe even that. If they try to get close enough to hurt us, we outrange them so much, we'll pound them to space dust before they can get a glove on us."

"But?"

"We're slow. Ponderous." Lionel put other numbers up on the board. "We can't catch anything, enemy units can run away. But we're immune to light units. They can't hurt us. And if we keep our light units in close, nothing can hurt them either. We're like this giant umbrella of safety that we can place over our fleet."

Devin sipped his wine. "What can hurt us?""

"Other battleships."

"Even I knew that."

"And major base defenses, if they are powerful enough."

"Meaning New Malaya?"

Lionel nodded. "New Malaya. Yes. Their defenses will chew up anything smaller than us. We can stand toe to toe with them. But that's not the most important thing. I don't know if you've looked at the supply requisitions from this morning."

"I skimmed them. That part, supplies, is what I have Prefects for. Thank you, Imin." Imin had returned with two small plates of canapes and served the two officers.

"Want to know the difference between a professional Naval commander and a…." Lionel's voice trailed off.

"Non-professional? Amateur?"

"I was going to say clueless noble pretending to be an officer." Lionel nodded. "But let's go with amateurs. Amateurs argue tactics, dilettantes argue strategy, professionals—"

"Talk about logistics. Yes. Yes." Devin leaned back as Imin dropped a cracker with red paste on his plate. "Know what Tribunes worry about?"

"What?"

"Money." Devin took another gulp. "Nervos belli, pecuniam infinitam."

"What's that mean?"

Imin pushed a plate in front of Lionel, and spoke. "Cicero. The sinews of war are infinite money."

The two officers stared at Imin. Imin returned their glances. "Sirs?"

Devin raised his eyebrows. "I know you didn't have a classical education. Where did you learn Latin?"

Imin shrugged. "I heard it in a movie once. More wine, Tribune?"

"No thank you." Devin sighed. "Do you know how difficult it is to be surrounded by people more competent than you, Prefect?"

"Absolutely not, no." Lionel grinned. "I've always got at least one person nearby that I can count on to make me feel superior."

Devin laughed. "I deserved that. But that's, what do you call it? Lazy-majesty?"

"Statement of fact. You're not any majesty yet."

"Thanks for the reminder." Devin leaned onto the table and potted another solid ball. "Remind me, why do you keep me around?"

"We need those execute, execute, execute words occasionally. Remind me again why you wanted to be Emperor?"

"Not want. Duty requires." Devin chewed his canapes. "Marvelous, Imin. How are you going to win this war?"

Lionel looked at the table. "How about bombarding a few dozen planets with our fancy battleship? Bet the rest will fall into line quickly."

"How we win matters more than winning."

"Not if you're losing." Lionel stared at Devin. "Nobody ever cares how you lost a war."

Devin glared. "We will win this war in an honorable way, because we are honorable men." He missed his next shot. "Jove's knees."

Lionel and Imin exchanged glances. Imin glided off. Lionel studied the pool table. "As you so recently said, that part is what I, Lionel, have a Tribune for. There's nothing I can do about money. Or strategy. That's on your desk."

"My desk is pretty busy—"

"Money will sink us later. Supplies will sink us now. You're gonna have to do more than skimming those reports. We're having issues. Fuel consumption is through the roof. Three of the corvettes ran out of fuel on a recent battle exercise."

"How does a corvette run out of fuel on an exercise?"

"Well, the officers that we'd assigned to them, previously in the Core fleet, had spent most of their time maneuvering within range of shore facilities. Now they have to do semi-deep penetrations, and they forgot to take fueling considerations into account."

Lionel detailed the problem. Two corvettes had to be refueled, meaning rescued, by a third, and one of the destroyers hadn't been able to reach the rendezvous with a tanker because of incorrect calculations. With the exception of his former crew from *Pollux,* most of the officers and crew were barely competent in shipboard operations, and useless in combat.

"So." Lionel pointed at the display. "Given the state of the light units, I'd like to point out that perhaps engaging a covering squadron of the Core fleet at this time may not be the best thing that we've ever planned. More training would help."

"We do have to do something, but an emperor who holds the provinces is no emperor at all. We have to get to the Core. Besides, as we've indicated here, the Core ships and their crews are just as badly trained as us."

"I'm not saying we're badly trained, Tribune, but we're well trained to run a frigate. Not a fleet or a battleship." Lionel spun an empty wine glass. "With respect, you make a great inspiration for all the troops, and you make a reasonable frigate captain. Not as good as me, of course, but luckily, you have me along."

"How lucky I am," Devin said. "Jove smiles on me."

"He does!" Lionel grinned. "But to follow that, I'll have to say you're no fleet admiral and this is my first time commanding a battleship, and on a scale of one to ten, I think I'm doing an excellent job. But. It's still my first time and I'm still making mistakes and we can't afford to make those mistakes in the face of the enemy."

"What do we do? Sit out here and wait for them to come to us?"

"I don't think they'll ever come to us."

The compartment door gonged and Imin stepped through. "Pino Grigio, gentlemen?"

"Yes, Imin. Thank you."

Imin served the two officers, pouring each a glass. "I'll leave the bottle, shall I sir?"

"Yes, please, Imin, thank you."

"Imin," Lionel interrupted. "How long have we been exercising the fleet here?"

"As the Prefect knows, we've been here for almost two weeks."

"And how long has our little semi-revolt been going on?"

"I wouldn't say it's only a semi-revolt, sir, but quite some time. Months, at least."

"I'm not expressing myself properly. Imin, have they heard in the Core about this?"

"Of course sir. One way or another, they know that the Tribune has proclaimed himself Emperor."

"How come they haven't sent out the fleet to squash us? We've got a battleship and some cruisers, but we're not exactly a militarily strong force. I would have expected they would have sent something on before now."

Imin loaded his tray with empty plates. "Maybe they need those fleet units in the Core to stay there sir."

"Whatever would they need fleet units to stay in the Core for when there's an Emperor in rebellion out in the provinces?"

"I don't know sir. I'm just a steward. But if I was the one in charge, I would ask myself, why were the Core fleets created in the first place?"

Devin and Lionel exchanged glances, then turned to look at the display.

Imin waited. "Will there be anything else sir?"

Devin shook his head. "No, not at this time. Thank you."

Imin closed the door behind him. Devin focused the screen display. "Right, it said 'Verge Sector.' Next, it's the... Let's cut the magnification down." He backed the display up.

The Verge sector was a huge expanse of space, a hundred times the volume of the Core sector. Core and the adjacent old Empire sectors were tiny, but densely populated. Even the adjacent Sarawak sector between the Core and the Verge occupied more space than all of the Core sectors combined.

Devin pointed at the display. "That is a good question. Why aren't they here? Why did they only send one old battleship and a couple small support ships and an admiral—an incompetent admiral—to squash us?"

Lionel nodded. "If nothing else, they could have sent out two battleships and squashed us."

"Battleships would have had a problem squashing us," Devin said. "Well, catching us at least."

Lionel shook his head. "They could easily have sent a destroyer squadron with a few light cruisers to back it up. *Pollux* couldn't run away from that, too many ships, and if they'd sent out a battle cruiser, that would have murdered us. They're as fast as *Pollux* is. And without us having all these support ships, they could chase us from system to system until we ran out of fuel."

"How come they didn't?"

"Bring the magnification up again." The screen changed. Now it showed all the known expanses of the Milky Way. "Rotate that." The galactic display shimmied on its y-axis, spinning in a circle. The capital was clearly visible, marked with a pulsing light. "Show the Confeds and the Nats as well." The display changed to show the Empire in green, the Confeds in red, and the Nats in a dark blue.

Spatial geometry was complicated. After the colonization wars, and after the destruction of Old Terra, known space had fragmented into empires and independent systems. Warships could traverse the distance between the capital planets in weeks, not months. Each empire expanded, and when they found their expansion blocked in one direction by another, simply expanded away in a different direction. The result was tendrils of settlement focused on jump lines that reached out in all directions.

The Verge was a particular mess. All of the main empires managed to get their claws into a planet or two. A dozen jump corridors snaked back to different Core sectors.

"You know," Devin said, "I think I've been away from the Core too long."

Lionel nodded. "You have. You've forgotten the main strategic constraints of the empire."

"The reason the fleets aren't coming out to get us is because they're needed elsewhere."

"But the capital fleets are corrupt and undercrewed and ineffective. Speaking from a devil's advocate point of view," Lionel said.

"That may be true," Devin said, "but they're also there. And even a corrupt, ineffective, undercrewed fleet will fight pretty hard when it's above their home capital planet, so they can't be disregarded. And quantity has a quality all its own as the man said." He looked back at the static pool table. "Are you going to take your shot?"

"In a minute. The reason that we haven't been squashed like a bug is—" Lionel ticked off his fingers. "First, they didn't know we needed squashing. Second, once they found out through the couriers or the merchant ships that you were here and needed squashing, they hesitated to move against you because of the political ramifications of dealing with your sister and the Emperor. Third, once they dealt with your sister and the Emperor, tracking you down and finding where you were was a challenge. Fourth, once they got a general idea of where you were and how strong you were, they sent the minimum capable force that they figured would be able to destroy you."

Devin twirled his own wine glass. "And this force was built by collecting together bits and pieces of ships from all over the sector, collecting the random Marine detachments from everywhere else and throwing them at us. Threatens us, but collectively weakening the entire Verge sector."

"Yes, that seems reasonable."

"So that means that the mainline fleet is needed in the Core for some reason, and that's why we're not getting chased by sixteen destroyers, three cruisers, and a battle squadron."

Lionel shook his head. "They don't have a battle squadron to spare. They need them all. The Empire only has, what, twenty battleships?"

"Not even that, if you check and see what's in service."

"Even sending one of the older ones out here is a noticeable disruption of their strength."

Devin spread his hands. "Good news is, we're not likely to meet much in the way of resistance when we get to the Sarawak sector."

"Bad news is, the reason that we're... not going

to meet that resistance is that they haven't bothered to send it out because they need the ships somewhere else."

"What else is going on?" Devin spun the display around side to side, up and down, and they stared at the colored lights.

"It's either the Nats or the Confeds," Lionel said. "They've been doing something. They took advantage of the chaos in the Core."

"Or they planned the chaos in the Core," Devin pointed out.

"And we're an unwelcome sidebar."

"Who is it? The Confeds or the Nats?"

Lionel grimaced. "Tribune, you're not going to want to hear it."

"Tell me anyways." Devin pointed. "And take your shot."

Lionel checked a few angles, then stepped up and ran the table, sinking all the striped balls in succession, and finishing with the eight.

"Never played before, you said."

"I never said that. You assumed. Bad habit for a fleet commander, assuming things."

"Good point. Well, is it Nats or Confeds?"

Lionel focused the map display on the Core Sector. "I think it's both."

Chapter 8

"Well, that explains the missiles," Lee said. "You have a warehouse full of maple syrup, the last thing you want is some pirate landing and stealing it."

Dena had identified the sap-bearing trees as maple trees. They crowded under the branches to examine the metal taps. Rocky sniffed a nearby oak tree, then dug at the roots.

"Pirates are going to steal maple syrup?" Scruggs licked her hands. Dena had dripped syrup on everyone. "I mean, it's tasty, but pretty watery. How much is it worth?"

"This is only the sap," Dena said. "You need to get rid of the water first. Concentrated maple syrup sap is fifty, or even a hundred credits a liter. One cubic meter of sap is a hundred thousand credits. Figure out how many of those you can fit in a standard container."

Scruggs did the math. "Five million credits a container?"

"Could be more, depending on the quality. That means the *Heart's Desire* could carry tens of millions of credits' worth."

"Yeah," Gavin said, "when you pirate a ship, people think the first thing you should steal is electronics or gold or something. But gold is heavy, and electronics are hard to sell, and there's maintenance and compatibility problems. Easier to take consumer products like toothpaste or shampoo or flour or something. Less security, easier to fence and the police don't chase you nearly as hard."

Lee raised an eyebrow. "You know a lot about pirate cargoes, friend Gavin?"

Gavin ducked his head and coughed. "I mean,

that's what I've been told, I heard it, or I think I read it somewhere."

"Like in a manual called 'Pirate operating procedures 101'?"

"Or in standing orders from your—" Scruggs cocked her head. "Your pirate leader. What's a pirate leader called?"

"Captain?" Dena asked. "Hegemon? Scourge of the spaceways?"

"Not the spaceways," Scruggs said. "Scourge of the... maple orchard?"

"Scourge of the orchards doesn't sound dangerous," Dena said. "More like a particularly nasty type of fungus."

Dust flew up as Rocky dug. He growled and pulled a bone out.

"What type of fungus shot this guy, then?" Dena wrestled the bone from Rocky. "And after it shot him, it dug a hole and buried him?"

"Maybe those were claim jumpers?" Scruggs asked.

"You only claim jump a mine."

"You told me that this is more expensive than gold.."

"Well, yes. Okay. Point."

"We'll have to be careful," Lee said. "The Maple Syrup Cartel has a reputation of being violent. Did you have them on Rockhaul, Dena?"

Dena shook her head. "No. They didn't grow there. I know that they're not part of the standard terraforming packages that the Empire uses. We tried, but they're impossible to grow most places. Not sure why, they should be able to grow anywhere that pine or spruce grow."

"Maybe they need some micro-nutrient that was only present on Old Earth," Scruggs said.

"Or they were excluded because somebody wanted to make money off them later in places like this. Either way, we need to walk small and keep sharp, avoid the planters."

"Everyone keep close together," Scruggs said. "If we run into them, we'll shoot first."

"Bad idea, Baby Marine," Dena said.

"What? The centurion always said start fights on your own terms—"

"The centurion's not here," Dena said. "Our job is to get into town and deal with those missiles, not start a fight in the woods. If we see them, we should avoid them."

"Dirk put me in charge—"

"Dirk's not here either. And he knows less than nothing about planet side tasks. When we're on a planet and follow his suggestions, we get attacked by snakes, or bombed by volcanoes, or drowned by rivers. I know the woods."

"I don't think—"

"She's right, Sister Scruggs," Lee said. "Dirk doesn't try to do everything himself, and the centurion never interferes in ship operations. Dena's giving good advice. You should take it."

Scruggs opened her mouth, then closed it. *Centurion did say to take the skills of troops into account.* "Fine. How do we do this"

"Me first," Dena said. "I'm the best tracker. I see things you others don't. Scruggs, you come next. Keep me in sight, and if I wave you down, you stop and wait until I say come up. Unless the shooting starts, then I'll hide and you can come up and fire away. You're our best long-range shooter."

Gavin raised an eyebrow. "You said you were better than Scruggs."

"Other than me, I meant." Dena looked at Scruggs. "She has been practicing. Say, half as good as me."

"Half?" Scruggs hefted her rifle. "Half?"

"Not now, Sister Scruggs," Lee said. "Then

Gavin and I follow?"

"As far back as you can," Dena said. "But keep her in view."

"You want us back there to keep us safe?" Gavin laughed. "Worried we might get all shy?"

"I want you as far back as possible because you march like a herd of drunken tabbos," Dena said. "You make so much noise, you and Lee both, it sounds like neo-moose in rutting season. Both of you never met a stick you didn't want to crack in half, or a pile of leaves that you didn't want to rustle."

"That's true," Gavin admitted. "Too much time on a ship. I don't have the knack of these woods."

"Me neither," Lee said. "Fine, we stay back. But what happens if we hear fighting, or shooting?"

"If Scruggs doesn't warn you back, come a-running. What do those Marines say? Run to the guns?"

"Current ad Bellum, we ran to the noise of battle." Lee said.

"No, it's *Currunt* ad Bellum," Gavin said. "Means run to war."

Scruggs shook her head. "Centurion says it's *Currant* ad Bellum. Run to the guns, like you're planning on doing it."

"Well, which is it? Current, Currant, or Currunt?" Dena asked.

The other three shrugged.

"What an Empire," Dena said. "Doesn't even know its own motto. Fine. Rocky, come here. I've got a special deal for you."

Rocky wagged his tail. Something exciting was happening. *Maybe there would be treats!*

The day wore on. Dena glided through the forest, guiding them uphill from the increasingly deepening ravine, but avoided the tops of the hills.

More rain made the forest floor slick and muddy, and she had to take care sneaking forward. She paused frequently to check the ground, or to climb a tree and get a view of the town.

Scruggs followed, rifle loaded and at the ready. She kept Dena in view, but had little time to survey her surroundings, concentrating on not falling on the rain-slicked hill. *I should be up front. I should be first. I'm in charge. But she's better at this than me.*

Gavin and Lee clumped along behind, slipping every third step, trying not to make noise and failing miserably. Rocky was their flanker. Dena had removed his bulky ship harness and given him a lightweight hiking one. She'd introduced him to a new game called 'roll in every pile of mud you find,' which he loved. A mud-covered black dog was invisible in the forest, and Dena let him roam as far ahead as he wanted, counting on him being mistaken for local wildlife.

"Never thought serving the Empress would involve this much mud," Lee muttered. "How does Dena stand it?"

"No worse than hydraulic fluid, I suppose," Gavin said.

"I hate it."

"Why?" Gavin dropped to one knee as he slipped on more leaves.

"It bothers me."

"But you deal with injuries and blood and all that all the time," Gavin said. "That never bothers you. Why not?"

"It doesn't, because, well, it doesn't," Lee said.

Gavin shrugged. "Dirt doesn't bother Dena, blood doesn't bother you, and hydraulic fluid doesn't bother me. But you know what does bother me?"

"I'm sure you'll tell me."

"Why you keep saying you're serving the

Empress, but you keep taking the Tribune's orders. Shouldn't you be going straight to the Empress?"

"He's her brother. He'll bring me to her."

"Not so far."

"There are other issues. I'm happy to be here for now. And since we're talking about this, how come you haven't headed back to go spying for… somebody."

Gavin shrugged. "Spying gets tiring. Always being somebody else. Here, I'm just Gavin the Engineer, hates mud."

"And likes hydraulic fluid."

"I'm used to it. Uh oh." Gavin pointed. Scruggs had dropped to one knee and was signaling. "That's her 'hold still' motion. Wait up."

After Dena waved, Scruggs dropped to one knee and made a fist. Dena dropped and wiggled uphill, then signaled. Scruggs turned to the others and pointed them up, then labored up under the trees. The hill was almost steeper than a person could climb here, but another yellow maple syrup tube ran uphill, and she used it to haul herself along. They'd crossed one of the tubes every few minutes, and she'd lost count of how many were in the woods.

Once she had climbed sufficiently high, she sneaked along until she could flop down next to Dena.

"Well?"

"That's a pretty impressive quantity of weapons, isn't it?" Dena pointed through the trees. A tiny creek splashed down the hill ahead of them, cutting a swath through the trees and overlooking a mountain meadow. Three hundred meters away, the meadow merged into another grove of maple trees. A crowd of armed soldiers stood in a semi-circle in front of a worker hammering taps into the trees. A second worker unrolled yellow cable and cut it to length. A third screwed the blue T-junction on, then attached a yellow drain hose to the tree spout.

Dena counted. "Three workers and ten, eleven, twelve guards. Why so many guards? And so few workers. It will take forever to get anything done."

Scruggs scanned with her sensor binoculars. "Are they afraid of animals?"

"What animals? The giraffes? They'll hardly charge that big a group."

"That's weird," Scruggs said. "Look at their weapons."

"Rifles, what about them? They're going hunting."

"They're not rifles. Sub-machine guns, the centurion would call them. They're not good at shooting long ranges, too inaccurate. Wrong thing to use to hunt animals."

"Unless the animals get close," Dena said. "The colors are different. These are blue hoses connected to yellow, the others were red to white. Watch it! Stay down!" Dena hauled a panting Gavin down next to her.

He splatted into the mud. "More mud, how exciting," Gavin said. "What are we looking at?"

Scruggs handed him the sensor binoculars. "Fifteen hostiles. Armed with short range semi-automatic weapons. No crew served weapons, anti-air or anti-armor visible. Deployed in protective formation."

"You spend too much time with the old man," Dena said. "You could have just said about twenty armed bad guys."

"It's important to be precise." Scruggs pointed uphill. "Gavin, Dena noticed the hoses are different colors than before. These are blue and yellow. Is that important?"

"Could be different size or materials," Gavin said. "It's that way with a lot of cables and hoses. Red is one diameter, blue bigger, so on. On a ship, it means the fluid going through them. Light blue is potable water. Yellow is hydraulic oil. Black is waste. White with stripes is cooling or heating. This isn't about size or type, though. It's gang colors. Most of the soldiers have a blue and yellow neck cloth, matches the pipes." He handed the binocs back. "Check it out."

Scruggs looked. The soldiers were all wearing colored neck cloths. "This is the maple syrup gang."

"One of them. Maybe different gangs run different tree sets?"

"Could be. What do we do? We're supposed to get into town tonight and deal with those missiles."

"Wait and see if they move, or where they go. If they go uphill or downhill, we can get around them."

"Could be other groups. We'll be careful—no, Rocky, no!"

Rocky had been rolling on his back in a puddle of mud. He was loving this new game. He stopped, sniffed once, then rolled upright. A low growl erupted from his throat.

"Stay here, Rocky. Don't chase the bad men," Scruggs hissed. Dena grabbed for his harness, but he swiveled free and dashed through the trees.

"Emperor's greasy—down, everybody, freeze. Lee, don't move." Dena shoved Gavin's face into the mud. "Keep down. Your face will give you away."

"Nurrrp," Gavin said.

Dena dropped. Scruggs did the same.

Rocky raced away through the bushes, leaped the tiny creek, and streaked uphill. One of the guards caught the motion, yelled, then fired.

The entire group of guards turned and blazed away. Trees and bushes shredded under the fusillade. The four crew members pressed deeper into the mud as the machine guns blasted away.

"You idiots!" a woman's voice cracked in the distance. "Wait until you can see to shoot."

"Did we get them?" another voice said.

"I don't know. I didn't see anything. Who can see them?"

Voices argued back and forth. Calls to check and re-load. Curses. Insults.

"Did they hurt Rocky?" Scruggs asked. "Is he okay?"

"What in the Emperor's name was that?" Dena's eyes were wide. "Who fires twenty machine guns after a whippet?"

"Can you see him? Is he hurt?"

Dena scanned the trees. Bits and pieces of bushes and branches dropped down. "I don't see any movement."

"If they hurt Rocky..." Scruggs slid back down the tiny ridge they were on. She rolled on her side and shrugged her pack off. "If they hurt Rocky, I'll kill them. All of them."

"Scruggs," Lee said. "Hang on, here, I love Rocky too, but we can't go shooting people because they killed our dog."

"Yes we can." Scruggs dug through her pack and pulled out a telescopic sight. "Centurion trained me for this. I can do it."

"Okay, I don't mean you can't do it. But we shouldn't do it."

"They killed our dog. I'm going to shoot them all." Scruggs snapped on the telescope. "Or as many as I can."

"This is a bad idea," Lee said.

"You going to help or not?" Scruggs cocked her rifle.

"Give me the binocs," Dena said. "I'll be your spotter."

Scruggs shoved them to Dena. She put them to her eyes. "I have a group of five downslope, your left, standing in the open in front of the pile of yellow hose. Easy target."

Scruggs moved her rifle to the left and sighted. "Give me a sec."

"Gavin," Lee said. "Some help here."

"Sure." Gavin unlimbered his rifle and laid it next to Scruggs. "Mine's loaded. Empty yours first, then use this. I'll re-load yours while you're shooting."

"That's not the help I meant," Lee said. "Scruggs!"

"No cap, brown hair and mustache at the far left." Dena swung the binoculars. "Then three more upslope, then there's one back in the trees. Take the left one first."

"Scruggs, this won't help Rocky."

Scruggs adjusted. "I got him. What's the wind?"

Dena looked at the foliage. "Some up high, nothing at head level. Firing downhill. Approximately three hundred yards."

"What's that in meters?"

"Scruggs," Lee said. "What about the mission? Think about the mission. You can't just shoot people. You need a reason."

"They killed Rocky. That's a reason. A good reason."

"A tactical reason, the centurion would say."

Scruggs stared down at the chattering soldiers in front of her. She took a deep breath, then another, then she dropped the rifle from her eyes. "Fine. Yes. The mission. Fine. Tactically, we can't do this."

"Not yet."

"Right," Scruggs said. "Right." Her eyes misted.

"Rocky. They shot Rocky."

"Look, we don't know, we need to check."

"I'll go and look—"

"Wait!" Dena held up her hand. "Listen."

Faintly, they could hear yelping.

"It's Rocky. He's alive. He's barking at something!"

"He's alive! Rocky." Scruggs stood and jumped down the hill. "He's hurt. Rocky, I'm coming. Hang on."

Lee grabbed for her, missed. Scruggs raced down the hill, splashing into the stream and powering uphill. Lee and Gavin came up on their knees and stared open-mouthed. Dena pushed them down.

"She's going to get killed!"

"We can't let her," Gavin said.

"But Jove's knees. There are twenty machine guns out there!"

The soldiers by the trees saw Scruggs, brought up their guns and yelled. But they didn't fire.

"They're not shooting," Lee said. "Why not? They let loose before."

More yelping drew everyone's attention. A limping Rocky staggered out of the bushes at the top of the ridge. Scruggs scrambled up the creek as Rocky stumbled down.

"We can't let her get shot," Gavin said. He pushed Dena's hand off and stumbled down the hill, following in Scruggs's footsteps.

"Why aren't they firing?" Lee shook her head. "They blasted everything before. Why not now?"

"Gavin, wait. Ah, Jove." Dena stood, put her hands on her hips. "That's done it. They can see us now."

The soldiers by the woods pointed their guns, but didn't fire. Cries of 'People' and 'A dog' could be made out.

"They don't want to hurt us, Lee. Let's go." Dena scrambled down the ridge and jogged up the creek. Lee shrugged and followed.

The downhill crowd continued to yell and gesticulate. They kept their guns pointed, but nobody fired.

"What in seven Empires is going on?" Lee asked. The group charged ahead. A limping Rocky had stopped short of Scruggs. She bent down to hug him. He yelped and she dropped him. "Sorry. Sorry, Rocky. You're hurt."

Rocky tried to leap up into her arms, but only made a sort of rolling hop. He yelped again.

"Lee, help him. Help him."

Lee arrived. Rocky plopped down beside her, his tongue lolling. She touched him and he whined, but as soon as she let go, he stopped and lay still, panting.

Lee felt the injury. Rocky howled again.

"Don't hurt him, Lee. He's hurt."

"Easy, Rocky. Easy. This will prick. ." Lee pulled out an auto-injector syrette and twisted the dosage to one-tenth, then stabbed. "It's going to hurt for a minute."

"Lee, he's a dog, he can't understand you," Dena said.

"Hang on, Rocky." Scruggs grabbed his shoulders and held him. "She's helping. It's okay. You're okay. You're okay."

"I need to clip and clean the wound, Scruggs. I need a better look. Easy, Rocky, I need to help. Let me see." She cradled his head gently. He whimpered, but settled. She dug into her kit and pulled out a hand sized box, then ran it over his flank. Clipped hair fluffed up.

"How is it? Is it bad?" Scruggs hovered over him.

"Bad enough." Lee moved his leg. "Not a

bullet. Shrapnel maybe, or a ricochet. And he's bleeding badly."

"Help him out!"

Lee poured the disinfectant on Rocky's legs. He yelped, then whimpered louder. He struggled against Scruggs's arms. He even snapped his teeth. She didn't move even as his mouth clamped on her arm. "It's okay, buddy. Lee, you're hurting him."

"Antiseptic. Have to clean the wound first so I can see."

"How bad is it?"

"Bad enough, I said. Pretty deep. I'll need to staple it. There might be some damage to tendons or nerves. I'll need better light, and until I can get a scan I can't tell if there is internal damage. We need to get him to the medpod in the ship."

"Hey!" a strange voice yelled. The four of them looked up from tending Rocky. Five soldiers with blue and yellow neck cloths stood near them. They all had sub-machine guns. "Who are you guys? What are you doing here?" The lead man glared down. "And what did you do to your dog?"

Chapter 9

"I said, don't move." The lead soldier pointed his sub-machine gun at them. "What's going on? What are you doing?"

Scruggs strained to point her weapon, but Dena kept her hands clamped tightly on it. The other soldiers weren't pointing guns at them, but they were armed. "I'm trying to stop my friend here from shooting you," she said. "How's your day going?" Dena strained to hold Scruggs still. The mud sucked at her arms. *He's got the drop on us. If Scruggs doesn't let go, he'll blast us. Don't start a fight we can't win.*

"Is that a dog?" the soldier asked. Lee and Gavin were fussing over Rocky downslope, next to the stream. "You brought a dog here?"

"Can't fool you, can we? Yes, it's a dog," Dena said. *Why didn't he shoot us? What's going on here?* "What gave it away? The four legs and the fur? Or the barking? And yes, we brought it here, and why the heck were you shooting at it?"

"Didn't know that it was a dog."

"Well, listen, screw-up," Scruggs said. "It is a dog. It's our dog. You shot it. And if he dies, we're going to shoot you."

"You call me boss man, little girl. And put that rifle down."

Scruggs kept straining to bring her rifle up. Dena's hands shook, trying to keep the barrel down. "Boss man screwed up, then. Back off while we fix Rocky up. Scruggs, not now."

Gavin climbed up and added his weight to Dena's hands. Scruggs stopped struggling. "I'm fine. I'm fine."

"Give us your rifle," Dena said. Scruggs let go and Gavin pulled it away from her. The sub-machine gun swiveled to point at Gavin. Gavin set Scruggs's rifle on the ground.

"How come you didn't know I'm the boss man? Everybody knows that. Who do you work for? And what are you doing with a rifle? Rifles aren't any good here."

"I don't need a rifle," Scruggs said. "Because I'm going to kill you for shooting my dog."

"Kill me, little girl." Boss Man laughed. "I'd like to see you try—"

Scruggs leaped uphill and knocked him down. She got both arms around his neck and squeezed. Gavin and Dena piled on a second later and restrained her arms, afraid she'd snap his neck. They all struggled for a few seconds. The other soldiers watched, bemused, then jumped to assist and pried Scruggs's fingers free. Dena and Gavin dragged her backwards.

"You tried to strangle me!"

"Give me a minute and it won't be a try."

"Scruggs!" Lee yelled. "I need you to hold Rocky. I have to give him a shot, then staple this shut."

Scruggs shook off the hands. "This isn't over. Soon as we fix Rocky up, we're finishing this talk." She slipped back down to help Lee.

Boss Man rubbed his neck. "What in Hades? Who are you? Why did you bring a dog here? You want to get us all killed?" He rubbed his neck some more. "And why are you skulking in the woods? And with a dog?"

"Why did you shoot at our dog?" Dena asked.

"Cause we thought he was a pig, of course."

"A pig? Like, a cow?"

"No, a pig. You know. Javelinas? Peccaries?"

Dena shook her head. "What?"

"Giant killer pigs. You don't know about the pigs?"

"No, we don't know about the pigs," Dena said. "Tell us about the pigs."

Boss Man fingered his neck. The other four guards raised their sub-machine guns.

"How come you don't know about the pigs? Everybody here knows about the pigs."

"We don't."

"What outfit are you with again? Are you with Lirk's people?"

"We're with our own." Dena let her hands drift down. She had a revolver in a leg holster under her coat. Gavin had Scruggs's rifle near his hands, and a shotgun on his pack. The guards hadn't noticed the shotgun. *If we can get both of those up and into the fight…*

The Boss Man's people jerked their guns up. "Hands up. Give me that." He took the rifle from Gavin. "Which one is your outfit? This is our territory, our colors on the trees. You should know better than to come up here. If you're not telling us which group you're with, we're deciding you're spies, and we'll take you into town. All the way to the starport, if we have to. They can deal with you there."

"Starport sounds great." Dena kept her hands up. *This isn't like you, snarling at everyone. Turn on your charm, girl. You can't help Rocky if you get shot.* "Maybe have some lunch. Get out of this mud." She twisted her arms slightly so her shirt tightened over her breasts.

His eyes tracked her chest. "You *want* to go to the starport? Now you're suicidal as well. Either way, you're coming with us. As soon as we get those taps hooked up."

Rocky yelped again. Lee dug out an anesthetic needle. "How much does he weigh?"

"Ten kilos a week ago," Scruggs said.

Lee sprayed ninety percent of the drugs out

then plunged the needle into his ruff, and pushed it in. Rocky's whimpers quieted. "Hold him still, Scruggs. Gavin, Dena, need another pair of hands."

Gavin looked at the gun-toting group and raised an eyebrow.

"Go ahead, help Rocky. We've got you covered." Gavin and Dena both jumped down to help Lee. The Boss Man ordered his troops into guard formation at the top of the streambed. "Keep watch, we got too caught up with these folks—Emperor's hairy armpits! Top of the hill. Fire. Fire. Fire!"

All of the soldiers jerked their weapons around and sprayed bullets over Dena's head. She ducked low to cover Rocky.

"Careful," Lee yelled. She finished giving Rocky his shot. His panting slowed. She had to scream over the sound of the guns. "Scruggs, hold his head. Gavin, hold the cuts closed. I'll need to staple." She ran a medical staple along the wound on his haunches, closing, sewing, and disinfecting as it went.

"Easy, furry buddy. You'll be fine." Dena patted Rocky's head. She couldn't hear her voice over the shooting. She turned to look uphill and her eyes widened. "Jove's tears."

The target of the shots roamed over the hilltop. It was a herd of wild boar. Giant pigs, each a meter or more high, and some two meters long grunted downhill. They were covered in coarse brown mud-spattered fur, and each mouth was framed by two giant tusks.

The gunfire slackened. The troops had spread out during their firefight and they were poorly distributed to defend. The trees blocked their shots. The group above them charged off into the trees.

Dena guessed thirty or more wild pigs, and

more still coming over the hill top. The pigs had spotted the crew driving the maple syrup taps, and charged. The three workers dropped everything and scampered downhill. The other fighters stood and sprayed bullets uphill. The lead boar staggered in a mist of blood as dozens of bullets impacted. Others jerked and howled as they were shot.

The crazed troops had terrible aim, spraying bullets all over the forest, and not correcting for the recoil. After the first shots, the guns rode up and sprayed bullets into the tree trunks or the branches. The few bullets that hit were too light to kill the pigs outright, and it took multiple shots to even slow the animals down.

Two soldiers farthest up the hill ran through their magazines. One dropped his gun and ran, but slipped in the mud. The herd of pigs swept down onto him, and their heads smashed up and down as they gored and stomped him.

The other swung his useless gun at the nearest pig and thwacked it on the nose, stunning it before the others rolled over him and savaged him.

The shooting dropped from continuous to bursts as magazines emptied, soldiers fled, or the marauding pack rolled down the hill.

"Lee," Dena yelled in a break. "We need to get out of here."

"Almost done," Lee said. "But I don't want to move Rocky."

"Look here." Dena pointed at the pigs. "They're attacking. We've got to get out of here."

"Need a minute. Gavin, keep holding."

"What are those?" Gavin gestured. "Pigs?"

"Wild pigs. Wild killer pigs."

"Pigs don't kill people. And wild animals are scared of humans."

The pigs made a high-pitched keening sound as they chased the humans. The hillside had devolved to a blood- and corpse-spattered field. A half-dozen or more pigs howled in pain. They'd been shot. Three times that number grunted and feasted on the fresh corpses. One used its tusks to dig at the stomach of a still groaning man, and pull out his entrails.

"Well, these pigs didn't get the message. They don't look scared at all. Fix up Rocky and let's get out of here. They haven't noticed us."

The soldiers had fled into the forest. The remainder were pig lunch, except for three that had climbed one of the oak trees down slope. They yelled curses.

"Stapled. Let me strap that leg." Lee sprayed quick seal foam on Rocky. The rapid-hardening plastic immobilized his lower body. "We'll have to carry him—"

"In here." Gavin upended his pack and dumped the contents on the ground. "He's small enough to fit. Push him in and I can tie him tight."

The pigs continued to browse on their meals. A group of five had circled the tree the soldiers were on. Some of the others stopped chewing and gave Dena a thoughtful look, then went back to chewing.

"How do you get killer pigs like that? Animals don't behave that way," Scruggs said.

"These are real wild animals," Dena said. "This planet is barely settled. On civilized planets, animals learn that humans are dangerous, and that human smell is something to be avoided, otherwise they get hunted to death. These ones don't have that reaction."

"Well, we can help them learn that."

"Might have to. Look there." A group of four pigs, led by a giant male, moved to the edge of the stomped maple syrup gang, and were chewing up the last of the corpses. "They keep looking at us, trying to decide if we're lunch."

"Lee," Scruggs yelled. "We need to get out of here."

Lee stuffed a groggy Rocky into Gavin's pack and helped him hoist it up. "We can move. Where are we going?"

"Let's try to climb up the hill." The four of them scrambled up the far bank of the stream, climbing higher into the woods, away from the developing pig fight. The slope was too much. Gavin slipped and fell face-first. Lee hauled him up and pushed him forward.

Dena made it to the top and turned. "Scruggs, they're coming at us." The big male had stopped eating. He trotted across the clearing toward the stream. His three friends followed behind.

"Keep climbing, slowly," Scruggs stopped at the top of the bank. She unlimbered her rifle and tracked the pigs. "I'll keep them off us."

"Jove's bowels." Gavin slipped and fell face forward a second time, landing on his hands in the mud. Rocky let out a single, strangled whimper. "It's too slippery. I keep skidding."

"Grab my hand." Dena tried to haul him up. He slipped again, and only regained his feet when Lee joined to help drag him up.

"Can't go uphill. Move downhill, follow that stream, slowly," Scruggs said. "If we get to the bottom, we can cross the big river. They won't be able to follow us."

"That isn't going to work," Gavin said. "It's too steep going downhill. If I fall backwards, I'll crush Rocky. If I fall forward, I'll kill myself."

"You want the pigs to get you? Get moving."

"Scruggs," Dena said. "Even if we get to the river, the pigs can follow us across."

BANG. The four pigs had snuffed forward. Scruggs shot the ground in front of them. They paused for a second, then shook their heads. The smaller male on the right snorted and continued.

BANG. Scruggs shot the first pig in the head. It dropped without a sound. The other pigs halted and sniffed the corpse.

"Great shot," Dena said.

"Better than you could do."

"I didn't say that. Jove's knees."

Curses erupted behind them. Gavin had slipped in the mud again. He'd nearly slammed Rocky into the ground, saving him at the last minute by rolling on his side and taking the hit on his shoulder. Lee slid down to help him.

"Go help them. I'll keep the pigs off." Scruggs aimed and shot another. This one didn't drop, but wailed in pain. Scruggs's second shot cut him off.

"I feel bad about shooting these pigs. They're just being pigs."

"I know. And we can't even cook them. Not enough time."

Scruggs turned to Dena. "That's pretty cruel. Eating them."

"What?" Dena shrugged. "You're the one shooting them. At least I'd make some good bacon out of it. Eyes front."

The herd of pigs had heard the keening, and now rushed to investigate. The big male snorted and attacked with his friends. Deprived of stationary targets, Scruggs took three tries to hit the smaller pig. The big male came on. Scruggs took careful aim, and fired shot after shot. She was sitting in the mud, and each shot slid her down an inch. The pig's inadvertent zigzags over fallen trees and past bushes threw her aim off. Six shots in, she got a body shot, but the pig kept coming.

Dena aimed her shotgun. "Scruggs, this is a problem."

"Tell me about it." Scruggs cursed as she slid an

inch in the mud. She recovered, aimed and fired again. Another hit. The big pig yowled, but kept coming.

Dena aimed her shotgun. BANG. Complete miss. "I can't hit anything at this range."

"Range will not be a problem in a few seconds." Scruggs fired again, missed. She took a deep breath, held it, and shot the pig again. He staggered, but kept coming, ducking around a bush and down into the streambed. Scruggs tracked him and fired, missing as the pig ducked behind a big rock. Dena fired and chipped the top off the rock. The pig splashed into the stream, only a dozen feet from them. Scruggs fired again, a hit, then her rifle clicked. Out of ammo. She let out a curse that the centurion sometimes used, and scrabbled in her belt pouch for another magazine. She fell onto her back, then slid down the muddy slope. Her heels skidded as she tried to dig in.

Dena plopped onto her butt, held the shotgun and aimed at the face of the upcoming pig. CLICKITY-BOOM. CLICKITY-BOOM. The pig yowled, and a spray of blood blew from one ear. The pig yowled again, splashed through the water and lunged at Scruggs's feet with a tusk.

CLICKITY-BOOM. Miss. CLICKITY-BOOM. CLICKITY-BOOM. She hit twice out of three shots. The third time, the pig dropped, and lay still, its tusk digging lightly into Scruggs's boot.

Scruggs yanked her legs back, then snapped a magazine in, and fired six shots into the pig from two feet away.

Dena wiped gunpowder from her face. "Not necessary, Baby Marine."

"Just wanted to make sure." Scruggs took a long, shuddering breath. "Just making sure." Scruggs pointed across the stream. "Look there. How much ammunition do you have?"

Dena's glance followed Scruggs's pointing finger. A second, fresh group of pigs had emerged from the trees above them.

"Not enough." She grasped Scruggs's proffered hand and yanked her upright. "Not nearly enough. Those pigs are going to keep coming. Let's get out of here."

Chapter 10

"Run, run." Dena climbed over the top of the bank and raced down the hill. The suns were setting, and Lee and Gavin were visible in the trees downslope. "The pigs are coming—Crap!"

She fell on her face. Great. Some hunter you are. A couple wild pigs and you run like a little girl.

Scruggs scrambled down, stooping to yank her up. "Lee, Gavin, run. Move it. All the pigs in the world are behind us." She windmilled downslope, overtaking Lee. As she passed, Gavin slipped again, catching himself on one knee.

Lee helped him upright. "Faster. I can't keep those pigs back. There's millions of them."

Gavin shook his head. "We can't go faster. I'll hurt Rocky."

"Those pigs will hurt all of us." Scruggs slid into a tree and cursed. The trunks were closer together now, the hill steeper. The mud made avoiding slamming into them impossible. "Or the trees will."

Dena slid in beside them and grasped the tree trunk. "Ouch. Watch the bark. It's sharp, but it should be easy to climb. I did this all the time as a kid." The oak tree's lower branches were shoulder high off the ground. "Once we're on the first branch, getting higher is like climbing a wooden ladder."

Rocky whimpered quietly. Everyone shut up and exchanged worried glances.

Scruggs slung her rifle, raced and hauled herself up to the first branch. "Let's try it." The others followed, grabbing Gavin by the shoulders and pulling him and Rocky along.

The herd of pigs followed, snorting and grunting as they flowed through the trees. Most stopped to munch on acorns lying on the forest floor. Others stuck their snouts in and dug.

A pig smashed the tree with its forelegs. They held fast as the trunk shook, then climbed higher.

Scruggs stopped twenty feet from the ground. "Hold up. Everyone okay?"

"Just my pride hurt," Gavin said, wiping mud from his face.

"And mine," Lee said. "Dena, you're bleeding."

Dena wiped her face. "Hit my nose when I fell. I'm fine." She draped one hand around the trunk and pinched her nose with the other. "Sabe. Theb is a brig tvee."

The oak tree ranged above them into the sky, at least sixty feet. The branches were large enough to take their weight, but narrow enough they could sit astride, legs dangling, and hold on with their hands.

"A very big tree." Scruggs nodded. "We can stay here for a while."

"Good idea." Lee said. "Let me look at Rocky. Turn around, Gavin."

A sleepy Rocky licked Lee's face when she petted him. Lee ran her hands over his cast. "The cast is holding. He's unhappy and confused about what's happening."

"Can you blame him?" Gavin asked. "If somebody stuck me in a sack and threw me over their shoulder, I'd be upset. And unhappy. And confused."

Lee lifted his sleepy head up. "I don't like his breathing. And he's warmer than he should be."

"Infection?" Gavin asked.

"Not this fast." Lee caressed Rocky's hair. "Could be internal damage. He got banged around pretty bad, and I just stapled him shut to stop the bleeding. I'll need a med pod to see if something is wrong inside."

"Can you give him more pills?" Scruggs asked.

Lee shook her head. "Not right now. He's so

small, I'm having problems with dosage. If I give him too much, I might kill him."

"You'll be okay, little buddy. We'll take care of you." Scruggs looked at Lee. "Should we go back?"

"It's serious," Lee said. "If this gets worse, he could die without proper treatment."

"We could turn around…" Scruggs bit her lip.

"Took us the better part of two days to get here," Gavin said. "That was without gangs of maple syrup thugs, and herds of killer pigs. Take just as long to get back. And when we do, we're still stuck in the woods with those missiles over us. We'll have to do this again."

"And you'll have to explain things to the old man," Dena said. "He won't be happy."

"I can stand his unhappiness."

"All evidence to the contrary," Dena said. "You've kinda been following his orders."

"I won't let Rocky die," Scruggs said. "We take care of our own. And after what he did for us—"

"If that's your goal," Lee said. "For the purpose of argument, we could find some of these thugs and ask for help. They have missiles and a spaceport, they'll have med pods."

Gavin grunted. "You think those thugs will help us?"

"Nope, but that's one of the questions the centurion will ask Scruggs here, if she considered aborting her mission to seek help."

"Look at the way they treated those pigs, and each other. Shot everything that moved. I saw at least one woman hit with friendly fire when they blazed away. They're not smart people. They'll shoot Rocky, probably shoot us, and then eat pancakes."

"Covered in maple syrup," Dena said. "Lee, we shouldn't do that."

"We need to talk about it. It's an option. We

need options. We're in a bit of a pickle."

Dena wiped the blood from her nose. Uh oh. Lee is always so calm. If she's worried, we're in trouble.

"We're not doing it," Scruggs said. "We go on. Downhill, to get into town and get those missiles. Weapons check." Scruggs reloaded her rifle and made sure to chamber a round. Dena had her shotgun, and Lee her revolver. Gavin had lost his shotgun, no idea where it was. He was fuzzy about what happened after the boss man. They all had the survival knives and compasses Dena had made them carry.

The tree shivered. Two pigs were plowing their tusks under one of the roots.

"What are they looking for?" Scruggs wondered.

"Fungus, usually," Dena said.

"Is this like the mold you put in cheese?"

"Different thing, but just as smelly." The tree shook, and shook again. "Um, Scruggs, they're digging up the roots."

"I see that. How long does it take a pig to dig far enough down to knock a tree over."

"No idea." Dena grabbed the trunk again as they swayed. "But it might not take as long as we thought."

Their weapons not having worked on the pigs before, the group debated what to do next as the tree swayed under them.

"Staying here is not an option," Scruggs said. "This tree will come down at some point. I don't think we can wait them out."

"Maybe they'll go away," Gavin said.

Scruggs counted thirty-five pigs in view. "Or maybe they'll set up a perimeter and dig this tree up and use it as a firebase and observation post."

"They're pigs, Baby Marine," Dena said. "They don't set up firebases, whatever that is."

"They don't swarm and attack people on the ground. These ones did. They don't attack in such big groups, these ones did. And they don't take ten hits to die, these ones did."

The tree gave a heave. They all grabbed for a branch. Two larger pigs had joined the medium-sized ones rooting below.

"Okay, so these are special pigs," Dena said. "We need to get away. Who volunteers to drop down?"

"I'm not getting out of this tree," Gavin said. "Not voluntarily."

"We don't need to." Lee said. "There are pigs everywhere, digging up all sorts of things, but they can't dig up every tree."

"They can dig up every tree we sit in."

"Then don't sit here. We can make it to that tree over there." Lee pointed downslope. "Climb out along that branch there, drop off to that branch below. We can move to another tree."

"This is a dense forest," Dena said. She balanced on the branch. "And it's easy to climb from one to the other. Drop your legs over and stretch down, you can go from tree to tree, they're that close."

"Let's do it," Scruggs said. "Get away from the killer pigs, and get down to that river. We can get across and up the other side to get to those missiles like we're supposed to."

Dena went first. She balanced on the branch, stepped lightly down to the end, then dropped to her butt. She flipped one leg over, stretched down and dropped her feet to the lower branch. Using her former tree home as guide, she scuttled along the new tree to the trunk.

"Easy peasy. Come on down."

Scruggs came next, heel and toeing along the trunk. She skittered when an especially vigorous pig shoved their tree, but recovered and dropped down next to Dena. She insisted Gavin come next, keeping Rocky on his back.

Gavin wasn't confident enough to stand, so he dropped down and slid sideways along the branch. Once above Scruggs, he pivoted and dropped his legs down. Scruggs set his feet on the branch. Once his feet settled, he could scramble along to the trunk.

Lee followed, walking the whole way, dropping onto the lower branch with a side hop.

"Jovians and their balance," Gavin said. "Forgot how good you are at that."

"I'm better in zero-G," Lee said. "But if I have time to get used to a gravity field, I can do it. Doesn't help with noise, though."

"Climb up higher, two more branches." Dena swarmed up their new tree. "It's all downslope, but we need to start higher each time."

The group moved along a half dozen trees. At first, a dozen pigs followed them along, looking up to see what the commotion was, and keep them in view.

"They're expecting one of us to fall," Dena said. "These are amazingly smart pigs. Like killer predator smart pigs. Wonder how they got that way."

"Wouldn't take too long," Lee said. "Pigs are smart enough. A few generations of training and they'll take orders, like dogs."

"Who did this?" Dena asked.

"Maple syrup people," Gavin said. "How better to keep people from going out in the woods and stealing your sap, because you'll get stomped and eaten by a killer pig."

"That's those graves we found," Scruggs said. "The pigs caught people out in the woods. That's why the locals only go out in armed gangs."

Dena climbed up another branch to get set for another branch walk. "Great. Trained killer attack pigs."

"Carnivorous killer attack pigs," Gavin said. "You saw them eating the corpses."

"Smart, dedicated, trained killer attack pigs." Dena pointed. "It's like some weird cheap low-grade sci-fi novel written by some hack writer."

"True," Gavin said. "But most modern writers are hacks. You can't get good sci-fi books anymore."

Dena looked below. "Well, the others have gone. But that one over there is keeping up."

Clusters of pigs had followed them down the mountain slope as they hopped from tree to tree. Most had drifted off, enticed by the numerous piles of acorns, or stopped to dig at the smell of root fungus. But one mid-size pig followed.

Scruggs unlimbered her rifle. "Shoot him?"

Dena shook her head. "Remember what happened last time. The shots brought more pigs along. Don't know why. They should be afraid of guns."

"Wrong type of conditioning," Gavin said. "These idiots were incompetent shots. Now when they hear shooting, the pigs think that there will be tasty people chow to eat. They aren't afraid of guns at all."

"Then that's a 'no' to shooting it, and climbing down?" Scruggs asked. "We go on in the trees?"

"I'm not getting out of this tree until I can climb back into the ship," Gavin said. "I hate planets."

The rest murmured agreement and kept moving.

They took an hour to reach the river, bouncing from tree to tree. They could move easily once they got the hang of it, but a slip and near fall made them proceed cautiously. Scruggs insisted on helping Gavin at every climb.

"You're not really interested in helping me, you're just worried about Rocky," Gavin said.

"Of course." Scruggs set his foot on a branch and stepped away. "If something happened to Rocky, I'd be devastated."

"And what if something happened to me?" Gavin asked. "What would you feel then?"

"Um." Scruggs looked at Dena. "I'd be… sad?"

"Very sad," Dena said. "Really, extremely, very, muchly sad, right, Scruggs?"

"Yes, that's true," Scruggs agreed. "I would be. Muchly."

"Good to know I'm not completely useless," Gavin said.

"You're not," Scruggs assured him. "We'll need you to help carry Rocky. He's too sick to walk right now."

The river surprised them. Not only was it larger than expected, on their side, the trees had been cleared away for a hundred meters. On the far side, it lapped against a steep cliff face, with a well-worn trail up to the ridge.

"Big," Dena said. "Looks deep in the middle. And fifty feet across, at least."

"Or thirteen meters, for you colonials," Lee said.

Dena wiped some mud from her pants and threw it at Lee. "You've been getting all Imperial snob, the closer we get to the Core, did you know that?"

Lee ducked. "Sorry, habit. We need to get

across that river."

"And up that slope and through the fence on top."

"And across that clearing without triggering that big guy down there." Dena pointed down. Their companion pig had followed them downslope, and was now snorting and pawing at the ground below their tree. "Think he can knock down the tree by himself?"

"Doesn't have to."

"We can shoot him."

"And bring the whole pack down?"

"Herd."

"Herd, pack, whatever."

"Well, we need to do all three. And get across the river, then get up that slope, and across that fence."

"How do we do that?" Dena asked.

Scruggs was scanning the far slope and the river bed with her sensor binoculars. "I think I know a way. We just have to be a little… friendly."

"Friendly like with each other." Dena raised her eyebrows.

"Not exactly." Scruggs pointed two trees over. "That one. Lots of leaves. We need to get over there."

"To do what?"

"Watch and learn, Nature Girl." Scruggs grinned. "And remember, you're the one who said the giraffes were cute."

Chapter 11

"This has got to be the stupidest stunt I've ever seen," Dena said. She'd pulled two dozen leaf-encrusted branches from higher in the trees and arranged them on her back. "The stupidest."

"Stupider than trashing an office on a station and escaping out the airlock?" Lee asked. They'd done that several planets back as part of an insurance scam when they needed money. She dragged her own bunch of branches behind her.

"Well, no."

"Or departing a building under fire by having the centurion blow out the rear wall with a rocket launcher like we did before?" Gavin said. They'd done that when a plan to get some scanning software had them accidentally destroying a spy safe-house.

"Well, no. Not that either." Dena wiped sticky sap from her fingers. The cut branches leaked. "What about you, Scruggs?"

"What?"

"Tell me what this is stupider than?"

"Nothing I can think of. It's pretty crazy." Scruggs led the group along the branches. The wide space fronting the river stretched before them. She'd had everybody cut fresh green branches from higher up in the trees and carry them along. Carrying cut foliage while balancing on a tree branch forty feet up was outside her personal experience. *It's dangerous, but that doesn't matter. I don't have time to worry now. Rocky needs help.*

"You think it's crazy? It was your idea."

"Improvise. Adapt Overcome. That's what the centurion says. And it's kind of your idea. You were talking about those giraffes liking the tenderest leaves."

"Saying that is a far cry from enticing them

close by feeding them."

"You said they were friendly," Scruggs said.

"I said they wouldn't attack us and wouldn't eat us. But nothing stopping them from kicking us to death if we get too close," Dena said. "Or chewing our arms off. They eat tree branches. You think our fingers will stop them?"

"You got any better ideas?" Scruggs asked

Dena stuck out her hands "No. Gimme one of your bundles."

Scruggs had picked the strongest and longest branch on the tree closest to the river. Dena walked to the end of the branch, dragging the bundle of freshly cut branches, which were engorged with leaves. Lee and Scruggs followed with their own bundles, Gavin bent double behind them using his hands to balance on the limb. He had branches stuffed in his belt, jacket, and under his backpack straps.

"I look like a chubby Saturnalia tree," Gavin said.

Dena slowed as the branch creaked below her. "Saturnalia trees are spruce or pine, not oak."

"Not for us." Lee pulled a branch from her bundle and waved it. "We always had oak trees. Here they come."

They had waited until a large herd of giraffes passed by and crossed the river. Different groups migrated in different directions, but this one was going to the river to drink, then crossing to the other side. Dena had identified that they liked oak leaves the best. She and the group had gathered as many new-growth oak leaf branches as they could carry, and were now waving them.

"Come and get the tasty leaves," Dena cooed. "Come here, little giraffe. We're your friends."

Lee waved her own branch. "Not so little. They're head high to us."

"Which is why they're not scared. There's nothing in the trees on this planet that lives in trees that can eat them."

"What does eat them? There's so many. Don't they have predators?"

"Maybe those predators died, so they kept expanding. That's why all the oak trees are stripped at the bottom. With so many of them roaming the woods, they'll eat through their food supply shortly and the population will crash. It used to happen all the time on Rockhaul. We kept records. Rabbits, neo-raccoons, neo-moose, big surges in population, eat all their food, a die off, repeat every thirty years or so."

"We'll, I'm glad there's a lot of them right now. Scruggs, what's the pig count?"

Scruggs turned her head to scan behind her. "I count seven. One group of five over there to the left, and two others behind me. Looks like they don't want to get near the giraffes."

"They're scared. Even if you're a big pig, a group of angry giraffes can cause you a lot of damage. Hooves are great for stomping short things. That's it, pretty girl. Try a snack."

A medium-size female, her head at waist level to them, stopped eight feet away. Her eyes followed the swaying branch for five seconds, then she trotted over and munched. Dena held the branch steady as the giraffe pulled the leaves off and chewed.

"Got one. Come closer, girl." Dena twisted the branch away, holding it closer to the tree. The giraffe followed, her head coming closer until she was chewing almost in Dena's face. Her tongue rasped out and dragged the leaves back.

"Jove! Her tongue is blue!" Dena kept twisting the branch to bring the tender, tasty leaves closer. At the same time, she patted the giraffe on the neck. "Good girl. Nice blue-tongued girl. We're friends. Friends. We'll give you some food if you take us across the river."

"Sun's going down." Gavin gestured at the horizon. "We need to speed it up. This will be harder to do in the dark."

The female giraffe continued to munch. Dena cooed in her ear, and fed her more. "Okay, let me try. Scruggs, how many pigs?"

Scruggs grimaced. "More. I can see shadows uphill. They're close. You ready?"

"Ready. Give her more food." Scruggs and Lee pushed more branches. Dena leaned in and patted the giraffe's neck. "Don't worry, little giraffe. I'm your friend Dena. We need to get across the river. It's okay. Have some more tasty leaves."

The giraffe regarded Dena, decided the strange noise and strange animals weren't a threat, and continued chewing.

Dena took a deep breath, then another, then put both arms around her new giraffe friend's neck. "Here we go. It's okay. It's okay."

Dena grabbed the giraffe's neck ruff, and slid down, landing on her back with plop. The fur was short and coarse, like a carpet. But long enough to grasp.

The giraffe froze, turned her head, and stared at this strange creature sitting on her back. What was going on? Should she be worried?

Dena grasped the giraffe's neck with one hand, and used the other to pull another branch out. She pushed the leaves up.

The giraffe tilted her head, sniffed once, then chewed on the leaves.

"Told you," Scruggs said. "They're so big, and we're so small. It's like we're a tiny cat on their back."

"I'd jump if I had a cat on my back," Lee said.

"Good thing we're not cats, then. Gavin, you ready?"

Gavin edged up next to them, keeping one hand on the branches. "As I'll ever be."

"Remember, don't let Rocky get hurt."

"What about me? Should I let me get hurt?"

"That's your best idea," Lee said. "Because if you get hurt, I might be able to help you. But if Rocky gets hurt, Scruggs will shoot you, and I can't fix that."

"I won't shoot him," Scruggs said.

Lee raised her eyes. "No?"

"Not right away. I'll check Rocky first. If Rocky's hurt bad, then I'll shoot him. Dena, you ready?"

"Yep. Me and Gina both."

"Gina?"

"I named her. Gina the giraffe. My new friend."

"At least as long as you keep feeding her."

"Shut up. Give her some of those choice branches. Gavin, go."

Gavin sat. Scruggs stepped past him—the branch was nearly wide enough for two. He edged sideways until he was near Gina's neck.

"Okay, Gina," Dena said. "One more small companion. Gavin, slide down the neck and hang on. I'll help you."

"This is not something that I learned in Engineering School." Gavin grasped Gina's neck, leaned in and fell. Dena cushioned him from below, and Scruggs grabbed his pack and balanced him as he slid down.

Gina froze and turned her head. Dena jabbed another bunch of leaves at her. Gina sniffed the leaves, then craned her head around to stare. Gavin had thrown both hands around her neck and leaned in tight. Dena's legs gripped the giraffe's flanks—she'd ridden horses on Rockhaul—and used her arms to feed leaves upwards.

"Hang tight, Gavin. She'll start moving with the herd as soon as we stop feeding her."

"Grawmpf." Gavin's head pressed into Gina's furry neck.

Gina's eyes roved over the two strange creatures on her back, then back to the leaves next to her mouth. She tilted her head right, then left, then started chomping on the leaves.

Dena thrust more leaves around her head, and away from the tree. That tilt must be what a giraffe shrug looks like. Now to get her focused on the herd.

By dint of careful extensions of the branches, Dena directed Gina's head away from the tree and back to the herd. Dena then tossed a bundle of tasty branches ahead into the middle of the herd. A passing yellow-dappled juvenile stopped to nibble on them, and Gina stepped forward to claim her share. Once she'd chewed her way through, she stuck her head up. The herd sauntered by, and Gina resumed her place in the middle, ignoring her passengers for the moment.

"It's working!" Lee said.

"A giraffe taxi," Scruggs said. "Safest way across the river."

"What about those pigs?" A group of two dozen collected behind them, snorting and pawing at the ground.

"They smell us." Scruggs pointed down. "But they're afraid of the herd. See, they're staying away."

The herd of pigs trotted past the edge of the trees, edging up to the giraffes. Several of the larger giraffes stopped and confronted the pigs. The pigs grunted and pawed the ground, but they didn't advance. The pigs might weigh more than five hundred kilograms, but the giraffes were twice that, and they had hooves too.

"Good. Okay, we need to get away ourselves. Just need to find another friendly giraffe-taxi."

Scruggs and Lee spent the next two minutes waving tasty leaves and calling to the giraffes. But the pigs had spooked the herd, and none came near.

"Scruggs, this could be a problem," Lee said. "If we can't get over there..."

"I know, I know. I thought it would work for all of us or none of us. Dena and Gavin are nearly at the river." Gina hadn't hurried, and stopped to exchange giraffe greetings with some others, who were probably asking, "What the heck is that on your back? Does it hurt? Want me to stomp it?"

"Should we wait them out?" Lee asked.

I wish we could. I'm tired of making decisions. But I need to do something. "Can't. We should get out of here now—wait, there's one."

Another female giraffe was enticed over by the display of tasty leaves. Scruggs and Lee cooed and waved their arms, and she ambled over and munched. Scruggs hopped out and slid down, clutching her neck.

"Thank you, Gabrielle." Scruggs patted her giraffe's neck.

Lee rolled her eyes. "Gabrielle the giraffe. Of course. If he was male, you'd call him George?"

"George is a stupid name for a giraffe. I'd call him Gordon."

"And that's better why?"

"It just is. Hurry up. This is harder than it looks. Dena makes it look so easy."

"You think she's ridden giraffes before?"

"Wouldn't put it past her. Will I fit?"

"It's not fitting." Scruggs swayed as Gabrielle stuck her nose around and grabbed branches out of her pack. "It's staying on."

"Relax, and I'll drop down there."

Lee readied herself. Gabrielle's back was six feet below. She was athletic enough to jump down and land two-footed, but what if the giraffe moved?

"Lee, hurry up. Before something happens."

Rocky yelped, ahead. The whole herd froze, eyes tracked around. With Rocky stuffed in a backpack, the giraffes had been smelling a predator close by but couldn't localize it. They balanced the proximity of the smell with the ready supply of tasty treats, and the immunity offered by the size of their herd.

Dena and Gavin were shushing an increasingly vocal Rocky ahead.

"Uh oh," Scruggs said. "This isn't going to turn out well."

"We'll be fine, as long as they don't panic."

Rocky stuck his head out of the backpack. The drugs had made him woozy, but he was worried about his people. He sniffed once and smelled dozens of strange creatures. Danger! Danger! He had to warn the pack. He opened his mouth and howled a warning.

Lee gasped in the tree. The giraffes unfroze and stampeded in all directions, kicking up dirt, shaking trees, charging through the river and into the trees, carrying Dena, Gavin, Rocky, and Scruggs off into the evening gloom.

Chapter 12

"Right, Prefect," Devin said. "Start the exercise."

"Stations for battle drill," Lionel said. Nothing happened. The dozen watch officers in view continued typing on comms. He swung his head left and right—the rest of the bridge work continued undisturbed. Lionel cursed and hit the intercom button. "Stations for battle drill."

The new helmsman—Devin couldn't remember his name. He didn't know half the names of the bridge crew even now—slammed down on the alarm. Lights pulsed red. The alarm bonged. "Battle drill, battle drill," rang out from the speakers. Screens flared to show crew members rushing to their stations throughout the ship. Water vapor condensed as atmospheric pressure dropped. Devin shivered as the temperature dropped. Less air meant less oxygen to burn in an emergency, and less pressure to lose after damage. But increasing the volume of the remaining air condensed the water out.

Devin waited patiently. And still more patiently. After three minutes, he looked to Lionel and raised an eyebrow. "Shouldn't there be an update?" *This bridge is bigger than Father's net-ball court. At least we can talk without the bridge crew hearing. I miss Pollux, but there are advantages to having a battleship as your flagship.*

Lionel swiped on his screen. "They should have been at their stations already. Everybody knew that there was a drill this morning."

"Isn't this supposed to be unscheduled?"

"Yes, but word always gets out. The smart officers quiz the bridge crew and cheat by getting their people in place ahead of time."

"You encourage cheating?"

"I encourage working as a team." Lionel glared

at his screen. "We're still only showing seventy percent readiness. Lieutenant, get the gun turrets on the channel. Ask them why they haven't closed up."

Devin leaned back and waited. He was supposed to be acting as a fleet commander. It wasn't his spot to start arguing with gunnery sergeants as to whether they should have closed up or not. *Treat it like a play at the Imperial Opera House in the Core. A play about being in the Imperial Navy.*

A display showed an apprentice operator in the forward sensor station twisting sideways to read a screen. She'd locked her helmet on the wrong set of suit rings. *A badly organized play peopled with poorly trained actors.*

Lionel dealt with several of those problems in the next few minutes. Eventually, he dispatched one of the junior lieutenants to run down to a battery starboard-3 forward to see why it still wasn't coming online.

"Tribune," Lionel said. "That's the best we're going to get. I suggest we continue with the fleet exercise while we troubleshoot the other issues."

"Very well. Helm." Devin cursed. He didn't know the helmsman's name either. "Helm, take the fleet in to the asteroid belt. Swing us past the targets. Execute."

Lionel coughed.

"Hold that. Send a time hack to the other ships. Let them know when you maneuver."

The helmsman acknowledged, transmitted the course changes, and started the countdown clock. Devin waited until all the other ships in his small fleet had acknowledged and nodded once. "Helm. Um... Helm. Execute."

Lionel brought a watch bill up on his screen, then leaned sideways. "Chuks. The helmsman is called Chuks."

Chuks pressed a button, waited for the other ships to acknowledge the pending maneuver, and then hammered the button again.

The flagship pivoted to the right. The escorting destroyers and corvettes swarmed out to the side. The fleet inched on course.

Space was huge. Spaceships were big and heavy, but complicated and fragile. Even a corvette could land a damaging blow on a battleship if it hit the right place. A glancing blow from any of the larger ships could destroy the smaller ones. It was worse in real combat. Warships were like eggs carrying hammers.

The *Canopus* took its place at the front of the battle line. Flanking and trailing her were the two light cruisers, *Fargo* and *Little Rock*. Three destroyers, *Rigorous*, *Romola*, and *Rowena* completed the formation. The corvettes and frigates swanned off in all directions, while the assault carriers, freighters and tankers peeled off on different vectors.

"Ship status," Lionel said. Three of the bridge officers tried to answer at once. "Strike that. Helm, status."

"On course, on target, in range in seven minutes," Chuks said.

Lionel waited, but nothing else came. "Very well. Weapons?"

"Batteries are charging sir. Not all are online." The weapons officer's name was Tapani. He was from the same planet as Lionel's old weapons officer Huusko, back on the *Pollux*. They even knew each other, so Lionel was prepared to cut him some slack. "What do you mean not all are online? How many are reporting?"

"Seventy-two percent report ready to fire. But only half are reporting full charges."

"How many will be fully powered when we get

to the target?"

Tapani tapped his screen. "Probably eighty percent online, sir, and almost all of those will be short-charged."

"On this ship," Lionel said, "we don't use the words 'probably' and 'maybe.' We use actual numbers. Get us some real numbers of how many will be online."

"Yes sir."

Lionel rubbed his forehead and shook his head.

Devin kept a poker face. *God help us if there was a real adversary out there. We would be in an enormous world of hurt.*

Lionel continued through his updates. "Engineering?"

"Engineering reports fully online sir. All drives functioning. All systems reporting ready."

"Very well," Lionel said.

"At least one of the departments seemed to have got their act together," Devin said. *Of course, that was after Lionel had gone down there yesterday with Imin in tow.* Bringing Imin to a meeting with a group of senior chiefs increased departmental efficiency by twenty to fifty percent, even when he didn't say anything. Devin wasn't sure exactly how that worked. Either Imin was imparting his enormous experience and detailed knowledge of battle operations via telepathy, or he was privately torturing the chiefs until they did their jobs. *It could be both. You never knew with Imin.*

Devin ran down his own checklist. "Navigation, status of the rest of the fleet."

The navigator, Villa, was an old *Pollux* hand. Her report was brief, crisp, and pointed. "Sir, tankers are clear. Assault ship is clear. Three of the freighters are clear. Two have suffered engineering casualties and are limping behind. One is not responding to hails."

"Jove's hairy armpits." Devin rubbed his forehead again. "Two of them? Very well. Resend the coordinates and instructions."

"We've already done so sir. Twice. I'd like to recommend that the *Valhalla* slow and dispatch a shuttle to board the trailing ships."

"To do what? Beat them until they comply?"

Villa grinned "Well, sir, the Marines can be very persuasive. They probably won't have to resort to beatings." She shrugged. "Probably."

"Very well. Tell the *Valhalla* to do what they need to do, at the brigadier's discretion."

The display showed three capital ships, two of them barely capital ships, heading into the asteroid belt. Lionel had picked three as their targets.

"In range in sixty seconds," Tapani said.

"In range of which target?" Lionel asked.

"Target one sir. Sorry."

"Don't apologize, just do it right next time. Engage target one as soon as we are at optimal range."

Tapani nodded and flapped through his board. "All weapons targeted sir. Counter is live."

"Very well." Lionel tapped his intercom. "Ship. This is a drill. Weapons disengage central control. All systems will fire under local control as they reach optimal range."

Tapani looked at Lionel and opened his mouth.

Lionel waved him silent. "I'm not looking for an argument, Lieutenant. I'm looking for you to disengage central control. Do it."

Tapani slapped his board. Lights changed from green to yellow. Some flashed to red. Devin had no idea what that meant. Did they all go off line? Just because they were set to local control? Was there no one at the turret controlling them? Do I really want to take this group of amateurs up against the Empire's main battle fleets?

"Weapons, give me a countdown to optimal range," Lionel said. "Put a timer up on the screen."

The timer came up and started counting. Fifteen, fourteen, thirteen, twelve…

Devin leaned over to Lionel. "Want to make a wager on how many will hit the target?"

"Only if I can take 'not enough,'" Lionel whispered. "And I think the better wager would be how many fire at all. Let's see if we can get that part working first."

The timer dropped. Five, four, three—lights flashed on the display. One of the lasers had fired early. Tapani jumped against his restraints. "Battery starboard-4 midships reports early release."

Lukas, more experienced than the others, had focused a telescope on the asteroid that they were purportedly aiming at. Lights flashed by. Not all of them hit. After a two-second pause, the asteroid exploded.

"Didn't see those shots," Devin said. "The last ones."

"Those were the positron beams," Lionel said. "Can't see them, no visible light. Sensors, play that back with false colors."

Devin watched the replay on the main screen. More than three-quarters of the lasers had missed. Three of the four positron beams had hit—but most of the *Canopus*'s weapons were old-school lasers. Devin grimaced. *I was spoiled on* Pollux. *We had all the latest weapons. And a crack crew. How's the Prefect going to whip this crew into shape? And for that matter, how am I going to whip my fleet into shape?*

"Very well." Lionel grimaced. "Run the board for us, weps."

"Turrets starboard-1 forward and port-2 forward fired early sir."

"Did they hit their target?"

The weapons officer gulped. "Sir, uh…"

"Let me guess," Lionel said. "You have no idea what they were supposed to be targeting, so you can't tell if they hit it. They didn't hit the asteroid, did they?"

"Uh, no, sir, they weren't even in the same quadrant."

"Very well. Next?"

"Turret starboard-3 forward did not fire under local control at all, reasons unknown." The weapons officer continued to the final summary. "Uh, seven percent hit rate overall sir."

"Well," Lionel said, "I've seen worse."

Devin perked up at that. "Really?"

"Yeah, when they're fresh out of the shipyard and there's no sensors installed, or the targeting software's the wrong type."

Lukas interrupted. "*Fargo* and *Little Rock* are firing sir."

"Very well." Lionel, Devin, and the rest of the bridge crew watched as the trailing cruisers fired in turn. Unsurprisingly, the flagship had the best shooting accuracy and time on target.

Only a third of the *Fargo*'s batteries came near the target. *Little Rock* managed a perfect time-on-target shot with its entire battery. At empty space. All the lasers zoomed out in the exact opposite direction to their assigned target.

"What happened there?" Devin asked.

"Somebody got a negative and a positive confused," Lionel said, "when they were transferring coordinates. They gave the opposite angle."

"Jove save us. They nearly clipped the corvettes."

The destroyers still lumbered along beside the fleet, but the corvettes had scattered at the misdirected shots. The corvette captains were disobeying orders, but they seemed to have the opinion that they would rather be alive and under charges rather than dead with a clean record.

"All right." Lionel rubbed his forehead. "Turn us around and do it again."

"We're not overthrowing any empire with this fleet," Devin said quietly.

"Nope."

"Will they get better?"

"Yes. We just have to do one thing."

"What's that?"

"Pray to the gods," Lionel said. "The problems we have, we need divine intervention. And soon."

Chapter 13

"Okay, Captain," Bronwin Hooper said. "Engineering says our hydrogen percentage is dropping, so they've programmed a vector change—"

"No." Franceska Monti shook her head. "They have control during fueling operations…"

"Countermand," Monti said. "Check the scans."

Hooper slapped her controls. An engineering voice squawked over the intercom. "Stand by." She ran through the screens on her board. "What? What do you see that I don't?" The two were alone on the bridge of the *Collingwood*. After scouting another inhabited system, they hadn't found any warships, or more potential Union of Nations spy ships. Their power consumption curve had gotten worse, so they'd stopped to suck some more fuel. "I don't see anything. The board is clear."

"Exactly. The board is clear. Now."

"Another great explanation by the captain. Oh—" Hooper tapped through a quick history. "There was a ship there before. Where did it go, Franky?"

"Don't call me Franky on duty."

"Fine, Captain. Tell me what's going on."

"There was a beacon when we came in." The *Collingwood* had jumped into this system far outside of the normal jump point and drifted, scanning all the while, and then gently eased themselves into this orbit. Only attentive ships with military-grade sensors could have seen them. Freighters wouldn't.

Hooper nodded. "We had a beacon. The *Terence Cochran* general freighter. You think it wasn't a general freighter?"

"Well, we can't exactly scan it, can we? But all of a sudden… Wait, it's back now."

"It's back now. How informative. So?"

"Yeah. Except that it's not the *Terence Cochran* anymore according to the beacon. It's squawking something different."

"Pirate or warship?"

"Warship." Hooper didn't hesitate.

"Why are you so certain?"

"Because if I were a pirate, I wouldn't have bothered to change the beacon. I would have come in, sailed through the system, loaded up, carried on to the next system. From a pirate's point of view, pretending to be one freighter is as good as pretending to be another freighter. They're going to attack other freighters, not warships, so they're not worried about sensor scans."

"Okay. Okay, that makes sense."

"Should we go to general quarters?"

"No." Monti frowned. "Too much chance of one of our crew turning on something they shouldn't turn on. We've never done a general quarters drill at EMP zero, and I don't want to try it right now."

"So we sit here like a sun-kissed wombat?"

"Keep watching it. What's our fuel status?"

"We're forty percent, so we could jump out if we had to, but then we'd run out of fuel before we got back to *Canopus* and the rest of the fleet."

"You realize," Hooper said, "that if that is an Imperial warship, we could turn a regular beacon on, meander up, and give him all the details of Tribune Devin and what he's doing."

"Do you want to do that?" Monti raised an eyebrow. "Quit the rebellion?"

"I'm... I'm not sure, I'm not. No."

"What? Tell me, Bron."

"That last admiral. Bracebridge. The collision that killed all those people in the destroyer, that was his fault. I'm kind of tired of dealing with these incompetent Core world twits. If they don't kill us one way, they'll kill us another. This rebellion will put an end to that." Hooper leaned back in her chair.

"Or maybe we'll replace one set of incompetent nobles with a different group. Should we want that?"

"What about you? You're the captain. What do you say?"

"We should stick with Tribune Devin and..."

"Why?"

Monti stared at the screen. Why did she want to stick with Tribune Devin? Because she liked the way he ran the Empire, or she liked the way he talked about how he would run the Empire. *Is that a good reason to start a revolt? Something good might happen? Is a nice speech worth getting lots of people killed?* "I think he's a better leader long term."

Bronwin groaned. "Oh good, let's plunge the galaxy into fire and flame so you can have a slightly better leader at the helm."

"Well, my impression is that we're going to be plunged into fire and flame whether we like it or not, or that we've already been plunged into fire and flame." Monti pointed to the course plot on the screen. "Let's say we do what you say. Let's say we fire up the engines, come into the nearest Imperial unit and say, let us tell you about Tribune Devin. What makes you think they won't blow us out of space as soon as we get close?"

"They might try, but given the accuracy I've seen from other Imperial warships, I doubt they'd be able to hit us even if we fed them targeting coordinates."

"Granted. But, second, even if they did take us in initially, what's to stop us from getting hauled up in front of some sort of court-martial board that's run by the Chancellor and his friends after they've extracted the information?"

"What you're saying is we're stuck if we do and we're stuck if we don't."

"What I'm saying is it's important we choose the right side in this conflict and that we're going to have to choose sides. Or have already. Maybe if we'd been in some Core ship on the other side of the Empire or some tanker in the far distance, or even back home on Melbourne sitting on the beach and grilling jellyfish, we wouldn't have had to make this decision. But unfortunately, we were here, with that crazy admiral who almost got everyone killed."

Hooper grimaced. "I'm glad I wasn't on that destroyer. Imagine getting killed because somebody else on some other ship did something stupid. Seems random."

"Tribune Devin is doing a good job, so I guess we're on Team Devin now."

"Not much of a reason to try and get killed."

"Well, if you can't take a joke, you shouldn't have joined the Navy."

"Copy that. What do we do now that we've seen this beacon change?"

"Go back, wake up someone in engineering. Farqan, he's one of the more intelligent people back there. Bring everything back online that doesn't emit any signal. Then go wake up Silaski and have her come up."

"Silaski? And have her come up and do what?"

"She's good at pirating newscasts and finding out what Susy the Newsy is doing. Maybe she can pick up some sort of emissions from that warship to tell us what type of ship it is."

"You're saying that because she watches a lot of lowbrow entertainment she's going to be a good sensor operator?"

"She does spend all her time tuning in on those video signals…"

"Copy that. Let's see what we can find out."

A half shift later, they were certain that the approaching ship was in fact a warship—a frigate. Not as new as Tribune Devin's old ship *Pollux* was, but still sufficient to smack them down. Especially given all the *Collingwood* carried was a single laser, some anti-missile-boat torpedoes and a disgruntled crew.

The other ship made a cursory sweep of the system with active sensors, then changed course directly for their gas giant, intending to take on fuel and jump out.

"Well," Hooper said, "from a philosophical point of view, at least we know the extent of how far out the Empire is patrolling from the base at New Malaya. Which would be here. They've obviously reached the end of their patrol pattern, and are getting ready to gas up, turn around and head back to where they started."

"They could be going farther out."

"They would have needed a tanker same way we did."

Monti nodded. Devin had positioned a tanker a few systems back to extend their patrol range. Another reason to respect Tribune Devin. Unlike a lot of those high-ranking noble twits, he understands that ships need fuel and parts. He gives them the tools they need to do their jobs without being asked. Unlike the rest of the Navy.

"We know they're checking in here to see if anybody like us showed up, and then they're turning around. The question is, how often will they be doing this?"

"Well, we need to—"

"Excuse me, Lieutenants," Silaski said from her station.

"Silaski, this better be important."

"Well, it is, kind of. I was reading about some of these things. Anyways, you know the energy, that blue light?"

"You mean the jump light?"

"Well, we just got some of it."

"Got some of it from who?"

"Well, I was thinking could be this frigate that you're talking about."

"Silaski, this frigate jumped in, hours and hours and hours ago. Old jump signatures aren't relevant."

"Well, I was seeing the jump light coming through, and well, there's these beacons."

"Oh, for Joves's sakes," Hooper said. She flipped over her screen and scanned it for four seconds. "Status change. Two new beacons. Imperial. One custodian class tanker and one frigate class unknown."

Monti grinned. "I thought you said they weren't going to patrol farther."

"Not with just one. But obviously, this is a deep penetration search that expects hostiles."

Silaski glanced between the two officers. "How can you tell they expect hostiles?"

Monti tapped her controls, putting course info up on the main screen. "A tanker and two warships. Have one ship hop into the next system, mosey around, then pop the tanker and the other frigate in behind them. The first ship will have detected anybody in the system. The second group jumps in far enough away that if any shooting has started, they can note the shooting, scan everything, then skedaddle back to where the main fleets are."

"Oh, that's clever," Silaski said.

"Thanks, Silaski, we're glad that you like Imperial Naval Doctrine. The planning staff has been waiting for your endorsement." Hooper shook her head. "What do we do now?"

"Gotta get out of here. Gotta get out of here without being seen."

"Orders, Captain?"

Now she's all business, for once. Grand. Monti put another course upon the screen. "Well, we're outside of the system jump limit, so all we need to do is get clear of the planetary influence and we're gone. How are we for gas?"

"Seventy-eight percent."

"We hop a couple systems. Get everything ready, we're going to get out of here. and head back and tell the Tribune."

"And what are we going to tell him, oh great commanding Lieutenant?"

"We're going to tell him that this sector is well patrolled with sufficient ships that even a main fleet hopping in here won't be able to get through before something takes a run out of here and warns the base."

"That's only a problem if there's something on the other side that can come up and challenge the fleet."

"Well, ask yourself this, if there wasn't some sort of fleet on the other side that could challenge the Tribune's fleet, who would bother sending any ships to protect the ingress points? That's the question."

Chapter 14

"Jove!" Scruggs gripped tight as Gabrielle dashed forward. Rocky's yelps had scattered the entire herd. Her legs bounced free and she tightened her grip on the neck fur. The river showed ahead. Scattered trees filled her peripheral vision. *Gotta hang on. Gotta hang on. Too high up. If I fall, I'm dead.*

Gabrielle swung right and Scruggs's legs bounced to the left. Her heels scrabbled on the giraffe's flanks. If she could hold on until the herd ran—

BANG. Gabrielle swung away from the rocky river bank and side-swiped a pine tree, catching Scruggs on a branch. The branch bent, bent more, bent even more, then snapped back. It snatched Scruggs clear of the giraffe's back and dropped her into the prickly branches. She dropped four feet and crashed through the collected boughs, smashing branches below her. She dropped again, six feet, snapping the smaller branches off. Then another six feet, landing on a thick carpet of boughs. The boughs bent, swayed, held, dipped again.

Thank Jove, the tree caught me. I'm safe here.

CRACK. The strained boughs snapped under her weight, and she plummeted down, smacking into the rocky riverbed.

Dena tightened her legs, squeezing the running giraffe's chest together. "Hang on, Gavin," she yelled. "Don't let go. Squeeze with your legs."

"Graamph." Gavin clasped Gina's neck and buried his face there.

Dena gripped tighter with her legs and leaned back. Holding on to Gavin would pull him off. She sat up straight, grabbed handfuls of fur, and tried to anticipate the bounces and jerks. She'd stayed on runaway horses before, and the giraffe wasn't as fast. As long as Gavin held on with Rocky, she should be fine behind them.

A puzzled Rocky licked Dena's face. "Woof?"

The giraffe had forgotten a team of carnivores sat on her back, but the woof reminded her. Dena felt the animal check its run, and gripped ever tighter with her legs. Gina slowed under the pressure, then decided she wasn't happy with these things on her back. She bucked every second stride. Dena shuddered—she had been in this situation before. *Gotta get off now, in control, before she drops me under her hooves.* She'd seen what was left of a friend on Rockhaul after falling under the hooves of a cattle herd.

Silver white river sand flashed ahead. Soft sugary sand, or hard packed dried sand? Doesn't matter. Better than trees or rocks.

Dena unclasped her legs and rolled right, diving as she came clear. She tucked and rolled, the sand softening the impact. She rolled over twice before bouncing up. She stagger-ran a few more steps, splashing into the river, stumbled once, then fell flat. Cold water took her breath away, but she got her hands in front of her, then rolled over and stood, dripping.

She shivered, then grinned. I rode a giraffe! That's why you go out into the galaxy—for giraffe adventures.

The herd splintered when Rocky's yelp startled them. The lead giraffes turned and waded into the river. The trailing animals obeyed their instinct and chased after them. Scruggs's giraffe, followed by a dozen others, swung left to go past the milling animals slowed by the river bank and water. Dena and Gavin's giraffe swung downstream.

Lee saw Scruggs swept off her ride, the entire crash-hold-crash-hold-crash through the trees. Scruggs landed on her back with a thud audible to her, three hundred meters away.

The scrambling herds had cleared the area in front of her. The wandering pigs had disappeared, frightened by the bigger grazers roaming wild.

Lee dropped to the next branch, landing at a crouch, and hopped down. The line between her and Scruggs's limp form was empty. She raced forward. A single giraffe charged across from her left, knocking her down. She rolled as she hit the ground and came up running. Two isolated trees blocked her, so she dodged left. Scruggs lay on her back, still, a rock bracing her.

Lee dropped down. Scruggs's eyes were closed. "Sister Scruggs, talk to me. Where does it hurt? Can you move?"

Scruggs's eyes flipped open. "I'm fine."

"You hit hard. There's a rock. Can you wiggle your toes? Wiggle your fingers?"

"I'm fine."

"Show me your hands. Wiggle your fingers." Lee bent over and ran her hands along Scruggs's chest, checking for breaks.

"I said I'm fine. Get off me."

"No, no." Lee pushed Scruggs back onto the rock. "Don't move. Show me your fingers."

Scruggs brought her right hand between them, and made a rude gesture. "Here. See that?"

"Okay." Lee sat back. "Fingers seem to work."

"Then move."

"I need to see your feet, and check you for broken bones."

"Get off me. You don't need to check."

"Yes, you may have hurt them."

"I didn't. I'm not. Get off me. I need to get

up."

"You don't need to get up."

"Yes I do." Scruggs glared at Lee. "I need to get up and shoot that stupid pig I see behind you."

Lee looked over her shoulder. One of the pigs had trotted up behind them. A juvenile, not nearly as big as the other pigs they'd faced. It couldn't have been more than a half meter tall, but it was built accordingly.

Lee crouched. "Careful, he's too close—Ouch." Scruggs had shoved her to one side. Lee bounced sideways. Scruggs reached over her shoulder, pulled the rifle over her head, and sighted at the pig.

Then she cursed. She'd had the gun strapped behind her as she fell, and the landing and smashing into the rock had bent the barrel left an inch.

"Imperial Anus mother-loving—" Scruggs cursed. And cursed. The centurion discouraged his troopers from cursing, and said it distracted them.

The centurion wasn't here now.

The pig snorted and snuffled forward.

"Go away, pig," Scruggs yelled. "Run, before I come up there and beat you."

"Scruggs," Lee said. "Be careful, that's a big pig and it might—"

Scruggs rolled onto her knees, reversed the rifle, grasped the barrel and smacked the questing pig on its snout. The pig squealed and backed up an inch. Scruggs swung the gun again, and again, smacking the pig's snout. The pig backed up, confused. Helpless prey wasn't supposed to act like this.

Scruggs stood, and smacked the pig again and again. "Go. Away." CRACK. "You. Stupid." CRACK. "Animal. I. Hate." CRACK. "Pigs. All. Pigs. Especially." CRACK. "You."

The pig squealed under the attack, then turned and ran.

Scruggs stood, breathing heavily. "Lee? You hurt?"

"No," Lee said in a small voice.

"Let's go find the others."

"What about the giraffes?"

"Bring 'em on."

Dena waded across the river. The herd was passing upstream of her. She was in the clear. She'd come out of her fall with only a slight limp and a pained shoulder. If she'd waited a few more seconds, she'd have smashed her head on the river rocks. *Good lesson. When you're going to do something stupid, do it quickly.*

There were no pigs nearby, so she headed to the far bank. She sniffed. Wild garlic. Must be a patch somewhere. Maybe that was why the pigs didn't cross the river. Lots of animals didn't like strange smells. The river sloped gently up to a twenty-foot cliff. The cliff was tumbled rock covered with dirt. Trees dotted the slope, and there were plenty of spots where she could clamber up.

"Gavin? Rocky? Where are you?" Dena splashed out of the water. The ground thrummed as the giraffes trundled upstream, stomping and splashing. Gavin wouldn't hear her over the thundering hooves. *The herd's heading upstream, no pigs on this side. Best follow.*

Dena traveled a hundred yards, waving clouds of dust away. She grabbed the branches of the next tree and pulled herself up six feet higher to escape the straggling giraffes. Gavin was ahead, farther uphill. He waved. She waved back and doubled her speed, but slowed after she slid six feet downhill onto the hoof-churned riverbank. "Are you okay?"

"Fine," Gavin said. "I'm fine. So is Rocky. We're both fine. How did you get here?"

"Dove off, slapped the ground, messed up my shoulder when I rolled, almost drowned in the river, sprained an ankle getting across when I slipped on a boulder, crawled onto the bank, banged my shoulder again when another giraffe bumped me into a tree, climbed up the hill, and slid down." Dena held up her right hand, bleeding from a deep scratch. "And looks like I cut my hand when I slipped on that scree over there and slid down the hill. You?"

"Gina the giraffe dropped me off there." Gavin pointed down to a grass-covered dirt ledge six feet below them.

"Dropped you off? You mean threw you off."

"Nope." Gavin shook his head. "We bounced around, then we ran into the water and splashed through the river. I couldn't see where the heck we were. We splashed out of the river, and I guess we ran into the bulk of the herd or something like that, because Gina slowed down. Then we got stuck in a giraffe rush hour, because she barely moved. I stuck my head up, and I saw that that ledge was right at foot level, so I rolled off, planted my feet and stood there. Then she walked away into the dust."

"You just... climbed off her?"

"Stepped off. No problem. Like a set of stairs."

"No falling? No dropping? No getting bitten or thrown off? No major injuries?"

"Well..."

"Well what?"

Gavin nodded. "I did have one thing."

"Show me," Dena said.

Gavin stuck his foot out. "See the coveralls? I tore the knee."

Dena looked down. The coveralls' knee was torn. "Did it bang up your knee?"

"Nope." Gavin looked Dena over. Her

coveralls were shredded and soaking wet. Her hair and upper body was covered with dust. Mud caked her legs up to her waist where she had slipped coming out of the river. She still had her pack, but she'd lost her rifle. She limped and was rubbing her shoulder. Blood covered her forehead where she'd used her bleeding hand to wipe it. "Knee's fine. But look at those pants." He stuck his leg out. "It will take me forever to sew that up."

Scruggs continued cursing as she stomped across the river, clutching the rifle. After smacking the young one away, she ignored the rest of the pigs and they had ignored her. The giraffes had churned the river bottom and the banks into mud, but Scruggs didn't slow. She waded across, Lee hurrying behind her. "Are you sure you're not hurt? You hit hard."

Scruggs didn't look back. "Bruises. I'm fine."

"Well, let me know if you need to—"

Scruggs stopped at the water's edge and rounded on Lee. "I'm fine. Completely fine. I see the others. Follow me." She stomped off.

Lee followed silently behind her. Scruggs slipped in the mud climbing the bank, but shook off Lee's hand as she hauled herself up, making sure to keep the bent rifle with her.

It took only two minutes to stomp along the river to where Dena and Gavin were sitting. Scruggs climbed up the slope, kicking her toes in and using the butt of the rifle to lever herself up.

"Dena. Are you hurt?"

Dena tried to wipe the blood from her face, but only smeared it more. "What do you think? How do I look?"

Scruggs gave her a once over. "You're standing, talking, and complaining. You're fine."

"My ankle hurts, my shoulder's bruised, and I'm bleeding. Sure."

"Cry me a river. Are you okay or not?"

Dena glared. "Fine, Baby Marine. I'm fine."

"Good. Where's your shotgun?"

"That's all you have to say? Where's your shotgun?"

"Did you lose it?"

Dena pointed "Back there."

"By accident or on purpose?"

"Why? You going to make me go back and get it?"

"Yes. If you know where it is." Scruggs held up her rifle, showing the bent barrel. "We're short of weapons now."

Dena's eyes tracked the rifle barrel, then Scruggs's face. "It dropped somewhere, either in the chase, or when I rolled, or bounced off. No idea where it is."

"Outstanding." Scruggs turned to Lee and held out her hand. "Check Rocky, and give me your revolver."

Lee looked at Dena. "Dena looks like she could—"

"She's fine. She said so herself. Check Rocky." Scruggs stuck her hand forward. "Revolver."

Lee handed her weapon to Scruggs. Scruggs was a better shot than her anyway. A cursory check of Rocky gave no good news. "His fever has gotten worse, and he's having trouble breathing. He's not doing well."

"Fine." Scruggs bent over the panting dog and kissed him. "Don't worry, little buddy. We'll get you to the ship and fixed up."

"Um, Scruggs," Gavin said. "We still have to get those missiles. The element of surprise is kind of gone now. They'll be alert, if not from this stampede, then from the other crews who met us and get shot up. They're going to be on alert, so we won't be able to sneak in like we planned."

"And we all smell like garlic," Dena said. "And I'm more of a floral girl."

"Doesn't matter. New plan. We'll bang our way in."

"Bang our way in with a revolver and a bent rifle?"

Scruggs shrugged. "Won't need the revolver." She turned and climbed up the bank. "Follow me."

Chapter 15

"You seem a little... uptight right now, Baby Marine." Dena trailed Scruggs up the steep hill. Gavin and Lee followed more carefully, Lee making sure Gavin didn't tumble and hurt Rocky.

Scruggs used the bent rifle like a walking stick, dragging herself up the sandy hill. "Missiles where there shouldn't be any. Two-day hike in the rain. Avoiding herds of feral giraffes, killer pigs, psychotic maple syrup thugs, nearly broke my back on a rock, Rocky's hurt and he might die, and, and—" She turned and brandished the bent rifle at Dena. "This was my favorite rifle. I had it custom made. Fit me like a glove."

Dena reared back. "You're kind of scary when you're like this." Dena grinned. "You know, the old man would be proud of you."

"He'll be prouder, shortly. Here we go. You down there, hurry it up."

"Scruggs," Gavin hissed from the hill. "Keep your voice down. We want to sneak up on them."

"No time for that. Both of you, get up here. Wait in the woods. I'm going next to the fence."

"They'll see you," Lee said.

"That's the point."

At the top of the bluffs was a fence. Parallel strands of metal, seven feet high, sunk deep into the sandy soil. Triple strands of barbed wire sat at the top, bent out. Dena bit her lip. *This could be a problem. How do we get across it without getting zapped?* None of the tree limbs extended over the fence. *I might be able to jump it with a pole, but no way Gavin can, or Rocky.*

Scruggs dragged the barrel along the struts. "Gavin, you said this fence is electrified?"

Gavin walked down the fence line until he came to the post. "There. Wooden posts, ceramic insulators, and live wires. Each wire likely has an alarm on it. If we cut the wires, they short to ground, and it will register in a central site."

"If we cut them quickly, we can walk through before they get here."

"We could," Gavin said. "If we had cutters."

"Where's the cutters?"

"In that pile of stuff that I dumped out when we put Rocky in my pack," Gavin said.

"No time anyways." Scruggs reversed her rifle, holding it by the bent barrel. She hammered away at the insulator holding the bottom wire. Once. Twice. Crack. The insulator smashed, and the wire sagged. Scruggs pushed it down with the butt of the rifle. Electricity flashed blue, and the wire grounded.

"There," Scruggs said. "They'll see that on their screens. How long 'til they come check it out?"

"Minutes, if they have a security operations center," Gavin said. "And a waiting patrol."

"Outstanding." Scruggs hammered away at the next insulator. It cracked, and she pushed it down. Next, she smashed the third insulator. There wasn't enough slack, so she moved to the next post and smashed that insulator.

Headlights flashed in the distance, and a motor roared.

"Scruggs," Gavin said. "Reaction force coming."

"Super." Scruggs turned. "Lee, Gavin, back into the woods, hide below the lip. Dena, get into the dark over there, and get your slingshot ready. Wait for me before you start anything." She bent over and pulled her boots off. Then she dumped her shirt, her belt holster and her pants.

"Scruggs," Dena said, "what are you doing?"

"Creating a distraction." Scruggs continued to strip until she was down to only her socks. Then she picked her bent rifle back up.

"I see lights. That's a patrol—"

"I know. Get back in the dark and wait there."

Scruggs walked to a third post and hammered the insulators off that one. She'd figured out the knack. It took only two thwacks before the wires hung loose. Methodically hammering away, she had five sets of wires knocked off in under a minute.

Headlights flashed past her, then returned and steadied.

Dena ducked back under a tree and loaded her slingshot. *What is that crazy kid up to? She'll get us shot. All of us shot.* The lights flashed over Scruggs's now naked body. *Well, not right away, not if they're male.*

Scruggs continued to hammer at the posts, knocking another set of insulators free.

A pickup truck pulled up forty feet away, and doors opened. Two shadowy figures stepped out from behind the lights. One trained a weapon at her, the other stood in front.

"Hands up or we shoot!" he called.

Scruggs stopped hammering. "Took you long enough to get here. Do you have a radio in that thing?"

"I said stop or we shoot."

"I stopped. But you'll need a radio to talk to base. It was a massacre out there. Dead bodies everywhere. The pigs ate them. It was horrible."

"Where? Who?" The man stepped into the light. He had the same kind of neckerchief the other group had, but with red and green rather than blue and yellow. He carried one of their short range sub-machine guns. "What are you doing here? Put down your rifle." He tilted his head. "Do you know you're naked?"

"All the trees got shot up. Sap everywhere—all over my clothes. That attracted the pigs, so I got rid of them. We shot at them. But they ate everyone."

"Ate everyone?" The man stepped closer. "Put your gun down."

Scruggs held up the rifle. The bent barrel was visible in the truck's headlights. "It's not a gun, it's a rifle. And it's not a rifle now, it's a hammer. Do you have a radio in there or not?"

"Why didn't you just call?"

"With what? I have a busted rifle and greasy clothes. I don't have a radio."

"What outfit are you with?" His radio squawked, and he spoke into a wrist comm.

"Not yours, obviously. Can we get to this radio? Or can you maybe take me to your boss?"

"Why were you hammering off the wires?"

"To get your attention. And I have to get through this stupid fence."

"What?"

"Worked, didn't it? Well?" Scruggs spread her hands. "I've knocked off enough wires I can jump through, above them." It was true. The bottom group of four electrified wires drooped low enough that a good jump would clear them.

The man shook his head and moved closer. "You're crazy."

"That's what they call me. Cute but crazy."

Rocky yelped in the woods. The man waved his gun. "What was that?"

"My dog, Dena. She's hurt," Scruggs said. "But she's okay for a minute. If I jump through, will you drive me to your boss? I need to talk to him."

"You're nuts." The man shook his head. "Fine. Come on through."

"Let me put on clothes first." Scruggs turned her head. "Don't worry, Dena girl, I'll only be gone for a minute. I need to talk to the man here, and I'll bet his friend will be able to help you."

She bent down and collected her pants, shirt,

and boots, and the revolver she had stashed under them. She stood, aimed through the clothes, and shot the closer man in the chest.

Dena sighted her slingshot and slammed a shot into the head of the figure behind the car door. She grabbed another metal ball bearing—she'd found them the best ammunition—and aimed into the dark. Nothing moved. "I think we got them, Baby Marine."

Scruggs dropped her clothes, ran two steps, and dove through the gap between the wires. She hit the ground on the far side, rolled, and stood. The first man was on the ground. She shot him again, then marched to the car, and shot the other man twice. "Everyone through. Gavin, hand me the pack with Rocky. I think we can lift him past."

Lee's eyes were wide. "Jove save us."

"Scruggs," Gavin said. His voice was quiet. "They'll have to call in or something. And there will be other patrols."

"That's why we have to move quickly."

Dena walked up to the fence. "This is crazy."

"Yes. That's my specialty," Scruggs said. "You got something to say about that?"

Dena looked at the two corpses, the damaged fence, and the bent rifle. "Not me. You want your clothes?"

Scruggs looked down. She was still naked. "Bring them. Toss me my boots."

Two minutes later, they were scooting down the perimeter road. It wasn't a road, more of a track in the field. But it had no obstructions, and they could maintain speed.

Scruggs drove, fast. "Gavin, get Dirk on the radio. Tell him to be here in ten minutes. Ten, not nine. Not twelve. Ten. Have him land on the southern pad."

"He'll want to know if the missiles will be down—"

"They will be. Tell him."

Gavin put on a head set and worked the radio. Lee fussed over Rocky. Scruggs strained to see—the primary moon dropped behind the horizon, casting long shadows.

Dena borrowed Scruggs's sensor-binocs. "Like we expected. Truck with radar. Cables from the truck to the shed. Big space between the shed and the missiles. Cables hanging from the side of the shed closest to the missiles, and an overhead power line running into the shed from town."

"How big a shed?"

"Smaller than it looked. I thought it was like a house. But it's more like one you'd use for ice fishing."

"Ice what?"

"Ice-fishing. You go out on a lake in the winter, dig a hole in the ice, drag a shed over it, hide inside and drink booze all day."

"Where's the fishing?"

"What?"

"Don't you try to catch fish or something?"

"No. What sort of idiot does that? You sit and drink alcohol. I drank corn whiskey myself."

"So no actual fish involved?"

Dena put the binocs down. "None. Why would you want that?"

"Never mind. The shed. Can I drive up to it?"

"Sure. Parking lot on the eastern side. Access road there as well. There's something like a hole—I think a trench. On the north side."

"Outstanding. Gavin, what's Dirk's ETA?"

Gavin held out a headset. "He wants to talk to you."

Scruggs stamped on the brakes. The crew

braced as they skidded to a stop, then Scruggs took the radio from Gavin. "What?"

Dirk's voice came over the radio. "Are the missiles offline?"

"They will be when you're two minutes out."

"I'd rather wait."

"I'd rather you didn't. Come in and land on the southern pad."

"If I come in for a landing and those missiles are live, they'll shoot me out of the sky."

"Yes."

"I'll die."

"Yes."

There was a long pause. "That's all you've got to say?"

"We've got our own problems out here. Put the centurion on."

"I don't think—"

The radio channel banged. Then the centurion answered. "Private?"

"It's acting temporary lieutenant now," Scruggs said. "Or cadet, if we're being formal."

"So it is. How can we help you?"

"Come and get us, now."

"The captain of the ship, the honorable Commander Durriken Friedel, duke of somewhere or other, I don't remember, expresses doubts about your abilities."

"The honorable Commander can kiss my—" Scruggs gave several examples of suggested activities.

Dena's grin got wider and wider. She lifted Scruggs's free hand and exchanged high slaps. "That's telling him, Baby Marine. Good for you."

Scruggs finished her diatribe. "But he does that after he gets here with the ship. In five minutes. Understood?"

"Acting Temporary Lieutenant, I'd like a little

more detail…"

"We're blown," Scruggs said. "They know about us. We have no weapons. We lost our explosives back in the woods. I have a plan to disable the missiles, but we need you airborne to keep their attention. And Rocky's hurt. He needs the med pod in the ship."

"Understood."

"We're heading in now, Centurion. I'm counting on you," Scruggs said.

"We'll be there in five."

"For sure?" Scruggs asked.

"Absolutely. Pilot will lift in one minute. You can count on it."

Dena leaned over and grabbed the microphone. "How you going to make him do that, Old Man."

"Easy, Nature Girl," Ana said. "I just have to make him more scared of me than he is of dying in a crash. Think I can do that?"

Scruggs cut the headlights and drove them another mile along the perimeter road, then cut back to the west. Dena gave directions using the infrared setting on the goggles until they intercepted the east-west road that ran into the base.

"Scruggs." Gavin had been peering out the back. "There's more activity down where we came in. I see headlights."

"Understood. We only need a few minutes." Their truck did have a radio, and they could hear at least three different groups arguing about what had happened and where the intruders were. The opposing trucks split up, doing a perimeter drive in opposite directions. One headed down the spaceport road.

Dena kept her binoculars moving. "The truck

following behind us is shining their lights at the fence, and scanning the fields. They'll be here in five, ten minutes at the most."

"Lights from the mountains." Gavin leaned out his window. "Drive plume. *Heart's Desire* is lifting."

"That's fine. Watch the missile battery, Dena. Centurion says once they detect *Heart's Desire*, they'll try to lock on, but they won't shoot right away. But we'll hear—" The wail of a siren broke out ahead of them. "A warning. And he says anybody with any sense will drop into those trenches or run away. Sometimes those missiles misfire, and when they launch, they blow burning rocket fuel around, and dust and smoke and rocks. Are they going for the trenches?"

"All sorts of motion there," Dena said. "Lots of scuttling, like people are diving into holes."

Lee looked up from patting a sleepy Rocky. "Why isn't the control room in a hole as well?"

"Centurion says that's why it's so far away. That and the fact that people are lazy and don't want to dig a big enough hole. Couple small trenches catch the stragglers."

"Radar stopped turning." Dena changed the focus on her binoculars. "It's jigging back and forth."

"They're tracking." Scruggs snapped on the headlights. "Anyone want out? Last chance."

"We're staying," Dena said.

"Strap in, then. And don't say I didn't warn you."

"Warn us about what?" Lee asked. "And you never said what you're going to do when you get there. We only have your revolver and Dena's slingshot."

Scruggs revved the engine. "We do have one other thing."

"Which is?" Dena asked

"Two tons of metal and plastic traveling at sixty kilometers an hour." Scruggs floored the truck and they roared off into the twilight.

Chapter 16

"You didn't need to point that shotgun at me." Dirk pulsed the *Heart's Desire*'s thrusters, and the ship rattled and tilted to the right. "Not to get me to fly."

"Need? Absolutely not. Want? Yes. Enjoy? Absolutely, yes." Ana finished strapping himself next to Dirk in the control room. He slapped his screens and brought the radar warning screens up. "Could you get this thing moving, Navy?"

Dirk pulsed the thrusters again, and the *Heart's Desire* lifted free of the muddy lake shore, then tilted hard left. Dirk cut the thrusters and dropped the ship back into the mud. "Pluto's ears."

"Now would be fine. What's the problem?"

"We're only lifting on one side."

"Thrusters bust?"

"Not according to the screens. Bring up the internal fuel schematic, and check the flow rates on the nozzles."

Ana folded his arms. "Do I look like a gas station attendant?"

"I guess it's stupid to think an army guy would understand fuel supply systems."

"I understand them very well. But I'm in the blowing things up line of work, not the fixing things type of work."

"Right." Dirk paged through his screens one-handed. "Thrusters look fine. Output is fine, according to this. Could be a sensor ghost. I need you to go back to the engineering console and check the rates from there—"

The intercom crackled. Whenever they were planet side, Lee slaved the commo channels to the intercom. They could both hear Scruggs's voice. "*Heart's Desire*, Scruggs. Engaging. confirm your status and ETA, over."

Dirk looked at Ana. Ana raised his eyebrows. Dirk cursed again, then flipped screens and typed in a long override code. He had to type it twice and confirm twice. Then he tapped the mic. "*Heart's Desire*, Scruggs. Lifting now. ETA six minutes, thirty seconds, over." He took a deep breath, then another, then slammed the throttles' levers all the way forward.

"Understood. Scruggs out." Scruggs kept both hands on the wheel.

Dena pulled the headset off her and handed it to Gavin. "Scruggs, what are you doing?"

"I'm going to ram that shed. We'll destroy it, cut the link with the control station and the power. The missiles won't be able to deploy." She swerved left to miss two porcupines that appeared in the headlights. "Sorry to scare you little guys. Don't worry, we'll leave you alone."

"Baby Marine," Dena said. "That's not a good idea. That building might be tough. If we crash into it, we might get killed."

"You said it was a shed. Sheds are sheet metal. The consoles are sheet metal. We'll plow right through it. You'll see."

"What if there're concrete blocks inside?"

"That's stupid. Who puts concrete inside a building?"

"What about if there're wooden supports inside? What if it's braced with tree trunks?"

"Did you see tree trunks?"

"No, but I'm well known to be an unreliable scout."

"That's not true. You're an excellent observer. You give detailed descriptions of what you see, count hostiles, and look for weapons. You're a great scout."

"I'm not. I make all that up."

"Gavin? Do you think she makes all her observations up?"

Gavin had been staring out the rear window. "No, not at all. I find her reliable and precise. What do you and the centurion mean when you say contact... contact rear?"

The truck bounced over a pothole. "You say that when there's somebody behind shooting at us."

Tracers appeared on their left. Bullets tinged off the metal. The rear window shattered, and a second later, so did the windshield. Everybody ducked. Tracer bullets faded off to the right.

Gavin stuck his head up. "Contact." He shook glass out of his hair, and put the headset back on. "Contact rear."

"I understand that you're a big-time Navy officer and all." Ana grasped his harness with both hands. The *Heart's Desire* was flying, sort of. It was climbing, but was stuck at a nearly ninety-degree bank. "And I'm just an ignorant trooper. But I would think that level flight is preferred to this."

"Shut up. I'm busy." Dirk's hands played with the throttles, and he pushed his control yoke back and forth. "I don't get a lot of practice flying in atmosphere, so I have to concentrate."

"Well, concentrate on this." Ana flipped through his screens. "We're losing some sort of fluid from the rear of the ship. The radar warning receiver just pinged hard, near max strength, and I just got a very garbled call from Gavin. They're taking fire and that battery is tracking us. Annnnd we're going to hit that cliff that has appeared in front of us."

Dirk had circled around their little valley, spiraling up to gain lift, and the threat radars had pinged them as they climbed. He jerked the ship to the left, losing altitude in the progress. "I'll never make it over that ridge. I need to circle the other direction and try the other ridge. What are we leaking? The fuel gauges look fine."

Ana focused the cameras on the spray dropping from the ship. "Looks like plain old water. It's not foaming or boiling like liquid H, and it hasn't exploded like oxygen." Ana tapped his screen. "Where is all that water coming from?"

Dirk kept the ship on its side as he pushed it to climb. "When we sucked out of the lake, how much did you pump in?"

"Tons and tons and tons. Hours the first day while you were sleeping. Much longer than usual. Did Gavin change something with the pumps?"

"Do I look like a gas station attendant to you?"

"Touche, mon ami." Ana paged through his screens again. "Oh, that explains it."

"Explains what?"

"Must have been a leak. Look here." Ana shared a camera. "The entire engineering compartment is full of water. We must have overfilled the water tanks, drained them into the cargo hold or something. Over massed with good old H_2O." Ana switched back to the forward screen. "So much so, in fact, that it appears that we won't make it over this ridge." Ana smiled. "Outstanding."

Scruggs weaved the truck from side to side down the access road. The first lucky group of shots wasn't repeated. The gunfire slackened.

"They're on the road behind us," Gavin reported. "Looks like they want to get closer before they give us a shot."

"Centurion says those sub-machine guns aren't accurate at distance." A line of single shots flashed ahead. "Nor are pistols, which is what those are."

Dena watched with the binocs. "Baby Marine, all it takes is one lucky shot."

"Well, let's hope they don't feel lucky today."

"Great news," Gavin said. "But aren't you planning on getting closer to, you know, destroy that radar? Won't that increase the accuracy?"

"Right." Scruggs pushed the accelerator to the floor. "Everybody hang on. Sorry about the trouble."

"What trouble?" Dena said. "I don't see any. Oh crap."

Scruggs swung back and forth across the road. Gunfire erupted from behind. Bullets streamed past them to the right. The pistol flashed ahead. Scruggs centered the truck. In the distance, bright lights surrounded the radar site, their beams spilling out across the fields.

"Scruggs," Gavin said, "they're shooting at us again."

"I know, I know, I can see. I can hear. Dena, what's to our right?"

Dena scanned. "Open fields. A few trees. Bushes. Some sort of crops."

"I'm going to change our axis of approach. I'll need you to scout an alternate ingress point."

Dena dropped her binoculars. "Axis of approach? Ingress? What the heck? You doing crossword puzzles again?"

"Centurion's been teaching me advanced tactics. We need another way in. I'm turning off the road and heading northeast. The berm of that landing field will protect us from shots from ahead, and that truck behind might miss us. Keep your binocs focused ahead, tell me if there's a problem. Gavin, keep an eye out the back."

Scruggs maneuvered to the edge of the road. Gotta make sure they see me in their lights before I turn. If I charge right in, they'll get me. Need to have them looking the wrong way.

Bullets flashed past to their right. One tinged off the trunk. Scruggs killed her headlights, then the driving lights, and slashed the wheel to the right.

A quick bump and the jeep bounced off the dirt road, down the bordering gravel, and into the fields.

"Dena, where's the radar unit?"

"Ahead left somewhere. I can't see it for the trees," Dena said. "Wait. Why can't I see it for the trees? How come there's trees ahead of us? Where did they come from? LEFT."

Scruggs spun to the left, bounced onto a bump and down a gully. Dirt fountained up behind the wheels.

Lights flashed behind her to her left. Then to her right. Then both sides. But no shots came near.

"Contact, well, no, never mind," Gavin yelled. "They're shooting at each other. Don't use the brakes."

"Don't encourage her, Gavin," Dena said. "She's crazy enough as it is. One bad bump and we're in trouble."

"If she uses the brakes," Gavin said, "then the brake lights come on, and those chowderheads back there will know they're shooting at each other."

"Instead of getting shot, we'll get crushed when we hit a tree." Dena resumed her scanning. "All sorts of options today."

"Can you see the radar?"

"Nope. But I can see the berm of the landing site, with the lights behind it. And I can see a road, or at least a notch in the berm that looks like the entry. Get us there and we should be able to drive right in." Dena gave Scruggs driving directions.

"Good, what's the ETA on the ship?"

Green fire bloomed ahead. A missile rocketed into the sky, arced left, then sped toward the hills behind.

"Not soon enough, I think." Lee said.

"This is all your fault. You flooded the engine room when you were pumping," Dirk said. "It's full of water." He fought the controls as they raced to the starport.

"You're just grandstanding," Ana said. "Stop your whining. Even if we filled the engine room, it's only a few tons. We can lift that."

"It's not how heavy it is, it's where it is. We have to balance loads when we're lifting. Make sure the containers are aligned properly. Otherwise, the thrusters are on weird angles and can't compensate. They're vectored to keep us on an even keel, not getting us up high enough."

BONG BONG BONG.

"Vampire!" Ana said. "Fast mover! That's one of the missiles." He laughed. "But of course you know that."

Dirk swung them back into his circle. "Is it tracking?"

"Oh, it surely is. Tracking well, too, almost mimicking your turns."

"Mimicking? Tell me about those missiles. Their story. How they got here."

"Their story? How they got here? Navy, you ask the stupidest things." Ana grinned. "Well, let's see. They were probably born in an Imperial factory on one of the Core planets. Papa was working-class type of chassis. Probably aluminum. Hard worker, Papa, a good union man. Oh sure, he would have liked to be one of those custom titanium jobs, but that's a lot of money for a workaday rocket casing.

Now Mama, she was a solid fuel rocket motor, real hot stuff, lights the place up. I'll bet they met at a work mixer where—"

"Shut up, you pompous, self-loathing timorous coward. We need to live. Otherwise, the others, and your precious Scruggs, will get killed. I need specifications. Think like the mercenary deserter you are. If you had to equip a unit on a low tech planet for protection against starships, what type of anti-starship weapons would you buy? How would they be directed? The missiles themselves. Radar? Infrared?"

Ana took a grip on himself. "Infrared. Cheapest and most reliable. Starships generate a lot of heat. The drives, the thrusters, re-entry. Big, bright burning hot spots in a cool sky. Radar's expensive and can be jammed unless you get high tech stuff. Radio control links can be disrupted. Video guidance can be masked with dust. But infrared? Use the ground radar to get a direction, launch thataway, then turn on the seeker five seconds out. Guaranteed you'll hit something."

"Infrared. Got it." Dirk flipped the controls, and the *Heart's Desire* turn tightened.

Ana pressed into his seat, unable to move with the G force, until Dirk straightened the ship. They were still on their side, but no longer turning.

"Pardon a self-loathing coward," Ana said. "But did you just turn us around to ram that missile?"

"Yes." Dirk tilted slightly. "Heading dead for it."

"And your plan is to evade at the last second?"

"No. I'm going to try to hit it head on. But I will blow up part of the ship before we hit."

"Outstanding." Ana flipped to an external camera view. A bright red light, dead ahead, grew in size. "An unusual plan. I'm dying to see how it turns out." He laughed again. "Literally dying, that is."

Chapter 17

"Well, that was bad," Devin said. The results of the latest exercise filled the display screen in his office. The computer had provided statistics on the last two days' drills. Lines of red and yellow overwhelmed the single green marking.

A light green, not even a dark green.

"Disagree," Lionel said. "It wasn't bad."

"Then what was it?"

"Shockingly bad. Incredibly, shockingly bad. I haven't seen this bad a result on a live-fire exercise since I was a battery commander on the old *Magdeburg*."

"But your shooting improved. So could theirs."

"My shooting was fine on *Magdeburg*, because we had regular force officers. It was the other training ship. The *Strassberg*, they had all the Imperial Volunteer Navy Reserve officers. She shot a chunk out of us by accident, her targeting was so bad. Nearly killed me and three others. A group of midshipmen trainees, all of them those useless noblemen who joined the volunteer reserve."

"The *Strassberg*, you say?" Devin paled. "Old light cruiser?"

"Yes, they did gunnery training for the volunteers." Lionel narrowed his eyes. "You know the *Strassberg*?"

"Yes, I mean, I've heard of it."

"Were you ever on the *Strassberg*?"

Devin bit his lip. "Not sure."

"Tribune, where did you take your gunnery training?"

"Um." Devin turned bright red. "Don't remember. Long time ago. Look here." He pointed to the board. "At least engineering came through."

Lionel gave Devin a long, searching look, then

shrugged and tapped a yellow light. "But tactical hasn't. We need more shooting exercises."

After yesterday's first fiasco, Lionel ordered the fleet to a parking orbit at the gas giant. Operations sucked fuel for two shifts. Engineering fixed all the weapons that hadn't come online, and tactical blamed everybody but themselves for poor performance.

"You've been giving them drills every shift. Are we running them too hard?"

"No." Lionel shook his head. "They're only getting two drills a day. They get the shooting drills, and then they get one other. That still gives everybody a chance to get at least one full shift of sleep. I've been timing it so that the same crews aren't woken up in the middle of the night every time, either at the end of one shift or the beginning of another. That way, even if somebody's in bed, they're only getting up a little early for their next shift."

"That should help them perform better."

"You'd think. But they're getting worse." Lionel grimaced. He had started drilling the ship's crew on ship issues over a week ago, before starting the fleet maneuvers. They improved for the first three days. Starting on day four, they flat-lined, and now in the second week, they were starting to deteriorate. "It's my fault," Lionel said. "I'm the captain. I need to fix it."

"You're the captain," Devin agreed. "But I'm the, well, what am I? Am I an admiral?"

"You're a Tribune. Tribunes outrank an admiral."

"True, but shouldn't I be appointed something?"

"Fine." Lionel flourished his hand. "I appoint you the fleet commander."

"Fleet commander is a position, Admiral is a

rank."

"You don't need a rank, you need a position. Either way, my position is captain. So I'm in charge and I'm not doing a good job."

"Well, it's your crew that's not doing a good job, not you." Devin looked at Lionel. *He looks bad. The crew gets rests between drills, but he doesn't.* Lionel designed all the drills himself. He spent all his time setting them up, grading them, or yelling about the results. He never seemed to sleep.

"I'm responsible for the crew. I need to fire some of them, but I need them."

"They're trying hard. Perhaps you should give them a break."

"Tribune." Lionel shook his head. "We've started a war. We need to make the hard decisions. If they're a problem, they have to be fixed."

"Can we let them go?"

"No replacements. We need to make them work."

"How do we do that? How do we motivate them?"

"The beatings will continue until morale improves, perhaps. I'm thinking of punishments now, not motivations."

"That's what it's come to? Punishing people for not being good enough?"

"Did I mention the war? And the hard decisions? And where we are…" Lionel's mouth contracted to a flat line. "Nothing but problems."

Need to cheer him up. "Has there been anywhere that's shown consistent improvement?"

"Engineering. The engineers are happy to have more toys to play with. They've started fixing everything in the ship, including things that haven't worked properly for years. Electrical consumption has gone down seven percent as they are replacing workarounds with proper maintenance."

"Anyone else?"

"Fleet maneuvering is up to standard. The maneuvers are getting crisper. But they were so bad initially, they had nowhere to go but up." Both light cruisers, *Fargo* and *Little Rock*, had clipped the tankers while refueling, and two of the destroyers had a mild but embarrassing collision while pivoting.

"What are we doing right there?"

"It's Rudnar. She called up a conference with the other navigating officers and the other ships and explained how she likes things done."

"She's only a midshipman. Why would they listen to her?"

"She told them that she was scared to death of you and your sword. She was going to steer the ship where she was told to, and if they happen to get in her way, she would run them over. They believed her. They're all paying a lot more attention to the flagship orders because they're afraid she's going to crush them."

"That's a methodology, I suppose. Good for her. Anyone else?"

"Sensors is solid, but that's Lukas, an old *Pollux* person, and let's see, life support, another *Pollux* person, and know what? All the *Pollux* people are doing better, or I should say all of their departments are doing better. No, that's not true." Lionel played with the numbers. "Any department where a *Pollux* person has direct oversight is doing well, but if it's indirect oversight, that is, if there's somebody between them and the actual people doing the job, then it's not going as well."

"They're not inspiring the troops."

"I don't know what they're doing. Jove save us, look at the sensor report for that battery. That's horrible."

"But this one—" Devin highlighted the next in

line. "Was excellent. Why is one doing well and not the other? We need more information." Devin tapped his intercom. "Let's get them down here. What was that name?"

The sensor operator, Strapakova, appeared in Devin's cabin twenty minutes later. Her uniform was pressed, her boots shined, and her eyes were clear. She saluted, the Naval salute, not the Imperial cross-chest salute.

Devin returned the salute. "I wanted to tell you you're doing a good job, Strapakova, and I'm pleased with the results."

"Thank you sir. The crew is working hard. Me too. I know this job is important."

"Do you?" Devin leaned back and looked at Lionel. "Do you indeed? Why is it important?"

"Well, sir, without the sensors providing adequate information, the navigation can get us in all sorts of trouble. If we're coming close to planets, tactical relies on us for accurate targeting information."

"No, no. I don't mean why the mechanics of your jobs are important to do well, or what mechanics are important to do well, or do… mechanics. Never mind that." Devin shook his head. "What I mean is, why bother? Why bother doing a good job on any of it?"

Strapakova's face blanked. "Because, sir, the Empire. We serve the Empire."

"Yes, we know that, but—"

"No, sir, I understand, but the Empire is necessary. We need to do things properly out here."

Did she just interrupt me? Do all my officers interrupt me? Should I let them? As long as they do their jobs, do I care? "Explain."

"Sir, I've been with you in the Verge for years. You're the only thing that was keeping the pirates from plundering those smaller colonies, or keeping those ship owners from turning into pirates themselves. Facilitating commerce. Without the ships traveling from colony to colony, there'd be no medical supplies, there'd be no education, there'd be no civilization. Civilization's important sir. You brought civilization to the Verge."

"Well, thank you. I think. But what about now?"

"Sir?"

"What about now? Who are we bringing civilization to?"

Strapakova shrugged. "I didn't think about it sir. It's not my pay grade. I expect you have a reason, a good reason for what you're doing, and I'm here to follow you. We trust you sir."

"Thank you for your loyalty. That'll be all." Strapakova braced, then marched out.

Lionel stood and stretched. "Well, what I heard was, you did a good job before, bringing law to the lawless. On the strength of that trust, we, meaning the crew who knows you, are going to assume that what you're doing now needs to be done for the sake of the lawful, the lawless. The Empire. Whatever. And that's why I joined the Navy, dammit."

"That's what they said." Devin stood and stretched himself. "Is that why you joined the Navy?"

"It was the dental plan. I had bad teeth."

"Why are these other people here? The non-*Pollux* people?"

"Don't know," Lionel said. "Let's ask them."

Asking them didn't turn out as positively as they expected. The first three officers that Devin called into question were shifty and gave canned responses. After they left Devin asked Lionel if there was a section in the officers' manual on what to say to the Tribune when he asked you dumb questions. Lionel pointed out he'd never know because he never read the officers' manual. Devin argued. Lionel gave him a reading list.

The fourth one spoke honestly, albeit by mistake.

Petty Officer Rebseman slouched into the office and saluted. When he used the cross-chest Imperial Salute, it exposed a hole in his uniform shirt's armpit.

"You're from Nouveau Galles, Rebseman?"

Rebseman sniffled into his hand, and wiped his nose with his sleeve. "Yes, Tribune."

"And you've been in the Navy twenty-three years."

"Yes, Tribune."

"How many on *Canopus*?"

"Last twelve sir."

Both Devin and Lionel looked up from their notes. Lionel spoke first. "You've been on the same ship for twelve years?"

"Yes sir. Great ship sir. Love it here." Rebseman wiped his nose again.

"Isn't that unusual, being on the same ship so long?"

"Oh, no sir. Pretty common, actually, in a lot of the Core squadrons. You get appointed to a ship, you either stay with the ship, either you're part of the ship crew or the admiral's crew."

"The what?" Devin asked

"Well, you follow an admiral sir. Some people do. Or you follow a ship. If you follow an admiral, then you go from ship to ship with them. And you come in with the admiral, leave with the admiral."

"What do the ship crew do?"

"Warrant officers and petty officers stay with the ship, sir, so we make sure it runs okay," Rebseman explained. Once the Imperial Navy gave someone a warrant officer's rank, they couldn't be decommissioned unless they did something incredibly stupid, like offending an admiral's sister. But as long as they did a reasonable job they couldn't be kicked out. They might not get promoted. It wasn't unusual to still be a lieutenant at a twenty-five year retirement.

"But you... Wait, I don't understand." Devin shook his head. "Don't you want to experience something new? Isn't that why you joined the Navy?"

"No sir. New things bother me."

New things bother him? Devin looked at his records from the screen in front of him. "It says here your father is Lord Constable of New Gaul."

"Yes sir."

"You would be the heir?"

"No, sir, my eldest sister, she's the heir. I'm, well, I'm nothing sir. I'm the spare. Fourth spare, actually. Unless all my sisters die, there's nothing for me there. My parents decided that I'd go into the Navy. So I went into the Navy. I went through the regional school. We couldn't afford the Capital College, you understand sir. New Gaul is not poor, but we're not particularly wealthy. So no commission for me."

"I see. And then once you enlisted…"

"Well, once I found a spot I liked, sir, I stayed. Most of the Core crews are like that."

Devin had never known this. The *Pollux* had been a crack frigate, and it never went anywhere that non-crazy people would consider fun. His crews spent all their times hobnobbing with barbarians, trudging through mud, and getting shot at by crazed pirates. Things that didn't sound like much fun to somebody who was only looking for a good dental plan.

Rebseman sniffed. "I know the sensors on the

ship, they're the same ones I've used for years. I understand my job." He wiped his nose again.

"You understand your job," Lionel said. "Except, last exercise but two, you targeted most of the port battery on the wrong asteroid."

"Yes sir. I've never used the targeting sensors until you came aboard."

"You've been here twelve years and you've never used the targeting sensors? You're a sensor operator."

"The first six I was assistant sensors sir. But since then, no. No need sir. Never had drills before you got here sir."

"Surely the original sensor officer would have shown you how to use the targeting sensors, at least once."

"She never used them either sir. I'm pretty good, though, with the long-range radars. I can map out a system and find you courses to targets pretty quickly. Or at least find the information that the navigators need."

"What else are you cross-trained in? Rebseman?"

"Nothing sir."

"You've been on the ship twelve years and you haven't cross-trained in any of the other positions?"

"No sir."

"And you never wanted to leave?"

Rebseman shrugged. "I like it here. *Canopus* is a good ship. We had a regular route through the Core sectors. I got to see my family once a year. It's home to me sir."

"I see. I see. And how many other ship crew are like you?"

"I would say a good percentage of them sir. More than half of them are the same people I saw the last ten years. Once you got on this, you didn't try to go anywhere else."

"But all those officers who quit, the ones that we offered transport back, all those were the…"

"Admiral's followers sir. They come and they go. Every year, we'd get a new commander. He'd bring his people in. They show up. They have shiny uniforms. They talk a lot, want to try all these new things." Rebseman sighed. "It's exhausting. We just keep the ship running while they play sir. Well, some of them aren't too bad. The last lieutenant commander in charge of sensors and navigation, she was pretty good. She left us alone, which is what we wanted."

"Let me understand this." Devin tapped both hands on the desk. "The Imperial Navy is crewed by a corps of long-serving officers and men who get on one ship and stay with it forever, and then small groups of admirals' followers who move around."

"Yes sir."

"But—"

Lionel interrupted. "Tribune, I need a word."

"Of course, Prefect. Thank you, Rebseman."

"Sir." Rebseman slunk out.

Lionel walked to the bar and tilted the wine bottle to read the label. "I can't read this. It's in Français. How do you know what we're drinking?"

"I had a private tutor, taught me when I was younger."

"Sexy woman with blue-green eyes and an intriguing accent?"

"Big hulking brute, ex-Marine. Hated every day of teaching a useless rich kid and let me know it."

"Bad teacher?"

"Best I've ever had. Outstanding. Nothing motivates you like a daily dose of contempt personally aimed at you by an expert."

"Odd way of teaching your children." Lionel

poured the wine and sipped. "Tastes good. Did your parents hate you that much? I mean, I can see why they would, from personal experience, but I'm curious."

"They wanted me to learn how to get along with people who despised me and didn't want to be in my presence. And prove to me that even if you hate somebody or something, you should always do your best." Devin held out his wine glass for a refill. "Well, now we know why engineering is doing so well. They've had a to-do list for the last ten years. But couldn't get permission."

"No wonder they're so happy. Everything they've wanted to fix or change or upgrade is available for all the people who want to fix things."

"Except it's extra work. But the rest of them, that's why all the more senior crew…"

"Let's call them what they are, old. He was at least ten years in his rank."

"He's never going to get promoted again. He was going to stay there until he retired."

"More likely died."

Lionel spun his wine glass. "All right, so we've got a ship full of people who don't want to be here."

"No, no, they want to be here on the ship. They don't want to do anything new."

"How are we, how am I, going to convert them into a fighting crew?"

"We could appeal to their patriotism."

"They don't have any patriotism. All they have is a great desire to have their teeth fixed. Most of them only have so many teeth, and they've gotten them fixed already. We don't have much to offer them."

"We need to offer them something." Devin held his own glass up. "Because if we don't, surely our enemies will."

Imperial Legionary

Chapter 18

"Keep everything quiet. I don't want them to detect us." Monti coughed and pulled her uniform collar tighter.

"It's been nearly an hour. We haven't seen them." Hooper wiped condensation from her display screen. "We're dying here."

"They haven't come out of jump yet."

"We must have gotten away." Hooper coughed and wiped her board clear of water again. "The system's empty. Not even any traffic from the inner planets. Please, please turn the environment controls back on."

"Not yet." Monti leaned back in the captain's chair and wiped the sweat from her face, then shivered. *Except it's not sweat, it's condensation. Temperature must have dropped ten degrees during the last shift. Even if I don't run the dehumidifiers, I'll have to turn something on to keep us from freezing.* "We can't take the chance. We saw them slowing before they came into jump."

"Which means they didn't jump. We beat them in. They've given up the hunt."

"They were only fifty minutes behind us in the last system. They would have improved on it in this one."

"They weren't more than a half an hour from the jump point by the time we got through. If they are following, they'd be here by now."

"Maybe they had a problem with their computers."

"Our computers are going to rust, or possibly liquefy if we don't fix the humidity."

"We're going to keep going until we get to the far side."

Two Imperial frigates had chased the *Collingwood*

across three systems. Outnumbered and outgunned, Monti had chosen the better part of valor and run like hell. She'd short jumped without even getting complete navigation fixes to save time. They hadn't seen the tanker again. One of the frigates had dropped off, but the other had continued its pursuit, drawing closer each jump. There had not been time to stop to gas up.

"Look, we can, we can—" Hooper coughed. "Damn it. We've got mold growing everywhere on this ship. Now it's growing in my lungs. I feel like a beach house when you open it up in the spring."

"Better to have mold growing everywhere than space growing everywhere, as in no oxygen growing anywhere."

"This killer space mold, it'll survive when we blow all the systems."

"It'll still be alive, but so will we," Monti said. "Keep the engines burning, and us heading for the jump point."

"Once we get past these asteroids and we're on a straight path for the next system."

"Good."

"Did you ever think that maybe letting them chase us right into the next system is exactly what we shouldn't be doing?" Hooper asked. "I mean, we're leading them into what's potentially an undefended tanker. They don't even have to go there. They can extrapolate we have forces there by our course."

"No we're not, because we had to jig that first time." Monti frowned. The *Collingwood* had made a double detour to avoid coming too close to the pursuing frigates. "By the time we get back, there'll be at least three other ships there. The tanker, and two other corvettes on scouting missions will be back. That's three ships. A single frigate won't take on three warships. Four with us." *I hope. If they stayed. If the tanker didn't send them back. If it hasn't chosen our alternative jump point rendezvous…*

"If the tanker is close to where we emerge, they could take the tanker."

"Yes, but they won't know it's a tanker and the others will be warships. They'll be in as much trouble as we are now. They won't be able to fight—they'll be out of fuel too, if my numbers are correct."

"We're betting our lives on that, so hopefully, your numbers are correct. At least turn the dehumidifier on low. Not for me. One of the emergency heating systems is already non-operational. Shorted out."

"No, we'll keep burning. I can't chance running out of fuel." Monti had disabled all the non-critical systems. They needed the fuel to be able to outrun the pursuing frigates. Last jump, she disabled some of the critical systems, or had them on half or quarter power. Now she had everything except maneuvering and jump shut off. The air conditioning was down, and she had also disabled the heating systems. The crew had snuggled together, six or eight to a stateroom to stay warm. The humidity had climbed so much that the whole ship felt like Bondi beach during typhoon season. And without the heat produced by the electronics, the lights, and the people, they were freezing.

Hooper stood and swung her arms. Her teeth were chattering. "If it was up to me, I'd have you turn the heat on."

"It's not up to you, it's up to me." *Why do I have to make these decisions? All I wanted was an easy career shuttling passengers around.* "And I say no heat." *But then why did I join that stupid volunteer reserve? I knew this could happen. I just hoped it wouldn't.*

"But the electronics are going to have

permanent damage if we keep them running in this steam bath. And we need functioning navigation computers to jump." She slapped her arms on her shoulders. "You know, it's not the cold, it's the humidity."

"I thought it was, it's not the heat, it's the humidity. Isn't that the saying?"

"That's not the saying by anybody who's been jammed into a spaceship with their atmospherics only running at ten percent. Franky, make a little detour, swing past that gas giant over there, and start to suck up some fuel. We'll get enough to run the systems for a little while."

"No, we need to—"

BONG. The main board lit up. Silaski, who'd been snoozing with her head lolling back, jumped up and banged her skull against the side of the display. She cursed a blue streak, then bent to sort through the sensor readings.

She'd been a big surprise. From a constantly whining, complaining, incompetent twit, she'd turned into a constantly whining, complaining, mildly competent twit. She could work the scanners now with only the occasional question.

"Status change," Silaski said. "Jump signature. Scanner's locked on. Details shortly."

"Put a telescope on it."

"I know, Captain. I've already got it slaved to the sensors."

"Very well." Monti sat back in her chair and waited.

Hooper whispered, "When did she learn how to slave the telescope to the sensors? Who taught her? I didn't."

"Everybody knows how to do that,", Monti whispered back.

"Yeah? How do you do it?" Hooper asked. "On this corvette, I mean. Not on a freighter."

"It's not the sort of thing that a captain needs to know."

"Sounds like exactly the sort of thing that a captain needs to know."

"It isn't, but that's not the part that should surprise you, that I don't know it."

"What then?"

"What surprised me is that neither of us taught her how to do it. Somebody else must have."

"Somebody else on this ship likes her enough to help her out?"

"Nobody's more surprised than me."

Silaski interrupted, "Beacon. Identity. Imperial frigate. ISS *Faulknor*."

"Confirm your scan, Silaski."

"Ma'am, they've turned on their beacon."

"You believe their beacon?"

"Not the first time in the first system, and not really the second time, but yeah, now it's the third and fourth time. Ma'am, unless somebody has hijacked an identical-looking frigate with a different name, somehow swapped beacons, and thrown in behind this, then yeah, I believe the beacon. It looks exactly like the same ship that's been chasing us."

"Very well. What's their course?" Monti leaned back and waited. She was expecting Silaski to say that their frigates course was either paralleling or converging to theirs, as it had been for the entire chase. *I have enough fuel for one more jump. Provided that I don't have to evade. If I burn fuel evading, we'll freeze in jump space. I'll have to surrender. I've run as far as I can.* Monti took a deep breath and leaned forward. "Bron, prepare a message for that frigate."

Hooper shook her head. She knew what was coming, as they'd talked about it before. At a certain point, surrender was the only option. "Don't do it, Franky. Keep running. Never mind the humidity."

"No sense killing everybody. Silaski, you asleep?"

"No ma'am, I'm having problems with the course."

"Silaski, you should recognize a converging course by now."

"Yes ma'am, except it's not converging."

Hooper and Monti exchanged glances. "Not converging?" Monti asked.

"No ma'am, it's definitely not. In fact, distance is opening and so is the angle."

"Where in Hades are they going?"

"Inner system ma'ams. Looks like they're targeted for fourth planet in the system."

"Gas giant, by any chance, Silaski?"

"I need to look it up in the sailing directions."

"Good to know there's still something she doesn't know how to do," Hooper muttered.

"Shut up. Shut up, Bron."

"You're not supposed to call me that on duty, Franky." Hooper tried to look stern, but failed. She grinned.

Monti grinned back. "I don't care. We might get out of this."

Monti ran the numbers herself. She didn't exactly not trust Silaski, but she just... Yeah, she didn't trust Silaski. Hooper did the same thing. The two officers and the helmsman slash sensor operator were now running the same checks. The bridge was dead silent for three minutes.

Silaski finished checking her numbers. "Ma'am, I ran the numbers again with the current data. It does look like they're aimed for the inner planets."

"They're out of gas," Hooper said. "Just like us. They're out of gas. They're turning around. They need to go gas up, and they're going to let us get away."

"If we can get away," Monti reached for the captain's control and hit emergency stop on the main engines.

The thrust came off, and she dealt with the frantic intercom call from engineering. The crew knew they were being chased by a potentially deadly adversary. And that, if caught, they were all for the high jump for being part of the rebellion. "Engineering wanted to know if that was a misorder or if they should bring the drive back online."

"No, no, we'll coast for now. Save the fuel."

They all sat silently for the next hour. After three separate recalculations by all three bridge crew, plus a guest appearance by an engineering rating who could navigate, they all agreed that the pursuing frigate, the *Faulknor*, had sheered off.

"They'd obviously sped up last system, hoping to catch us right at the jump limit and overwhelm us," Hooper said.

"Is there any way they can catch us now with the current parameters?"

"Skipper." Hooper brought up her screen. "Even if they pivot and rocket out again, we'd still make it clear of the asteroid debris. On the far side, we could jump again well before they can catch us."

"Why are they letting us get away?"

"They're not. Or they think they aren't. They don't know how much fuel we have. We might be faking it. They think they can refuel and then chase us across this system, and we can't jump out."

"Well, we can't go down to the planet and get more while they're there."

"Yup." Hooper ran another calculation. "They can scoot around that planet for three or four days or three or four weeks, so they're all topped up and can come out and chase us down anytime."

"We have two choices," Monti said. "Roll the dice and hope we have enough fuel to make the next jump at the limit. Because the velocity we're going to need to carry through is going to be considerable to get out of the planetary gravitational area of control. We won't have enough for a second try."

"Or," Hooper said, "we can coast and orbit the system and wait for those"—she used a word meaning sons of a sexually deranged kangaroo offspring—"to fuel up and head back where they came from."

"What makes you think after they've fueled up they're going to head back where they came from? After fueling up, by definition, they'll have lots of fuel. They'll be able to start scooting out and chasing us. And we won't have enough fuel to outrun them forever."

"Which means if we stay, they're bound to catch us eventually."

"Depends on how bad they want to catch us. They might have changed their minds."

"How many systems have they chased us through so far? You want to bet our future on them changing now?"

"Nope."

"Didn't think so." Monti hit the intercom. "Ship, this is the captain speaking. The Imperial frigate chasing us has broken off and is retiring to the inner system to refuel. We're continuing to the jump point. We will jump and meet other elements of the fleet. All hands, be aware that we are at a critical fuel level and it will be necessary to continue the fuel and environmental restrictions that we have implemented. That is all." Monti turned off the intercom. She was almost certain she could hear the screeches coming through the ship.

"Franky," Hooper said quietly, "when we get to

the jump point, let's say we make the jump."

"Yeah?"

"Are we gonna be alive when we come out, or will we be frozen?"

"Not according to the numbers I ran. I've made some assumptions. If nothing goes wrong, then we should come out the other side tickety-boo with enough fuel to send out a distress call. Hopefully, we'll be close enough to the tanker or one of the frigates so they can come over and render assistance."

"Provided, of course, nothing breaks along the way and that we don't have any issues with any of the remaining fuel, the whole systems not being calibrated properly in months?"

"As long as nothing goes wrong, we'll be fine."

"If it does?"

"Anything bad happens, anything at all, we're dead women. Either frozen, starved, burned or asphyxiated."

"That's why you're the captain. I knew you'd cheer me up."

"How long 'til our new jump points?"

Silaski answered instantly. "Two hours, thirteen minutes, seven seconds."

"Silaski, that's highly specific."

"You're saying that's unusual in me, Franky? Being precise?"

Hooper smirked.

Monti's eyes widened. "Yes. And so is using my first name. It's disrespectful. Don't do that."

"Make me."

Hooper smirked some more.

"Listen, spaceman." Monti glared. "You keep talking like that, you know what's going to happen?"

"Well, Franky," Silaski looked up. "One of two things is going to happen here. We're going to make it, in which case you won't care what I said to you. Or we're not going to make it, in which case I won't care what I said. So let's see how this plays out, shall we?"

Chapter 19

"Scruggs," Dena said, "maybe we can slow down."

"No, we need the velocity. Besides, they'll see the lights." The truck careened across the darkened field, all lights out. Scruggs swept the wheel from side to side as black shadows—trees and bushes—appeared from the gloom.

"Velocity? You mean speed?"

"Well, velocity has a direction, speed is just—"

Dena yelped and ducked as a tree branch scraped the side window. "Jove's ears, Baby Marine. We're not at school. Stop accelerating. Then we'll slow enough to—"

"CONTACT REAR!" Gavin yelled. "They've got—" A yellow line of fire streaked by and exploded two hundred meters ahead. "They've got a rocket."

"New plan!" Dena yelled. "Faster, Faster."

"Make up your mind." Scruggs spun the truck left, aiming for the slot leading to the landing pad. A mist of sand from the explosion patterned onto the windshield. "Gavin, what are they firing?"

"A rocket-propelled grenade."

Centurion said they're not accurate over one hundred meters. Easier to believe that when we're not being fired at. "How close are they?"

"Back on the road. They're firing from there."

The defenders had finally figured out that they were going a different direction. Another rocket slid by, detonating ahead.

"Scruggs, they've got the range. Get us out of here. They'll get lucky."

"Understood." Scruggs spun left and aimed for the bright spot in the landing berm. "We'll cut through the pad and hit the missile. Dena, where's the ship?"

"Get ready to yank the fire suppression system," Dirk said. "We're going to blow the rear hatch."

"So when we go boom, the hatch will be okay? Good for the hatch." Ana slipped through screens. "Need to put in a code. Is it worth it?"

"Are you going to do what I say?"

"Of course. You're the expert, this is what you do. The pilot. Up here, I do what you want." Ana tapped in his code. His screen glowed red with warning, and a single 'execute' pulsed in the middle.

Dirk tilted the ship more. The burning light of the oncoming missile flared on the camera. "You're pretty calm for a guy who might die in the next fifteen seconds."

"I died a long time ago. This is inertia." Ana's finger hovered over the screen. "Ready to pop the hatch. And for a guy who might die in the next ten seconds, you're pretty calm as well."

"This is what I do, like you said. Isn't that what life's about? Doing your job?"

"Odd time for me to be agreeing with you." Ana centered the camera on the oncoming missile. "Say when."

Dirk counted, "Three, two, one. When."

Ana slapped his screen. In the engine room, a solenoid in the manual locking system reversed polarity. Four spring-loaded bolts that extended from the hatch retracted as their magnetic field reversed. Dirk fired the Z thrusters, and the ship pitched hard onto its nose as the tons of water slammed forward, kicking the nose down. The ground swelled in the camera.

Is this idiot going to power us into the ground? Stupid way to die. Ana held on to his straps. *Stupid or not, it was out of his control. At least we'll duck below that missile.*

Dirk cut the stern lifters, but left the bow firing. Now the stern dropped and the *Heart's Desire* spiraled right. Dirk waited long enough for the stern to drop below the bow, then he feathered the main drive.

Heart's Desire climbed. On the camera screen, the missile corrected and aimed at their drive plume.

"Navy, you're climbing into the blast radius—"

Dirk slammed the main drive on full. The ship bumped, shook itself like a dog, then leaped upward.

"And now you're in it—"

BOOM. The ship jerked, then settled. Dirk cut the engines and the thrusters, and let the ship coast.

Ana checked the radar warning screen. Nothing. The front camera showed only sky, the rear, trees. "What did you do? How are we alive?"

"Popped the hatch. Rocked the water forward, then back. Water flushed below us. Fired the main drive, vaporized the water. Very hot. Infrared targeted that. Blew up the water."

"Well." Ana nodded. "Outstanding, Navy. Outstanding."

"Problem solved." Dirk feathered the controls, and the ship settled back to the horizontal, and turned back to the spaceport.

"You know, Navy, we only thought that was water. It could have been hydrogen, or oxygen leaking out there."

"Could have been."

"Which means when you fired the drive, we could have blown up in ball of expanding gasses."

"Could have. Didn't."

"What if we did?"

Dirk shrugged. "From our point of view, also problem solved."

A bright light flashed behind the truck. "Crap," Gavin said. "Big explosion."

Scruggs aimed at the break in the landing berm. "Did the ship blow up?"

"Something did."

"Problem for later." *Focus on the now, girl. Thinking will get you killed.* The truck cleared the berm and passed onto the landing pad. This wasn't a concrete berm like advanced starports, but a six-foot ridge of dirt that kept spaceship main drives from cooking nearby equipment. The access road cut offset from the center. Trucks could drive in, load from a ship, and drive out again without turning. A single tanker truck sat to one side. Lights lit the far exit. Scruggs aimed for the lit slot, and floored the accelerator again.

"Scruggs," Dena said. "What do we do when we get there? We don't have any guns. You can't just crash into the whatever. What are you even going to hit?"

"I'm going to crash into whatever I want. You told me that building wasn't big enough to stop the truck, so it's not going to stop the truck."

"I didn't say that."

"You said that."

"I said I could see it. I didn't say it looked like it was made from metal. I said it looked like, ah, Jove's testicles."

The truck screamed through the slot and into the plaza between the three landing pads. They were coming from the east. Dead ahead sat the radar van, a squat metal eight-wheeled truck. An antenna topped mast extended up thirty meters. Four red metal stabilizing legs extended out three feet on each side.

Scruggs eased right. Crap. Can't knock that over. Not without us crashing.

A radar dish sat on a swivel at the rear of the

truck. It tilted upwards at a thirty-degree angle and skittered from side to side, tracking.

The main one is the search radar. Back one is the targeting radar. And it's tracking the ship. The centurion and the pilot.

The back of the truck had a flatbed which contained one large metal box with grids on the side connected with power cables to the radar. Bundled blue and yellow fiber cables dropped off, wrapped in a circle, and came off the side of the truck. The cables snaked out to their left, running along the ground toward a hut in the middle of the clearing. Simple, metal, no windows, a door. Something to keep equipment out of the weather.

To the left, visible between the truck and the shed, was the missile launching battery. The missiles were housed in a rectangular metal canister with six lids. Two lids—the expended missiles—hung open. The other four were shut.

Scruggs swung the truck to the left and aimed at the hut.

"Concrete," Dena yelled, "concrete, don't." Somebody smarter than the others they'd met had surrounded the hut with four substantial concrete bollards.

Scruggs swung away from the hut and started cursing. Lights flashed around them, and people ran from the hut, or dove out of the truck parked next to the hut.

Gunfire rang out. Good luck hitting us at this speed. I have to stop the missiles. Have to get Rocky to the ship. Can't hit the truck. Can't hit the hut. Help Rocky.

Dena yelled, "Don't hit the building. It'll kill all of us. Don't hit the building."

"I'm going to aim for the launcher," Scruggs said. She swung left to thread the needle between the two.

"There's another berm. They're behind it." Dena gestured. A three-foot-high dirt mound surrounded the missiles themselves. "Scruggs, that'll kill us as well. We've got to save Rocky. We can't save Rocky by killing him. Drive away. Drive away."

"But—"

Dena grabbed Scruggs's arm. "We'll get away. Drive on. We'll figure something out."

Gavin's pointing hand extended between the two arguing women. "Control cables. Hit the fiber links connecting them. Shock will shatter the glass, or pull it out."

In the headlights, a group of red, yellow, and purple cables ran from the hut building to the radar. They stretched along the ground between the hut and the missiles, and climbed onto a sawhorse before they reached the berm.

The sawhorse lifted the cables three feet off the ground. Bumper height.

"Hit the bundle. Hit the cables."

Scruggs swung right. "Got it," she said.

The grill of the truck smashed into the sawhorse. Splintered wood bounced off the hood. The cables caught on the bumper and dragged. Scruggs kept the truck powering forward. Cables stretched, a clinking sound. The truck slowed.

"Don't stop, don't stop," Gavin said. "Keep going. Don't let it stop. We'll pull them out."

CRUNCH. The back wall panel of the shed snapped open as the cables pulled a metal console through.

"Keep going, keep going."

The truck stalled and hung against the cable line. Scruggs depressed the clutch, dropped into first gear, then popped it. The engine whined and the truck shoved and skidded sideways. The left rear wheel spun. The truck tipped to the right as the cables pulled.

ZIIIIT.

Electricity arced behind them, and they were moving again. The cable slithered along the front of the truck, then the front end dropped free.

Gavin looked behind. "Looks like the console's been shredded or beaten to pieces. It's on fire. You've done it. Now where's the ship?"

Smoke billowed behind them. All four remaining lids opened, the remaining missiles burped out of the cannister, then their rocket motors fired.

"I understand your concern," Dirk said. "But it worked the first time, skipping around, letting them impact the mountain, so that sort of thing should work the second time. These missiles aren't sophisticated—you told me that."

"I guessed." Ana checked his screens. "Primitive colony and all that. No radar warnings. I see small arms ahead. Get us down there. Take the pad on the right."

"Understood." Dirk played the thrusters. The main drive was difficult to control in atmosphere, so he feathered it and coasted. "On the ground in sixty seconds."

"Still, we could have had a problem."

"In the Navy, I trained extensively in counter-missile actions. Most non-Imperial Navy missiles aren't that great." Dirk slewed the ship left, then down, gliding in for landing.

"What if they were Imperial Navy missiles?"

"Then we wouldn't be having this conversation. Jove!"

A plume of fire exploded ahead of them, dead between the three landing pads. "Incoming!"

"No radar warning," Ana chanted. "Other

sensors—ow." The forward camera flashed yellow. Something big had blown up there.

"What happened?"

"Fratricide when they launched. They're all—there's one. Incoming. Incoming."

"They're too close. That one's going to hit."

"We're not—"

THUNK.

The *Heart's Desire* shook. The forward screen cleared, and the landing pad appeared in the center. The sensors were silent.

"Radar warning?" Dirk asked.

Ana tapped the screen. "Nope. Let me run the cameras." Ana swapped through the different cameras. "Nothing. We're alone up here."

The radio squawked. Ana hit the button. "*Heart's Desire.*"

Dena answered. "Come get us. Baby Marine blew up everything. Whole place is on fire. Random shooting. She's careening around like a crazy lady, and Rocky's still hurt."

"We're landing in ten seconds. East pad."

"Great—what?" Dena went off line. Five seconds later. "Be advised, Baby Marine's words not mine, be advised there is a tanker truck on the east end of the pad—"

The *Heart's Desire* cleared the berm, then burped up. Something dragged on the rear landing struts, then Dirk centered them again, and they thumped down.

"Outstanding," Ana said. He unbuckled and raced back to the ramp. Dirk had already dropped it. He ran down and dropped the last few feet. The tanker truck on the far end of the pad leaked a brown liquid from the smashed tank, and a fire burned on the hood.

A battered quad cab truck pulled up, trailing random fiber cables from the bumper. His four crew mates leapt out and charged for the ramp.

"Out of the way, have to get Rocky in a pod." Lee ran by.

Gavin followed, then stopped, backed up, and stared up at the drives. "Why is the engineering hatch hanging open?"

"We had to blow it." Ana shrugged. "I'll explain later. Can you fix it?"

"I'll try." Gavin raced away. "Let me know when Rocky's set, and I'll lift."

Ana regarded Scruggs. "Your uniform shirt is offset, Cadet."

Scruggs fingers scrabbled at her shirt. "Sorry, I had to take it off. Cadet?"

"Can't call you Private. You're an officer cadet. So cadet it is."

"Thank you, Centurion."

"What's that hanging from your pocket?"

Scruggs pulled a white fabric out. "Oh, that's my panties. I had to take them off too."

Ana put his hands on his hips. "You took your underwear off as well? In the middle of a firefight?"

"Not in the middle. Before."

"You got naked before a firefight? Why?"

"It wasn't because of the firefight, it was because of the giraffes."

"The what?"

"Giraffes. They're a tall, yellow—"

"I know what a giraffe is. What were you doing?"

"Riding them."

"Riding them?"

"Kind of like a horse…"

Ana shook his head. "Doesn't matter. How did Rocky get hurt?"

"Battling killer carnivorous wild pigs."

"Wild pigs?"

"Killer carnivorous wild pigs, yes."

"Battling killer carnivorous wild pigs. I see. Was this before or after riding the giraffes?"

"Before. But after we got in the firefight in the woods with the Maple Syrup Thugs."

"Maple Syrup Thugs?"

"Yes."

"Yes? Yes what?"

"Yes, Cen—" Scruggs paused. "Yes. Ana. That's what I did."

Ana let a grin play on his face. "Fair enough. They'll have Rocky strapped in by now. Let's get out here."

BOOM. The truck at the other side of the pad exploded. Brown liquid fountained up into the air, and splattered over the whole pad.

Ana ducked, then put his head back up. A light patter of golden brown pieces rained down on them. "This isn't shrapnel. And it's sticky. What in Zeus's name is it?"

Scruggs picked a piece off her arm, sniffed it, then stuck it in her mouth. "Mmmpgh. Good. It's maple candy." She picked a piece off Ana's arm and held it out. "Want some?"

Chapter 20

"It has to go farther, Cadet," Ana said. "Need to get better suction."

"I suppose you expect me to do it?" Scruggs finished unwinding the fueling hose and dropped it into the tranquil mountain lake. Unbroken fields of snow covered the ground and placid peaks throttled the horizon. Cheery green pine trees spotted the gray granite landscape. "Wade out into this freezing lake?" Scruggs shivered and her breath condensed in the cold air. "I guess it can't be much colder than the air."

"Well, you are…"

"Junior? Not anymore, Centurion."

Ana huffed. Clear skies, but not enough oxygen this high. It's not me, It must be this thin air and light gravity. "I was going to say younger. Or more flexible."

"Of course you were." Scruggs stared at the water. "It's beautiful here, so quiet."

"Happy to have a rest?" Ana asked. "Drop your responsibilities for a while?"

Scruggs bit her lip. "You said I did well stopping those missiles, Centurion."

"You did. Achieved the objective. Adapted. Overcame. Improvised. It's just that…"

Scruggs waited. "Not like you to be short of words, Centurion."

"You did your job. But you took the most direct, most violent route to achieving it."

"What's wrong with that?"

"Nothing if it works," Ana said. "But that was a straightforward mission. Sometimes things can be muddy. Sometimes the direct path is not the best."

"All the time you've been training me, you've been encouraging me to act, not think."

"Too much thinking and not enough action is

bad. Too much action and not enough thinking is bad."

"That's not helpful." Scruggs dropped the hose. "How do I figure out which is which? I lose both ways."

"Now you're starting to understand." Ana grinned. "Isn't growing up grand?" He looked at the hose, floating in the water. "We're not going to get enough flow with that hose there."

"Fine." Scruggs kicked off her boots and pulled off her socks.

"Is this getting naked going to become a habit for you?"

"All I'm doing is rolling up my pants. And what if it is?"

"I suppose it's rather healthy." Ana fed the hose out to her as she walked in the water. "I think you could use a little more activity in that area."

"Wow." Dena stepped out from behind the landing strut, dragging a cable behind her. "Did he just say what I thought he said? Is he telling you that you need a boyfriend?"

"More or less," Ana said. "I mean, let's face it. Our little girl is growing up. At some point, someone's going to have to explain the birds and the bees to her. I nominate you for that."

"Speaking of bees, both of you can buzz off." Scruggs threw the hose forward in a splash. "There, it's underwater. Let me stake it down, and you can start sucking the water. Then I'm going for a walk." Scruggs splashed away from the ship. "Ow. Cold. My feet hurt. I'll want a towel later."

Ana folded his hands and watched Scruggs kick the water.

Dena sprayed her cable with insta-glue and stuck it to the strut, but left the end hanging. "Gee, Old Man, she's talking back to you now. Bet you never expected that."

"I planned for it."

"Don't believe you."

"It happens to all of them eventually," Ana said. "It's a natural part of the progression. First, they're dependent and seeking approval. Then they start to get some minor amount of independence and start making their own decisions. She'll be back for advice after the first destructive decision, second-guessing herself."

"You talking about soldiers or kids?"

"Soldiers are my kids."

"You've got her that much figured out?"

"No, not her. Everyone. It's the same for all of us. I've got you all figured out. Her, you. Two different sides of the same coin."

"We're a coin, are we? Different sides? Which side am I?"

"You both ran away from something, but you're much more confident in yourself, have been from the start. You have skills and drive. You didn't run away so much as fight yourself out. It shows in your actions. You'll do well, within your limitations."

"And what are my limitations, annoying old teacher?"

"Poor education, and only average intelligence. Education can be compensated for, and so can the other with hard work."

"That sounds like an insult."

"You already know that it's a handicap, but you compensate using physical attractiveness, brashness, and good hair."

Dena twirled the end of a wire. "I never claimed to be brilliant. I'm not dumb, but there is a reason they didn't send me off planet when I was younger, and it wasn't only that I'd run away."

"Don't think you'd make a good engineer. Or navigator. Or doctor or scientist. Gun salesman, that's where I see you."

"There are non-military jobs in the galaxy, you know."

Ana shrugged. "I never see 'em."

"Now I'm curious. What about Scruggs? What's your plan for her?"

"Smart, dedicated, hardworking. Lacks confidence. That's why she ran away. She wanted to get out from under the shadow of something."

"What shadow?"

"Her family in the Core is rich, or famous, or both. Anything that she got back there, she'd always wonder if was because of her own skills or because of who she was related to. Out here, away from everything, she sinks or swims on her own. Her confidence has already improved, and the longer she stays out here, and the more difficult the jobs she takes on, the better she'll grow. Same thing the pilot did."

"Dirk lacked confidence?"

"Why do you think he became a Navy pilot and seconded to the Scouts, rather than going into the Senate or working in the capital? Out here, he's his own man."

"Listen to you. Almost sounds like you like him."

Ana laughed. "Not at all. I understand him. I understand you. I even understand Scruggs. We all pass through the same peaks and valleys in our life, and I get that. But I still hate all of you."

"Wow, you're not just a cranky old man. You're a cranky old philosopher."

"Most philosophers were cranky old men," Ana said. "But even if I'm a cranky old man, I'm not looking forward to the day that Scruggs comes back and says that she messed up."

"Why? Because you don't think you'll be able to handle her self-doubt?"

"No, because it only comes after some huge screw-up, which means a whole bunch of people will be killed. Her friends, her squad, her troops, maybe me."

"And you'd be sad to be killed?"

"Some days, not others."

"Maybe she'll get Dirk killed instead."

"I wouldn't be that lucky, but I suppose there's always hope. What are you doing out here? Aren't you supposed to be fixing the sensor lines?"

"If by fixing you mean running the wires that Gavin gave me in the places that Gavin told me and laying them there so he can connect them to the things he told me he'd connect them to, then yes, more or less. I can staple them to the hull, but I don't know how to run the testing system software yet. He said he'd show me."

"You'll figure it out. You're not nearly as stupid as you first pretended."

"Thanks. You're being pleasant for a change today."

"I mean, you're still as dumb as a rifle stock, and as much use as a drunken first-year recruit riding a demented ostrich, but even drunken ostriches have their uses."

"And there's the old man back again. You couldn't even stay pleasant for five minutes?"

Ana shook his head. "Don't see the reason to."

CLANG. A bent circle of metal dropped onto the rock behind the ship. Gavin slid down the ladder from the rear hatch and kicked it. "Huh, you and the skipper did a number on that hatch. "

"Either a broken hatch or a broken ship." Ana shrugged. "Broken hatch is less trouble. Oh-ho! Look at who's returning to duty! Everybody, heads up."

At the top of the ramp, a furry black form appeared.

"Rocky," Scruggs said. She waded back in, splashing water, and ran up to the hatch. "You're okay."

Lee appeared above him. "Careful, Scruggs. He's not okay. He's still in bad shape, but at least I was able to bring the fever down."

"Is he still sick?"

"A little, but I got the drug dosage right. Eight hours in the pod and he's almost good as new."

"That's great. He's walking."

Rocky limped down the ramp. His hind leg was immobilized by a cast, and he more rocked than walked, but he made progress.

"He's got to keep the cast on, but he's able to move and it's best that he moves as much as he can because that'll keep the muscles around the legs from atrophying."

Rocky settled down to the bottom. Scruggs dropped to her knees and gave him a hug. He licked her face. Dena came over and cooed over him as well and leaned down and ruffled his fur. Even Ana wandered over and gave him a friendly pat. Rocky wagged his tail. The pack was all here. His stomach felt strange, and something was wrong with his leg. But it didn't hurt, and there were smells to be discovered. He hobbled off the ramp and then went to the landing strut. It was difficult cocking a leg, but he managed to sort of lean into it and lift his hip and pee.

"He always favors the starboard one," Ana said. "Wonder why."

Lee walked down and stood next to them. "Do you need a hand with the fueling?"

"No, Scruggs has it under control. Dena's got the line stapled to the hull. Gavin has to connect them once he's finished hammering the hatch back into shape. Don't see how it's going to be airtight if he has to hammer it."

"He took the seals off first." Lee said. "He needs the metal underneath them flatter, and then he'll be able to get new seals back on it."

"Are we going to fill the engine room with water again?"

"Nope. That was a crack on a pipe we hit last time. He's gone through and strapped that."

"I've added a new item to our checklist," Dena said. "Now when we land, we have to go through and check all the pipes." Dena was now their official checklist person. She'd been studying up on ship operations and was able to stand a watch, read a control board, and do surveys after landing and takeoff. She couldn't fix anything yet, but that would be for the future. For now, she could identify a problem and find the right person to take care of it.

"Well, the gang's all here. What do we do now?"

"Well, two shifts to suck up some water," Ana said. "Get some sleep. All of you are a little banged up."

"Centurion," Scruggs said, "you're in the best shape of all of us. You can take the first watch up on the roof, on the dorsal side, with your rifle."

"You think someone's going to find us out here in the woods, Cadet?"

"No, but it's best to be safe. We all need a break. I could use some sleep."

"Well, we'll hang out here until the ship gets fixed up, until Rocky gets fixed up, and then we'll head off to see the Tribune."

"Who says we'll be seeing the Tribune?" Dirk wandered down the steps, yawning. "Time for my nap. I've got a complete list of other military units to meet up with, and orders to give. Now, as we're fueling, I shut down the board. And I've turned off all the electronics except for the pump. So even if they come looking for us, they won't find us."

"I don't think they're going to come looking for us," Scruggs said. "All their missiles are blown up."

"Yes, about that," Dirk said. "Why did you launch them all at me at the last minute?"

"We didn't," Scruggs said. She explained what happened when they had crashed the truck through and hit the control lines and then banged off the berm.

"Good work," Ana said. "As soon as you cut the control lines, they went in an auto-destruct sequence. That's why they fired off. The idea is to pop them up into the air, fire the rockets for a few seconds, and then let them explode."

"Why didn't they blow up the *Heart's Desire*?"

"Hadn't armed yet," Ana said. "Good call on the pilot's part."

"Wow. That's a first," Dirk said. "Am I asleep already? Is this a dream?"

Ana ignored him. "When they came up, they were only in the air for three or four seconds. They needed a twenty-second vertical climb before they'd blow up."

"Which leads to another question," Dirk said. "Why is there a bunch of missiles here protecting the starport?"

"Clearly, they were protecting the maple syrup," Lee said.

"But that leads to another question. Why was there a maple syrup gang here?"

"Maple syrup is expensive." Gavin returned from behind the hull. "People want maple syrup. It's worth money. So the criminals come down here, they harvest the maple syrup, they take off."

"Yes, that's fine, they harvest the maple syrup, but that means they'd have held the starport hostage—at least part of the population hostage or have part of the population in on it."

"So part of the population was in on it." Gavin

shrugged. "So what?"

"We're not out in the Verge anymore where they don't see a warship for years and years and years. We're almost in the Core. Or at least in the Sarawak sector. In fact, I'm sure that we're on a direct route for the fleet units heading to the other sectors, so there should be ships through here on a regular basis. That's why the Tribune sent us here, to check out if he could infiltrate a real fleet in this direction. Those ships would have noticed something, or somebody could have commed them and let them know, or a freighter would have figured it out."

"Well, maybe there haven't been ships here for a few months or a year or some time." Gavin shrugged again. "Lee?"

"I don't know either, but the fact that the closer we get to the Core, the more I expected the Imperial presence to increase, but instead, we're seeing more and more bandit activity."

"Bandit activity? You mean private military activity," Ana said. "Non-Imperial troops."

"You know what I mean," Lee said. "This is unusual. This is something we have to tell the Tribune."

"Well, we don't have to tell the Tribune yet," Dirk said. "But we've got good recordings, we know where we're at, and there's nothing here now that will stop even a corvette. He can send his tankers and refueling ships through here, along with his regular units, without any trouble. There's not gonna be any word getting back to the Core. It's perfectly safe for a rebellious fleet to fly through here."

"Yeah, that's true," Lee said. "That's what bothers me. It's perfectly safe for a rebellious fleet to come through here. Which the Navy should be stopping. Where're the units that are supposed to be stopping that?"

Chapter 21

The gunnery chief saluted. "Lens functioning correctly sir."

Lionel returned the salute. *Never been saluted in a turret before. Not without banging an elbow.* His walk from the bridge to starboard-3forward had been a trot, and he needed a second to catch his breath. *My God, these battleships are big. And to the size of the crew. So many unfamiliar faces. Can I trust them?* "Very well, carry on, Chief Petty Officer…" Scuffs on her hard suit concealed the name tape.

"Agra sir."

Lionel fixed her name in his head. "Take aim, Agra, and prepare to discharge the capacitors."

"Sir." The chief turned to the rating at the console. "Take aim."

The targeting rating gulped. "I don't have a target designation, Chief."

The chief turned to Lionel. "Do you have a target sir?"

Lionel couldn't believe it. They hadn't even downloaded the exercise parameters to the turret. "Target any asteroid in view," Lionel ordered.

"Yes sir." The rating typed a sequence through his targeting console.

Lionel waited. *I don't have time for this, I need to be on the bridge dealing with the whole ship, not a single battery. But I don't have enough experienced officers. And the Tribune's busy organizing our scout ships and plotting the route to New Malaya. At least, I think that's what he's doing. He does seem to spend a lot of time with those female officers from Collingwood, and they sure get good dinners.*

Lionel had seen the quality of the wine Devin served the *Collingwood* command team. High quality stuff. And he spent a lot of time talking strategy with them. *Devin always had an eye for the ladies, worse since his wife died. But subordinates? I thought he got that out of the way with that internal security woman...*

Nothing happened for twenty seconds. "Spaceman, what are you doing?"

"Searching for a secondary target sir."

"Searching? You mean, you don't already have one?"

"Well, sir, the sensors take some time to respond, well—

I had no idea how good I had it on Pollux. Lionel closed his eyes. *I'm not sure I can do this. This crew isn't reacting properly. Maybe I'll never have them battle ready.* "Surely you were cross-linked to the sensors at the start."

"We don't normally cross-link to the sensors sir."

"Why not?"

The rating looked at his chief. The chief stood at parade rest, her eyes not meeting Lionel's. "It's not part of the procedure sir. We don't upload the sensor's information to the local targeting computer."

Lionel crossed his arms. "You're telling me that even though the sensor information is freely available from the main computer, and it even breaks it down by quadrant, that you don't bother loading that up and scanning it and at least identifying tentative targets?"

"It's not part of the procedure sir."

Lionel glared at Lieutenant Slusky, behind him. Slusky shrugged. " The chief is... correct sir."

Lionel's lips tightened. *I should have court-martialed him just for that shrug, but I can't go firing every officer who's lazy.* "We did it all the time on the *Pollux*. In fact, every individual gun downloaded their targeting information constantly."

"Yes sir." Unspoken was, you're not on the

Pollux, big boy. You're in the real Navy now.

"I see," Lionel said. "We'll be making it part of procedure from now on. Understood? Now, spaceman. Tell me when you have a target."

"Sir, we've located an asteroid."

"Target and fire." Lionel put a hand out so that he was grounded to the wall and made sure that his boots were magnetized. Lasers didn't generate recoil, but sometimes things happened. Bad things. Arcing or sparking could electrify a whole compartment. And being sturdily anchored so that if you had to jump or duck made a big difference.

The gun crew was not anchored. They were mostly just relaxing in their restraints. One of them didn't appear to have his buckle set.

"Chief, you need to check everyone's restraints and make sure they're buckled in."

The chief's eyes tracked to the weapons-grade second in the corner and frowned. She hurriedly cinched up her buckle. "I'll speak to her later sir."

Lionel's lips tightened further. *That wasn't what I meant either. But I'll take what I can get.* Thrumming noise filled the compartment. Lionel felt the magnetics releasing into the laser and the laser spitting a charge. Whatever it was—ozone, changes in electrical fields, or some sort of short-lived magnetic sense that people responded to—anyone who stood next to a major laser weapon swore they felt when it fired.

"Wow," the spaceman second-class said. "What was that?"

"That's what victory feels like, son," Lionel said. "That's the sound of freedom."

"Yes sir."

Lionel turned back to the chief. "Chief, this weapon appears to be functional."

"Yes sir. Thank you sir."

"In fact, it seems not only functional but in

good working order." Lionel took a breath. "So explain to me why the threat board on the bridge continues to report that this mounting and the one adjacent to it are offline?"

"I don't know sir. As you can see here, we're online."

Lionel looked over his shoulder. "Any thoughts, Slusky?"

"No sir. I haven't been notified by the battery commander concerning any issues."

"Who's the battery commander?"

"We don't have one assigned sir."

"You don't have a battery commander?"

"No sir."

"If you don't have one, how are they going to notify you of issues?"

Slusky gave his maddening shrug. "Protocol dictates that we only respond to issues provided by the battery commander."

"Even if there isn't one?"

"I don't believe that is in the operating instructions sir."

"And if the battery commander is killed in combat, what do you do then? Just sit there? In the middle of a battle while your buddies are dying?"

Lieutenant Slusky's neck reddened. "I would imagine. I don't..."

"Have you ever been in combat, Lieutenant?"

"Not as to say, per se, sir. Not, you know, for any extended length."

"I'm going to take that as a no," Lionel said. He turned to the assembled crew. "Raise your hand if you've never been in combat." Of the four-man gun crew, three of them raised their hands. Of the three who raised their hands, two had forgotten to anchor themselves, and the jerking motion caused them to drift away from the bulkheads.

Jove bless us, how much zero-G time have they

had? Every first-year spaceman knows to anchor after their first cruise. The chief hadn't raised her hand, but looked doubtful. "You've been in combat, Chief?"

"Yes sir. I have the C-Star Campaign Medal."

"C-Star Campaign." Lionel raised his eyebrows. "Wasn't that a pirate incursion?"

"Yes sir."

"That was overrun when a fleet unit on a scheduled maneuver, accidentally entered the system they were in and blasted one of them?"

"Yes sir. Extremely successful operation."

"Didn't three of the pirates get away?"

"Well, yes sir, but we managed to destroy one and chase off the others."

"This was an entire battle squadron with escorts? You only caught one pirate?"

"Well sir, we were surprised when we arrived in-system."

Lionel opened his mouth to ask why they were surprised, then realized he didn't want to know. "If I understand things correctly here, there is nothing wrong with these two batteries. They should have come up on the weapons board in green, but there is a missing level of supervision."

"Yes sir, that's correct," Lieutenant Slusky said.

"I see. Well, I have two ways to go about fixing this, Lieutenant," Lionel said. "One is to appoint a new battery leader over these two batteries."

"That would be wonderful sir."

"That strikes me as inefficient. We don't need someone whose job it is to watch two batteries and report when they're online, especially given that you can see that on your board."

"Yes sir. But that's procedure sir."

"This—" Lionel made a rude hand gesture— "To procedure. Number two option would be to indicate that you're gonna fill in for the battery commander for the remainder of this cruise. Not only for this battery commander but any of your battery commanders who are not present either through sickness, battle injuries, or magic tricks. You are responsible for all of these turrets, and for reporting timely and accurate information to the bridge. Do you understand me, Lieutenant?"

"Yes sir, that would decrease my efficiency if I was forced to take over the duty of the eight battery commanders underneath me."

"Sixteen lasers." Lionel counted on his fingers. "Eight battery commanders, one for every two lasers, with a lieutenant above them. Whose only job is to report the status to the computer?"

"Yes sir."

"I see. Well, my other option is to demote you and put you in charge of this battery. How would that be, Lieutenant?"

"That would be fine sir."

Lionel started. Fine? Fine? I offered to demote this man, and ruin his career, and he thinks it's fine? "You're fine with this? I should do that?"

"Yes sir. It would certainly simplify my life."

Lionel rubbed his eyes. *That's the worst attitude I've ever seen. How am I going to fix this?* "And that's what you strive for in the Navy? Simplification?"

"Sure sir." Lieutenant Slusky shook his head. "I mean, isn't that how we all join the Navy? To make things simple?"

Lionel looked for a wall to bang his head on. This was going to be a long exercise.

Chapter 22

"I think," Scruggs said, "that it's a pirate."

"I think," Dena said, "that it's a privateer."

"I think," Ana said, "that the two of you don't know the difference between the two."

The three were sitting in the lounge, looking at the sensor readings of the ships docked at the orbital station in orbit of Chyura-1c.

Tribune Devin had arranged for troop carrying ships to arrive at the edge of the Sarawak sector and await further instructions. He'd sent *Heart's Desire* to help provide routing information. Ana decided that Scruggs and Dena should handle the initial location and contacts, to 'further their military education.' And to get used to dynamic, non-violent situations.

"Check this out." Scruggs dragged the display pointer to the left, then tapped the ship icon. She navigated two menus deep to bring up the ship specifications. "That's a freighter. It's bigger than us but doesn't seem to have as many containers. According to its length, it should ship an extra fifty containers. But instead," Scruggs brought up the manifest of the other ship. She grimaced. It took three taps before she got the display to stick, "it's showing higher acceleration but lower cargo. Gotta be a pirate."

"There's no way," Dena said, "they'd allow pirates to operate this far inside the Empire. It's got to be a privateer."

"You used to live in a tree on a mud planet," Scruggs said. "What do you know about privateers?"

"I know more about privateers than some spoiled Core-bred girl with an addiction to cut-rate Basic."

"That's what I love to see in the crew," Ana

said. "Mutual disrespect. Makes the whole divide and conquer thing easier. But to answer your question, mud-girl—"

"Next time we're on planet, I'll bury you in a mudslide, and only way you'll get out is if Rocky pees it clear."

Ana ignored Dena. "There's no way they'd let privateers hop this far in. I'll tell you what it is—it's a high-speed mercenary transport."

"What's a high-speed mercenary transport?" Dena asked.

"Yes, Centurion, what's that?" Scruggs chimed in.

"It's for transporting mercenaries at high speed," Ana said. *And if two newbie sensor girls can figure out it's not what it seems, then so can any Imperial spies watching. So much for the Tribune's 'secret' troops.*

"Thanks, Old Man," Dena replied. "Informative as always. Glad you're here to explain things."

Dirk's voice crackled on the intercom. "Centurion, I direct your attention to the supposed freighter docked in Berth 7A ahead."

Ana grinned and thumbed the intercom. "Gosh, Navy. You want to talk about a ship? A groundpounder like me can't tell one ship from another. Is the paint a nice color?"

"It looks like an auxiliary transport. A high-speed attack transport."

"For the sake of the young ladies down here still learning—what are such things?"

"It's a cargo ship with extra engines and more life support. It's designed to be a regular ship that can be requisitioned by the local governor if he needs to move troops in a hurry."

"I thought the Empire had dedicated troop transports," Scruggs said. She cursed as her display fritzed again.

"They do," Dirk replied. "Come to think of it, Miss Sandra Caroline Ruger-Gascoigne, your family probably builds a lot of them. They are extremely fast, strongly protected, equipped with excellent computers and defensive weapons, a reasonable amount of offensive weapons, and practically no cargo space. They're constantly in use transporting Imperial assets—Marines or Imperial Army troops—from station to station, or from Core world to Core world, or from a Core world to a sector capital. They move with a task force."

"But that looks like a freighter." Scruggs had refocused her display. "Not a dedicated transport."

"Dedicated transports cost Jove's own jewels to build. Freighters are cheap, the Navy pays for a few modifications so they can be used to move troops in an emergency, and they don't have to cover maintenance. Bring it up on your screen."

Dena worked her board. It took two tries to get it right. "Got it."

"That," Dirk continued, "is an armed auxiliary transport. Check out the oversized main drive. And the paired thrusters. You can see where the hull is reinforced—It probably ships a gun or two, maybe a laser, to keep the real pirates away. It can ferry a platoon or three of Imperial auxiliaries from planet to planet."

"So what's it doing here?"

"Ferrying Imperial auxiliaries from planet to planet."

Dena shook her head. "You had to say it that way, didn't you? You and the old man both think you're funny."

"We've got a good scan of the station," Lee's voice came from the control room. "Nothing threatening. Lots of traffic. We can't afford to get closer to the inner planets. Their scanners will be better."

The plot they had been monitoring showed no fewer than thirty-seven merchant ships moving in-system. Two habitable planets coreward, each with populations in the tens of millions. Both planets had extensive satellite networks, including separate stations for cargo and passengers. And an active customs department with several inspection cutters.

"Why go to the station, then?" Dena said. "Can't we talk to them on the radio?"

"Bad idea," Lee replied. "First off, what would we say? 'Do you have those illegal troops we're supposed to be meeting?' Not great security if somebody heard us. We need to blend in. A crew on this type of freighter would expect some shore leave, so..."

"Yay shore leave!" Dena's fist punched the air.

"More importantly," Lee said. "We can't rush over there and babble on about a rebellion. How do we know that they're our troops, and not the Chancellor's troops?"

"She's right," Dirk added. "We need to dock, and have people be seen going on shore leave. Then we'll meet up with our agent to talk about that ship."

"Aren't we supposed to be running a rebellion or something? Why do we have to hide?"

"The Tribune is running a rebellion. The guy with a battleship and swarm of warships. He can't hide what he's doing, so he doesn't. We're a barely armed freighter trying to sneak some troops around before anybody figures things out, what we're doing or where they're going."

Everyone was silent. Rocky trotted in and dropped his ball for Scruggs to throw. He still limped, but he got better every day.

"Do we have IDs that will hold up?" Scruggs

asked.

Ana frowned. "The crew IDs, yes. The ship? Ask Gavin."

Scruggs called down to the engine room. "Gavin, will our IDs stand Core world inspection?"

"Yes," Gavin said. "As long as they don't hold us too long. Our specifications are close enough, but if we get boarded by customs, they might notice we're not as big as we're listed. They can hold us while they call back for confirmation. And we've got weapons and sensors that we shouldn't have."

"So we don't discharge anything," Dirk said. "We say we're carrying traffic in bond for the base at New Malaya."

"What would the base at New Malaya need from farther out in the Verge?"

"Luxuries," Dirk said. "Specialty fruits. Small, light, expensive, and long-lasting. If we fake our manifest to show we've flooded two dozen containers with carbon dioxide-covered fruit, we're safe. They won't have the facilities to handle it here. And that's the type of thing a tramp freighter like us would be carrying."

"That's what we should do, then," Scruggs said.

"I give you permission," Dirk said.

Ana rolled his eyes. "I wasn't aware that she was asking you," Ana said. "Being as I'm in charge of security and all."

"Centurion," Dirk said, "remember the rules. When we're in space, I'm in charge."

"Sorry," Ana replied. "Habit."

"Taking charge?"

"Thinking you're useless. Let's get to it."

It took the better part of a ship shift and a half for the *Heart's Desire*—now registered as *Heavyweight Items*—to get assigned a dock at the cargo station. A waiting list of ships hovered nearby ready to offload and reload. Dirk negotiated at length with the station controllers. When they discovered that *Heavyweight Items* would only be staying for two days to top off consumables and give the crew shore leave, they assigned the ship a slot originally meant for a larger bulk carrier.

None of the waiting cargo ships wanted the space. They couldn't complete their offloading within the limited time or didn't want to pay the higher fees for the larger docking slot. Dirk, ever cheerful about spending the Tribune's money, happily took the opportunity.

"We'll only need it for thirty-six hours," Dirk said. "That's four shifts. One shift to arrive, one shift to do our work, one shift to recover and have some fun, and one final shift to party before we leave."

"What do you think, Cadet?" Ana asked.

"Pardon, Centurion?" Scruggs said.

"What the Navy guy here said." Ana pointed at Dirk.

"You're asking me, but the pilot—"

"The pilot isn't in charge dirtside, we all agreed that. We're dirtside now, so I want to know, do you agree? Stay four shifts, don't drop cargo, shore leave, meet the contact, all of that."

"I... think so, Centurion."

"Think or—"

"Yes. I agree. That's the plan. Everyone suit up." Scruggs left to get station side clothes on, and the rest scattered to their rooms.

Dirk paused before he left. "You sure about this, Centurion? This is an important meetup."

"That's why I pushed," Ana said. "She needs to be in a fluid situation where there are consequences if she doesn't adapt quickly."

"She screws this up, we might not be able to fix things."

Ana shrugged. "Only way to learn."

Ten minutes later, everyone had assembled at the lock. Ana glared at Scruggs until she cleared her throat. "Everyone," she said, "be on your best behavior. Officially, we're here to have some station food, and Lee to pick up more supplies. Right?"

Lee and Dena had ordered most of the consumables they needed—food trays, some basic supplies, and a couple of specialized parts Gavin had requested.

"We don't need them," Gavin said, "but it'll add to the verisimilitude."

"The vermali-what?" Dena asked.

"Sorry," Gavin replied. "Lee's been giving me books to read."

Everyone looked at Lee.

"I mean...you know, I like literature," she said. "I'd like to have someone to talk to about it."

"You can talk to me," Ana offered.

"Are we sure you can read?" Dena asked.

"In six languages," Ana said. "Well, six well. I get by in four others."

"Cursing doesn't count, Old Man."

"I don't see why not. I always thought Cantonese curses were almost magical."

"Where did you learn all these languages?" Dena asked. "And why?"

"I worked with a lot of different troopers," Ana said. "And for different commanders. I had them teach me, and then I studied some more. Helps pass the time in jump. And the better you all understand each other, the less likely you are to get killed by accident. I didn't want to get killed by accident."

"You chose a strange profession, then."

"I don't want to be killed by accident." Ana

shrugged. "On purpose, that's a different herd of tabbos."

Despite Ana's protests that someone should stay behind to guard the ship, Dirk and Gavin had overridden him.

"It won't look right," Gavin said. "Any sort of freighter coming in, the whole crew gets off. Everyone. They want to party and have fun for as long as they can before the ship leaves. No one stays on board unless they're moving cargo. We're not moving cargo, and our supplies won't be here until the start of the next shift anyway. People can count, and they'll notice if we don't disembark."

"And Rocky will guard the ship for us," Scruggs said.

Rocky wagged his tail. Guarding the den was an important job. And he'd be able to search the rooms for treats, or smelly socks.

The dockmaster who checked them in sported extensive hair braids, a pristine uniform, and a skeptical attitude. She listened to their story that the station didn't have the facilities to unload the carbon dioxide-screened containers, but clearly didn't believe them. She re-tied her braid while Dirk requested embargoing any removals from the ship but allowing loading of their cargo.

"Fine." She checked her hair in a pocket mirror, and adjusted the neck kerchief. This station used patterned neck and wrist ruffles to signify department, and the different neck knots signified rank. Their IDs had already scanned green at her station, but she switched to another unit and re-typed the names and ID numbers.

"What's the delay, officer?" Dirk asked.

"We're scanning these against the central computers planet side to see if there's anything attached to them."

"Why would you do that?"

"Are you kidding me?" She pulled a mirror from her pocket and checked her neck knot for the third time. "We've already got one mercenary unit on the station, over at 7-B. You're clearly another. You've got trouble stamped all over you."

Dirk raised an eyebrow. "An old man, a Jovian, a couple of merchant crew, and two young girls—that's a mercenary unit?"

"It's not the ages that are of interest." She closed one eye and scrunched her face up. "I think I got robbed. This is dark scarlet, not brick red." She flipped the hand mirror closed. "First of all, that young girl over there"—she pointed at Dena, who was wearing her usual leather outfit—"looks like she just climbed down from the nearest tree. By her accent, I'd guess she's from a planet where everyone lives in the trees. Or eats them. The way she's dressed means she's looking for all sorts of trouble. And the Jovian lady next to her?" She pointed at Lee, who was wearing a sleek skinsuit under basic ship coveralls. "Her uniform is entirely too new. What was her last one? An Imperial Jovian suit perhaps?"

"I'm not wearing a uniform," Lee protested.

The clerk ignored her. "Three of you have the same coveralls," she continued, pointing at Gavin, Ana, and Scruggs. "And you're all wearing military utility belts. I see knives, a shock stick, and other weapons—not the hidden, clipped-down kind either, but quick-draw holsters."

She looked at Gavin. "That's the biggest wrench I've ever seen on someone's belt. And while there's no law against carrying tools, I doubt he uses it just to hammer nails."

Then her eyes landed on Ana. "And you, old fella—you're a walking armory. Let's see...a knife in one boot, a pistol in the other, a revolver on your hip, something that looks like a bayonet, a shotgun, and another cut-down shotgun on that pack you're carrying. So yes, the three of you look like a mercenary unit."

She nodded at Dirk. "And this guy? He's wearing an Imperial Naval spacesuit with all the identifying flashes removed. If that's not suspicious, I don't know what is."

Dirk looked down at himself. It was true—they were just spare ship coveralls, but they were clearly Imperial Naval coveralls.

"And Jovians," the station clerk continued. "They travel in packs of six, ten, or twenty. So having one of them with you means somebody's up to no good. Just so we're clear—we've got plenty of cameras, we've got a quick reaction force, and we've got your ship chained to our hull. Any issues from you, and we'll shoot first."

"And ask questions later?" Dirk asked.

"No. You only ask questions if you care about the answers. We don't. Especially given the current circumstances."

"What would those current circumstances be?" Ana asked.

"The Rebellion, of course," the clerk said, raising her eyebrows. "Haven't you heard? The evil Tribune Devin has declared rebellion against the Empire. He's busily destroying trade, burning Verge planets, stabbing people with his sword, skipping out on parking tickets, and generally laying havoc and waste to the region."

"Really?" Ana said flatly.

"That's what I heard. It doesn't matter. What does matter is this: we haven't seen any regular forces through here in forever, but we have seen two different mercenary units pass through in the last two months—one of which is docked with their supply ship right now. Two Imperial Auxiliary warships passed through without stopping, and the number of Nat cargo ships transiting the system has doubled. And now, we've got you guys, who are clearly some sort of special operations team."

"We're not a special operations team," Ana insisted.

"Walks like a tabbo, quacks like a tabbo," the clerk replied. She tapped something into her computer. "All right, your IDs came back clean—for now. But we're watching everything, we're counting everything, and we're going to charge you for everything."

"Thanks for the welcome," Ana muttered. The group gathered and walked down the corridor. "I think we need to stop at the first bar we find and get some idea of what's going on," Ana said. "She figured us out way too quickly."

"What's wrong with my accent?" Dena asked. "I talk good."

"It's distinctive," Ana said. "Regardless, we're not in the Verge anymore. Maybe next time, we should come off a little less...hard."

"You think?" Dirk said.

"We've made a tactical error," Ana admitted. "We're used to warding off trouble by appearing dangerous. Now that we're back in more civilized places, we need to ward off trouble by not appearing dangerous. It's a mistake we can't make twice."

"Come on, Centurion," Lee said. "You're worried about what a clerk thinks?"

"I am worried," Ana said. "What a clerk figures out, anybody else can figure out. Like a mercenary unit in the pay of the Chancellor. If they figure it out, they can cause us problems." Ana set his mouth in a grim line. "And a full company of mercenaries can cause us a lot of problems."

Chapter 23

"Well, your accent, for one thing," Scruggs said. "You sound—"

"Watch it." Dena caressed her shotgun. "What do I sound like?" After clearing the customs check, they'd headed for the nearest bar, no longer bothering to try to hide weapons. Their boots tramped loudly in the metal corridors as Dena demanded they explain how everyone knew she was from the Verge. She was so upset, she didn't even flirt with the men they stopped for directions.

"You sound like you grew up on a remote planet with only limited Imperial connections," Scruggs said. "You don't have the mainline Core accent…"

"You talk like you're from a colony," Lee said. "Not your fault. I've picked up the local accent since I've been in the Verge. So has Scruggs. But now that we're surrounded by Core speakers, we're losing it."

Dena's eyes narrowed. "Are you saying I talk wrong?"

"Not wrong, Dena. Not wrong." Scruggs shook her head. "But different. Distinctive. You won't pass for somebody from the Core." And not just your accent either. We're all a bit… harder than they're used to here. I'm so used to dealing with aggressive people, I've gotten used to it.

"You never mentioned this before."

"No need. All sorts of accents in the Verge. You don't stand out. Core side, you will."

Dena rounded on Gavin. "Do I sound that different?"

"Yes." Gavin nodded. "Not bad, just different. Your pronunciation is kind of country."

"And yours isn't?"

Gavin shook his head. "I've got a middle

Empire accent. Lee and Scruggs both sound like Core people who lived in the Verge, but they'll revert to middle Empire soon enough. But we all sound generic. Not like, say, Dirk or the Tribune. They sound like aristocrats."

"Nobody mentioned this."

Gavin shrugged. "It wasn't an issue. So many colonies in the Verge, so many different accents, mostly Imperial-related ones, one more in a group didn't make any difference. But in the Core, you'll find people talk much more similarly."

"Much more similarly? I have to talk like that? Use stupid word choices?"

"It doesn't matter right now. However we pronounce it, and however we measure it, we need to find out about that ship and see if we should contact the crew."

"All right," Dena said, "but what do we do now?"

"Let's go have a drink and get the news," Ana replied. He led them down the station's outer ring. Wall-size display screens blazed advertisements for ground-based vacation resorts. Pictures of sunny beaches with eye-catching deep-blue water, mountain streams tumbling down rocky waterfalls, and fields of blue flowers surrounding rustic log houses flowed past them.

Scruggs sniffed. "What's that smell? It smells… fresh and happy."

"Pine trees," Dena said. "Reminds you of what you're missing planet side. Things like hunting in the woods in the fall, cooking over an open fire. "

Ana grunted. "Fog, mud and freezing rain. Crouching in foxholes and not eating for days."

"Sliding in the dirt, being chased by packs of killer animals, and nearly being eaten," Gavin said.

Lee shuddered. "Near death experiences, falling out of trees."

"Floods, snakes, and deadly dust storms," Dirk said. "Marching for days in snow storms and getting attacked by wild dogs."

Scruggs sniffed again. "Pine scent. I'll bet they'll sell me some sort of air freshener like that. Hey." She bit her lip. "Do you think I can get pine-flavored Basic? To remind me?"

"Centurion," Dirk said. "I thought part of your training was to crush the optimism out of your cadets."

"It is," Ana said. "She should have been thoroughly miserable after all this time. I must be slipping."

"Or maybe," Scruggs said, "I'm tougher than you think. Or I've gotten tougher, I know my own mind, and I don't care what the rest of you say."

Ana grimaced. "Harrumph." But he smiled.

Dirk and Lee exchanged glances and Lee winked at him.

Scruggs stomped down the hall. *They're manipulating me. And I'm not sure which bothers me the most, that they're doing it, that I know they're doing it, that they know that I know but they don't care, that they know that...Jove damn them.* She slowed and stopped stamping. *Focus. The meeting. Meet the troops, get them on the Tribune's side. Remember the mission.*

"Well, we're here." Lee gestured to the double door entrance to the spacer's bar. Bright neon lined the walls, leading them down another corridor to the bar. "They're bound to be a local media station playing. Let's see how your optimism survives the news."

The news, as they discovered, was uniformly bad—at least for the Tribune. The Empire was united behind the ruling family and his designate, the Chancellor. The Tribune was a desperate dirtbag degenerate for attempting to overthrow his sister's husband. Reports of horrible atrocities in the Verge were rampant, and the gallant Imperial Navy was supposedly gearing up to crush the rebellious Tribune.

There was no mention of Admiral Bracebridge's defeat, any Union of Nations' incursions, or the pirate activity. Official statements from the Empire were sparse—only written missives from the Chancellor and Empress, with nothing directly from the Emperor himself.

"It's not looking good," Ana said.

"Do we need to stay here and watch this?" Dena asked. "It's depressing."

"Look at you, Nature Girl," Ana said. "All on the Tribune's side now. When did you start caring about what happens to the Empire?"

"You folks care. Dirk and Lee especially—they know the Empress, seems like, and they're worried about what this Chancellor guy might do. Scruggs is so worried about what she'll find with her family that she jumps at every opportunity to not go back to them. Gavin's had plenty of opportunity to foul things up, but when push comes to shove, he backs Dirk and Lee. He must have a reason. And you, Old Man, you're a big supporter of the Tribune and the Empire. You want him to win."

"I don't care who wins," Ana said. "Those high muckety-mucks and their problem have nothing to do with me. I'm just a working soldier."

"A working soldier who does everything the Tribune asks without question. And you've never threatened to strangle him with his own liver, unlike every other person you meet."

"You can't strangle somebody with their liver," Scruggs said. "Not long enough. Need intestines, or an esophagus."

"Esophagus." Ana nodded. "Never thought of using that, might be long enough. But it could work, and that's a new one for me. Well done, Cadet. Good out-of-the-box thinking."

"You needed a new hobby, Centurion."

Dena shook her head. "Baby Marine, you've been spending far too much time with the old man. But the point is, you've both bought into this Save-the-Empire thing that Tribune Devin is pushing."

"And you haven't?" Lee asked.

"Not completely. But it's important to you five, so I guess it's important to me now. Cause we're all in this together."

The crew sat in silence.

Ana blinked once. "Is this where we hug and sing supportive songs and talk about our feelings?"

Dena shuddered. "I'll need a lot more to drink before that happens. And looking at the swill that's on the table here, a lot better quality of booze. Lee, you're my expert on space station behavior. Do we have to stay here?"

"We do," Lee replied. "If we show up, go to one bar, and then run away, we'll draw attention."

"We're already drawing attention," Dena said, nodding toward the other patrons.

As soon as they'd ordered drinks, it became obvious that nearly every table was watching them. Conversations quieted when the crew stared, but got louder after they looked away.

"Jove," Dirk muttered. "This isn't what I expected. Look at their clothes."

Everyone looked. Business suits. Ship coveralls over skinsuits. Lots of fashion ruffs. And not a holstered revolver to be seen.

"We've been out of the Core too long," Ana said.

"We're not in the Core," Dirk replied.

"Close enough. Maybe we should have come in as Duke and Company," Ana mused.

"I assumed—never mind," Dirk muttered.

"We're too used to rough places. Look how we're sitting."

The crew, as was their habit, had taken a circular table in the corner but arranged themselves so everyone faced an exit.

"We're giving off all the wrong vibes," Ana muttered.

"Uh-oh," Gavin said suddenly.

"Uh-oh what?" Dena asked.

"Here comes trouble."

Three men in uniform had appeared in the doorway. The uniform wasn't unlike theirs—combat fatigues worn over skinsuits, complete with utility belts, shiny boots, and weapons. They looked until they located the crew, then sauntered toward them.

"Scruggs, your play," Ana said. "Stay seated and try to be inconspicuous, stand up and confront them with drawn weapons, or open fire?"

Scruggs's eyes widened. "We could, I mean. No." She took a breath. "Everyone ready, but don't fire yet. Clear weapons, but no shooting unless they do. We talk to them, see if they're who we're supposed to see. If trouble starts, Dena take the farthest, everyone else take whoever is closest to you."

Dena smirked. "Take the one closest? Huh, the old guy you can have, but the two younger ones? I wouldn't mind one of those." She glanced at Scruggs. "You pick first."

"Pick what?" Scruggs flushed.

"You know what I mean," Dena replied. "I don't feel like fighting you over them. Neither of them looks bad—they both look quite...yummy."

Scruggs flushed more.

"Now, now, Scruggs," Dirk interjected, his tone teasing. "We understand you've been having some trouble this trip. But maybe work on figuring out what should be done in this situation."

Scruggs swallowed. "This is hardly the time—"

"Any time is a good time," Dena said. "I want the one on the left, the brunette. Scruggs, you take the blond."

"You do realize," Dirk said, "that they might have preferences of their own in this matter?"

Ana laughed. "Seriously? After all your years in the service, you think they'll have much of a choice one way or the other?"

The group of men slouched to a stop in front of their table. They looked relaxed, but their sidearms and gear told another story. Their holstered pistols had no barrel, only an optical sight and a huge battery behind. One cradled a peculiar weapon with a cable running to a backpack.

Dirk leaned toward Scruggs. "Those sidearms are low-tech knockoff of Imperial officers' laser pistols. They look similar, but only have a dozen shots before they need to be recharged. And that mini-plasma rifle is another low-tech knockoff. It's only got a couple shots, but that thing could take out the whole table if he fires it."

"Won't it blow the station up too?"

"High temperature, low penetration. Skin and bone burns much faster than metal," Ana said. "Good for clearing a station corridor, if you don't mind the smell."

"Morning," the leader said.

"Is it?" Dirk asked. "We just got here. We don't know what shift it is."

"It's morning. Early morning. First shift," the man clarified. He was tall, nearly as tall as Ana, but slim. His uniform, while neat, seemed ill-fitting— too broad in the shoulders and cinched tightly at the belt, which still hung loosely.

"Didn't expect to see you here," the man said.

"I'm not sure we've met," Dirk replied.

"You're the captain of the..." The man glanced over his shoulder, snapping his fingers. The second man, the blond Dena had been eying, said, "*Heavyweight Items*, out of Pallas. Greek-speaking crew."

"For native Greek speakers," the man continued, "none of you seem to have much of an accent."

"We've got accents." Dena grinned at him. "In fact, I'm so good with accents. I could teach you all sorts of new words—or teach your friends here."

The man laughed. "I'm sure you could. But you can sort that out later. We have business first."

"What can we do for you?" Dirk asked. "And who are you?"

"I'm Captain Gutu of Imperial Auxiliary Regiment 237, Company C," the man said. "These are Lieutenants Scheve and Kaul."

"I didn't know a space station needed an auxiliary regiment," Dirk replied.

"It doesn't. We're in transit—stopped here to take on supplies."

"Supplies. Good for you. Don't see how it's any of our concern, though."

"Would you like to know what kind of supplies we're taking on?" Gutu asked.

Dirk shrugged. "No. But you're going to tell us, aren't you."

"We're taking on rations for a three-month voyage."

"Do tell," Ana said, raising an eyebrow. "Three months is a long voyage."

"And we're supposed to meet a liaison officer with some comm equipment."

"Are you?" Dirk asked. "Liaison to what?"

The man smirked. "Auxiliary regiments don't get liaison officers normally. Or comm equipment. If they're giving us Imperial comm equipment, it means we're operating directly with Imperial forces. And given that we're ground forces, the only thing requiring special coordination would be..."

"A starship," Ana interjected.

"Got it in one," the man confirmed. "You're our contact."

"Why do you say that?" Dirk asked.

"Couple things," Gutu said. "You're here, dressed for trouble, and off a starship. And two, we've met."

"I don't think so," Dirk said. "I'd remember you."

"Oh, it's not you specifically. It's your type." Gutu pulled a chair from a nearby table and sat down, facing Ana directly. "So," he said, a wry smile on his face. "You're the rebels. Do you want to have a drink, or are you going to try to kill me first?"

Chapter 24

"If I'd wanted to kill you," Ana said. "You'd be dead already."

"Guess I'm a lucky man," Gutu said. "Not being dead and all." He fingered his holstered laser pistol, as did Scheve. Kaul, with the knock-off plasma rifle, remained standing and kept it pointed at the ceiling. The bar had quieted.

Ana stretched. "You should celebrate that. And soon."

"Why soon?"

"Well, I don't want to kill you. But I could be convinced otherwise."

"Who'd do the convincing?"

Ana gestured at his table—a round one. He sat side on, watching both the front door and the rear exit. Gavin and Dirk to his left, Scruggs, Dena and Lee to his right. At first glance, they were crowded together, but each had their weapon arm free. "The crew here will eat you up."

"An old man, two girls, a skinny Jovian, an engineer with his back to us, and a pilot who looks like he sleeps all day."

"We prefer it when Dirk does that," Dena said. "Otherwise, he tries to do combat landings in atmosphere. I don't like those. I puke all the time."

The younger, blond man laughed. "You puke, do you? Don't worry, pretty girl, I'll hold your hair while you do that."

"Thanks." Dena smiled. "I hate it when my hair gets messy."

"What will you do for me, then, pretty girl?"

"What are you thinking?"

"How about a kiss?"

Dena grinned. "It better be a good one."

"Or what?"

"If I'm not impressed, I'll shoot you in the head

with this metal ball bearing?" Dena flexed her slingshot.

Gutu laughed. "That's not much of a threat. Scheve doesn't use his head much. He probably won't miss it." He turned to Ana. "That's all you got, Sergeant?"

"Senior Centurion," Ana said.

"Oh, my pardon, Senior Centurion." Gutu laughed again. "Congratulations, Senior Centurion." He leaned back and crossed his arms. "I'm supposed to meet a crack team of Imperial Operatives sent by Tribune Devin and take on equipment and payment. I wasn't expecting a bunch of amateurs and has-beens. I'm not impressed. Maybe I'll kick your butt, take the money and equipment, and move on. I'll square it with the Tribune later."

"Not going to happen." Ana glanced around the table. *Lee's got a poker face. Navy and the punk don't look scared. Dena's having fun. What about Scruggs? Does she know this is all a dominance game? Best we prove we're in charge.*

"Why not? What are you going to do about it? We've got you covered. You're unarmed. And weak. And old. I'm going to pull you out from behind that table. You'll be lucky if I don't let the boys put you out an airlock when we're done."

"Not going to happen," Ana repeated. "You want to know why?"

"Enlighten me."

"First of all, it's a good thing that your friend there doesn't need his forehead, because Dena here is a dead shot. Soon as he reaches for his pistol, she's going to blast him across the bar. If he's lucky, his brains will follow along. If he's unlucky, they'll stay behind and leak out along the way. Now as for you, it's entirely possible that you might also have no use for your head, but I'll bet you have a use for your crotch, and that's where Cadet Scruggs has the shotgun she has under the table pointed at."

"You're bluffing. I've never seen anybody knocked out with a metal ball before. And this little girl hasn't moved since we got here."

Scruggs grunted. "Don't call me little girl."

"Why not, little girl? You going to threaten me with the non-existent weapon you have down there?"

"Yes," Scruggs said. Her voice cracked and her fingers were white.

Ana blinked. *He's not going to believe her. She's never been scared in combat before. Why's she acting weird now?* "Because since we sat here, she's been holding a shotgun under the table. Which is why you don't see her hands. Right now, it's pointed at your crotch. Do you already have kids?"

"Still bluffing," Gutu said.

"What's your load, Cadet?" Ana asked.

"Boarding shot, Centurion," Scruggs said. "Non-lethal, but not much dispersal at this range."

"Don't believe you, little girl."

"Well, you, you should." Scruggs's voice cracked again. "We can take you easily."

Kaul swung the plasma rifle down and pointed it at Ana. Gutu grinned wider. "No you can't. Kaul here will melt you to pieces with the plasma rifle." He raised his eyebrows. "I'm not impressed, Sergeant. Not the way to treat a contact. I don't think you're up for this. We don't need your liaison services. Hand over the money and our gear, and we won't hurt you."

"Plasma rifles are outstanding weapons," Ana agreed. "Even low-tech ones, like what you have, are powerful, but short ranged. Deadly to unarmored crew, and doesn't damage hulls. Favorite weapons of pirates, in fact. But not much range or penetration."

"Don't see any armor on you. You'll fry like an emu egg. We'll be scraping you up with a spatula. And why are we talking about this? We're going to your ship, and you'll give us our money and supplies."

"The thing about plasma rifles, though," Ana said. "Is that they take thirty seconds to power up the capacitor unless they're already charged. And once the capacitor is charged, it makes a very slight hum. Only a trained ear can hear it, and even then, they have to be close. I couldn't hear it from this side of the table. But the engineer there—" Ana nodded at Gavin— "He's an annoying punk. But he's been on a lot of ships. And he knows engines, and capacitors, and he doesn't look worried. Are you worried, Engineer?"

Gavin shook his head. "Not really, no."

Dirk held up a hand. "For the record, I'm worried."

"Shut up, Navy. Engineer, hear any buzzing noises?"

"Not a one. No buzzing."

"You know," Dirk said, "rather than discussing our hearing loss—"

"Shut up, Navy." Ana smiled. "No buzzing means that your boy is at least thirty seconds away from firing a shot. We can do a lot in thirty seconds. Dena can break a hand before it reaches for a pistol, Scruggs can knock you down a dozen ways, and the others have weapons to cover you after. We don't even need to kill you all. We can immobilize you, take you prisoner."

Gutu looked at the three of them. Then he boomed a laugh. "I don't believe a word you say. Get up, Sergeant, I'm going to kick your ass."

"Centurion. Senior Centurion. I already told you that."

"Blast you, Sergeant." Gutu laughed. "This is going to be fun. Take him, boys."

Dena's slingshot flicked out, taking Scheve in the hand. He screamed as his wrist shattered. Scruggs shoved her shotgun forward and down and shot Gutu in the foot. His boots were reinforced, but the shot broke his ankle. He yelled and grabbed his foot.

Dirk grabbed the barrel of the plasma gun and pushed. Kaul struggled for control. Gavin grasped his wrench and made an awkward swing. Kaul ducked and yanked the plasma gun away.

And fired it.

A spray of high temperature plasma splayed out. It was hot. Burning hot. But the stream didn't have time to disperse, and it stuck to the first thing it hit—the ceiling.

Lights flickered and burned. Retardant foam flashed to flame. Paint blistered. The whole corner of the room flash heated. Scruggs kicked her chair back and rolled under the table, kicking Gutu's ankle as she did. Gavin swung again and knocked the gunner down. He dropped, dragging the gun behind. Dirk stooped, unclipped it from its power supply, and pulled it away.

Lee produced a revolver and stuck it into Gutu's face. "No, no, no. Stay there. I'll see to your feet later." Dena and Scruggs disarmed him and Scheve, pocketing their pistols. Dirk checked that the plasma rifle was safe.

The bar emptied, patrons stampeding to the door, proceeded by the staff.

Ana looked at the burning ceiling, then wiped ash from his face. "That went well. Cadet, we'll talk later."

Scruggs nodded but stayed silent.

Ana glowered at a sweating Gavin. "Engineer, you said you didn't hear a buzz."

"I didn't," Gavin said. "Not a single b."

"Centurion," Dirk said, "only the older models buzzed. It was a known problem. The newer ones don't make a noise when they are armed. I tried to tell you I was worried."

"I did not know that." Ana shrugged. "I guess the engineer didn't either. That's why he wasn't worried."

"I knew the newer ones don't make noises," Gavin said. "Ever since series 63. They're all quiet now."

Ana raised an eyebrow at Gavin. "You knew that it wouldn't make noise?"

"Yep."

"So it could have been armed?"

"It was armed."

"But you said you weren't worried."

"I wasn't." A burning fluff of ceiling insulation dropped onto Gavin's arm and he beat it out. "I wasn't worried," he repeated.

"And why not?"

"No need to be." Gavin grinned. "It was pointed at you, not me."

Chapter 25

"Don't call the captain stupid, Bron, and don't call me Franky," Monti said.

"First, I wasn't saying the captain was stupid. I was saying this activity is stupid," Hooper said.

"Fine, fair enough."

"But since you asked, yeah, I think you're being stupid."

The *Collingwood* crew had survived to make their rendezvous with the tanker. And, surprise, found the flagship and the others there, doing more maneuvers. After topping their fuel tanks up, they loaded an extra fuel bladder into one of the cargo holds for even longer range. And vented as much of their air as they possibly could, so they didn't stink like a three-day-old tabbo corpse, and rejoined the fleet.

Devin had given the two of them a sumptuous dinner, a low-level medal, and an alcohol-fueled pep talk where he demonstrated how he would attack the base at New Malaya. He was pleased with their efforts, and wanted to reward them, but time and tide waited for no man, and he was short scouting ships, and he did need some other paths scouted, so…

Franceska Monti, Captain Under God, had turned the *Collingwood* around and scouted another path in. One that was uncomfortably close to where they had seen the Imperial frigates.

Because that's what I do now. Do what the Tribune says, help the rebellion, make decisions that put us in danger. Because that's my job now. And I hate it.

"I understand you might have a death wish," Bron said, "going back to chase the frigates that had nearly killed us, but did you have to bring all of us along with you?"

"I don't have a death wish. Yes, the first part of this, we might run into our old friend the frigate, but the last part is a different branch path. And as I recall, I asked for volunteers, and you volunteered."

"I surprised myself on that one. Never know what I'll get up to these days. What do you think, Silaski?"

Silaski looked up from the helm position. "I think you shouldn't call the captain stupid ma'am."

"I didn't call the captain stupid."

"Not initially, but then you corrected yourself to say she was stupid."

"And you called her by her first name."

"Didn't seem to bother her, at the time. Did it bother you, Captain?"

Monti looked up from her course plot. "It's Captain now, is it? Change of heart after I threatened to disrate you? And kick you out?"

"I don't think you'll do that ma'am."

"You don't, do you? And why in Jove's name not?"

Silaski nodded. "Because I'm still here. I volunteered, and you let me come along. I must be doing something right."

Hooper scowled. "Silaski, you're only a helmsman. You need to stay out of these conversations."

"Didn't you ask me to come into the conversation?"

"Leave her alone, Bron."

"Silaski, shut up."

"Yes ma'am."

"How come we never got leave?" Hooper asked. "Or at least a break?"

"Like the Tribune said, he's short scouting ships."

"There were some with the fleet. One of them could go."

"Remember, the Tribune said we were one of his most effective teams."

"I saw that." Hooper nodded. "I also saw that the other commanders that were with him earlier have been promoted. In charge of destroyers, or a cruiser. And their first officers got to take over the old ships."

"You have a point, Bron?"

"Just a data point. Jump course laid in and proceeding."

Monti checked the course on her board. "Got it. Silaski, put the jump counter on the screen. Bron, call everyone to action stations."

Hooper raised an eyebrow. "Action stations? What, so that we'll all be in our pressure suits when we get blown up by the destroyer escort and other ships that'll be lurking at our jump exit as we come through?"

"They won't be lurking at our jump exit as we come through. We saw them break off first. They needed fuel as badly as we did."

"This is true," Bron nodded. "But so what?"

"If they're not following us, they must be going back to where they came from." *I hope.* "We need to find out where."

Monti had picked a non-standard emergence point, where she was sure there wouldn't be any enemies lounging, waiting for her. Her hope was to sneak in while the enemy frigate was fueling, and sneak past it. To her surprise, when they returned, the pursuing frigate was nowhere to be seen.

Monti grimaced at the board. "They must have left as soon as they had minimal fuel." *Which means we need to find out where they went.* She checked her nav screens. Nothing in the way, and they were still outside of the jump limit. She gave orders for an immediate pursuing jump.

Hooper was running numbers on her screen. "That means it's assuming a tanker is coming after it. So why would it be assuming that?"

"Same reason we assumed our tanker is coming after us?"

"Because...?"

Monti nodded. "We had a pre-planned exploration and scouting path, and the tanker was arranged weeks ahead of time."

Hooper shook her head. "They didn't. They reacted when another ship blundered into the middle of their operation. But why did they react?"

"A rebel ship scanned them, so they chased it away."

"They didn't see a rebel ship. They saw an Imperial corvette."

"Well, they must have known that we were with the Rebel Tribune Devin, as they say now."

Hooper made an elaborate shrug. "Must they? How would they know that?"

"The direction we were coming from—they would have come from New Mayala, the Core. They would assume any ships coming from direction of the Verge were rebels."

"They didn't know that."

"Well, surely Devin's activities have gotten back. Surely they should have challenged us."

"But they didn't challenge us. They came after us like the proverbial tabbo of hell."

"Do tabbos go to hell?" Silaski asked.

"Yes, Silaski. Bad tabbos go to hell, along with bad helmsmen who interject themselves in conversations that they're not supposed to be in. Now get us into jump and chase that frigate."

"Captain?" Silaski said.
"Yes?"
"Sixty seconds 'til emergence."

"Hooper?" Monti asked.

"Ship is at action stations, Captain. We are prepared for battle. All weapons, or I should say our weapon, is manned and ready, and we have a full supply of anti-missile missiles ready to go out. For all the good that will do."

"We want to be ready."

"That frigate could be waiting at the jump limit, wait 'til we emerge, and blast us to pieces. And what have we accomplished?"

"They won't be waiting. We could emerge from anywhere, anytime. They can't watch everything."

"Ten seconds to emergence," Silaski said.

"Or instant death," Hooper muttered.

"What's that, Hooper?"

"It's a delight to be here, Captain. An instant delight. Happy you're in charge."

Silaski smothered a laugh. "Emergence. Request power to the scanning consoles."

Scanners flickered to life on the bridge. Last battle stations drill, Monti had tried getting everyone to shut down all of the active scanning systems so they could go dark. After two embarrassing mistakes in the drills, she had ordered engineering to pull the breakers on all the active scanning systems and leave them turned off unless she specifically called for them.

"Well," Monti said. "I got nothing."

Hooper ran her board. "I got nothing close by neither. No radar sources. No infrared."

"Silaski, you see anything?"

Silaski was still flipping through screens. "I, um, which—"

"Never mind. Silaski, double-check us as you can. See what you can find."

Monti methodically searched the near space. *Nobody waiting. We live another day. Or do we...*

"Silaski, point a telescope on the far side of the

system. Hooper, figure out the direct course they'd take to go back to where we found that tanker originally, and see where the jump point would be." This system was a triple star system. When they were originally chased through it, they had to transit the system in a bizarre corkscrew course to get a clear path away. They'd have to do the same going backwards."

"Uh, Captain, that'll take..."

"I know, I know. Do your best."

Forty minutes passed before they had a course that all three agreed was direct to the next jump point.

"All right. Point the passives in that direction. I'm going to head down to the engineering stations."

"We'll put the— status change," Silaski said. "Jump light across the system."

"Where at?"

"Right where you told me to point the telescope, Captain."

"Somebody jumped in?"

"No," Silaski said. "Somebody jumped out."

"Did you see the ship?"

"No ma'am. But the jump flash showed like you said it would."

"Good. We know where they went, and they don't know we're following them."

"How does that work?"

"Even light takes time, Silaski. So the light from our arrival wouldn't have crossed the light from their departure. They're so far away, the fact that we got that flash within, what, one hour, sixteen minutes after emergence? All right, and they're on the other side of the system. That means they got out before we got in. So unless there's a second ship—"

"They didn't have two ships before."

"They could now. Point us at that jump light and get the drive up. Set us up for a least time cross. We're going to follow that ship into the next system."

"You're the captain."

"Glad you remember, Bron. Settle in for a chase."

"Great news!" Hooper rolled her eyes. "Weeks of increasing humidity and the constant smell of mold and wet dog."

"That's what I don't get," Monti said. "Why does it smell like wet dog? We've never even had a dog."

"Some sort of dog mildew or something? We only cleaned out as much of the ship as we could, but we didn't open to vacuum. Next time we get by that tanker, we're doing it. Otherwise, everything in here is going to smell like old socks."

"Everything here already smells like old socks."

Collingwood crossed the system and entered jump space again, scouting yet another path to New Malaya. They came out of jump space in the next system with the weapon ready. When they flashed out, there was activity nearby.

Monti looked at her display. "Alerts. What have you got?"

Hooper flashed her screen output onto the main. "Got a ship. Could be a tanker."

"Imperial tanker?"

"Not sure. Not in the warbook."

"Is it the one that was there before?"

"No, different class. It's a strange shape. Too long. Stand by. Well, looky look. Another tanker."

"I only see one."

"Overlapping. And there's another one, offset from the first," Hooper said.

Monti raised an eyebrow. "Three tankers?"

"Another. Four. Four tankers. There's four tankers in an empty system."

"Where's that frigate?"

"Don't know."

"Could be sitting beside us."

"We'd be blown up by now. Four tankers. That's a lot of tankers."

"Have they seen us?"

"Not yet."

"What are they doing?"

"They're in dispersed orbits outside the jump limit. Anybody coming in that wants to rendezvous with them should be able to make a quick shot and then head out."

"They're orbiting the primary?"

"No, they're orbiting some rocky planet out there. Planet number 7. Just a designation."

"What's in that direction?"

"Uh, nothing."

"Nothing?"

"Well, nothing Imperial. There's a border system claimed by the Empire, but also claimed by the Nats. And then there's a Nat system. Not heavily trafficked. And then you hit one of the main Nat trading lanes."

"So those ships are deployed to refuel ships going to the Union of Nations?"

"Could be. If any ever go that way. Which they don't. There's no trade route. Jumps are too long."

Silaski spoke. "I know what type of tankers those are."

"Did you look them up in the warbook?"

"I did," Silaski said.

"So did I," Hooper said. "And they weren't there. You're mistaken."

"I'm not, you are."

"How is that?"

"Because you looked them up in the Imperial warbook. I didn't. I looked them up in the Union of Nations warbook." Silaski put a note on the screen. "Those aren't Imperial tankers, they're Union of Nations tankers. Fleet support tankers. There's a Nat fleet around here somewhere."

Chapter 26

"Happy to be commanding a battleship, Prefect?" Tribune Devin sat in his bridge command chair. Keyboards clacked, watch-standers conferred, palms slapped and warning alarms bonged for attention. On his previous flag ship, the frigate *Pollux*, officers had murmured quietly, and most alarms muted to visual only. Here, it seemed like everyone competed to have the most numerous and loudest notifications.

Lionel frowned at his display.

"Prefect," Devin repeated.

Lionel continued to mark up his report. Devin tilted his head until he could see Lionel's screen—a schematic of a piping system, marked up with red and green text.

Devin raised his voice. "Pipes more interesting than a fleet commander, Prefect?"

Lionel jerked up. "Sorry, Tribune. Administrative and maintenance details. How may I serve the Empire? And how may I serve your august presence, emperor-declarant?"

"Had to get a dig in there, didn't you, Prefect?"

"It's my job. Didn't the old-school Romans have somebody behind their—"

"Yes, yes, they had someone on a chariot holding the famous crown of leaves and saying, 'Remember thou art but a mortal man.'"

"I don't want to hold a crown of leaves over your head," Lionel said. "Especially not on a chariot. You'd crash it swerving into the nearest wine shop. But I'm sorry, Tribune. I should have been paying better attention. What was it you asked?"

"I asked if you enjoy commanding this battleship." Devin waved at the room. "Commanding all this."

On *Pollux*, he and Lionel had sat side by side, directly behind the watch officers and their heads-up displays. On *Canopus*, he and Lionel brooded on a raised central dais. Eight senior officers—offensive weapons, defensive weapons, sensors, navigation, helm, life support, engineering and security sat in a semicircle in front of them. Junior ratings, and officers under training lined a second circle beyond that, with two levels of display screens in front and above them. *It's like a theater with two rows of tall people between me and the screen, except a theater has only one screen I need to keep track of. Here, there's two dozen of them spouting information all the time.*

"Yes, no, and no."

"An oddly specific structure of answers, especially given that there are three of them and I only asked one question. What do you mean?"

"Well… I like commanding ships because I like being a commander. I don't like having to command a fleet, because I've never been trained for it, and no, I don't like commanding this particular battleship because my days are spent on something like the following."

Lionel sent a copy of a report to Devin's screen. It was the quarterly report of sewage treatment facilities on *Canopus*, with a special notice for pipe flow analysis and the necessity of replacing and updating flow meters and valves.

"What is all this crap?"

"Exactly," Lionel said. "It's all crap. I'm reading a report about crap."

"Don't you have an engineering staff to take care of this?"

"In theory," Lionel said. "In practice, they've been doing things the same way for the last twenty years, so they don't know any other way. Dockyard maintenance supposedly happens every two years, but that maintenance is overdue. By three years. They don't have enough parts to do regular maintenance, and even if they did, they don't have the expertise to do the fixes. And now, I've confronted the staff with an unusual circumstance: we're twenty percent over the Empire standard crew."

"Are we going to overwhelm the life support?" Devin shook his head. "But we're not fully crewed, you told me, that we still need more…"

"We are not over-crewed." Lionel pulled up another note. "We're under establishment according to what this class is rated for. But it's never been crewed to this level."

"Even though we're under—wait, I don't get it."

"The sewage system never worked properly. Nobody noticed because there was never more than a thousand people on the ship, even though it was rated for two thousand. Now that we've added more people, we're overwhelming the system. Not because it isn't rated for it, but because it's not functioning properly. And the current crop of engineers sees no way to update or support more crew."

"Well," Devin said, "can't you just…" He paused. "Fire them?"

"Nope."

"Why not?"

"Because there's no one else in the fleet with big ship experience. All our expertise is on small ships."

"Surely the engineering staff on *Pollux*—"

"The engineering staff from *Pollux* is amazing—talented, experienced, educated."

"Laying it on a bit thick, aren't you?"

"Laying it on thick would be adding that they're attractive, and smell nice." Lionel blanked his screen. "Actually," he said, "that's probably true too. They were better at getting the water system running, so they got to take more showers. Unlike now."

"Right, I heard about that," Devin said. Lionel had sent out a ship-wide decree cutting the number of showers. Previously, *Canopus*'s crew members were allocated one shower every two days, which was standard on most starships. Now, with the additional crew, they were limited to one a week.

"Nobody's going to like that," Devin said.

"Pulling crew from *Pollux* won't work," Lionel continued. "I can't transfer more of them. We've got them spread across the fleet, and we've already promoted every command team that we had, and split the officers up. I note that the Commander of the *Collingwood*, and her first officer, remain together. We could take one of them—"

"No. They have to stay together," Devin said. "I need them on that ship to do scouting."

"And as dinner companions?"

"They're volunteer reserve officers, not regular officers. They have some unique insight into the fleet and how it's being used. I discuss a lot of our strategies with them. Their answers are…illuminating."

"You're discussing fleet maneuvers and strategies with junior officers. Junior volunteer reserve officers?"

"I discuss my plans with whom I please, Prefect."

"Tribune." Lionel nodded. "Doesn't hurt that they're both good-looking."

"Looks are not an issue. They need to stay on that ship. I have plans for them in the future." *Plans that you don't need to know about.*

Lionel waited. Devin didn't elaborate.

"Understood." Lionel nodded again. "Besides,

if we brought them back, there'd be seniority issues, even more seniority issues, which is another problem."

"What seniority issues?"

"Everyone from *Pollux* has been promoted. By you. That's good, because they're occupying key positions on the other ships in the fleet, and we can count on them. But there's a general sense that anyone who was with me got rewarded with a promotion because they were part of our group—not because they were competent."

"I need people I can trust in senior positions."

"And the fact that they are competent," Lionel added, "is obscured by the jealousy it's engendered. Except for the Sluskys out there. And I will admit, not all of them are Slusky-like."

"I never thought of that," Devin admitted.

"Me neither," Lionel said. "I've never commanded a ship this big or a task force this large before."

"I remind the Prefect," Devin said, "that you do not command the task force. You command the flagship."

"And I remind the Tribune," Lionel added, "that I've spent a good part of my career making up for your lack of interest in Naval and military activities, so I'm expecting you'll dump fleet command on me at some point."

"Golly," Devin said. "I was hoping you hadn't noticed that. I planned to get away with being the Tribune playboy."

"I was hoping you could too," Lionel replied. "Leave the military thing to me. You can handle the politics and the money issues."

"I'm the Fleet's banker now?"

"Well, I can't be. I don't have enough money."

"I don't either," Devin said.

"But the bankers don't know that."

"Not yet." But they will. I could make that to my advantage, perhaps. I wonder... "Sorry, Prefect?"

"I've got some ideas for updating our... crap-producing system. Want to hear them?"

"Do I have to—"

A loud bong interrupted him.

"Contact! Status change," the sensor operator announced.

"Thank Jove!" Devin muttered.

"*Fargo* reports a jump signature in their sector, heading in-system," the communication rating said.

"*Fargo* reports a jump signature in their sector, heading in-system," her officer repeated.

Devin grunted. Saying I heard it the first time will just confuse things. Big ships are hard to manage.

"Sensors?" Lionel said. "What do you see?"

The sensor officer, one of the *Canopus*' original crew, looked confused. "*Fargo* reports—"

"I don't want to know what the destroyer reports. Tell me what you see. Use our sensors."

"Yes sir. Sorry sir."

"Get your Bejoved butt in gear. Move it. Now."

The sensor operator's face turned red as she switched back to the screen and typed frantically.

"Everyone, see to your duties. Helm, what's our new course?"

"Sir?" the helmsman, unfortunately not Rudnar, asked.

"Our course to intercept the target."

"Ahhh..."

"Get an intercept course. Plot it now."

"Sir."

"Sensors," Lionel continued. "Scan that incoming ship. Communications, monitor *Fargo*'s comms and send a note to the rest of the squadron to follow us. We're closing in to see what it is.

Action stations, set Level One. Move it, people."

The alarm bonged, and the bridge crew double-checked their straps, ensuring their helmets were close at hand. Devin unclipped himself from his seat and stepped next to a glaring Lionel.

"Prefect?"

"I know, Tribune. I know," Lionel sighed. "I'm sorry. I have too many things going on right now. I can't believe the lack of resourcefulness—or willingness to act. But it won't happen again."

"Likely it will," Devin muttered, "but at least we were warned."

Devin carefully clipped himself into his seat. Muttered commands passed between sections heads and their crews. They spoke quietly and nobody contacted him directly.

Sure is different from the Pollux. By now, every station would have reported directly to either me or Lionel. They would know who to send which information. Lionel would already have tactical control.

He noted that the small section of the ship he was directly responsible for on his own screen—his quarters and the pantry where Imin was stationed, had almost immediately flashed green as locked up at action stations. *Imin doesn't let grass grow under his feet—or any other vegetable, for that matter. In fact, he probably would plant special tasty vegetables that he'd use in a casserole—*

Devin slapped himself mentally. He never daydreamed on the bridge, but it was so Joved boring being the fleet commander.

He missed the Pollux. Things were easier before. No bankers, no rebellion, no mutinous officers.

But still people trying to kill him.

Lionel was giving instructions. "All right, bring the fleet around. Release the escorts. General chase."

Devin waited. A battleship as large as the *Canopus* was powerful and carried a stunning array of weapons. But it was ponderous to maneuver and couldn't turn on a dime. Lionel's decision to release the smaller ships to chase and develop the pursuit was sound.

"Helm, give us 3G from the mains," Lionel ordered.

The acceleration alarm bonged again. The helmsman pivoted the ship. The *Canopus* rounded to its new course. There was a pause as the ship floated in zero gravity.

"Helm?" Lionel asked, his voice flat.

"Sir, we're on course. The board is set for 3G."

"Why aren't the engines firing?"

"Unknown sir."

"Well, contact engineering and find out."

Devin spent the next fifteen minutes watching his flotilla chase down the intruder. *Canopus*'s screen interface was different than he was used to, and he was having problems getting good information on the pursuit. Next to him, Lionel's voice got louder and louder as he worked his way through a series of engineering staff trying to find out what was going on. The chief engineer kept repeating he was 'contacting the watch officer' and the watch officer continued to not respond.

Don't get involved. Lionel has to fix it. Your job is to keep an eye on the fleet.

The engines finally engaged, but instead of slamming on, they accelerated gently. Devin felt himself being slowly pushed back into his seat. He glanced at Lionel, who shook his head, eyes fixed on the board.

"*Pollux* would never have done that," Lionel muttered. "When given a course, they'd flip the ship and go to max power. This meandering has to stop."

The sensor operator spoke up. "*Fargo* is overhauling sir. They say it's a frigate—an Imperial frigate."

"Are they requesting assistance?"

"Uh, stand by... No sir."

"Well..." Lionel rolled his eyes. "Tell the other three ships to set a pursuit cone at maximum speed. Repeat maximum speed twice."

Fargo, a light cruiser and the least maneuverable, grabbed the center of the pursuit cone, putting itself on a least-time course to intercept the retreating frigate. The remaining escorts, *Rigorous*, *Romola*, and *Rowena* angled off the base course at diverging angles. This formation allowed the escorts to cover the space around the target. If the target frigate ran straight, *Fargo*, the light cruiser, would eventually overhaul it. If it tried to dodge, it would come into gunfire range of another. *Canopus* lumbered behind, preventing the target from pivoting and slowing to engaging the direct pursuers and slug it out. Unless it wanted to risk an encounter with the battleship's massive firepower.

Devin observed the maneuver for a few minutes. "I will say, Prefect, the fleet is performing well. That's a textbook execution for those three." He highlighted *Fargo*, *Rowena* and *Romola* racing after the target.

"Yes, I agree," Lionel said. "A well-executed pursuit."

"Send my congratulations," Devin replied. "And send my displeasure to *Rigorous*. She's lagging."

Lionel's eyes flicked toward Devin. He grimaced and shook his head.

Uh-oh. What don't I know? Devin raised his eyebrows.

Lionel opened a private channel. "*Fargo, Rowena,*

and *Romola* executed a perfect maneuver and are boxing the target in. *Rigorous* didn't react quickly enough. I've sent her two instructions already, but I don't think their captain or navigator knows what they're doing."

"What's wrong with stating that publicly?"

"The other three are commanded by officers formerly from *Pollux*. *Rigorous* still has its original command team. If I criticize them publicly, it'll look like more denigration of their abilities. More favoritism."

"Cancel the order, then."

"Too late," Lionel said, shaking his head. He waved his arm, indicating the bridge.

Devin cursed under his breath. At least twenty-five people from different departments had heard. Word of his comments would spread throughout the fleet, whether announced formally or not.

Before he could say more, *Fargo* reported, "Target One has surrendered and cut its acceleration."

"Very well," Devin said.

The ship's acceleration ceased, and Devin drifted in his straps.

Lionel's head snapped up. "Have we suffered an engineering casualty? Helm, what's going on?"

"Sir, I've reduced thrust to cut stress on the ship and crew, since the enemy has surrendered."

"Countermand that," Lionel said. "Continue course and speed until we're sure they can't escape our weapons envelope. In case they change their minds."

"Yes sir. Understood sir."

Lionel reopened the private channel. "Reduce stress on the ship and crew?" he scoffed. "This isn't the Navy I'm used to. We need to fix this."

"Yes, but how?"

"Not sure, but I know one thing we'll have

more of, Tribune, if this continues."
"What's that, Prefect?" Devin asked.
"Stress. Lots more stress."

Chapter 27

The intercom burped Dena's voice. "Old Man, is Lee in the lounge with you?"

Ana bounced Rocky's ball off the lounge wall. "Why? Problems with jump emergence? And when will you stop using the computer so much? I want hot water." The *Heart's Desire* had emerged from jump en route to Ast Station. Dena was helping Lee navigate. Which, given her lack of math skills, her help had presented itself as obsessive checking of basic computations, and a drain on life support as she diverted power to frantically unnecessary computations.

"We need good navigation solutions more than hot showers."

"Wasn't asking for me. Have you smelled yourself lately? That leather outfit needs a good hosing down, as does your hair. You stink of smoke and bad decisions." They'd managed to retreat from their last encounter only after paying a huge fine, leaving instantly without taking on supplies or recharging their life support systems. The mercenary unit had taken their instructions and left. "Besides, the navigator can do calculations with no strain on the systems."

"I'm not her."

"Sadly, yes. Should have left you behind." Ana clicked the microphone off as Gavin arrived with a weapons case and unloaded the contents on the table. He and Gavin had arranged to strip and clean the crew weapons. "Those for me?" He sniffed. "I love the smell of gun oil."

Gavin lined up the revolvers on a white cloth. "Both of us. Need to service them. And they need more than oil."

Dena made several rude comments on the intercom about centurions who smelled so bad, even pressure washes wouldn't help. Ana suggested Dena drown herself in perfume, or just drown, and told her Lee was in her bunk.

Rocky retrieved his ball and returned it to Ana's outstretched hand. Ana bounced it off the overhead, stripped the first revolver and looked at the course plot on the lounge screen. "And if Scruggs is with you, tell her I want to talk to her."

Ana had spoken to Scruggs earlier about her failure with the other troops. "He didn't buy your story, you didn't sell it. That voice break wasn't good. You've never wavered before. What happened?"

"I got worried, Centurion," Scruggs said.

"Scared?"

"Not for myself, but for the others. What if something went wrong?"

"They'd die."

"Yes." Scruggs nodded. "I mean, I know that can happen to me, but I didn't realize the others, I mean, I didn't think…"

"Being personally brave is one thing," Ana said. "Being brave for others is different."

"If I did something wrong, one of my friends might die."

"Even if you do everything right, all your friends can die. Things happen. Ever think of that?"

Scruggs's eyes widened. "No."

"Better work on that. Things happen. I won't always be here. And you need to learn that fighting through isn't always the way to go. You can't lose your confidence in a crisis, whatever sort it is."

"I'm sorry, Centurion, it won't happen again."

"Yes it will." Ana sighed. "Do better next time."

Scruggs had slunk off.

After reporting back to the frigate covering the

scouting ships, they'd received fresh orders from Tribune Devin to transit to the Ast system and help pick up some troops for occupation duties. Ana pushed Lee and Dirk to assign as much work on the girls as possible, while he assisted Gavin with weapons maintenance.

Lee stopped by on her way to the bridge. "Did I hear Dena looking for me?"

"Problems with the jump?" Ana asked.

"Let's find out." Lee called the bridge on the intercom. "Dena? Is there a problem up there?"

"No, the board is green. But could you come up?"

"Whatever for?"

"We may have a problem...with our course."

Ana grinned at Lee. Finally, they noticed. *Much longer and I would have to step in. Let's see how they deal with it.*

Lee nodded. "Well, I'm sure you'll figure it out. Besides, I'm busy right now."

Dena's voice came back. "Uh, how busy are you, Lee?"

"Very busy. Very, very busy. Super-duper very duper busy." Lee grabbed Rocky's ball from Ana and tossed it. "Can this wait, say, half a shift?"

"I guess so."

"Good. See you later. Lee out." Lee clicked off the intercom and nodded to Ana.

Ana nodded back. *I asked her to let them figure it out. Dena's smarter than she acts. They both just need experience.*

An array of gun parts cluttered the lounge table. Gavin and Ana handed pieces back and forth. Ana had disassembled their personal arms, including the revolvers, and was showing the wear patterns to Gavin.

"There's a surprising amount of corrosion." Ana handed Gavin a barrel. "See? Even when I clean every day, look at the pitting. And some of these springs are almost gone. The pull is a lot looser than it should be."

"I can fix this," Gavin said. "I've got the materials in the shop. But do you have specifications for how strong it's supposed to be? I'll need to know what type of alloy to use."

"I don't have specs, no," Ana admitted. "I suppose you could take apart one of the other revolvers and measure it somehow?"

"I can do that," Gavin said. "I've got some testing equipment in the shop."

"Metallurgical testing equipment? On a starship?"

"Gavin set that up," Lee interjected. "The last few places we've been, he's been buying all sorts of odd parts and equipment. He's got a complete gunsmithing shop in there."

Gavin and Ana delved into a technical discussion about metallurgy, firing pins, and firearms in general. Lee sipped her drink and threw Rocky's ball. She was off-watch, her share of the chores finished, and their navigation path was straightforward—except for one little bump that Dena and Scruggs had just noticed.

A quarter shift later, Ana and Gavin had laid out a schedule for weapon repairs. They'd lost several firearms during their last planetary expedition, and of the ones that returned, some were damaged, others were filthy, and others worn out. Most tramp freighters had a shotgun and two revolvers in the ship's locker. The *Heart's Desire* had three dozen different common firearms clipped in there and sixteen crates of diverse ammunition, belts, holsters, backpacks, tents, and a worrying amount of grenades. Plus Ana's special crates that he reserved for 'ship-wide area defense.'

Jove alone knew what was hidden away in crew

cabins. I could probably equip an entire Marine platoon just from my closet. If I cared about Marines.

"With our spares," Gavin waved his comm, "and some of the random pieces I picked up, if I machine a few things, I can bring us up to standard. What do we really need?"

Ana held up a finger. "Boarding shotguns for everybody."

"Yes."

Ana held up two fingers. "And two spares, in case."

"Sure."

Three fingers. "Twelve regular revolvers. Two for everyone."

Gavin made a note. "Need more holsters for those. Twin holsters."

"Holsters we've got. There's a crate in back. And six mini-revolvers. For the girls."

"They don't like being called girls."

"Don't care what they like. I can call them kids instead."

"They'll like that even less."

"Kids it is." Ana tapped another finger. "Couple of scoped rifles. Couple of carbines. Three submachine guns. Or at least machine pistols."

"Only you and Scruggs can hit anything with a rifle, scoped or not."

"I saw you shooting some pigs previously."

"Luck. I'm not as good as you."

"Nobody is. And the navigator can shoot. I've seen her with long arms. She looked surprisingly comfortable with the automatic weapons."

"Must be a Jovian thing. I think the Marines teach them." Gavin made another note.

"Dena's good with hand weapons at short range. But she never takes a long gun."

Gavin opened one of the revolver cylinders and

checked the spin. "She's used to lighter weapons. She jerks."

"Scruggs doesn't."

"You taught Scruggs. Dena had to learn herself."

Ana tapped his own comm and made a note. "I need to get Dena to practice with those."

"On your own time, not mine." Gavin made another note. "You have those other crates back there..."

"The automatic mortar, yes. Scruggs can use that. The rocket launchers, of course. Don't worry about those, I take good care of them." Ana tilted his head. "I should do some practice with that. Want to learn how to fire a mortar?"

Gavin raised his eyebrows. "What makes you think I don't know already?"

Ana laughed. "Good point. You lie about everything else. Why not this? Navigator." Ana turned. "Have you ever fired an anti-tank rocket?"

"Not an anti-tank rocket, no." Lee said. "And it's amazing how well you two get along when you're talking about something technical."

Gavin shrugged. "I don't have to like him to appreciate that he knows a lot about firearms. He should—at his advanced age."

"Thanks, punk," Ana said. "I'm glad that some of the younger generation, instead of wasting all their time on women and beer, actually learn useful skills like metallurgy."

"Metallurgy?" Gavin snorted. "That's nothing. What about engineering? Systems repair? Fusion equipment maintenance? Computer skills?"

"Yeah, yeah," Ana replied. "But none of those help me with shooting people."

"Speaking of people getting along," Gavin said, "I would have expected Scruggs or Dena to come down at some point to grab their mid-rats."

"What could they be talking about up there for hours?" Ana wondered. "And miss eating. Rumbling young stomachs should remind them."

"They made a navigation error," Lee said. "We're going the wrong direction."

"We're not heading for the station?" Ana asked.

"Oh, we're heading for *a* station," Lee clarified. "But they thought we were heading for a different station. When I checked their plan for the system, they had us arriving at the planetary station to refuel, top up on supplies, spend a shift exploring, and then head out to the jump limit. The problem is, with the new orders, that station isn't the one we need to be at."

"And you know this how?" Gavin asked.

"Because I'm the navigator, because I always double check, and because Dirk told me the agent we're meeting will be out at the belt station. We're supposed to go there and be visible and they'll approach us."

Dirk had gotten the instructions from Tribune Devin. Go to Ast System, meet their agent, and arrange the transport of a battalion of auxiliary troops. "And he told Dena to make sure they went to 'the station.' They were using an outdated version of the sailing directions, and didn't ask me to be specific. There used to be a refueling station above the planet, but it's closed now. All those services have been moved to the belt station on the far side of the system."

"Where does that leave us?" Ana asked.

"We're on a least-time course to the planet—Ast-1-D. We'll reach it in three shifts. But if we need to get to the belt station, it'll take another six shifts and some fairly radical course corrections."

Ast System was unremarkable. The only reason for their presence was its location on the jump route—one of the planets between Tribune

Devin's fleet and the New Malaya fleet base. Devin planned to scout for ways to slip a fleet past any picket ships and approach the Malaya system undetected.

"Is this bad?"

"Nope." Lee shook her head. "More time to get scans. And so far, this route looks like a strong candidate for bringing a fleet through. There's a gas giant for refueling beyond the jump limit, we haven't seen any regular Imperial warships, and everything looks peaceful."

"Another step closer to New Malaya," Ana said.

"And closer to meeting Devin's troop carriers," Lee said. "And the Core. Eventually."

"Figured it out yet?" Lee asked Scruggs and Dena when they finally entered the lounge.

Ana had gone up to watch the board, and Gavin was in engineering machining springs.

"Yes," Scruggs admitted. "Didn't read the notes. We booked us to planetary orbit. Now we're heading to the asteroid station, not the planet."

"Is this going to be a problem?"

"No. It'll work. But I'll admit, it scared me at first," Scruggs said. "I worried we'd made a huge mistake."

"Are we going to starve?" Lee asked. "Or did you not check?"

Scruggs shook her head. "We've got supplies for months, and as long as we've got fuel, life support will keep running. We're fine for weeks, at least."

"Twenty-three point two days," Dena corrected. "I logged it this morning." Dena was in charge of keeping records.

"All right," Lee said, "so we're not landing on the planet. Tell me what I need to know about this asteroid station, since it wasn't in the course briefing you gave earlier."

"It's big-ish," Scruggs replied. "There's a mine, a smelter, and a station. The station's stuck on the surface of the asteroid, so there's no real spaceport. You land near the main entrance and walk in."

"No docks?"

"A truss for the mining ships. No information on docking there. Sailing direction says to ask control when you land."

"What type of services does it have for merchants like us? Does it make sense that a tramp-freighter like we're supposed to be would port there, or are we going to attract notice?"

Scruggs paused to bring up a map. "Well, the first thing we'll see when we walk in? A bar. Then a casino, a restaurant, another bar—"

"Brothel," Dena said.

"You don't know that."

"The menu is online. It's called the Venus bar, and the online menu says drinks are triple the price of the other places."

"Well, we won't be going there," Scruggs said.

"Why not?" Dena asked. "Somebody might buy us expensive drinks."

"Somebody might ask us to, well…"

"Don't worry, Baby Marine." Dena patted Scruggs's shoulder. "I'll protect you. Tell you what, we'll tell them you and I are together. A couple."

"Good." Scruggs's shoulders sagged. "That will make them go away."

"Nope." Dena shook her head. "That will make them buy us even more drinks. We'll drink all night for free."

"But…" Scruggs said. "Really? They'll…"

Dena bit her lip and nodded.

Scruggs shook her head. "I don't understand people."

Lee chimed in. "That's pretty evident. Back to the briefing. After the entertainment district, what else?"

"Well, ship supplies and a bunch of maintenance companies. Beyond that, the main part of the station, which has regular merchants. Clothes, tools, kitchen goods type of things."

"Plenty of reasons for a crew on shore leave to be wandering there, then."

"Right." Scruggs nodded. "Doesn't seem like many options for the merchants, though. I only found one gun shop."

"And only a single clothing store," Dena said. "I mean, what's a girl to do?"

Lee grinned. "Stop shopping with the centurion on leave for one thing. There's usually only one of each kind of shop in a place this small. The existing merchants don't like competition. They form a guild, and the guild controls licensing. If you want to sell something, you need to apply for a license. And the guild doesn't give out multiple licenses for the same product or service."

"Kind of makes sense," Dena said.

"It works on corporate or small stations," Lee agreed. "It also means there's not much worthwhile for us to buy here. Everything is overpriced. It'd be worse if there wasn't a planet in the system. With the planet nearby, anybody who needs something can hop on a shuttle or get a friend to go pick it up. That keeps things manageable and prevents too much price gouging on the asteroid."

"Fair enough," Dena said. "Um, do we still need to go to the planet and check things out for the Tribune?"

"The planet doesn't matter," Lee said. "Dirk says we meet the agent at the outer station. Other than that, we need to get a feel for the system—what kind of weapon systems are here, if any. So far, we haven't picked up any beacons or seen anything resembling a warship. We'll get a better look at the station when we land, but we don't see anything military there so far. If there aren't defense systems this far out, there won't be anything on the planet either."

"Stations are easier to attack," Dena pointed out. "Pirates could target this place. What's stopping them?"

"Nothing," Lee replied. "But let's say pirates come in, land, and steal a bunch of stuff. Then what? They'd need a planet nearby to sell it, and there's nothing close enough. This is Sarawak sector, not the Verge, and the Empire keeps a solid presence."

"The only thing stopping piracy is somewhere to sell things?" Dena asked.

"Piracy is all about economics, in the end." Lee said. "Like most things."

"All right, ops, we're down now," Dirk said, shutting off the thrusters. *Heart's Desire* tilted as the landing legs settled into the dust. "What do you want to know now?"

"Huh, snippy type, aren't we?" the voice on the other end replied. "All right, you're cleared into the station. How many are you?"

"Not snippy," Dirk said. "Just confused. I don't understand why you wouldn't let us dock on the truss and use the airlocks there."

"You don't understand why we wouldn't let you dock on the truss, huh?" The voice chuckled. "Well, take a look out your window and see what's happening up there."

Dirk swapped his cameras to check the truss. Runabouts loaded with ore docked and fed crushed rock into grinders. A conveyor belt moved the crushed ore to a stage-one processing mill. Lights flashed near the truss, to the right of the main mine building. "You running your solar distillation plant?" Dirk asked.

"Twenty-four seven," the voice said. "And we're not stopping it for some tramp freighter. We've got an ore carrier arriving in eight shifts. All the ore containers need to be prepped and lined up for pickup. And most importantly—we don't care what you think. That's where you're parking. You don't like it? Find another station."

"I can see why you don't get many visitors," Dirk muttered. "With that attitude."

"Son," the voice replied, "even if we had the best attitude, we wouldn't get visitors. The only reason people come here is that they need something. No point wasting good humor on folks who have no choice but to deal with us."

"Understood," Dirk said. "What are the rules?"

"We're sending you a document. Read it. But the gist is: no firearms, no edged weapons, no trouble. You pay a thousand-credit deposit at the station office. Before you leave, we'll make sure you've paid all your bills. If you have, you get the deposit back. If not, we keep what we need. Simple."

"A thousand credits? That's a steep deposit," Dirk said.

"Like I said—find another station if you don't like it."

Dirk cut the comms. "Everybody hear that?"

"Yeah," Ana replied.

"I'm not thrilled about leaving the ship unguarded. Centurion, what's your take?"

"No," Ana said. "We're not all going in at once. We'll leave enough people on board to defend the ship. I don't trust these people any farther than I can throw them."

"That's what I was thinking," Dirk agreed. "All

right, Centurion. We're grounded. What's your plan?"

"Two groups of three," Ana said. "I'll lead one group, Scruggs will lead the other. When we're on the ship, we keep our full weapons at hand in case someone tries to sneak on board. How many weapons shops in the market?"

"Only one, Centurion," Scruggs said.

"Hardly worth visiting, then. And we can't have both the captain and navigator in the same group. If someone gets snatched, we'll need enough people to pilot the ship. Pilot, you'll stay with me. The navigator will go with Scruggs. Gavin, Dena, where do you want to go?"

"I'll go with Scruggs," Dena said.

"Huh," Ana said. "Girls and boys—interesting division. Well, at least you can get into gender-appropriate trouble without a disapproving audience."

"I can't imagine disapproving of anything you've done, Centurion," Scruggs said.

"Clearly, I haven't been trying hard enough." Ana smirked. "I could give you a list. I'm sure you'd disapprove of some of it."

"I've watched you drag a man's guts out with a hook and blow up a platoon of soldiers with a mortar shell," Scruggs said.

"True," Ana said. "What about you, Cadet Scruggs? Planning anything Dena would disapprove of?"

Dena laughed. "I saw her run people down with construction equipment, try to kill someone with a can of beans, steal a bunch of trucks, break into an office, blow up a tank with a rocket, and set some buildings on fire. What's left to disapprove of?"

"No fair!" Scruggs shook her head. "The office thing was a job!"

"Sure."

"And the can of beans saved Hernandez and Weeks."

"Uh-huh."

"We needed the trucks to get away!"

"Um-humm."

Scruggs shook her head, then smiled. "I am kind of proud of the tank, though, except it wasn't a tank, it was—"

"A wheeled self-propelled casemated tank-destroyer, I know. You told us. Repeatedly." Dena shrugged. "Still looks like a tank to me."

"All right," Ana said. "Enough self-congratulation. Let's suit up."

Scruggs, Dena, and Lee donned their skinsuits, sturdy walking boots for traversing the rocky surface, stained coveralls, and crowded utility belts.

"You can't take that," Dena said, pointing at Scruggs's holstered revolver.

"Oh. Right," Scruggs said, unbuckling it.

"Actually," Lee interrupted, "take it. Strap it in and hand it over when they ask for weapons. Use an older holster and a gun you don't mind losing."

"I'll take one of the ship guns," Scruggs said. "Not one of mine."

"Good. They'll focus on what's visible and won't look for anything you've hidden in your boot," Lee said.

"Good point," Scruggs said, checking her boot knife.

Dena adjusted her utility belt, her slingshot hanging openly. She shrugged when Scruggs pointed at it. "People always think it's just some weird tool," Dena said.

"Exactly," Lee said. She hefted a small med kit and a repair kit.

"What's the repair kit for?" Dena asked.

Lee pulled out a wrench. "Just in case. I don't enjoy hitting people with it, but I'll do it if I have to." She hefted the wrench. "And given the way things are going for us, we might need to crack a few heads. I want it in case." She spun the wrench again. "Just in case."

Chapter 28

"Right." Lee removed her helmet and clipped it to her harness, then tried to wipe the dust off her gloves. They'd had to hop along the asteroid's surface, through clouds of pulverized grey rock from the smelter. "First, we go and have a drink. We expect the contact to find us. We'll start in the bar, then head to the restaurant for dinner, and afterward, come back to the bar. That'll give them plenty of time to spot us."

"I'm not going anywhere looking like this," Dena said, dragging her fingers through her hair.

"You look fine."

"Scruggs, do I look fine?"

"If you like the covered in gray dust look," Scruggs said. She leaned forward and spat. "It's even in the air. Tastes like extra-gritty baking soda."

"Keep your helmet on," Lee said.

In the airlock, they had been blasted by a high-speed fan meant to clean off surface dust. The fan blew the dust not only off their suits but into Dena's carefully styled hair.

"No way I'm going to sit in a bar full of attractive men and let them see me like this," Dena said. "I look like a greasy river otter."

"Some men like that. And how do you know they'll be attractive?"

"For weeks, I haven't seen any men other than Centurion, the engineer and the greasy Navy guy. Everyone here's attractive to me."

"The pilot's not greasy," Lee said. "He keeps very clean."

"I didn't mean physical cleanliness—never mind. The point is, I'm not ruining my chance of a man hitting on me because I didn't have time to fix my hair."

"You sure they'll find you attractive?" Scruggs

asked.

Dena spun the airlock handle and stepped through. "We're on a mining station, and men outnumber women five to one. I'll be attractive to somebody."

"But if the men find you attractive, even with your hair—"

"What will the women think?" Dena asked.

"You're interested in the men…"

"Yes. But I don't want to give the women the satisfaction of sneering at me."

"I don't understand people," Scruggs said.

"People will teach you, don't worry," Dena said.

A bleak corridor stretched ahead. Metal doors framed by scuffed windows lined each side. The floor and ceiling were unpainted metal gratings, slathered with dust. Pipes and cable raceways festooned the walls. Two of the windows were covered with plastic. Somebody with more optimism than patience had painted a red and blue checkerboard pattern on one wall, but stopped after six rows.

Scruggs pointed at the red-painted closet next to the airlock, empty except for a broken axe-handle. "Hope we don't have to fight a fire." The extinguishers and rescue tools were missing.

"Place like this, they would seal the locks and vent the pod," Lee said. "And us along with it."

Dena leaned on the door lever. "If they can even get the doors closed." It took Scruggs helping before they got the green light.

The first door to the left was propped open, the words 'station security' scrawled on it. They poked their heads in, handed over their fake IDs for registration, and paid the required deposit. The clerk, a woman, looked them over critically. "What happened to you? You like rolling in the dust?"

"Where can I get my hair done?" Dena asked.

"You know, fixed up?"

The woman raised an eyebrow. "Why do you want to do that?"

"There's going to be a lot of men here, right?" Dena said.

"Girl," the clerk replied, "the men are not going to be looking at your hair. Unzip your skinsuit."

"Good point." Dena unzipped her coveralls. "You too, Scruggs."

The clerk gave Scruggs a once-over. "She doesn't even need to do that." Then she looked at Lee. "Huh. We don't get many Jovians here."

"Oh?" Lee asked.

"Not normally. They usually stick to the more Imperial-friendly stations."

"We are in the Empire, aren't we?" Lee asked.

"That we are," the clerk said, handing back their IDs. "Unfortunately. Deposit's down. You're all set. We keep track of everything."

"Understood." Dena fiddled with her hair.

"All right," Lee said. "Let's go get a drink."

The first section of wall was covered with commercial notices. They headed for the closest bar. The next section of the wall was all community notices. "Volleyball on Tuesday, start of third shift." Scruggs peered at the display. "And a note that the station medical doesn't cover injuries from fights."

"Full contact volleyball. My kind of game." Dena pointed at the door. "I think this is the bar."

"Because the door has the word 'bar' written on it?" Scruggs asked.

Dena put on her suit gloves before opening the door. "Yes. And because it smells like vomit."

Lee's feet stuck to the floor as she stepped to a table. *Do they clean in here, or just blow more dust on top of the grime? Wonder how much gets in the beer.*

The waitress strode over. "Drinks? Five-credit minimum."

"Five-credit minimum?" Dena repeated. "Fine. What do we get for five credits?"

"You can have beer."

"I'd like some Basic, please," Scruggs said. "How much is that?"

"Basic? After coming off a ship?"

"Yes, please."

"Five credits."

"That seems excessive."

"That's the price," the waitress said. "You want it or not?"

"Three beers," Dena interjected. "One for each of us."

"Good enough," the waitress said.

"Dena," Scruggs whispered, "I don't like beer."

"Then don't drink it."

"But I don't want it to go to waste."

"Trust me, Scruggs." Dena smirked. "It's not going to go to waste. Not while I'm here."

A comm unit blinked behind the bar. The bartender interrupted pouring to take the call, then called the waitress over. She leaned in, listening to someone, then turned to glare at the three women. "I understand," she said into the comm.

She returned, slamming three beers down hard enough to splash the liquid onto the table.

"Hey!" Dena exclaimed. "Watch it!"

"Fifteen credits," the waitress snapped. "Either from you or out of your station deposit."

"We'll pay." Dena reached for her credit chip. "Can we run a tab?"

"Pay now," the waitress demanded, extending a reader.

"What about the tab?"

"No tabs. These are your last drinks."

"Huh?" Dena said. "We just got here."

Imperial Legionary

"Doesn't matter. Drink up and go."

"You don't want to sell us more beer? We haven't caused any problems," Dena protested.

"Well, didn't know you had a Jovian with you. We don't like Imperial killers here. There's your beer. Thumb here."

"I don't like the way we're being treated."

"Or don't thumb." The woman took the comm back. "We'll take it off your station tab anyway." She walked away.

The three crew members exchanged glances.

"Lee, have you been here before?" Dena asked.

"No," Lee replied.

"I thought Jovians were fine in the Empire."

"They are. We are. I am. I don't understand it." Lee frowned

"Well, let's move along, then," Dena said. "What's the plan? Go to the restaurant next?"

"Yes," Lee said. "That's where we'll go."

"Good." Dena eyed the drinks in front of her. "Of course, there's no need for these to go to waste, is there?"

Ten minutes later, a scowling Lee, a bewildered Scruggs, and a belching Dena pushed open the crash doors to the next pod. It differed only in the checkered paint job being black and yellow, and having half as many ceiling lights lit. They yanked open a door labeled 'Bob's Burgers.' Another set of fans blasted them as they walked in, kicking the ever present dust off their feet.

The hostess blocked the entrance. "Sorry, we're closed."

"Closed?" Dena asked. "The station map says you're open 'til next shift."

"Station map's wrong. We're closed."

"We checked when we came in." Dena stretched to look behind the hostess. "And you've got a dozen customers."

"Yeah, we just closed. Just this minute. They're finishing up and then they're going home."

A waiter delivered an order to four men in coveralls in the corner. Dena pointed. "What about them over there?"

The hostess shook her head. "Sorry, no room."

"Gotcha." Dena beamed a grin. "Thanks so much for your help. Anywhere else in here we can get some food?"

"You might try Chuck's."

"Where's Chuck's?"

"End of the hall. Left, down through two pods, right, second pod." The hostess crossed her arms and waited.

Lee draped her arms around the women. "It's okay. We're not that hungry."

"I'm hungry," Scruggs said.

"Not now, Sister Scruggs." Lee led them out and into the next pod.

Dena belched the whole way. "What did they put in that beer?"

"Don't ask questions you don't want to know the answer to," Lee said. The walk took them into the heart of the station, past darkened shipping offices and shops. Each shop had a table full of items outside, a comm reader, and a circle split into three equal parts. One part was filled in to show opening hours—first, second, or third shift.

Dena pointed at a counter covered with liquid tooth cleaner, shower perfume, and industrial cleaning soap. "Anybody need some cleaning sundries? Ripe for the taking."

Lee jerked her head at the ceiling. "Cameras. I'll bet security is watching us the whole way."

"But why leave them outside? It's like they want people to take them."

"They do," Lee said. "Three different shifts on station, but they don't want to staff stores all the time. If you work night shift and don't want to wait for the shop to open, just take what you need and get it to read your comm. They charge your account. That's why the big deposit. In case you try to be sneaky, they get you on the way out."

"Overcharge you on the way out, you mean," Dena said.

"Good business," Scruggs said. "You can hardly complain being overcharged for something you were trying to steal."

Dena laughed. "I forget sometimes that you're a rich business woman. This is how you take advantage of the plebes, right?"

Lee looked over her shoulder. "If you don't steal things, then it's not a problem."

"Makes sense," Dena said. "From now on, I'm going to limit my stealing to other women's boyfriends."

The restaurant, grandiosely named 'Auberge Charles V,' aka 'Chuck's,' had an actual wooden door, a fancy yellow light set in an iron frame adjacent, and gold lettering on its frosted glass window.

Dena shook her head. "This will cost a lot more than five credits for a beer."

"You're right," Lee said. "But we need to do something. Be somewhere so that our contact can find us."

The three women marched in. A tall, dapper man stood behind the counter. He wore an actual suit, with a tie. If he had on a skinsuit, it was hidden under his clothes.

"Party of three? For dinner?"

"That's us," Dena said. "We tried the other place, but they're closed. Funny that, they were open when we landed."

"Sometimes they close on short notice," the

man said, smiling faintly. "Follow me."

He led them to a table and seated them. Only one other group—a pair of well-dressed couples, two women and two men—were inside. They had a bottle of wine on their table.

"A glass bottle. That costs a lot to lift out of gravity. And that's an expensive wine."

"How do you know?" Dena asked.

"I've seen the Tribune drink it before," Lee explained.

"It's pricey and pretentious, like he is."

"You don't know the Tribune."

"I wouldn't mind knowing him. He's good-looking. And his clothes are snazzy. Especially those togas. Wonder what he wears under them?"

"He's twice your age," Lee said.

"I know. Think of all the things he's learned." Dena smiled.

"Why is everybody at that table staring at us?" Scruggs tilted her head. The patrons at the far table glared at them.

Dena flipped her hair. "They're attracted to the dusty look."

The other diners were dressed for a party. The men wore jackets over loose, embroidered blouses, and the women had similar outfits, all in solid colors. Both had beads woven into collars and cuffs. They went silent when the crew entered, but now leaned in and conversed in low voices.

The waiter handed them menus. "I'm afraid we're out of the specials, but we do have the prix fixe."

"The price is fixed?" Dena asked. "The price is fixed to what?"

"It's a set menu," Lee said. "You don't get to pick what you want. They serve what they have."

"We're getting leftovers?" Dena asked.

The waiter suppressed a snort. "Will the three

of you have that?"

"We'd like to see the menus," Dena said.

"We're all out of everything else."

"I understand," Lee said.

"I don't," Scruggs muttered.

"Not now, Sister Scruggs. Not now," Lee said, exhaling. "All right. I see what's happening here. We'll take three."

"And a bottle of wine," the waiter added.

"Do we have to?" Lee asked.

"Yes. Really, you do."

"Fine. The specials and the wine." He disappeared into the back.

"What's going on?" Scruggs asked. "Why is everyone so mean?"

"I don't get this." Lee shook her head. "Most people are happy enough to take your money, but they want you to come back. These folks are making sure that we spend some, but never come back." *Which means they want something else to happen. Where is that contact? I haven't seen any troops at all.*

Dena had kept her menu. "Holy expensive bear livers. Look at these prices."

"No food here is worth that," Scruggs said. "We're being robbed."

"Doesn't make sense. There's others on our ship. They know that. A little less hostility, and they'd get more cash. Something's up."

The waiter returned to the other table, spoke briefly, and the other four diners got up. They straightened their jackets, took a final sip of wine, and left the restaurant. As they passed, the men flicked their thumbs, and the women swept their fingers under their chins.

"Dena, do you know what that means?" Scruggs whispered.

"It's not important," Lee replied. "But I don't think we should eat here. Who knows what they'll put in the food."

The waiter reappeared. "The food will be here in sixty minutes."

"Sixty minutes?" Lee asked. "We're the only people here!"

"That's right. It takes time to produce quality," the waiter said.

"I don't think we're hungry now," Lee said.

"All right," the waiter replied indifferently. "We're still going to charge you."

"Of course you are," Lee muttered. "Let's go, ladies."

"But I want to stay for dinner," Scruggs said. "I'm hungry."

"You don't want to eat what they're going to give us," Lee said, pulling her up.

The three women left the restaurant, and walked down the corridor.

"Too quiet," Lee said. "Where did they go? We're not that far behind them."

"We haven't seen anybody in the corridors since we got here," Dena said. "It's third shift, but there should still be people up. And somebody shut off half the lights since we went in."

The three of them headed back to the entrance. As they approached the main corridor, a group of four people stepped out of the shadows. It was the couples from earlier.

"Uh-oh," Lee muttered.

"Listen, you Imperial freighter scum," a green-shirted man said. "We've had enough of your kind here."

"We were just leaving," Lee said.

"Not so brave without your troops around, are you?" Green Shirt asked.

"Dena," Scruggs whispered, "the woman on the left, red blouse, is holding a shock stick behind her right leg. The man behind has a knife. I can take them, but I can't see your side. They might have anything."

Dena moved right and fingered her slingshot. "I don't see any weapons. Lee? Your play here."

"No violence if we can avoid it." Lee put her hand on the wrench on her belt. "We need to meet our contact, not start a brawl. Don't draw any weapons, or we'll be blamed for this."

The restaurant door clanked behind Scruggs. She turned. The waiter and the cook stepped out. Both were carrying frying pans. "Dena. Contact rear."

Dena glanced back. "Beaver crap. And all I wanted was a beer."

"New plan," Lee said. "We need to get out of here. Back to the ship. Fast."

"Right," Scruggs said. "Here's what we do." She explained her idea.

"Got it," Lee said.

"Super-duper," Dena said.

Scruggs nodded. "Let's do it."

The three women turned their backs to the couple in the main corridor and charged down the hallway.

"Yaaag!" Scruggs screamed as she sprinted.

Lee cursed. *Too much noise. All I wanted was a quiet meeting.*

Scruggs jumped up and shoved off the wall.

The cook stabbed with the pan like he would with a sword. And missed. Lee grinned. *Sister Scruggs was right. He can't stab with a pot, and he can't swing if he doesn't have room. They're not used to fighting. Not like Scruggs and Dena are.*

Dena, two steps behind her, did the same on her side.

Scruggs's man swung his pan but didn't connect. She grabbed an overhead pipe, pivoted, and thumped her legs into his chest, knocking him down. The second man managed to clip Dena's leg before she crashed into him. Momentum sent him sprawling.

Scruggs dropped then kicked her man again, sending his pan rolling. Lee scooped it up, and then spun and brandished it at the couples down the corridor. The two couples froze at the unexpected level of resistance.

Lee glanced back. The man Scruggs had struck wasn't moving. The other scrambled up and swung at her. He fell flat when Dena swept his legs out from under him. Scruggs stepped on his arm, grabbed his wrist, and twisted hard, breaking it.

Lee returned her attention to the couples, waving her frying pan menacingly. *Two out of the fight already. Centurion would be proud of his girl.*

Dena stepped up next to Lee. She'd retrieved the other pan.

The woman on the left showed her shock stick. "Any farther, Dusty, and we'll zap you," she threatened.

"Don't call me Dusty," Dena said.

Lee handed her pan to Scruggs and held her hands wide. "Look, we don't want any trouble—any more trouble. We only want to get back to our ship."

"Get him, Sua! Give it to her!" The man behind her pulled out a knife. "Zap her!"

"You're not zapping anyone," Dena held up her pan. "Unless you want a clank to the head first."

"We've had enough of your Imperial Jovian types here," the woman with the shock stick snarled.

Dena cocked her arm, readying her pan. "Lee, keep them busy."

"What have you got against Jovians?" Lee yelled. "We're people like you! Normal people!"

"No, you're not!" the woman shouted. "You'll

never be—"

Dena threw the frying pan. It hit the woman squarely on the forehead, sending her crumpling to the ground. When she hit, the shock stick triggered, zapping her.

"That's gotta hurt," Scruggs said.

Dena grabbed her nose. "Smells like burning chicken. Going to leave a mark."

The man with the knife screamed, "You hurt Sua! You hurt Sua!" He advanced down the hall.

Scruggs rushed to meet him. "Centurion always warned me about bringing a knife to a gunfight. And here I am, bringing a pan to a knife fight."

The man lunged at her. Scruggs waited until the knife came close, then swung.

CRUNCH.

The man jumped back. "Ha! That didn't even hurt."

"Wasn't supposed to," Scruggs said.

It couldn't have been a very good knife—Scruggs's slam with the frying pan had snapped the blade clean off. Instead of a knife, he now held a half-inch piece of metal. It might scratch someone if he jabbed it into their chest, but it wouldn't puncture anything.

"Crap," the man muttered, staring at the broken knife. Then he turned and ran. His friends followed.

Scruggs charged. "Dena, Lee, follow me!" Scruggs hopped over the stunned woman and chased. Her quarry ducked right, then left, darting down the corridor.

Dena grabbed the frying pan. "Lee, get the shock stick!" Lee was already on her comm, speaking with the ship and explaining the situation. She nodded, scooped it up, and followed.

Scruggs continued her pursuit of the fleeing assailants, screaming and waving the frying pan above her head like a war banner. At the next intersection, the couple split right, the broken-knife man left.

"Scruggs! Follow the couple! Head for the airlock," Lee yelled.

Once around the corner, the man and woman ducked into a side room, slamming the hatch behind them.

Scruggs reached the door and started banging on it with the pan.

Dena and Lee caught up five seconds later. "Scruggs! Enough," Lee snapped. "You won't get in."

"I know," Scruggs said, still hammering the door. "But I'm trying to suppress them while we figure out what's going on!"

"I don't think we're going to meet our contact tonight," Lee said. "We need to retreat back to the ship."

"They can't get out without us seeing them," Scruggs protested.

"No," Lee corrected, "but they can make a radio call."

"Right." Scruggs sighed. "Well, as Centurion always says, 'In the face of superior opposition, retreat.' So, let's retreat."

The three of them jogged to the airlock. A few people peeked out from nearby doors but quickly slammed them shut as the women jogged past.

They zigzagged through corridors back toward the airlock, passing more closed doors. They turned left, then right. It was now a straight shot ahead to the airlock at the end of the next pod.

Scruggs and Dena slowed to a jog. They exchanged grins, then started laughing. "You hurt Sua!" Dena warbled, and Scruggs giggled even more.

Lee rolled her eyes. "Focus, children! Focus!"

Pilot told me we need to treat her like a potential officer. She's got a long way to go.

As they approached the airlock, the door clanged open, and three short, fair-haired men stepped out. They wore identical skinsuits, draped with military utility belts. The two in the front carried shotguns, while the rear man had a sidearm.

"Jove," Scruggs muttered, skidding to a stop. "Lee, Dena, turn around. The other way!"

The three of them turned, but Bob's Burgers had reopened. Streaming out of its door was a crowd of a dozen miners, armed with hammers, a wrench, and even a sword.

"Outstanding," Scruggs said, surveying the situation. "But not going the way I expected."

She glanced back at the men with the shotguns, who were now pointing their weapons at them.

"I wonder," Scruggs said, "if we'll get our deposit back."

Chapter 29

Two men in patched skinsuits brandished shotguns at Scruggs. "Down." The third, shorter, but with more patches on his suit, waved. "Make down!"

She dropped her shock stick and held up her hands. "Look, we don't want any trouble. "

The two men in front kept their guns pointed at them. The other waved again. "I said, make down! On the ground, now."

"What did we do?" Scruggs asked.

BAM!

Shotgun fire blasted into the ceiling above them.

"All right. Hold up." Scruggs dropped, and the others thudded next to her. She curled her fingers into the floor grill and looked up at their captors. *Normally, the Tribune plans better than this. Is this a setup? We're stuck on this stupid station. How do we get out of here?*

As soon as they were out of way, two shotguns fired. CLICKETY-BOOM. CLICKETY-BOOM.

Shotgun blasts ricocheted down the hallway. Lights shot out and cables sparked as they shorted. Metallic pings from ricocheting pellets filled the air as the pursuing crowd yelled, dove for cover, and then turned tail to flee.

Scruggs stuck her head into her arms. Burning sparks danced down from the ceiling, singeing her hair. Is this the unit we were supposed to meet? Those skinsuits could be uniforms. Those colored patches on the shoulders—rank markings? Those could be the Imperial markings the centurion showed me. Their saviors—still armed and ready—remained standing, their guns aimed past Scruggs's group.

"Move it, please! Let go!" the leader shouted.

"We can fit in the airlock. They'll come back soon. Move it!"

Scruggs shrugged, climbed upright, and slapped dust off her skinsuit.

"You good?" the man asked.

"Fine." Scruggs rubbed her ears. "That was loud."

"Into the airlock."

All six of them—Scruggs, Dena and Lee, plus their three rescuers, scrambled through the pod door and raced down the hall, past the now closed station office door. They piled into the airlock. Dena pulled the locking bar down and leaned on it for extra security, ensuring it was locked tight.

The leader moved to initiate the evacuation sequence. The rest slapped on helmets and gloves. The indicator light shifted from green to red. Air bled out, a faint hiss growing quieter as the pressure dropped.

CLANK. All the lights in the airlock died. The fans stopped spinning. The door wheel froze.

Scruggs and Dena activated their suit lights. The two men with shotguns stood there, seemingly confused. The leader continued to tug at the wheel. This airlock was double the usual size, with a primary door big enough to take two people. Like all airlocks, it opened inward, and that wasn't going to happen without dumping the internal pressure.

Dena touched helmets with Scruggs. "Why aren't they opening the emergency vent?"

"Same reason you wouldn't have done it two months ago. They don't know what they're doing." Scruggs came up on the all-suits channel. "Open the emergency release!"

The leader didn't hear. He kept straining at the wheel.

Scruggs pushed him aside and opened a panel, exposing another lever and a smaller wheel. She yanked that lever down, then pointed to the wheel. "There. Now you can crank the vent open."

The leader looked at Scruggs, shaking his head. She pointed at the wheel. He tapped the two men with the shotguns, gesturing for them to assist. They grasped the wheel together and started cranking it open

The smaller vent opened. Fog formed, then changed to frost when pressure and temperature dropped. The men continued cranking until the vent was fully open.

"You don't need to keep cranking, fellas," Dena said, tapping the lead man on the shoulder. She held up three fingers, then four, then two. She meant for them all to switch to channel 342.

Scruggs and Lee adjusted their suit radios. Dena repeated the gesture to the leader.

He shook his head.

Scruggs faced the leader so he could see her lips. "Three-four-two," she said.

The man shook his head.

"Is he stupid?" Dena asked. "He looks like a moon-struck field mouse."

"I don't know if he's stupid, but he's definitely confused," Scruggs replied. "We need to get the main door open."

Dena grabbed one of the men by the shoulders and guided his hand to the primary hatch wheel. He worked the mechanism. His friends joined. One minute later, the main hatch cracked open.

"Let's go," Scruggs said, waving at the men again and pointing to the channel number on her helmet.

The men shook their heads, grabbed their weapons, and marched out of the airlock. Their leader waved at Scruggs, Dena, and Lee to follow.

"Don't they have radios?" Scruggs asked.

"They should," Lee said, frowning. "Those are

standard merchant ship suits. Comm systems should be built in."

The men pointed toward the horizon. Lee gestured back toward the *Heart's Desire*.

"This is us," she said. "We need to go to the *Heart's Desire* to sort this out."

The leader shook his head and pointed to his own ship, making a silencing gesture before motioning for them to follow.

"Huh. Well, nothing ventured, nothing gained," Lee said with a shrug. "Let's go, ladies."

The six of them trudged across the asteroid's dusty surface, the fine powder billowing up and clinging to every crevice of their suits.

"This is one dusty asteroid," Scruggs muttered.

"Yeah," Dena agreed. "Worse than the plains in the dry season."

As they marched, Scruggs opened a line to their ship. "*Heart's Desire*. Scruggs reporting. Station crew assaulted us and we fought free. We've been rescued by a group of armed soldiers and we're going to their ship." She explained in more detail what happened, which ship they were approaching, and their status. "Standing by," Scruggs finished.

"Copy all that," the centurion's voice said. "Any injuries?"

"Dena got hit with a frying pan."

"Nothing a few beers won't fix," Dena said.

Ana grunted. "Won't be the first frying pan some angry wife hit her with."

"Shut up, Old Man," Dena said. "Make yourself useful. Tell us about this ship and these guys here."

Dirk had set up a camera pointed at the ship they were approaching. "I can't identify registration," Dirk said. "But it's a medium-sized freighter."

"How big is medium-sized?" Lee asked.

"A little bigger than us," Dirk replied. "Crew no

more than a dozen."

"I still don't understand why they shot at the crowd back there," Ana said.

"I don't understand why the crowd chased you to begin with," Dirk said. "Something's not as reported."

The short horizon had that cut off feeling that small diameter planetoids have. After a five-hundred-meter trek, only the top of the station and the ore truss were visible. The three men had no problem opening the airlock on their ship. It had a similar design to *Heart's Desire*, only bigger. It had three additional life support rings, and its containers appeared to be part of the ship's air volume.

"Look there," Lee pointed. "See those connections? The containers with cables attached?"

"Yeah," Dena said. "More containers. So what? We've got lots of containers too."

"Those are habitat containers. Extra life support and berthing. Plug them into ship power, and they give you everything you need: air, power, heat."

"Neat." Dena counted. "Half of their container load. Why do they have so many?"

"Extra life support means more people. Could be a troop ship?"

The men with them still weren't responding over the radio. Lee followed them into the airlock, noting, "We're going to have to clean off this dust. Otherwise, it'll get everywhere inside the ship."

As soon as the outer airlock door closed, one of the gunmen—Lee couldn't tell them apart—spun the locking mechanism and secured it. Then he turned and saluted the first man.

Scruggs grinned. Oh-ho. Military. Maybe these are the people we're looking for.

The man returned the salute and moved to the

inner door.

"Wait," Scruggs said. "We need to dust this off first."

She gestured at their suits, hoping to emphasize the importance of cleaning the dust off before entering the rest of the ship. But the man ignored her, punching the button to pressurize the airlock.

"Don't—" Lee started, but the door swung open as soon as the light turned green. Dust billowed around them. The man removed his helmet and stepped inside.

Scruggs pulled off her helmet, but before she could thank him, the stench hit her. "Whoa." She recoiled.

Dena and Lee had followed suit. Dena grabbed her nose. "That's vile."

"Worst I've ever smelled," Lee agreed.

"My God," Dena said. "It smells like a thousand neo-moose crapped all over the deck."

"We're sorry," the man leading them said apologetically. "We've had issues with the recycling system and waste disposal. This ship wasn't designed for this many people."

"This many people?" Lee asked.

"Yes, we are one hundred forty-three. I mean, we have one hundred forty-three on strength, or should." He turned to the others and spoke rapidly in Français.

"One hundred forty-three?" Lee repeated. "That's too many for a ship this size."

"We needed to keep our unit together."

"Your unit?"

Scruggs piped up. "That's the standard size of an Imperial Auxiliary Company, isn't it?"

"Why, yes, it is, young lady," the man said. "You have the look of a military person about you."

Scruggs preened. "I'm Cadet Scruggs."

"I see. And the rest you are?"

Lee introduced herself as the navigator of *Heart's Desire* and Dena as the ship's sensor operator.

"*Bien sur.*" The man smiled. "We have been here awaiting contact for some time. You must be here about our employment."

"How can you be sure that we're your contact?" Lee asked.

The man laughed. "You are clearly a Jovian, one of the Empire's most trusted. Of course you represent the Empire, no matter what ship you travel in. Here is—" He pointed at the tallest of the three men— "Captain Daille, commanding 1st Platoon, first battalion, Imperial Auxiliary Brigade 271. His Standard is not good, sorry."

Captain Daille braced to attention. "*Enchante.*"

"I am Lieutenant Isere, and this is Lieutenant Fornet." They all shook hands. A group of men and women arrived from the bowels of the ship and glanced at them curiously. Daille addressed them in Français, and they clapped and smiled at the newcomers.

Isere turned back to Lee. "Do you have an order package for us?"

"Our orders were verbal," Lee said. "Perhaps we should discuss this in private."

"Of course, of course." Isere translated for Daille, who pointed forward. "We will go to the office. You three." He frowned at them. "You are Spacepeople. Do you not have ground officers among your crew? Marines, perhaps?"

"Oh, yes," Lee said. "We have some experienced army personnel, as well as a pilot who's ex-Imperial Navy."

"Excellent," the man said. "We are tasked to follow the Navy's instructions."

"But why are you here?" Lee asked. "I mean,

stuck in your ship. What happened back at the station?"

"We had some… issues," Isere admitted. "The station rules—the thousand-credit deposits, the payments in advance—those may have been our fault. Few of us speak Standard, and there were many confusions. We've been banned from the station and refused more supplies. We've been waiting for you for almost three weeks. The troops are bored, and money was running low. We worried you weren't coming."

"Well, we weren't supposed to meet an auxiliary unit here," Lee said, "only their leaders, but I don't think we're late, at least not according to our orders."

"That's no matter. You're here now. If we can go to the bridge, perhaps your crew can establish communication with your pilot, and we can receive our orders."

"Of course," Lee said. "But which unit are you exactly?"

"Imperial Auxiliary Brigade 271," the man replied. "From the planet Rhone. You've heard of it?"

"Afraid not," Lee said.

"No matter. We fulfill our obligations."

"Yes," Lee said. "Well, I'm sure you have our thanks—and probably Tribune Devin's thanks as well."

Isere laughed. "Ha! You jest! But of course, it's funny, isn't it? Coming all this way to pick up the likes of us to fight?"

"Yes, indeed," Lee said. "You're a long way from home."

"Yes, a very long way. But we support the Empire. May I present—"

The man swept his hand toward the group of soldiers who had crowded into the room.

"Imperial Auxiliary Brigade 271, the Rhone Brigade," he announced, "here to fight for the Empire!" He raised his fist in the air and shouted, "Death to the traitor Devin!"

"Death to the traitor Devin!" the troops roared back. "Death!"

Chapter 30

"Tribune," Lionel's voice echoed over the intercom. "Could I join you in your cabin for a few moments, please?"

Devin put down his wine glass and sniffed his stew—he smelled paprika and mace. Imin cooked up big batches of Devin's favorites, vacuum-froze the excess, then doled them out when Devin ate alone. Imin said the workaday bulk cooking allowed him to concentrate on more artistic meals when Devin had guests. And it gave him more time to 'see to the Tribune's other concerns.' *I never ask which of my other interests he's seeing to. I'm scared he'll tell me.*

"I've just started dinner, Prefect. Why don't you come join me?"

"Thank you sir. I don't believe I have time for dinner right now. But I do need to see you. Right now, please."

"Right now?" Devin blinked. "All right. Come down."

"Yes sir. I'm bringing Rudnar with me. And I'm assuming Imin is there?"

Imin stopped filling Devin's glass. "I'm with the Tribune sir."

"Very well. We'll see you shortly."

Devin looked at Imin. "Any idea why they're coming down to speak to you, Imin?"

"No sir," Imin said. "I have none. Should I set another place for the Prefect anyway?"

"Set two. Rudnar can eat as well."

"Yes sir."

Devin spooned up his stew. Imin always seemed to know what was going on. If he didn't, it had to be either recent or critical for Lionel not to have shared it with him. *Why does he need to see me in person? It has to be bad. What's so bad he can't say it over the radio?*

Five minutes later, the door chimed.

"Tribune's quarters," Imin said at the intercom.

"Imin," Lionel's voice came through. "I'm here with Rudnar. We need to speak to the Tribune right away. And the Bosun and two Marines are with me."

Imin reached under his tunic. A pistol appeared in his hand. "The Bosun and two Marines sir?" Imin's tone was mild, but he checked the pistol. "I'm sorry. Why would that be?"

"They're going to watch the door while we have a discussion with the Tribune."

"A discussion with him sir? Watch the door?"

"Yes, Imin. A discussion. Let me in, please."

Devin looked over. "Imin, let them in."

"Sir—" Imin said.

"Imin, put the pistol away. It's the Prefect."

"Yes sir." Imin's tone was reluctant. "Sir. Things are just... a little confused."

Imin's pistol disappeared somewhere in his clothes and he unlocked the hatch. *When did he start locking the hatch? And when did he start carrying a pistol in my quarters? Everything is going to Hades.*

Lionel and Rudnar entered, both coming to attention and giving the full Imperial salute. Devin gaped. Lionel never saluted in his private quarters.

"What's going on?" Devin asked. He stood, dropped his napkin, and returned the salute. "Prefect, Midshipman, please be seated. Imin will serve us some stew."

"No thank you sir," Rudnar said. "I don't have time for stew right now."

Devin stared at her. "Did you just turn down a dinner invitation from the commander of the fleet?"

Rudnar gulped. "Sir, we don't have time."

Imin's hands disappeared under the table.

Devin grabbed Imin's shoulder. "No."

"What?" Rudnar asked, confused.

"Imin was about to pull a pistol on you. That will only confuse things further."

Imin ignored the hand on his shoulder. His eyes never left Rudnar.

"Imin," Devin said firmly. "Give me your pistol."

"I'm not sure I can do that sir," Imin replied. "Something's going on here, and I'm confused. I don't like being confused."

"Imin, wait." Devin raised his voice. "Bosun McSanchez, front and center."

The Bosun stepped inside, the two Marines visible behind him.

"I'm not sure what's going on either," Devin continued, "but everyone seems a little tense. Imin, you're either going to hand me your pistol or I'm going to have the Bosun and those Marines take it from you."

Imin laughed. "Take my pistol? He won't be able to. Neither him nor the Marines."

"If I tell them to, they'll try. And if they try, you'll have to stop them. Do you want everyone shooting each other because you're confused? Perhaps we should ask some questions first. Bosun, what are your orders?"

The Bosun snapped to attention. "The Prefect instructed me to guard the door with these two Marines, and let no one in until relieved by either you or him sir."

Imin relaxed. "My apologies." He removed his hands from under the table.

"Thank you," Devin said. "Now, stew for our guests—and some wine. Bosun, anything else?"

"No sir. Though I will say, sir, I'm glad you didn't ask us to disarm Mr. Imin."

"Would you have tried?"

"Yes sir. I'm pretty sure we'd fail."

Devin nodded. "No harm in failing. The harm is in not trying."

"Understood sir."

Devin waved him off. "I've changed my mind. Wine for everyone, including you, Bosun. And, Imin, not that swill you usually give my guests—get something out of the green cabinet."

"The green cabinet? Are you sure—yes sir."

"Sir," Rudnar interrupted, "time is of the essence."

Devin held up a hand. "You've made your point. You're here to tell me something important. Whatever it is, the time it takes to pour a glass of wine won't make much difference—and it'll give us a moment to calm down and think more clearly."

Imin returned with a bottle. Devin's eyes widened. "A Napa-Bordeaux? You know something I don't, Imin?"

"The Tribune did say the green cabinet…"

"Never mind," Devin said. "Just pour."

Imin complied. The Bosun stepped outside with the Marines, the door clicking shut behind them. Imin walked to the bulkhead and typed in a sequence. The lock engaged with a soft click, and then a second, louder thunk. *I'm not sure what security he engaged. Knowing Imin, probably something with explosives.*

"Speak," Devin ordered.

"A member of the engineering crew sabotaged the main drive during the recent maneuver," Rudnar said. "When we attempted to pursue that Imperial ship we flushed out, one of the engineering ratings manually decoupled the fuel system from the main drive. The manual decoupling read like battle damage, and the damage control systems shut down the drive until the error could be rectified."

"You sure it was sabotage and not an accident?" Devin asked.

"Yes sir. That procedure simulates battle damage—or as close to battle damage as you can get without an actual explosion. It has to be done manually. Pulling a big red lever. No chance of misunderstanding."

"I see." Devin stared at Rudnar. "And how did you decide to go looking for this information, Rudnar?"

"Sir, I didn't. The Prefect instructed me to look for anomalies in the system related to our loss of acceleration during the recent battle. He also asked me to be discreet."

Devin turned to Lionel. "Why didn't you simply ask for the logs?"

"Because then everyone would know I was looking at the logs," Lionel explained. "If I went looking, the whole bridge staff on the next watch would know. But each helmsman accesses the logs of the previous watch when they arrive. It's standard procedure to check system parameters, make notes, and review repair details. Unremarkable. I caught Rudnar before her shift, told her what to look for, then went back to my cabin and brooded. When she came off shift, she reported to me."

"Well, then, arrest the rating in question."

"Can't. There's more than one."

"So arrest the other one. Wait, you didn't say 'two.' You said, 'more than one.' What aren't you telling me?"

"Sir." Lionel hesitated. "It's likely this sabotage was observed—or even aided—by other members of the engineering crew."

"How many others?"

"The entire watch was either complicit or

turned a blind eye."

Devin's jaw tightened. "Marvelous. Not just one saboteur—we've got a whole nest of them. And why? What do they think I'm going to do?"

"That's why I wanted Imin to be here." Lionel nodded. "He has a better feel for what the crew is saying."

All the diners at the table turned to face Imin. "Well?" Devin asked.

"I have been worried about the crew for a while sir. Nothing concrete, no actions I observed, just a general feeling. Conversations that stopped when I arrived. People wouldn't meet my eye."

"But nothing concrete?" Lionel asked. "No plans?"

Imin continued pouring the wine. "No specific plans as such, sir, but a lot of grousing. The crew thought this was some sort of fight between nobles. That you were disobeying some orders out of spite, because you hadn't been invited to some party, or some such thing."

"They think the Tribune would rebel over a party invitation?"

"Well," Devin said. "It would depend on the party, I suppose. I mean, not a christening, but maybe a Halloween ball. But in any event, you're my steward. You'd be the last to know."

"They would have told me sir," Imin said. "If I asked."

"If there were actual plans, they wouldn't have told you just because you asked."

"Not true sir." Imin shook his head. "Depends on how you ask. I can be very persuasive."

Imin finished pouring the glasses and handed them around. The three officers took the glasses in silence.

Devin sipped his wine and scowled. *None of us is going to ask him what persuasive means. If we* know, we'll be complicit. Things were easier before I rebelled. "In any event. Are you saying the crew is no longer loyal, Imin?"

"They weren't loyal to start with, Tribune. Just time servers. They were willing to go along with some upper-class shenanigans when they thought it was harmless. Now they're in the middle of a real live revolt, and they're not sure what to think."

"Yes sir," Lionel interrupted. "It appears there's a consensus that staying uninvolved—or silently hindering us—is safer in the long run. The logic is unclear, but it seems rooted in fear of future reprisals."

"It's too late for them now," Devin said. "There is no going back."

"They don't believe that. Or at least some of them don't." Lionel sipped his wine and made a face. "I think this bottle is off."

Devin leaned back, drained his glass in one motion, and grimaced. "It tastes like I remembered," he said. "I remember savoring a bottle like this with my father when I was younger. At my graduation from university."

"Graduation sir?" Rudnar asked.

"Enjoy it, Rudnar." Devin sighed. "You'll never drink another wine this old. This bottle was seventy years old when I first had it. I have less than half a case left—probably closer to a third. This might be one of the last bottles in existence."

"Second to last sir," Imin said.

Rudnar pushed her glass forward. "No need to waste it on us sir."

"It wasn't wasted," Devin said. "This is Imin's way of saying he understands the situation and is apologizing for earlier. Please, take a drink."

Rudnar sniffed the wine and took a gulp. Her eyes widened, and she gagged, then had to spit it back in the cup. "Sorry sir. Very sorry sir." She licked her lips. "It's, it's, perhaps it's too sophisticated a taste for me sir. I can't adequately describe the feeling..."

"It tastes like vinegar mixed half with tabbo urine and left out in the sun to rot," Devin said. "Doesn't it?"

"It must have been better before sir." Rudnar said.

"Nope." Devin shook his head. "It was horrible before, and it's horrible now. But it's a well-known old Earth brand, and it's sought after, and it's incredibly expensive. People pay a fortune for it. And I think Imin opened it for the same reason my father shared the bottle with me. When there's a lot of money and danger on the line, people can get confused with what's real and what's not. This wine is so expensive that people think it must be good, just because. The reality is it's not. That's what those junior mutineers don't understand. They think this is a game between nobles. Reality wins in the end."

"I don't understand either sir," Rudnar said. "Why did they sabotage a battle?"

"That's because you're not a noble," Devin replied. "It's not about changing the outcome of a battle. It's about changing the outcome of the court-martials, especially for the officers. When they're hauled in front of the Emperor's or Chancellor's justices, they can claim they sabotaged us out of loyalty to the Empire. They'll say they stayed aboard to clandestinely undermine me as a supposed traitor."

"But, sir," Rudnar argued, "the outcome was never in question. That ship we were pursuing was outnumbered ten to one—or more."

"True," Devin said. "But they needed something to make themselves look like patriots."

Lionel interjected, "We need to recall loyal

Imperial Legionary

officers from the other ships. We know we can trust the former *Pollux* crew and others from smaller ships. I'll make a list."

"No," Imin said quietly.

"Why not?" Lionel asked.

"If an entire engineering watch is involved, it's more widespread than I thought, Prefect," Imin said. "Bringing loyal troops back from other ships could provoke an incident. Even if we win, the cost could be catastrophic. Someone might sabotage the reactors or worse."

Devin nodded. "I see. And if we lose…"

"We're dead, or in prison," Imin finished. "That won't help us, your sister, or the Empire."

"Recall the Marines only," Lionel suggested.

"No," Devin said. "Marines can't crew a ship. They may be loyal, but they're not navigators or engineers."

"True," Lionel conceded.

Devin turned to Rudnar. "You did everything right. Keep doing your duties, keep your eyes open, and report only to me, the Prefect, Imin, or McSanchez—unless Lionel or I tell you otherwise. Understood?"

"Yes sir," Rudnar said, saluting.

"Well done, Rudnar. Wait here for a moment," Devin said. "Bring out your comm unit. I'm giving you some commo codes that can reach me anytime—" Devin fussed with his tablet. "How to sort the commo codes…too complicated. I'll give you the full set. There you go, Rudnar, don't abuse them. Not unless it's an emergency."

"I promise sir," Rudnar said."

Lionel's mouth gaped open. "Did you just give a midshipman fleet commander codes?"

Devin shrugged. "She said she wouldn't abuse them. I believe her. I trust my officers, Prefect. This isn't good news, but you did right bringing it to me. For now, keep maneuvering the fleet like nothing has happened. I need time to think. This is a political matter, not a military one, and I need to take steps."

"Tribune." Lionel gave the full formal cross-chest salute. "The Empire."

Devin stood. "The Empire. And, Rudnar?"

"Sir?"

"Sit down. Imin will get you some soup and some decent wine. This might be the last good meal you get for a while."

Chapter 31

"Signal from the flagship," Silaski said. "Switch to engaged side. Dispersed formation number three."

"Understood," Monti said. "Take a random vector off the flagship's course."

"Weapons online—such as they are," Hooper said from her seat at the backup helm, which also served as the weapons board.

Upon encountering the Nat tankers, Monti had hot-footed it back to the fleet. Tribune Devin had accepted their report and dismissed it as unimportant. He continued exercising the fleet, promising to do something about it later, after their next meeting.

Monti wasn't happy that they weren't doing something about a possible Nat incursion, but she did agree the fleet needed practice. Two of the destroyers had nearly destroyed each other when they misinterpreted a turning maneuver. Only half of the battleship batteries fired regularly. A small ship in the firing or maneuvering arc of the larger ones took its life in its hands.

"Do we have a target?"

"Yes." Hooper popped the information onto the main board.

"Are we going to hit it?"

"No."

Monti rubbed condensation from her screen. The dehumidifiers were on the fritz—again. "You're supposed to encourage us, not discourage us."

"Encourage this, Senior Lieutenant, Acting Captain. Our laser targeting software can't target a red wallaby on a white beach. Our sensors can't distinguish between a wombat and a weasel, never mind two different asteroids. And our relay from the flagship is suspect. We're missing data most of the time."

"Then why do the other two corvettes keep beating us? They have the same sensors and targeting software. This doesn't make sense."

"Couldn't it just be personal inadequacy on my part?" Hooper said. "Except for the missing data part, I think that's you. You must have peeved somebody on the sensors side on the flagship."

"I don't know why I put up with you."

"You have to. Tribune won't split us up for some reason."

Monti rubbed her head again. That's a problem. Bron should have her own ship right now. Why were she and I the only command crew that had stayed together? All the other commanders got larger ships. Why not her? And why is she the only ship not getting a full sensor readout? Doesn't the Tribune trust her? And why isn't he doing something about those Nat ships? He said he'd take care of them after he dealt with the emperor, but what about now?

"Firing in thirty seconds," Silaski said.

Monti glared at Hooper. "And now Silaski is firing?"

"I also mirrored the weapons board to her, so she's weapons officer now too," Hooper said. "Good cross-training exercise."

They approached a set of asteroids. The exercise required multiple passes, firing each time.

"On screen," Hooper said. "And three, two, one—"

Bang. Hit.

"Direct hit," Silaski said.

Monti clapped. "Well done, Silaski. Well done, Bron."

"Thank you, Franky."

"How'd you do it?"

"I've got a new technique I'm trying out."

"What's that?"

"Ignore the flagship's telemetry. There's something not right with it."

"What do you mean, 'not right'?"

"I mean the positions are off. It shows our position as incorrect. It shows their position as incorrect."

"Why would it do that?"

"Sheer incompetence? Somebody misprogrammed something and hasn't caught it yet."

"That's why we've been missing?"

"I know that's why we've been missing. I couldn't figure it out until now."

"Glad you found that out." *And why didn't any of the flagship crew catch it? Or are they so incompetent that they didn't notice? Are they just as bad as the old crew? Have I traded one incompetent group for another?*

Now that they were ignoring the flagship's data, their targeting sharpened. Hooper achieved a seventy-two percent hit rate—unrealistic in battle but much better than the single-digit and low double-digit percentages they had been hitting in the exercises up to now.

"Much better," Monti said. "Much better."

The fleet shifted into maneuver drills, changing directions on command. Silaski adjusted their course, pitching down two degrees, without being told.

"You're doing much better, Silaski. I saw you were doing more of the sims."

"Thank you ma'am. Not much else to do out here. It's not like we have shore leave."

"Another point against our Tribune." Hooper didn't look up from her display. "Why won't he let us have leave? He's rotated some of the other ships back to planets, and we've been stuck doing all this courier and scouting work. Has he got something against us?"

Silaski's hands moved again, adjusting the pitch by three more degrees. "I had some interesting bits from Susy the Newsy ma'am."

"Silaski, we're seven systems away from where you got your last Susy the Newsy broadcast. How are you getting more?"

"The couriers bring copies. We pass them through the fleet ma'am. Us Susy Stars."

"Susy Stars?"

"That's what we call ourselves. We think Susy's a star."

"Of course you do."

"Anyway, ma'am, do you want to hear about the latest Susy broadcast?"

"Not particularly, Silaski."

"Susy was talking about the rebellion, and she had an interview with a friend of the Tribune."

"Really? An interview with a friend of the Tribune? From an Imperial news source?" Hooper asked.

"Bron, don't encourage her."

"No, no, I want to hear this. Tell me more, Silaski."

"Well, the guy they were interviewing—he was handsome. Tall. Broad shoulders—" Silaski blathered on about the interview—what Susy was wearing, what the man was wearing, what the set was wearing, the color of the drapes. Monti kept her eye on the course plot and the communications from the flagship.

Midway through Silaski's discussion about the bejeweled microphone Susy had been using—it was covered in glitter—communications from the flagship came in.

"New course: 270 degrees X, 17 degrees Z,

positive galactic north. Execute in 30 seconds. Countdown."

"Countdown on the screen. But I didn't think it was glitter. I thought it looked more like stardust. You know stardust ma'am?"

"No, I don't know stardust. You mean dust from actual stars?"

"Well, that's what they call it ma'am. It's like glitter, only smaller."

"So it's small glitter."

"No, ma'am, it's stardust. Glitter's bigger."

"So it's like glitter, but smaller. Why don't you call it small glitter?"

"It's not small glitter ma'am. It's stardust." Silaski typed on her board. "Executing in 5, 4, 3, 2, 1."

The main engine cut out. The thrusters fired, and the ship pivoted to its new course, adjusting its aspect and holding the drift. The accompanying big ships were so heavy and ponderous that they couldn't turn easily. They had to stop, orient themselves, then maneuver on command.

"Executing," Silaski said. "On course as per flagship."

Monti looked over at Hooper. Hooper nodded once—she had been tracking the maneuver on her screen, and it had been performed properly.

"All right, so it was covered with stardust," Monti said.

"Yeah, but the fellow was really interesting," Silaski continued. "He said the Tribune is actually an agent of the Nats and that he was sent in here as a clone when he was a kid. They cloned the original Tribune and replaced him with a Nat agent."

"Of course they did," Franky said. "And his sister, the Empress? For that matter, the Emperor and the entire rest of the Imperial Navy never noticed this?"

"No ma'am," Silaski said. "None of them did. Isn't that amazing?"

"That's not the word I'd use."

"Yes ma'am. More course corrections coming in."

"Carry on, Silaski."

"Yeah, amazing," Monti muttered. She looked at Hooper. "What would you call it?"

"Interesting." Hooper wiped her screen. "Any word from engineering as to when our wet hell will stop dripping over?"

"They're working on it. Do you think that Imperial Tribune Devin—brother of the Empress, commander of the fleet, governor of the Verge, Lord Lyon—has been replaced by a clone who's a Nat spy?"

"No, not the clone part," Hooper said. "The rest is... interesting."

"What? You believe this claptrap?"

"Some odd things happening," Hooper said. "The timing of the rebellion. Do we really know that the Empress has disappeared? And, well... we found a Nat fleet."

"We didn't find a fleet. We found four tankers."

"We found four tankers, which means a fleet out there somewhere."

"We found four tankers, which means we found a lot of gas. There's no fleet until we see a fleet."

"Fine, Captain. We saw four tankers. Four Union of Nations tankers in an Imperial system. What's being done about it?"

"They don't tell us everything."

"You can count. So can I. Every ship that Tribune Devin has is out here. We're exercising nowhere near where that incursion is. In fact, we're deliberately avoiding it. And we're going to take a different path to New Malaya. If we even ever get there."

"That's because they need to pick up the troops—"

"I haven't seen any troops, and neither have you. All I've seen is that somewhere out there might be a Nat fleet entering Imperial space—and we're not doing anything to stop."

"Well, maybe... maybe the Empire—"

"The Empire we're being told we have to overthrow—that Empire?"

"What are you saying, Bron? Spit it out."

"I'm not saying anything. Well... maybe. What I am saying is, we need to keep an eye on things. Maybe we don't have the whole story."

"We probably—we definitely don't have the whole story."

"I've asked before. Why are we doing this? This rebellion thing?"

"We went over this before. The Empire is corrupt. We've seen that. The Empire is incompetent. We've seen that."

"Yeah, but it's still our Empire. It's not somebody else's. It's not the Nats'."

"I don't think the Tribune is involved with the Nats."

"I don't think he is either."

"But here's something to ask yourself."

"What's that?"

"If he is... if there is a Nat fleet out there... and the Tribune ignores it…what are we going to do about it?"

Chapter 32

"Kill the Tribune?" Dirk asked. "Did I hear that right?"

"Yes," Scruggs said. "They've been recruited from their home planet. They're called the Rhone Brigade. They've been enlisted to fight in the war against the rebel Tribune Devin, as they call him. A direct request from the Chancellor."

"These are the people we were supposed to pick up?"

"Maybe someone got their codes scrambled."

"This is a little more than someone getting their code scrambled. It's serious, like being at an Imperial Levee and eating your fish with the salad fork. That's a major problem, and nobody will forgive you." Dirk and Ana sat in the control room of the *Heart's Desire*. Dirk and Gavin had brought the engines to standby, but hadn't lit anything. Ana was checking sensors, but the dusty surface blocked most video and infrared.

"Navy," Ana said. "Did you just equate being captured by opposing troops and maybe killed with eating your salad with the wrong fork?"

"They're not the same thing, Centurion."

"Good, I worried that you had lost perspective."

"Not at all. Nobody cares what fork you eat your salad with. That's personal choice. But fish—" Dirk shook his head— "You have to eat fish only with a fish fork. Otherwise, people will talk."

"I wonder why we don't just rise up and kill all the nobles," Ana said. "Since you're obviously so clueless and useless."

"Can't," Dirk said. "We'd stab you with all our fish forks." A light flashed on his screen. "Somebody has jumped in-system."

Ana's fingers flew. "Imperial beacon. Freighter.

Name is… OTES. Capital letters too. Weird name."

"Means 'On the Emperor's service.' A warship under direct Imperial Orders. Can't be ordered around by a fleet commander. How big?"

"I can get a mass rating from the newer sensors." Ana played with a screen. "Half our size. Moving faster than we would."

"A freighter in a hurry?"

"Or a warship seeing what it can see." Ana played with the screens again. "Warbook says right size for an R-class destroyer."

"Someday, Centurion, you're going to tell me how you're so good at scanning, and finding Imperial warships in a warbook."

"Right after you teach me which forks to use and take me to a formal Imperial banquet."

"As a guest or as a prisoner?"

"Will you be a prisoner too?"

"If you want."

Ana grinned. "Works for me. If that's a destroyer, we can't outrun it if it gets too close."

"How truly good." Dirk brought the channel back up again. "Scruggs, we're on a schedule here." Dirk explained their situation, surreptitiously, in case he was overheard.

"Understood, Pilot," Scruggs interrupted. "We might have some supply issues ourselves, so it's best to get moving. But it will take some time to sort things out with our crew, because most of them don't speak Standard. Luckily, Lieutenant Isere does, *and he's right here next to me.*"

"Standby." Dirk clicked off and turned to Ana. *No secure communications. Marvelous. But we can't leave people behind.* "What can we do with a regular company of Imperial troops who want to kill us?"

"Kill them all first and let Jove sort it out?" Ana said.

"We have to get our people back first."

"Don't think that's an option." Ana clicked the radio back on. "Cadet, this sounds like a non-standard operations challenge."

"Say again, Centurion?" Scruggs asked.

"It's an opportunity to excel, Cadet."

Noise blanketed the channel and Dena's voice came on. "Stop it with the military flim-flam," Dena said. "Speak Standard."

"There are a few problems."

"You think it's a problem?" Dena sneezed. "You know what it smells like back here?"

Dirk rubbed his forehead. "Can I talk to Lee?"

"Yes, Lee is right here," Scruggs' voice said, "along with all of the others, including the officers. They're discussing how to execute the rebel Tribune when they catch him." Scruggs paused. "I think the three of us can handle staying here. The situation is fluid, but I think I can help produce a positive outcome. Ask the centurion for details if you need any."

"Got it," Dirk said. "Stand by." He muted the channel and looked at Ana. "We've managed to collect a battalion—or a partial battalion—of troops who are dead set on killing the Tribune. And there's an unknown ship, possibly an Imperial warship, heading our way, and half our crew is more or less hostage on another ship. What's going to happen now?"

Ana shrugged. "Good leadership opportunity for Scruggs. She seems willing to take it on, so we let her. But that's only some of our problems," Ana said. "Gavin, you see what's coming out of the airlock behind us?"

The screens flashed as Gavin popped a camera view of a six-foot cylinder—a water tank—with seats on top, controls on the front, and thruster at the rear. "Broomsticks. Personal transports."

"Are they armed?"

"I'm not a weapons scanner. But I don't see any serious weapons in their hands."

"So not a threat?"

"A few station people don't worry me," Dirk said. "It's pretty hard for suited people in a vacuum to fight against unsuited people operating from a starship." Dirk ran through a launch checklist. "All we have to do is close the airlocks."

"Skipper," Gavin said, "they could send someone with a pry-bar or a wrench and try to hack their way into the ship."

"They can't damage the main drive."

"They could pull control wires 'til we can't lift. You give me a wrench, a pry-bar, and sixty seconds, and I'll take out all your thrusters and your sensors. Then you're not going anywhere."

Dirk cursed again.

"And, Navy," Ana said.

"What?"

"The first group is heading right for us. But there's a second group heading to Scruggs's ship."

"Just had to make my day better, didn't you."

"Nope, just wanted to give you a sense of how deep a hole you've climbed into."

"Me? Don't you mean you?"

"I'm the security coordinator when we're on the ground, but you're in charge of spaceport operations."

"We're on the ground now."

"At a spaceport. Your problem, not mine."

Dirk cursed again. "Okay, ground security adviser. Give me some options. Could those Rhone troops seize the station for us? And take out those broomsticks?"

"I bet they could, that many," Ana said, "especially if we let Scruggs lead them. But where would that leave us? We'll have a bunch of stinking

Imperial troops taking over the only place nearby where we can collect air, water, and supplies. Think they'll give us any when they know who we are? And there's that warship…"

"There's that," Dirk said. "Options, we need options. Gavin, can we lift?"

"We can lift. We can even get out of this system."

Dirk switched to the comm. "Scruggs, could you and the other two come back here, please, while we discuss our coordination?"

"Negative on that, Pilot," Scruggs said. "They want our help here, and want us to stay. I'd be happy to give it to them."

"Well, we'd like to have you back here," Dirk said.

"I don't think that's feasible at this point," Scruggs replied. "We've just started discussing some… other matters. And Lee wants to talk to you."

Lee came up on the channel. "I've just come from their bridge. Life support is stressed. There are a lot of red lights up here. It could fail, and soon. We need to ground somewhere and make repairs."

"What type of repairs?"

"Repairs that require atmosphere. Breathable atmosphere. We need to shut down and re-tool a bunch of things, and we need air to do that. Did you notice that bunch of angry-looking broomsticks heading our way—"

"Yes. Ignore them. If we find a planet, can they do the repairs?"

"Maybe. But I'm not sure they can fly it there. This crew is a bit…"

"A bit what?"

"Incompetent."

"You don't think they've been starship

trained?" Dirk asked.

"I'm not sure they've ever seen a starship before. I'm not sure they've even seen a picture of a starship. I have no idea how they got this far without dying. They've been using auto-sequencing for everything, including navigation. The computers are ancient, the software is buggy, and most of the sensors don't work."

"Can they read beacons? Beacons of ships entering the system?"

"Why would they want to read beacons…oh." Lee paused. "They cannot. Fixing those scanners is not a priority right now."

"Just as well," Dirk said. "Best leave that 'til other things are fixed."

"Navy," Ana came up on the channel. "A third group of those broomsticks is coming out of the lock. The other two are holding short. I can see prybars, axes, and this thing—" Ana popped a picture on the screen. "Not sure what that is—"

"Welding torch," Gavin said. "Cuts steel, it will melt all our control lines. They get next to us and we're not going anywhere."

Dirk groaned. "Lee, that crew flew that ship. It got here. Do you think they can land it on a planet?"

"Nope."

"Okay, so... do you think you can land it?"

A long pause. Lee sighed. "I'm going to have to, aren't I?"

"Yes," Dirk said. "You are. All right. Here's what we're going to do. There's a habitable but mostly empty planet two hops from here. So we're going to head there, and do repairs."

"Pilot," Scruggs said. "I just had a conversation with the officers, via Lieutenant Isere. They're short on everything. Food, water, Hydrogen. Parts. Also money. They don't think they'll have enough equipment to do repairs. Captain Daille wants to know what supplies he'll get from you there."

"Scruggs, there are people coming—"

"He won't lift unless he gets guarantees. He's also asking why we're afraid of these locals, why we don't just use our Imperial connections to deal with them."

Dirk switched off the channel, cursed once, banged his head, then switched the channel back on. "Please tell the gallant Captain Daille that we will be providing him with food, fuel, and such like when he arrives at his destination. It's not expedient to remain here right now. We have an extensive set of training exercises that need to be performed at the target planet," Dirk gave the catalog number. "Once there, we will both land and do some familiarization exercises, training, and transfer supplies. And fuel up, of course. Plenty of time to flush their life-support while we are there. They have the personal word of an Imperial Duke. But we need to lift as soon as possible so we don't stress their, or our, existing supplies and the stellar geography is such that our launch window is right now. Otherwise, we have to wait two more weeks. Ask Lee for details."

Dirk clicked off.

Ana laughed. "A launch window, for a jump? Even I know that isn't a thing. Get to the jump limit, as long as you have a clear route, jump whenever."

"It's only important for certain types of maneuvers."

"What type of maneuvers?"

"Whatever maneuvers Lee makes up."

Scruggs came back online. "They understood, Pilot. Lee explained the stellar conjunctions. They do want some details on the training."

Ana flicked the channel back on. "Cadet, this is

your opportunity. The pilot and I have full confidence in your ability to oversee a company-sized training program. Lay it all out, and you can assume proper non-commissioned support when we arrive at the destination."

"I do?" Dirk asked. "I mean, I do, yes. But what—"

Ana pointed at the screen. The new beacon was flashing. It had changed course and was closing the station.

Dirk sucked in a breath. "Attention, ship *Esprit*," Dirk said. "I am the Duke Dirk Friedel. By Imperial order, you are to convoy with us until released. Immediate lift and sprint to jump limit. We will escort you to your next station. Understood?"

"Understood," Scruggs said. Lee echoed that a second later.

"Lifting," Dirk said. He punched the screen. "Jove save the Empire!"

Chapter 33

"Oh my God. I'm going to puke." Dena slammed the compartment door. "I don't know how much longer I can stand the smell."

"You get used to it," Lee said. "Once you've been on a ship for a week, all the smells fade into the background and become normal. You won't notice it again until you get to a planet, and then you might think it's the planet smells bad."

"There is no way that this will ever fade into the background," Dena said. "I tried to eat a tray. It tasted like frosted barf."

"You always hate the trays," Scruggs said. "It's not that bad in here. We can handle it." I went without a shower for weeks when I ran away, all those months ago. I can handle a few more days. Besides, we have bigger problems. How do I get these troops on our side?

"How can it possibly not smell bad?" Dena asked. "None of these people have had a shower in—what? Weeks? Months?"

"Twenty-six days," Lee said. "We need to tune their environmental systems, but I don't want to do it right now because if they mess something up, they might make things worse."

"What does 'making it worse' mean?"

"We run out of air. Flop around gasping like stranded fish. Asphyxiate. Die in agony."

"No making it worse, then. It's going to stay that way?" Dena said.

"Yes," Lee said. "Until we get to that planet."

The three of them were sharing a compartment on the mercenary transport ship, the *Esprit*. The merchant officers in charge hadn't been keen on lifting, but Lee's garbled discussion of jump windows and Dirk's Imperial Orders had convinced them of the necessity of moving quickly.

Imperial Legionary

Scruggs and Dena had convinced Lieutenant Isere to lock everyone down into their quarters while Lee took them to the jump limit.

"I've been talking to some of the troops," Scruggs said. "Sort of talking. Their Standard isn't great. These are not regular soldiers, they're farmers or something. They've never been trained in anything. They've got weapons on the ship for them—or at least, they have been told they have weapons meant for them—but I don't think they've fired them. Or seen them."

Dena raised an eyebrow. "And why does this matter to us?"

"We're here to train them. Lieutenant Isere said they were waiting for an Imperial contact who would provide training and supplies. That's us. And we can use that to our advantage." *I hope. What would the centurion do? Improvise. Adapt Overcome. I can do that.*

"We're here because we got chased away from a space station that supported the rebellion who thought we were Imperial sympathizers, and these people rescued us."

"And now we're with real Imperial troops," Scruggs said. "The officers might want to space us when they figure out whose side we're on. We have to have them think that we're on their side." Scruggs leaned forward. "But the troops themselves are a different story. They're not loyal Imperial troops. Either mercenaries or adventurers, or former criminals. They may be interested in other options."

"We can't convince a shipload of troops to change sides." Dena hissed.

"Why not?" Scruggs shrugged. "We can be persuasive." *And this is a chance to make up for my screw-ups.*

"And either way," Lee said. "We need to do

something during jump. They won't expect us to sit here."

"What would real Imperial trainers do? What should we do?"

"Lay low for a few jumps, sneak off when we get to that planet," Dena said "Won't be the first time I've been lazy for two weeks."

"I can't be lazy," Lee said. "I've got to be on that bridge most of the trip. I don't trust that crew not to suffocate us. We need to get this ship somewhere with atmosphere, as quickly and as smoothly as possible."

"Which traps no neo-moose with me," Dena said. "But because I'm a wonderful person, when I'm not napping and trying to ignore the smell, I can sit on the bridge and watch a board."

"It'll take more than that. I'll probably have to live there. And there's another point—"

"It's not enough to sit here," Scruggs said. "We need allies. If we train these folks, they'll be happy. That's what they expect. That's what I'm going to do."

"Scruggs," Dena said. "These are enemy troops. Training them would make them better soldiers."

"Well, yes, but if we get them on our side, that means I—"

"Wasn't thinking clearly," Dena said. "That's a bad idea. We want them to get worse."

Lee raised her hand. "As I mentioned, there is one other thing—"

Scruggs shook her head. "We can do this."

Dena threw her hands wide. "The old man's not here, and he's the one who knows training. Sit down, shut up, be quiet and try not to—"

"He spaced half the bridge crew," Lee said.

The two other women stopped talking. Both heads swiveled to Lee.

"What?" Scruggs asked.

"The captain. Captain Daille. Half of the crew were pro-Empire, half weren't. When he found out, he spaced the rebels, or even the ones who were only lukewarm. They're gone. That's why the ship crew is so overwhelmed."

"He won't space us," Scruggs said. "Then he won't get supplies or fuel."

"Two of the people he spaced were the navigator and engineer. The rest can barely keep the ship going. They're all junior and they're scared flameless. He's a total fanatic on being pro-Empire. He wanted to attack that station, but his officers talked him out of it, said he couldn't launch military operations without direct Imperial orders."

"So he doesn't like rebels," Dena said. "He thinks we're Imperials. Won't affect us."

"Crew said he shot some others who were supposed to follow orders, but didn't. If he expects us to be doing training, you'll have to do it, or out the airlock you go."

Dena closed her eyes. "Fine. Tell me how this training thing works."

Scruggs discussed what the centurion had shown her before. Lee added her own comments. Keep them busy. Give them contests. Not too difficult, not too easy. Lots of physical work.

"And even a cursory inspection says they're lousy," Scruggs said.

"Do all Imperial troops suck this bad?" Dena asked.

"All the auxiliary regiments are like this." Lee shrugged. "Pretty standard. The locals raise troops to help support the Empire. The Empire kicks in money for their training and support, and when there's an emergency, they can grab them and transport them."

"But why are they so badly trained?" Scruggs asked. "I mean, they should at least be able to fire a gun."

"Money." Dena nodded. "It's always money, isn't it. I'll bet you the local officers have been pocketing the cash, right?"

"Yes," Lee said. "That's the way it is. The money goes to the planetary government. The planetary government that promises to provide the troops, and then they do what they want with it. Some minister or deputy minister got the cash. The more competent officers want to stay on the planet or go into the Imperial forces. These guys here? They're not the best officers you'll ever meet."

"I already figured that out," Scruggs said. "The troops may not be able to do any sort of shooting, and not the officers either. I get the impression the captain guy is a landlord and these troops are his farm workers."

"We did that with the ranches." Dena said. "The rancher's in charge. There'll be a few that are his bully boys—his cowboys. They get good food, good money, and know what they're doing. They'll be like the palace guard. The rest will be whoever they picked up. Kids looking for adventure. Failed workers desperate for money. Losers running away from their problems. Joining the planetary guard and then hooking up with the Imperial Auxiliary is a big way to disappear."

"You seem to know a heck of a lot about how this planetary guard thing works," Scruggs said.

"I thought about it myself. I wanted to get away from my farm. I wanted to get away from my family. And I didn't want to get married. This was one of the options."

"I didn't know you had a planetary guard or whatever on Mud Pit."

"Rockhaul," Dena said. "The planet is called Rockhaul. You've been listening to the old man for too long."

"Well, Mud Pit, Mud Dirt, whatever," Scruggs said. "Listen, Nature Girl, nobody cares what you call that stupid planet you were born on."

Dena raised a fist, then smiled and dropped it. "Ah, got me. Good for you. You sound like the old man when he's abusing people during training."

"We're going to have to help each other with this training that Dirk and the centurion suggested," Scruggs said. "We'll both be doing things like that. As long as they think we're following orders and getting them ready for fighting, we'll be fine."

"What if we don't want to?" Dena asked.

"You've kind of forgotten the little problem that they think we're, you know, not exactly who we said we were... or who we let them think we were."

"You mean," Dena said, "they're going to go kill the Tribune, but we're working for him?"

"Don't say that out loud," Scruggs muttered. "Maybe the cabin's bugged."

"Don't think so," Lee said. "That was the first thing I checked—scanning through the internal sensors."

"What kind of internal sensors do they have?"

"None," Lee replied. "The whole board was dark. Either the modules are missing, the software's not there, or something else is wrong. I couldn't figure out more without being obvious, but I was happy to see that nothing was working."

"Maybe it's a secret surveillance system," Dena said. "Maybe they're listening to us right now."

"If it's a secret," Lee said, "it'd be a secret to them too. They've barely got the basic software package. This ship was obviously bought used—very used. It's got the minimum necessary to operate in Imperial space. None of the remaining crew has any idea what they're doing." Lee tapped a note into her comm. "My impression," she continued, "is that this was maybe built as a jump-capable ship, but it was used for in-system operations. Might not have jumped in years."

"Let's summarize," Scruggs said. "We're stuck on a stinking hole of a ship that smells like three weeks' worth of human feces."

"Twenty-six days," Dena corrected. "Let's be exact."

"Sorry—twenty-six days' worth of human feces. And we've got only a quarter of the people we expected to be here, but still too many for the ship. They're supposed to be troops, but they have no training. We're led by officers who aren't competent and also don't speak Standard well. Oh, and they're on the wrong side of the conflict we were supposed to be recruiting them for—and they don't know that yet. If they did, they would space us instantly."

"We need a plan," Lee said. "For the training, and for not getting shot."

"We need more information," Scruggs said. "First we learn, then we plan. Let's get out and talk to everyone we can. And try not to get shot."

"Yay," Dena said. "Adventure awaits."

Scruggs and Dena spent the next two shifts prowling through the *Esprit*. Lee spent most of her time sitting in the co-pilot's chair, running checks and asking questions. She wasn't happy with the answers she got, and the crew—who she had to identify by position, their Standard was so bad—weren't happy with her questions. The more they answered, the more worried she got.

"Things are better than I thought," Dena said when they met back at the end of the first shift. "There are a whole bunch of opportunities here."

"You mean for training and helping out the Tribune?" *Dena helping! That's a positive development.*

"Huh?" Dena said. "No, I mean some of these guys are hot. The trooper lead guys."

Scruggs blinked. "Those... uh, you mean those special trooper attendant guys with Lieutenant What's-His-Name? The other guy."

"Lieutenant Fornet," Dena said. "Bertrand, Alain, and Claude. They're good-looking, especially Alain. If I could get him hosed down somehow, get the crap smell off him, I think we could have a good time."

"Dena," Scruggs groaned. "These people might tear us limb from limb when they find out who we work for."

"True," Dena said. "All the more reason to have fun while we can."

"What sort of upbringing did you have where this is all you consider?" Lee asked.

"One that was a lot more fun than yours," Dena said. "But fine, I'd rather not be killed for being an evil, rebellious mutineer."

"Technically, you're not a mutineer," Lee corrected. "You're a rebel."

"Are they going to shoot us any differently?"

"No," Lee said. "But the Tribune is more likely to get his head cut off than be hanged."

"Well, we got that to look forward to," Scruggs said. "I've been thinking."

"This isn't going to end well," Dena groaned. "I see my fun going out the window."

"What?"

"Every time you start thinking, you come up with some sort of grand plan that's excessively dangerous, fits right in with all this Empire stuff that Lee, Dirk, and the Tribune want to do, and requires a whole bunch of effort."

"Yeah," Scruggs admitted. "That's true. But I

think it'll be exciting. You in?"

Dena shrugged. "Why not? Adventure awaits."

Scruggs explained. "The whole thing is based on three habits of an effective and respected leader, like the centurion always said."

"You mean kill, maim, destroy?" Dena asked.

"He didn't say that."

Dena raised her eyebrows.

"Okay, he said that. But the other things he said…"

"I never listen to what the centurion says, except to make fun of him."

"I mean competence, pro-activeness, and responsibility."

"Now I'm sorry I asked. That sounds boring."

"It is boring," Scruggs admitted. "But do you respect the centurion?"

"I don't like him that much," Dena said.

"I know. That's not what I asked. Do you respect him?"

"Yeah," Dena conceded. "He knows how to shoot. He knows how to fight. And the things that are important to him—he's great at them. I've learned lots from him, I'll give him that much."

"We may not like somebody, but we respect them if they're competent. So we need to make ourselves seem competent and the officers in charge of the ship seem incompetent—without ticking them off, or ideally, them noticing."

"Making them look incompetent will be easy," Dena said. "But how do we handle the not ticking them off?"

"With the second part. Pro-activeness. We're going to go out and start doing their job for them, and give the officers plenty of time to lounge. We're going to start training these troops, giving them opportunities to learn."

"That's not going to work," Dena said. "The

officers in charge have had plenty of opportunities to do this. They haven't."

"Yes, they haven't. And why is that?" Scruggs asked.

"They're lazy and stupid?"

"Exactly. They're lazy and stupid. We're neither. Lee is smart, and she's a Jovian, one of the Emperor's premier bodyguards. They'll listen to her when she tells them something. When she says 'that's how we do it in the Praetorians,' who will disagree with that?"

"The bridge crew might listen to me," Lee said. "But they're scared. They don't want to step on the toes of the other officers and get spaced."

"But." Scruggs raised her eyebrows. "We're going to get them supplies. Dirk promised them supplies in the next system. If they don't do what you say, they'll run out of hydrogen, and they know it."

"We don't have enough fuel on *Heart's Desire*," Dena said. "Gavin's aways complaining that we're short and we refuel every week."

"Because the pilot makes him. Full fuel tanks give us full tactical flexibility, Dirk says. And *Heart's Desire* has something they don't have. A fuel processing plant. Land both ships on a world with water, and we can crack enough hydrogen to fill their tanks and ours, and exercise the troops while we do it. That will give us time to prove ourselves to the troops. Make them think we know what we're doing, get them used to taking instruction from us, and go from there."

"That's great for them," Dena said. "Not a problem. But what exactly are we going to do?"

"Easy," Scruggs said. "First, we're going to gamble."

"And win?"

"And lose," Scruggs said. "Lose big."

Andrew Moriarty

Chapter 34

"My captain asks why we should start the training now?" Lieutenant Isere said.

Scruggs tilted her chin up to look in Isere's eyes. "We have time during the jumps and system transits to do some training." The three ground officers had quarters in the main habitat ring with the starship's crew. In addition to his own stateroom and private dining room, Daille had commandeered another room as an office. He made Scruggs stand at near-attention in front of his desk—there were no visitors' chairs. He had an expensive wooden desk, elaborate wall displays, and scent dispenser that hid the ship's stench behind fresh pine sprays. It reminded Scruggs of a prissy school principal's office from the private school she'd attended when she was five.

Isere turned and spoke to Daille. Scruggs's eyes swiveled down to look at Daille's face. Isere was a head taller than Scruggs, Daille a head shorter. *It's like doing constant neck stretches to listen to the two of them.*

Daille frowned, shook his head, and answered at length. Isere turned back to Scruggs. "It is difficult. I do not know the word. We have a problem with compactness, we cannot exercise the way we should. Why not wait 'til we arrive at the training planet?"

"The troops will be bored, and they will lose their edge if they have nothing to do. This will help to keep them sharp."

Isere translated and Daille flipped his hand and laughed, then spoke at length, gesturing with his arms. Scruggs's eyes zeroed in on his cuff. Something bothered her. *He's wearing a skinsuit under his uniform. His troops don't have skinsuits. They don't care what happens to the crew if there is a hull breach. I can use that, spread it around.*

"My captain says the troops never were sharp, nor will they be. They are peasants, farmers. They are best marginally efficient. He says they are—" Isere checked a phrase with Daille— "the scum of the earth. The mere scum of the earth."

"That was good enough for Old Earth generals, wasn't it?" Centurion had made Scruggs read old histories as part of her training. A famous old Terra general had said that.

"Pardon?"

Scruggs shrugged. "Not important. Are you wearing a skinsuit, Lieutenant?"

Isere nodded. "We all are."

"All of your troops have skinsuits?"

"Only the officers, of course."

Of course. Why give poor farmers who are destined to be cannon fodder good protection equipment. No wonder they're not motivated. Scruggs nodded. "Very well. But even if the captain is hesitant, I propose we should do some sort of training. I've spoken with Praetorian Lee—" Scruggs emphasized Lee's title— "and she confirms that the Praetorians are always training. If it's good enough for them…"

This time, Daille's laugh was louder and lasted longer. Isere kept his face blank. "My captain says that you are not…smart…I am sorry, those were his words, if you think anything in common between these troops and Praetorians."

Scruggs bit her lip and glanced around the office. Daille did himself well—plush wooden office chair, solid wood-topped desk. His I-love-me wall behind her had photos of Daille with presumably famous people, and a glass-fronted box containing numerous medals—his shadowbox. *The large center one is the Imperial Order of Truth and Purity, fourth class. The one Centurion called the order of sweeping the barracks. This is not a combat officer's office. I need to make it easy for him.*

Scruggs shrugged. "Could I ask for volunteers?"

Daille crossed his arms. He stared at Scruggs and spoke slowly. The translation software kept up. "You are a bit of a conundrum, student officer."

Scruggs nodded. Conundrum? What a lousy translation program.

"Most Imperial officers do not care for the Auxiliary Brigades. I do not blame them, these people are one of the least good. But you seem concerned for their welfare. That is strange. I wonder at that. Are you really Imperial officers?"

Scruggs shifted her stance slightly. *If I grab my revolver, I can take him out before he shoots. Then get the others. But there will be too much noise.* "We've worked with Auxiliaries before. They have their challenges, true. But they can learn."

Daille raised his eyebrows. "That is not my experience." He drummed his fingers on the table and stared into space.

Scruggs felt sweat run down her back. I need him to believe me. They're too many of them to take on, especially in jump. But if we can get in with the troops.

Daille shrugged in the Français style, nodded, then spoke faster to the others. The translation program cut out. Isere translated. "You may ask for volunteers, but only for volunteers. We have enough problems of our own, you must do this without our help." Isere shrugged. "And personally, I do not think the motivations of the troops will be there."

"Of course," Scruggs said. "But I can try. I have your permission to arrange contests and suchlike?"

"Yes. Do your worst." Isere grinned, and winked at her. "I am interested to see how the Imperial Navy's representatives handle this."

Scruggs started with the poker games. "Oh, is that poker?" she asked a group of soldiers. "I've heard of that. Maybe you can teach me how to play."

The squad was only too happy to teach her. They were all hot-bunking—sixteen men shared eight berths in a container. Half slept or lounged in bed, the others eight had to be elsewhere in the ship until their turn came. They loafed in the hallways or exercised in the cargo hold. Poker passed the time.

Scruggs identified the local shark and let him beat her up until the last hand, where she double-bluffed him and took the whole pot, plus all his previous winnings.

"Beginner's luck," she said. "Thanks, guys."

She moved through the second and third groups. By the time she returned next shift, word had spread throughout the ship.

"You are a poker expert, Miss Scruggs," one of the men said. "We don't play you. You always win."

"Well," she said, "I have won, but I don't seem to have a lot of credits. All I've got is this scrip."

The Rhone Brigade was paid in Rhone Dollars, issued by the government of planet Rhone and overprinted with the words "Valid only on Planet Rhone. Not exchangeable for Imperial Currency." The on-board store only took the fake dollars, so it forced the troops to buy supplies at inflated prices. The troops treated it like funny money, not caring how much they won or lost.

Scruggs next cornered the other lieutenant, Fornet, who guarded the main store's container shop. His Standard didn't stand up to the discussion about buying alcohol, and a translation program didn't help.

"Je ne compronde pas," he said repeatedly.

Dena came by as a frustrated Scruggs was asking what type of profit margin he needed for the third time.

"Baby Marine, you're doing this all wrong." Dena smiled at Fornet, who grinned back. She pushed him gently aside and grabbed a bottle of cheap brandy from the shelf, then put it on the table.

Fornet's eyebrows rose. He nodded.

Dena turned Scruggs around and grabbed a handful of the Rhone script, and showed it to Fornet, then pointed at the brandy. Fornet held up ten fingers.

"Count out ten of the red ones," Dena said. "Those are lower denomination. See what he says."

Fornet nodded, and pushed the bottle at her. Dena reached behind him, grabbed another one and set it on the table. Fornet shook his head and pulled it back.

"Only one per customer, huh?" Dena grinned. "Now, count out twenty."

Scruggs did. Fornet nodded and reached for the twenty. Dena grabbed his hand. "Wait. Scruggs?"

"Yes?"

"Grab the four cases back there and drag them out. The cases with the double-size bottles."

Dena held Fornet's hand and waited until Scruggs dragged out the four cases. Now there were forty-eight bottles piled next to the table.

"Count out one hundred of those blue ones," Dena said. "Slowly. Lay them on the table as you do."

Fornet's eyes widened as Scruggs counted, and he counted along as the numbers went up.

"Ninety-eight, ninety-nine, one hundred." Scruggs left the money on the table.

Dena let Fornet's hands go. "Money for booze. This is more than you'll see in a year. And you can spend it on your planet, or send it to somebody there. It's worth real cash to you, eventually."

He looked at the pile of money, then at the stacks of brandy. "Mon capitaine…"

"Isn't here right now." Dena picked up the wad of currency and waved it under his nose. "He doesn't need to know. You do the books, lose them in transit, something like that. What do you say?"

Fornet wiped his brow. This side of the ship was empty. There was only him, Dena, Scruggs, a pile of money and a pile of brandy.

"Mon Dieu." He coughed, then looked at Scruggs. "Two hundred. Give it to me now."

Chapter 35

"I'm Cadet Scruggs," Scruggs told the soldiers in the first container nearest the bridge. She and Dena had dressed in their custom skinsuits, and hung every weapon they could carry from a holster, belt, or boot. Scruggs had a portable projection unit, and Dena carried a rifle and a sealed bag. "I've been assigned to handle your training. Cadet Dena and I are looking for volunteers to learn more about your weapons."

Those with some Standard translated for the others. A buzz passed through the compartment. One man raised his hand.

"Yes?"

"This is, ah, an order? From the captain?"

"No. Volunteers only."

The man translated. Others fired questions at him. "What would we learn?"

"Field-stripping the rifle, zero-G combat, marksmanship drills—" Scruggs documented a list of things that they could manage in the close quarters.

The men and women laughed. "No training, but we would like to learn to play poker like you."

"Do you have more money?"

"No."

"Then no poker for you." Scruggs grinned, and they mostly grinned back, jostling the more experienced poker players who had lost to her. They appreciated her skill in fleecing the others. "We'd start with a lecture on your rifle, then practice stripping it."

"Will you give us money?"

"No."

"Then no lecture for you."

Everyone, including the two women, laughed.

"No money for you." Scruggs tilted her head.

The questions had been in Standard, and some of the crew clearly didn't need translations. "How many of you speak Standard?"

The crew's faces blanked.

"Comprend Standard?"

Every single one of them shook their head 'no.'

Scruggs nodded. "I see. Dena?"

Dena opened her bag and pulled out a bottle. "Smell this."

A woman in the front took and sniffed it. She called out a name, and the crowd perked up. "Brandy. Tres bien brandy."

"Anybody who can ask for a shot, in good Standard, gets one. How many of you understand that?"

This time, a dozen hands went up. Scruggs chatted with each as they stepped up, and if she was satisfied, Dena poured them a shot. Most had some Standard, several were fluent.

"You were a fireman back on Rhone?" Scruggs asked one.

"Section chief," the man said. "Got in fight with my boss, next thing you know, I was transferred to the 'military fire detachment.' And here I am."

Scruggs called him 'Fireman Joe.' The crew laughed at that. Then one woman introduced herself as 'Cargo Jenny' and told Scruggs about her time working at a shipping warehouse on Rhone.

"A valuable shipment went missing, and I was blamed, so they sent me to this stupid Brigade."

"Did you steal the cargo?" Scruggs asked.

"I wish I had," Cargo Jenny said, "then I would have bribed my way out of this." Everyone laughed.

"Well, if I need anything stolen, it's good to know I can count on you." Scruggs surveyed the group. "Anybody else?" The others shook their head gloomily.

"Well," Scruggs said. "Too bad. But, please translate this. There is still hope. Dena?"

"Yep." Dena held up the bottle. "Cadet Scruggs wants to show you how to use that rifle. She's going to show you how to strip it and put it back together. Then we'll let you try, and if you can do it in under two minutes, and answer the questions, you get a drink."

The woman in front clapped her hands. "Since I was child, I have always wanted to learn about rifles."

"Really?"

"Yes." The woman smiled. "And since I was a child, I have always loved brandy. Show me."

Daille had been reluctant to give her any rifles to practice with. Scruggs solved the problem by buying them.

"I'm sure you can make up the shortages," Scruggs said. "I'm willing to pay Imperial credits for, say, eight of your carbines. Then they will be our carbines. We're allies, after all."

Dena and Scruggs lectured each group and demonstrated. The troops were bored, and initially treated it as entertainment. She encouraged betting on it. The troops hadn't lost all their money on poker, and what else would they spend their fake money on?

Each squad got one carbine to practice with. Scruggs consistently beat them all. Then, she took the winner from one squad and pitted them against the winner of the next squad. By handing the rifles out judiciously, she ensured that each squad spent a good portion of their day practicing and trying to outdo the others.

"This is a good idea," Lee said, "but you need

to mix it up."

"What do you mean?" Scruggs asked.

"Someone is going to be the fastest, beat everybody. The others will stop trying. If we want to keep this interesting for betting, we need to add some variety. Do it this way—have multiple rounds in the contest. Put a player from one company against one from another in a round-robin format. Everybody competes with everybody else at least once. That way, everyone gets multiple chances to compete, and to bet on it."

It took some explanation. Each squad practiced stripping and assembling the rifle during their shift, and then one would compete against another squad. The results were recorded, and points were assigned to the individual and to the entire squad. This way, even less skilled squad members had a chance to earn points for their buddies.

The competition was fierce and continued for the rest of jump time. Point totals were updated after every shift. The winning squad each got a shot of brandy. The high scorer got a triple shot.

Lee taught them zero-G boarding skills—acrobatics, and seeing who could go the longest down the central corridor of the ship without touching the walls. None of them were any good at it, but it was harder than it looked, and took the place of physical exercise.

By the end of the week, every single member of every squad was competing in at least one of the contests. Some wanted to stay in their bunks, but then their squadmates missed out on squad points. Anyone who slacked off was harassed by their friends.

"The centurion talked about this," Scruggs said. She held one of the troopers while Lee helped splint a broken arm. "You need to have them win or lose as a team so they fight as a team."

"Well, it's working." Lee applied the quick-dry cast to the sweating trooper. "How did you break your arm again?"

The trooper clenched his teeth. "Fell."

"In quarter-G acceleration?"

The man's eyes drifted to the med bay door. Four other poker-faced troops stood there, arms folded. "Fell. Fell hard."

One unfortunate side effect was that the ship stank even more. Vigorously exercising—rushing to strip a weapon, practicing zero-G or low-G maneuvers, or trying to hit a target with a slingshot—generated a lot of heat, sweat, and smell.

"I should be complaining," Dena said. "But I don't notice it as much now."

"Told you," Lee said.

The slingshot program proved especially popular. Dena bent some truss reinforcement struts into a slingshot shape, and the troops used fabric waistbands from underwear to made an acceptable sling.

Scruggs didn't ask how they acquired the underwear.

By mid-second jump, they had established a pattern. Every squad had one shift in a container resting, one shift practicing drills, and one shift competing. The three *Heart's Desire* crew members spent most of their time supervising contests, overseeing drills, or answering technical questions. Scruggs even allowed some of the top winners of the rifle contest to examine her personal weapons and even disassemble them.

"Will we have guns like this?" one trooper asked.

"Sure," Scruggs said, "once you're under regular Imperial command, officers like us, I'm sure you'll be issued better weapons than the ones you have."

"Our own officers are maudit," he said.

Scruggs shrugged. Finally. I was worried this wasn't working. If one of you is saying it, half you are thinking it. "They don't have expertise in training. That's why we're here."

"I hope we work for you."

"Not up to us," Scruggs said. Even better. They know we're competent, now let them think we're important. "The Duke will tell us what the plan is."

"The Duke?" the man asked.

"Our pilot. Duke Friedel. He's an Imperial Duke, and he's in charge of our ship. He assigns duties. Maybe he'll assign all of you to my squad."

"You are tough," the man said, "but you are skilled and work hard. I hope we work for you."

"I'm not tough," Scruggs said. "I'm filling time 'til we get to the real training. On planet. Wait 'til you see what's in store for you there."

The night before they came out of the jump, Scruggs called a meeting with her two crew mates. "Right," she said. "What's our status?"

"The boys and girls are much happier than before," Dena said. "They've got some skills now, soldier skills. We've got the more energetic ones involved, and they've whipped the others into shape."

"You mean that metaphorically?" Lee asked.

"Nope," Dena said. "At least that one broken arm that you know of, and a couple of the non-performers were pummeled in their beds at night. They're covered in bruises."

"Men can be so mean to each other," Scruggs said.

"Baby Marine, that was the girls who did the pummeling." Dena smirked. "They understand stripping a rifle doesn't take much physical strength. After they found something they could dominate in, they dominated. Unless I miss my guess, out of the top ten fastest rifle strippers, seven will be female."

"Outstanding," Scruggs said. "I mean, that's good."

"Nah, you meant outstanding," Dena said. "You've turned into the old man, you might as well start talking like him. You've whipped these troops into shape by example, like he would."

"Well, you two helped me."

"After you showed us how."

Scruggs reddened. "I don't, I mean—"

"Don't get all up on yourself," Dena said. "Lee and I know what you did. You're the big leader. I'm the exotic weirdo, and Lee was the Imperial presence. You played them like a fiddle, but it's not like you invented this. You did what the old man did to you, and passed it on."

Scruggs muttered a denial, but she had a warm feeling inside. *I trained these folks. They're better soldiers now. I'm proud of how they worked. Is the centurion proud of me like that? I'll have to think about it.* "What do we do now?"

"Of course," Dena said. "Whether they'll be willing to shoot anybody is an open question. Except maybe us, when they discover that we're rebels." Dena frowned. "Why aren't those officers more in our face about this?"

"Greed," Lee said. "I talked to the Daille on the bridge last shift. As soon as we come out of the jump, he expects us to head to that training planet. He expects a bucket of Imperial credits when we land there."

"Are we going to be able to come up with them?"

"Not at all."

"Won't he get upset if he's not paid?"

"Extremely," Lee said. "I'm counting on that."

Scruggs narrowed her eyes. "And then?"

"Then I figure you need to fix it."

"Me?" Scruggs said. "What am I supposed to do about it?"

"You're the one whipping this company into shape," Lee said. "Once we land, they're going to look more to you and the centurion than anyone else." A timer beeped. "Gotta go. I have to supervise this emergence. "

Lee left. Scruggs and Dena went over the list of supplies they needed for the next phase of the training she and Scruggs had planned.

"This part is fun," Dena said.

"You like being in the army?" Scruggs asked.

"Nope. But I like doing things I'm good at, and being in charge. These kids all look up to me. And they look up to you. You're the boss now. Your plan has worked."

"These kids are all older than you?"

"Haven't done what I've done, haven't seen what I've seen. They respect us both because we did what they want to do."

"What's that?" Scruggs asked.

"Escape," Dena said. "We ran away from something. That's what they all want."

Two hours later, Lee's voice cut in over the ship's comms. "We are in-system. All parameters are normal. We are 1.5 shifts from orbital insertion. We will be on the ground for training in two shifts total. Everybody has thirty minutes to deal with bodily issues. After that, you'll need to strap in because we will be maneuvering for the next full shift. We will have a break and issue some food, but I suggest eating lightly—landings tend to be a little rough. There are storms in the forecast."

"She sounds like Dirk," Dena said.

Scruggs nodded. "Yeah, she does, doesn't she?" She opened a channel to the bridge. "Sister Lee?"

"Yes, Sister Scruggs?"

"Where did you learn to land a starship from orbit? Have you done it before?"

"It's been a long time," Lee admitted. "But I'm current on my simulations. Besides, I've had an excellent mentor to show me how to land."

"Oh? Someone from the Tribune's staff? One of the other Praetorians?"

"No, no," Lee said. "I've been watching Pilot land. He has an interesting technique. A little rough, but it gets us down fast and in one piece." Lee clicked off.

Scruggs and Dena exchanged glances—then dove for their bunks, strapping themselves in as fast as they could. "This won't be so bad, will it?" Dena said.

"We won't feel a thing," Scruggs said.

"You mean when Lee will give us a smooth landing?" Dena asked.

"Sure," Scruggs said. "Or crashes. Or if we crash and blow up, we won't feel a thing either way."

Chapter 36

"And what exactly is this, Imin? Do we need it?" Devin adjusted the strap holding him in his office chair, and pointed at the line item on the display screen. He tried to get comfortable and failed. He hated this chair, this desk, this office. *Battleships have great comm and big display units, but my office is tiny, this chair is uncomfortable, and I need a bigger wine fridge. The problems of revolt.*

Lionel was maneuvering the fleet. Imin, Devin's steward, was also strapped in on the other side of the desk. He was helping the Tribune sort through personal expenses.

"That would be food sir. I don't think we can cut that out. You need some of it every day."

"Every day? Huh." Devin drummed his fingers on the desk. "Perhaps I could eat only every other day."

"Not an entirely bad idea sir." Imin nodded. "You have been complaining about your weight recently."

"I was being facetious, Imin."

"Yes sir."

"And you were being facetious, weren't you? About my weight?"

"As the Tribune says, of course."

Devin narrowed his eyes. "Do you seriously believe I should only eat every other day?"

"Oh no sir," Imin replied. "Hard to get any benefit from that at all. Now, every third day—"

Devin's glare cut him off mid-sentence. "I have put on a little weight recently," he admitted. "I assume because I spend so much time brooding about this sorry excuse for a fleet instead of working out in the gym."

"Stations for extreme maneuvering." Lionel's voice came over the intercom.

Devin and Imin reflexively slapped their hands down onto the chair arms and let them stick. When the ship maneuvered normally, a fall could snap a wrist. Extreme maneuvering would snap an arm or smash a head.

"Any idea what he's doing up there?" Devin asked.

"I could ask, Tribune."

"No. More exercises, I suppose."

Imin remained silent.

"And of course, I shouldn't ask him because that's acting like the commander of a single ship instead of the task force commander. I'll let my flag captain carry out his duties."

Imin ran Devin through the list of expenses. Most were reasonable—at least, as reasonable as one could expect from a pompous Tribune with a wine fetish, under the circumstances. Devin examined the lines at the bottom.

"If I understand this correctly," Devin said, "I'm flat broke?"

"Oh no sir. You're not flat broke," Imin assured him.

"Well, that's good to know. What does this really mean?"

"You were flat broke months ago sir. I've been borrowing money, extending payments, and juggling all sorts of things. You're way beyond flat broke. You're deep in debt, and the sunlight's a distant memory from the abyss you're in."

"Thank you for that colorful, albeit concerning, explanation, Imin. Any suggestions?"

"Talk to your banker sir. Ask for more money."

"Marvelous suggestion. And how, pray tell, do I go about doing that?"

The intercom chimed. "What do you need, Prefect?"

"Tribune," came Lionel's voice. "One of the

destroyers has intercepted a freighter that entered the system—a tramp freighter. The *Anna Mazaraki*. They're asking for you."

"Asking for me? Why?"

"They claim to have a cargo of nutmeg for you."

"Nutmeg? What am I going to do with nutmeg?" Devin turned to Imin, who coughed into his fist. "Never mind. Imin obviously has a plan for it. Very well, can we transship the cargo?"

"They've also requested to dock with us. One of the passengers wants to speak with you. In person."

"In person? Have they identified themselves?"

"They claim to be your banker."

Devin clicked off the intercom and stared at Imin, who stared back with his usual unflappable demeanor.

"Well, isn't that a coincidence?"

"Fortuitous sir."

"I know you never went to college, Imin. Where did you learn words like fortuitous?"

"I listen to you and the Prefect talk, Tribune. I learn a lot."

"I'll bet you do. Well, isn't that fortuitous. Bring my banker aboard." *More fortuitous than you can imagine.*

An hour later, the intercom chimed again. Imin checked. "Your banker is here sir."

"Send her in."

The same blousy woman, Raka Flintheart, that Devin had met weeks before on Planet Pekak, strode in, all confidence and disheveled clothes.

"Tribune, good to see you. How are things?"

"How did you find us?" Devin asked. "The location of this fleet is highly classified. We've implemented stringent security protocols—"

"I asked the last tramp freighter that delivered

Imperial Legionary

supplies to you," she interrupted. "They told me where you'd be next."

"What?"

"Well, you need supplies, right? Your logistics people tell freighters where to go, so we track their movements to predict your location."

"I see," Devin said darkly. "I'll have a word with my logistics team—and by word, I mean I'll hit them with my sword until either their heads or my sword breaks. Now, why are you here?" He sniffed. "And what is that smell?"

"Nutmeg. It gets everywhere. And I'm here to remind you that you owe us money," she said. "We were expecting repayments through tax credits in the Emperor's name, but…"

"But what? You got your tax credits." Devin grimaced. "Your extensive, long-lasting tax credits. You're living in a herd of fattened tabbos now."

"Well, tax credits only work if you're in charge of a sufficient portion of the Empire to tax them. Right now, there's concern you might not be in that position for much longer."

Devin's jaw tightened. "And who exactly is concerned? I'll send Imin to deal with them."

"Not important, Tribune. It's not who's worried today. It's what the Chancellor might do tomorrow. To you."

"Be specific."

"Specifically, we think you're losing."

"I'm not losing!"

"You're not winning either."

"Not yet. These things take time."

Flintheart shrugged.

"Why don't they think I'll win?"

"A few months ago, you were rampaging across the Verge—defeating Imperial units, killing pirates, stabbing people, and making excellent soup. But now, your momentum has stalled. You're duffing around in the Empire's backwaters instead of advancing toward the Core. And you haven't offered me any soup."

Devin frowned. "I can't saunter in and attack the first major Imperial base I see?"

"Why not?"

"Because we're not ready. We need training. Practice. Ammunition."

"Then you're going to lose. If you can't take a sector base, you can't win a revolution. Which means eventually you'll fade back into the Verge, and be hunted down on some border planet and hung by the local Marine Commander."

"Nobody is hanging me."

Flintheart shrugged again. "I'll bet you plan on killing yourself privately, not giving them the satisfaction."

I was thinking that, what I could do if I lose. That's a dangerous attitude. "I don't have any money I can access. What would you have me do?"

"It's not about the money, it's about the winning. People need to believe you're still winning."

"First time I've ever heard a banker say they weren't interested in money."

"At this level, money has nothing to do with it. When this is done," Flintheart smiled, "I'll be a duchess, or I'll be dead. And I want to be a duchess."

"That's your view of how to become a noble? Crime and rebellion?"

"Sure." Flintheart smile widened. "How did your great-great-great-grandrelative become the Lord Lyon? The first one."

"I don't know." It had involved smuggling, a large number of bribes, and outright theft of three cargo freighters. Devin suspected she knew that already. "I asked before, what would you have me do?"

"We don't want to tell you what to do. You're the combat leader, after all. We don't want to upset you, but to be diplomatic—"

Devin leaned forward. "I'm leading a battleship, in open rebellion against the Empire. I carry a sword. What about me suggests I don't appreciate blunt answers?"

"Capture New Malaya."

"The biggest fleet base in this sector? That one? That New Malaya?"

"That would be wonderful." Flintheart smiled. "Yes, please. Can we count on that by the end of the month?"

"No, you can't count on it by the end of the month. We're not ready."

"When are you going to be ready? It better be soon."

Devin opened his mouth, then shut it. *She's serious. And worried. But she doesn't know if I'm telling the truth about whether we're ready. And everybody who can read a map knows I have to attack New Malaya, eventually, just not when. Can I work with that?* "You expect me to launch a rebellion with inadequate troops, poorly trained crews, an insufficient number of hulls, and a shortage of military supplies?"

"Yes, that is exactly what we expect, and that was exactly our agreement. You showed up needing money. We gave you money. You said you'd use the money to get ships and go conquer the Empire."

"I didn't say conquer. I said release my sister from bondage."

"Whatever. We heard conquer. When it's done, you'll be in charge, and we'd get our tax credits. If we don't get our tax credits, then we'll have to look at supporting somebody else."

"You're pretty brave, coming all alone on a flagship to shake me down for some money."

"We're pragmatic. Either we get you mad at us now, or we get the Chancellor mad at us later. You might stab me to death with your famous sword—or you might not. But the Chancellor surely will stab me to death, or hang me, or electrocute me, or feed me to a vat full of lobsters. He's done it before."

"He's done that before? Really?" Devin laughed. "Imin, do you think the Chancellor has fed people to vats full of lobsters before?"

Imin nodded. "Oh yes sir. You have to be very careful where you source your lobsters. They'll eat all manner of things. That's why I like the natural ones. The ones from some shipping companies—you're never sure where they've been."

"The Chancellor actually feeds people to lobsters? Wait, lobsters are carnivorous?"

Imin's hand twitched. "Yes, and yes, Tribune."

Devin hadn't missed the twitch. He's got a pistol there. Flintheart must have seen it and she didn't even blink. Cool customer. I wonder if she'd like to command a warship? "Well, I learn something new every day. Plainly speaking, you're telling me I'd better make some progress toward winning this war soon by taking New Malaya. How do your great military minds suggest I do that?"

"We're not going to suggest anything because we're not great military minds. That's supposed to be your job. We gave you the money. You're supposed to spend it on something that gives us what we want."

"Which is what?"

"More money, of course. We'll be extracting it in a different manner than you're used to."

"I don't see how you're making a profit off this."

"You don't have to. We don't see how you're winning the war, and we don't have to. What matters is we're making a profit, and you're winning the war. As long as those two statements are true, everyone is happy—except the Chancellor, but we don't care about him."

"I started this war for the best of reasons. I started this war to liberate my sister. Free the Empire. Uphold the right." *At least I tell myself that.*

"Good for you, and good for your reasons. Are you willing to lose because you had the best of reasons, or do you want to win with slightly less noble ones?"

"That sentence doesn't even make sense."

Flintheart spread her hands wide. "You get the point. I'm delivering supplies for your fleet and payments for another thirty days. After that, we expect news of a great victory—of Tribune Devin sweeping toward the Core, slaughtering his enemies, beheading their leaders, and driving all before him."

"Slaughtering all my enemies? Do I have to do it personally?"

"You don't even have to slaughter all of them. Just a representative sample. Could you video it, perhaps?"

"How should I do that? Take videos as I cut people to pieces, sever their heads, and swing them from ropes behind my ships?"

Flintheart nodded. "That would be great. I'm not sure how well the swinging would work in zero gravity, but you're resourceful. Maybe your video people can edit something."

"You're serious, aren't you?"

"Deadly serious." Flintheart grimaced. "I'm not particularly bloodthirsty. I'm not keen on seeing anyone's head cut off—except I am keen on not having my neck cut off. The deal was money for protection. Protection means winning a war."

"I can't do it in a month."

"How long do you need?"

Devin stared her down. She didn't blink first, he did. "Ninety days. I will occupy a major fleet base in ninety days."

"Which one?"

"New Malaya. But not for three months." He named a date. "That's when I'll attack."

"Why so long? Can you do it sooner?"

"No." Devin shook his head. "I'll need all that time. I'm finalizing my routes now, I'll be taking some roundabout paths to get there to avoid Imperial patrols. Once my scouts and detached ships rejoin, I'll need another month to finish drilling, and up to two months of travel time. We'll drop into the system where they won't expect us, and take 'em from behind. The plans are almost complete. I just need to show them to my officers."

"Can I see those plans?"

"I'm not sharing my plans with you. But you have my word, I'll be running into the New Malaya system ninety days from now. But not before."

The banker stood. "We will supply you until then."

"And when I occupy said fleet base," Devin said, steepling his fingers, "you and your colleagues—a list I'll provide—will make a public announcement of support for me and denounce the Chancellor. The announcement will be phrased so there's no backing out. We sink or swim together."

The banker blinked, sitting silently. "What names will be on this list?"

"Whatever names I want. I'll tell you this, it'll be long. If I forget anyone, I'm sure you'll make sure they're added."

"Fine. Ninety days. We're reasonable people.

Pleasure doing business with you."

"Thanks. Go back to your ship now."

"Do I have to?"

"What do you mean?"

"I was hoping you'd make me stay for lunch." She smiled slightly. "Maybe have some soup."

Devin escorted her to the shuttle, and waited until she left to board her ship, *Anna Mazaraki*. It was a mark of respect, a sign of goodwill, and an assurance that the escorting Marines would intervene before he throttled her. The clanking hatch marked her departure.

Devin sighed. "Imin."

"Yes sir?"

"Contact Captain Monti and invite her for dinner. Get a couple others. Rudnar, some of the younger officers. Put out good wine. Configure a presentation of the latest plan the Prefect and I put together."

"Should I invite the Prefect?"

"Not this time. He's seen the plan. And I need input from my junior officers right away. Next shift. Two at the latest."

"Right now sir? I believe the lady said ninety days sir."

"Well, I've got other plans. And take my sword—make sure it's sharpened. I'll need it for those other plans."

Chapter 37

Monti slumped in the bridge chair. "I told him," she muttered.

Hooper sniffed. "Are you drunk? I smell wine." She had the bridge watch while Monti was away at the flagship. Which mostly meant watching the boards, and trying to keep warm. Silaski sat at the helm, watching a sim and keeping her hands in her pockets.

"Are you wearing mittens?"

"My hands are cold. And it's so damp."

"Where did you get them?"

"My gram sent them to me. She knitted them herself."

"Is that even allowed—"

"It's required, because with mittens, you can't see which fingers I'm holding up." Hooper extended her hand. "Never mind the mittens. Tell me about dinner."

"We talked for almost three hours," Monti said. "He talked about his plans. I gave him the report on the potential Nat fleet entering Imperial space." Tribune Devin had invited her and several others over for another drunken dinner. They were so short crewed, Hooper had to stay behind.

"What did he say?"

"I told him. I told him what I saw. I gave him the scans."

Hooper sniffed again. "Red wine, I think. Fruity. What type was it?"

"He didn't believe me. Even though I told him, I don't think he believed me."

"Definitely red wine. Are you sure he didn't believe you?"

"Well… kind of."

"What do you mean, kind of? He either believed you or he didn't."

"He said he wasn't going to—quote—'reposition the fleet on the basis of a single scouting report.' He said he had a plan to take New Malaya."

"Even a scouting report that included scans and beacon codes?"

"Even that."

"You know, it's got this tannic, dark tannic red quality," Hooper mused. "Was it another one of those Napa Bordeaux he offered before?"

"Hooper, this is serious."

"I know, Franky. I know."

"I told you not to call me—"

"Yes, I know. Don't call you Franky while you're on duty. All your stupid rules. Don't call you Franky. Don't sleep on watch. Don't let Silaski calculate the jumps—"

"That's not fair!" Silaski spoke up from the helm. "I'm doing much better now. I've only made, like, three major mistakes."

"Yes, but they were all the same three mistakes, and on the same jump," Hooper said. "But never mind. You showed him the scans, and he said he didn't believe you?"

"Well, it's not so much that he didn't believe me. He didn't care. He gave me a long speech about the needs of the Empire, the needs of the rebellion, worries about the Empress, and logistical concerns."

"A reasoned and valid argument?"

"No clue. I'd had a lot of wine by then. It seemed to make sense."

"You've had a lot of wine now."

"Yep. I think I'm going to go to my bunk and try to sleep it off."

"You can't sleep it off. You're on watch."

"I can't be on watch. I've been drinking. Wait—who's on watch now?"

"Silaski."

"Silaski's not allowed to be on watch."

"What I meant to say was, I'm on watch. But I've been sitting here doing other stuff while Silaski runs the watch."

"Why do we only have three watch-capable people?"

"We don't. We have two watch-capable people. Actually, we have one watch-capable person. That's one watch-capable, non-drunk person. That's me. You, on the other hand, may be watch-qualified, but you're not watch-capable."

"I need a nap. We'll talk in the morning."

"It is morning. You were gone two shifts. It's already morning."

"Fine. We'll talk second shift."

Monti slept for a full shift. When she woke, she felt horrible. "Serves you right," she muttered to herself.

She wandered up to the bridge and found Hooper asleep in her chair, while Silaski was running through scans.

"Silaski," Monti said, careful not to wake Hooper. "Who's flying the ship?"

"That would be Lieutenant Hooper ma'am."

"Lieutenant Hooper is asleep."

"Yes ma'am."

Monti waited, but no further explanation came.

"It doesn't bother you that the watch officer is asleep?"

"Well, ma'am," Silaski said, looking up, "since the last reorganization, we've lost... what, thirty percent of our crew? Sent to other ships?"

"Yes, that's true."

"And the only remaining bridge officers are you and Hooper. Although I don't understand why they haven't put her in charge of another ship."

"Me neither," Monti said. "I asked the Tribune, and he said he thought it was best that the two of us stay together. That we make better decisions that way."

"Does that mean he doesn't trust you?"

"No, I... I don't know. And anyway, I'm not discussing this with you. You're just a helmsman." Monti sat. "I'm going to comm the flagship and ask for more people."

"But we kind of have a system working now, right? I'm learning all sorts of new stuff. You two are getting some sleep. And we haven't run into any trouble yet. I know enough to wake the lieutenant when the bells go off."

"Uh-huh. And?"

"What if, you know, when we ask for new people... we get new people?"

"That's the point, Silaski. We need new people."

"Yeah, but you want, like, good people. People like you and the lieutenant."

"Uh-huh. And?"

"Well... what if you just get more people like me? What do you think is gonna happen then?"

"Ah, crap," Monti muttered.

She looked at the sleeping Hooper.

"How much longer can you stay awake?"

"At least another half shift."

"Silaski, I'm going to take a shower. I was never here."

"Understood."

A half shift later, after a longer nap and a shower, Monti sat in her chair and checked supplies. Fuel and water were plentiful, the tankers were on the job. And a shipment of trays and basic had been delivered while she slept.

"Thank you for helping us out, Silaski."

"Yes. Ma'am."

"Shows strength of character. I'm glad I didn't

ask for more people."

Silaski shrugged. "Wouldn't have mattered if you did ma'am. The flag wouldn't have sent anybody."

"What makes you say that?"

"Well, they don't like you for some reason. Or don't trust us, maybe."

"They trust us. The Tribune showed us his battle plan. He asked for questions. Even gave me a secret copy to review. He trusts us."

"Then how come every other ship gets shore leave, and breaks, and how come they won't give you and Lieutenant Hooper bigger, better ships? I've seen what those chowderheads out there are doing. I couldn't tell earlier, but you two are better ship handlers than all of them, except that scary woman on the flagship. And once you started ignoring their 'help,' you started doing really well on those combat drills. I didn't understand before, but now I do. Somebody over there has it in for you two."

"Nobody has it in for us, Silaski. You're imagining things again."

"Ma'am." Silaski yawned. "I've been awake three shifts ma'am. Can I go get some sleep?"

"Of course, and thanks again."

Monti waited until Silaski was out, then brought up the results of the last ten drills, careful not to wake Hooper. Neither of them ever got enough sleep. The numbers didn't lie. As soon as they stopped taking the flagship's data, they did better in the drills.

Tribune didn't mention that. He talked about not moving the fleet for a single scouting report. She looked at the sleeping Hooper. Was showing us his plans a way of manipulating us to work harder? Why are we busting our ass for a rebel? One who sabotages us at every turn? And one who isn't taking a possible Nat incursion seriously. Have I misjudged this Devin guy? Is he really loyal to the Empire? And if he wasn't, what was she going to do about it?

She brought up the drive performance specs, and then displayed some course plots on the main screen. Knowing what your ship was capable of gave you options, and it was looking like she'd need some more options in a hurry, and soon.

Chapter 38

"Three, two, one, touchdown," Dirk said. "Shutting off. Centurion, let's get those fuel hoses deployed, pronto."

"Navy, you can take your fuel hose—" Ana gave Dirk detailed instructions on an anatomically impossible action— "Do that pronto if you like. As for me, the punk can get a hose into that lake over there himself. I'm putting out flares and a beacon to set a landing point for the Navigator in front of us."

"Do we need to do that?"

"I assume all Navy pilots are incompetent idiots who don't know where to land, so I help them out by directing their landings."

They had crunched onto tundra adjacent to a stream-fed lake, surrounded by dense shoulder high scrub brush and low pine trees. Meadows alternated with steep hills—the one on the horizon was at least three hundred meters tall. Dirk's landing hop over it had impressed even Ana.

"We need fuel."

"We've got days to suck fuel," Ana said. "But I want that other ship landed where we can cover it with our laser cannon, while Scruggs and I discuss things with them." He regarded the bush-covered meadow. "Superior firepower always helps with getting agreement in negotiations."

"Our laser is tiny, and it will barely scorch anything in atmosphere."

"A laser pointing at them looks impressive. They don't need to know how powerful it is. But we need Lee to land within an angle that we can cover, and we can't tell her that over the radio. Tell her we've scoped out a landing spot for her, and that she can proceed with her plan."

"Shouldn't we wait 'til they're on the ground

and we know what their plan is?"

"Scruggs will try to seize the ship and kill the officers."

"You have no proof of that." Except that's the way I'd bet. She's all action and motion, that one. Spent too much time with the centurion.

"You've met her. She wants to be an officer." Ana shrugged. "You're used to young officer candidates. She did well on her first test, screwed up her second. What do you think she'll do on her third detached command? Sit around and wait for orders? She knows we need troops for the Tribune, so she'll figure out a way to get them for him. Besides, what did you do when you had to plan things?"

Dirk remembered being a young officer, and some stupid things he had done. Junior commanders had to learn by doing. "Made a complete mess out of things. Got a lot of good people killed."

Ana shrugged. "That's what officers do. Think she'll do better than you?"

Dirk sighed. "Fine. I'll tell Lee where to land when I'm talking to her." Dirk hit the intercom. "Gavin, you ready?"

"Not yet. I need to drop the ramp, but it looks like everything is on fire out there."

The main drives had ignited the foliage as they landed, and the *Heart's Desire* sat in the middle of a growing circle of burning bushes.

"We'll tell her to aim for the fires." Dirk called Lee on the radio. "When you get close to the co-ordinates, look for a beacon and flares. Centurion has picked a place for you to touch down."

"A clear spot with landing access?" Lee said. "Easy to find?"

Dirk looked at the fires surrounding the *Heart's Desire* and the steep hills nearby. "You'll have no problems seeing it."

"That's got to be the worst landing I've ever seen." Dirk coughed and waved the smoke away. "How long is that skid? Three, four hundred meters?"

Ana coughed as well. "Don't you watch your own landings, Navy? You've done way worse than that."

"I may have hit harder," Dirk said, "but I never skidded that far."

"You remember that time—"

"Okay, I don't often skid that far, but she should have adjusted for not landing on concrete."

"Good thing she didn't. I need time to adjust to these clothes." Ana pointed to his clean uniform. "Was all this necessary?"

"I'm in charge of presentation and diplomacy," Dirk said. "You worry about who to shoot." Dirk had made them dress up in formal uniforms to overawe the troops and officers on *Esprit*.

Lee had brought the *Esprit* down according to Dirk's instructions. Unfortunately, Dirk's instructions came from a former assault boat pilot, and the only way he knew how to land a freighter was fast, hard, and—faster and harder.

The *Esprit* had hit the pegged landing area exactly where Ana had specified and then skidded across a stream, over a small hill, and into another stream, finally coming to rest beyond it. The entire landing field was now a collection of burning and smoking bushes, scenting the air with a dark cherry smell.

"Well, good news," Ana said. "It's still in the arc of the laser. Top two-thirds."

"Bad news," Dirk said. "We're going to have a problem fueling it. Can we even get a hose that far?"

"That might not be such a bad thing," Ana said. "Keeps them dependent on us. Let's see how it plays out. Gavin, you ready back there?"

Gavin fussed behind them, tightening a pipe fitting with a wrench. "Yep, all set."

"You sure this is going to work?" Dirk asked. "The water thing, I mean."

"I'm sure it's not going to work," Gavin said, "which is the point. And they're not going to be able to figure out why. Even if they do get the hoses together, they're going to get almost nothing. And the first hydrogen explosion is going to cause them to—"

"Hydrogen explosion? Cause them to what? Blow us up?"

"We'll work on that later," Gavin said. "If they can't get a tight seal, I won't pump the hydrogen."

"Those boxes I asked you about…"

Gavin pointed at some piled a distance from the ship, next to the hoses. They were stenciled 'Hydrogen pump extension units' and the open top showed more hoses. "Rifles and ammo, like you said. Under the false bottoms."

"Well done. It's time for you to man the main batteries, as it were," Dirk said. "We'll wait here for the, uh, representatives of the Rhone Brigade."

Dirk and Ana waited while the small fires started by the *Esprit* burned out. Half of the bushes and trees were now festooning the top and front of the *Esprit*—and they were also burning.

Dirk tried his communicator. "*Esprit*, this is *Heart's Desire*. You're on fire."

Lee's voice came back. "Understood, Pilot. We'll need a few minutes to clear the exits and wait for things to burn down. The crew is excessively interested in getting off the ship, given the way things smell."

"No doubt," Dirk said and clicked out. "What do you think, Centurion?"

"An interesting tactical problem to get everyone out. I don't see a ramp."

"It's not a custom-built assault boat. It's a Verge freighter," Dirk said. "No ramps, cranes, nothing. This is purely a Core world ship—a big container carrier. An intra-system barge."

"Well, it's a heavily loaded intra-system barge," Ana said. "Given the number of troops that—here they come."

A small pile of smoldering brush heaved off the top of the bow of the ship, and a figure's head appeared, pushing them away.

"Trust the flight crew to get their first shot of fresh air," Ana said. "Just like the Navy. Always leaving the poor grunts hauling behind."

The upper midship's airlock opened. With the landing legs extended, the ventral airlock was blocked. A group of uniformed figures pressed forward, then one yelled and fell out, landing on the ground with a thud.

"That's got to hurt," Ana said. "What is that, twenty feet? Why don't they put a ladder down?"

"They don't know how to put the ladder down. They've never done it," Dirk said. "They haven't practiced how to exit in atmosphere away from a landing port. Lee should have warned them."

"Glad she didn't. We don't want them all getting out in a hurry," Ana said.

A familiar figure had dropped out of the aft belly hatch.

"Dena found the engineering hatch," Dirk said. "Smart girl."

Dena jogged across the intervening smoldering bushes.

Rocky had accompanied them down onto the bushes, sniffing and peeing. He had ignored Lee's landing. He was used to loud explosions, fire, and violent maneuvering. After all, he flew with Dirk a lot.

But when he saw the woman running toward him, he barked once and then took off like a shot, leaping over the piles of still-smoldering trees.

Rocky missed his friends.

The jogging form met the torpedoing dog partway through. Even from this distance, they could hear her grunt as Rocky slammed into her chest. She cradled him in her arms and continued jogging toward them.

"Fellow crewmates."

Ana sniffed. "What is that stench? Did you forget to wipe your—"

"The life support system isn't working well. The clothes pick up the smell. And we're lucky, the three of us got to shower once in the last week. The others didn't."

"We'll talk hygiene later," Dirk said. "Where's Scruggs? Where's Lee?"

"I love you too, Rocky, but please stop." Dena tried to avoid the dog's slurping tongue. "Did the two of you rob a costume store on the way here?"

"Rob a costume store? What are you—?"

Dena pointed. "Is that fur?"

Dirk had on something approximating the full ceremonial regalia of an Imperial Duke. Dark blue tunic, dark blue pants, gold buttons—and a dead animal wrapped around his shoulder.

"It's fake fur," Dirk said. "It's called a pelisse."

"Well, you better police it up somewhere else because it looks pretty scraggly."

"I'll have you know that most pelisses are passed down through Imperial families from generation to generation. Why, they were originally—"

"They're going to be used to gag a babbling

duke if you keep talking," Ana said. "Nature Girl, where's Scruggs? And where's Lee? What forces do we face? What's the tactical situation? What's the briefing?"

"We had problems. The officers are incompetent, and Scruggs says these are the worst troops she's ever seen." Dena explained the whole trip there—the company's original confrontation with the commander, the demand for their orders, the demand for money, Scruggs's plan to play poker, the training they'd been able to do.

"The head captain guy is suspicious, but he's greedy and lazy. We found out he's getting a cut of the everything the troops buy, and eat, so he's pocketing a fortune on this cruise. We think his plan is to take your supplies and fuel, then later claim he paid for it. He'll make even more. As far as whether we're rebels or Imperials, we've managed to put them off. They're still suspicious—they made a point of making sure that Lee is secured on the bridge and that Scruggs is back with the officers. She's being held for 'consultations.' The captain guy is pretty sure that something's not right, but he didn't object when I volunteered to help in engineering. They can barely fly that ship. The crew is so incompetent that they didn't know there was a hatch there."

Dena waved at the *Esprit*. They'd finally managed to get a ladder down from the main hatch, and a group of soldiers approached.

"You know, maybe you're not the worst pilot in the history of pilots," Dena said. "Her landing skid was, what, four hundred meters long?"

"She didn't account for the vegetation," Dirk said. "Starport pads are flat concrete, not wet wood. Easy mistake to make your first combat-style landing."

"Or your hundredth," Ana muttered.

"Good camouflage," Dirk said. "And she cleared a workspace between the two ships."

"Outstanding," Ana said. "If you like uncontrolled forest fires."

Dena shook her head. "Either way, your police thing—"

"Pelisse."

"Whatever. Looks like you crossed a drunken beaver with a dead badger. Look at this." She displayed her shoulder, marked with a strip. "Scruggs made me a cadet!"

"Good for Scruggs," Ana said. "Not that it counts for anything."

"If I'm a cadet, then I get a uniform too." Dena grinned. "I'll put a fur collar on my leathers. That will look sexy." She frowned. "Or maybe my cuffs. Hard to decide."

"There's a group of mercenaries approaching who probably want to kill us," Dirk said. "And you're worried about your future clothes?"

"Collar and cuffs." Dena tilted her head. "I'll do both. That will look amazing. And shouldn't I be proud to be a cadet?"

"Somebody should be," Dirk said. "I'm not." He pointed to the approaching Rhone Brigade officers. "What do we do with these guys?"

"Lie," Dena said. "Assign them more training under Scruggs."

"Does Scruggs have a plan?" Dirk asked.

Dena explained. She and Scruggs had decided to try to get the Rhone Brigade to revolt and follow them, if they could find the right moment. Two of the squads, now friends, should follow Scruggs's orders. They hoped Dirk could confuse the officers while they tried to get the other officers away from Isere. "Give them fake orders. Act like a clueless duke. One of those empty-headed pompous types that continually screw things up and count on your subordinates to fix it."

"Shouldn't be hard," Ana said. "He does that already."

"Not now, Centurion," Dirk said. "Scruggs and Lee are on that ship, and there's a hundred-ish somewhat trained troops who may want to kill us, and we're alone with them on an uninhabited planet. Everybody act sharp."

"I always act sharp," Ana said.

"What do you want me to do?" Dena said.

"Well, Cadet," Dirk said, straightening and throwing a full Imperial cross-chest salute. "Parade your troops. And Jove save the Empire."

Chapter 39

"All right, so what do we do here?" Dirk said. Three uniformed figures had dropped out of the other starship and marched toward them. "Ana, can we handle this?"

Ana nodded. "Going to have to. As much as I'd like to, I can't shoot all of them."

"Lacking faith in your abilities?" Dena said. "What a surprise. Never would have expected that."

"Not abilities, mass. All that ammunition is too much to carry. There's, what, two hundred men on that ship? I mean, even if I limited myself to one bullet per, I'd still have to carry a pretty substantial amount of ammunition. And they're unlikely to stand still the whole time."

"Unfair of them," Dirk said. "Ruins your day."

"Wait, you mean shoot everyone on the ship, not only those three?" Dena asked.

"Let me do the calculation." Ana scrunched up his face. "And I should double-tap. So—two to the chest, one to the head to make sure. A hundred cartridges is a kilogram...what's the official total of the starship crew?"

"Not now," Dirk said. "Meet first. Shoot later. Follow my lead."

The two groups met halfway between the two ships, on a spot of scraped rock. The *Esprit*'s landing legs had pushed the dirt and bushes clear. The ones on the side were either knocked over or almost on fire.

Dirk gagged as the smell hit him. *Did they crap in their pants? It's worse than a dead body. And speaking of dead bodies, let's not become one.* He stepped to the front. "Good morning," he said. "I am Duke Durriken Friedel. Cadet Scruggs tells me you are the officers of the Rhone Brigade."

"Yes, uh…"

"My lord Duke is the proper form of address."

"I am Lieutenant Isere, my lord Duke." The first officer introduced Captain Daille, and translated the responses. He didn't introduce the other man dressed as a soldier, complete with pistol in a belt holster. Dena had told Dirk about Alain and the other bully-boys, so Dirk didn't push it.

Daille said something, and Isere nodded and turned to Dirk. "Captain Daille asks if he has met you before. He says you are familiar."

"I have been in Imperial Service all my working life. Perhaps we served together in the past."

"This is the captain's first time off planet. The Rhone Brigade has never deployed before."

"Can't be that, then." *Thieving weasel. Why discomfort yourself when you can steal your men's pay from the comfort of your chair?*

Isere cocked his head. "You do look familiar to me. Have you ever been on the vids, perhaps?"

Dirk laughed. "I'm no actor. I've never been on any video show." *Not as an actor. Now, as a criminal charged with treason…*

Isere gave Dirk a long look, then shrugged. "I understand you have orders from the Empire for us."

"We do," Dirk said. He produced a message cube and handed it to the captain, trying hard not to touch him. "It is not tuned personally to your DNA, but it uses an Imperial code. You should be able to read it with your ship equipment."

"I see." The captain queried the lieutenant. Isere turned to them. "The captain asks if you give me the gist of it? We will have to unpack our coding equipment."

"Gist?" Dirk grinned. "That's an excellent word to know in a second language. Where did you learn your Standard?"

Isere blushed. "Cartoons, my lord Duke. When I was a child, I was fond of Chilly Harold, you know…"

"The penguin and his friend." Dirk grinned. "I watched it as well. Great fun."

"There was not a lot of entertainment on Rhone, and the video displayed the spelled words in Français, but the spoken ones were of course in Standard."

"Which explains your excellent pronunciation and accent," Dirk said. "Well done, Lieutenant. The Empire needs resourceful officers like you." Dirk chatted some more to give Scruggs and Dena time to do whatever they were going to do.

The captain snapped a stream of Français. Isere blanked his face. "The captain asks about our orders…"

"Of course," Dirk said. "You have been assigned as an area of my responsibility for the next while for training. Once training is complete to my satisfaction, we will have other tasks. I have additional duties from the Emperor, so I will not be directly involved. Cadet Scruggs and her staff will take that over." *How are they going to make this work? This is going sideways as we speak.*

"Her staff?"

"First Centurion Anastasios will assist her. And, of course, our engineer will provide the technical support where necessary. And young Dena as well, of course."

Dena had stepped away behind them and was playing with Rocky, keeping within hearing but out of smell range. Daille glared at her and spoke to Isere.

Isere translated. "Dena is part of her staff as well? I was under the impression—yes, that she was a companion. She is not very military."

"She is still young. But she has skills that your

troops will need. That will be part of your training. By the way, where are Cadet Scruggs and Praetorian Lee?"

The captain's answer to Isere was much longer this time. Isere nodded several times, then turned to Dirk. "The captain says that they are required on the ship, my lord Duke. Praetorian Lee is assisting the crew on some needed repairs, and Cadet Scruggs has decided to stay with them to continue the crew's training."

"I'm not surprised. Praetorian Lee always has some ship-related task or other to attend to. Cadet Scruggs is, of course, dedicated to her job. She loves training, did she tell you that? She's expert at it."

"She said something like that," Isere admitted, "but I was uncertain, given her age."

"Her age is of no matter," Dirk said. "She has all the appropriate experience. She is a youngster, compared to me, but most of you are now. Especially to old folks like us, Captain. Isn't that so?"

Dirk clapped the captain on the shoulder, but kept his face blank. He was holding his breath. *The smell…don't vomit.*

The captain barked a reply.

Sweat beaded Isere's brow. "The captain, he says he is not that old—"

"I know, I know. It creeps up on you," Dirk said, leaning in closer. "I'll tell you, though, I'm glad that the girls will be staying with you. When they're on board our ship, they're somewhat… energetic. Noisy. Why, several times, they've interrupted my afternoon nap. But they can hardly train your troops if they're not living with them and exercising them, is that not so?"

Isere translated. "Of course, my lord Duke. I have been in conference with them. They have a full set of training exercises prepared. Perhaps we can discuss."

"And I'm sure they're excellent ones. I can count on you and the centurion to take care of that, can I not?"

"Yes, yes." Isere looked to his captain. The captain spoke a phrase, then repeated it. "We'd like confirmation of your authority—"

"Our authority is in your orders, Captain. Don't you recognize an Imperial code?"

Isere floundered. "We will validate the codes, but perhaps we can meet to discuss things."

"A weekly update would be fine, would it not?"

"The captain would like you to come on board right now—"

"I'm sure you can speak to the cadet and the senior centurion. They're here to handle the training of your brigade, after all. And if you have some ship matters, you can speak to Praetorian Lee," Dirk said. "Is there anything else?"

"We are in need of hydrogen fuel, as you know."

"Of course, of course. Our engineer has indicated that our fueling system is operable and we can crack the hydrogen you need. We have plenty of time, so if you can arrange a party to haul the hoses over, we can start sending you the hydrogen as we crack it." *And hope it's the crew Scruggs wants.*

Isere paused for translation, and then Daille spoke on his radio, then queried Isere again.

"The captain has sent for crew to move the hydrogen. And supplies?"

"We have those too. Once the hydrogen is flowing, we will drop one of the containers that contains food trays, and you can transfer things to your ship. Or so the engineer tells me." Dirk examined the *Esprit*. "I note you have neither a crane nor a loading ramp, so this might be difficult for you. But I'm sure your ship's crew can assist you with that. But that's enough for now. I'll retire to the ship." Dirk made to turn.

Captain Daille reached over and grabbed Dirk's arm. His voice was loud, and the trooper with him put his hand on his holster.

Sweat ran down Isere's face, and his voice cracked. "The captain, the captain he insists that you accompany him to the ship to discuss this further. He finds this lack of regular training facilities irregular. Why are we on this out-of-the way planet? Why so few officers? Why did you send only three people to train us? And where are our supplies?"

Dirk glared at the arm, then up at Isere. "Translate this carefully. We will provide you with fuel, if you can be bothered to send a working party to our ship. We have resupply for you, several containers, but my engineer tells me they will be difficult with your ship configuration. That is also your problem. He also told me that you needed a planet with breathable air to conduct your own repairs." Dirk pointed his finger at Daille. "Translate that."

Isere did. Daille started to speak. Dirk held up his hand. "And remind him that I am an Imperial Duke. I understand he is confused. But you are not the only ones armed here." Dirk glared. "The centurion is armed. I am armed. We will provide you what you need, but we will not be ordered around. I serve the Empire, not you. Understood?" *And we need those troops out here where we can talk to them.*

Daille glared back at Dirk, then released his hand.

Dirk nodded. "We will help you prepare for your upcoming fights. But remember this— you serve at the Emperor's pleasure. It is your responsibility to be ready for the upcoming conflict. And, if this peasant," Dirk pointed to the captain, "handles me again, he will feel the Empire's wrath."

Chapter 40

"Plug them together like this." Gavin mated the female end of the hose with the male one, and twisted the holder into place. "Pull the quick snap first. If it's water, then you're done. But if it's hydrogen, you need to screw on the insulated pipe." He slid the heavier metal coupling to the end of the hose. "It twists onto the hose on each side to make a seal. The screw pitch is much smaller, and it's cone-shaped, so the more you twist, the tighter the seal. Once it's finger-tight, step on the riser plate to hold it into place, and use the ratchets and your body weight to lever it tighter." Gavin demonstrated, then held up the mated hoses. "Questions?"

The four troopers sent over from the *Esprit* stared at Gavin, looked at each other, and exchanged shrugs.

"Pardon," the shortest man said. "Ne comprend pas."

"Jove save us," Gavin said. Most of the fires from the *Esprit*'s skidding landing had burned out. He'd opened the outer lockers on *Heart's Desire* to get at the water pumps and fuel cracker. "Any of you speak Standard? Comprend Standard?" *How am I going to talk to them? I need more than hand gestures to say 'kill your officers and join us.'*

The four men shook their heads, and muttered in Français.

"We need to get this set up for you to get your fuel. Lieutenant?" He called the group in the middle of the field. Captain Daille had hissed his displeasure and stalked back to the *Esprit*. Lieutenant Isere was left to deal with all the loading and unloading issues.

Isere held up his hand. "Un moment, please." He turned back to Dena and Ana. "I am sorry, but

I have my orders. Cadet Scruggs and Navigator Lee must remain onboard to consult with the captain. I cannot change that."

"Whatever you say, Lieutenant, it's fine by me. I'm only a senior centurion after all, not an officer. No need to follow my suggestions. I'm sure your people know best."

Isere winced. He wasn't much of a solider, but even he knew that not following a centurion's suggestions didn't end well. "I can pass her questions—"

"Lieutenant," Gavin yelled. "We need some translation over here. If you want to get any hydrogen, ever, I need water to crack. And if you want your water system flushed, you need water too, and if I can't explain to these troops."

"Un moment—"

Ana interrupted. "I still need a platoon, or at least a couple of your squads to move the supplies. When can I have them?"

"I will have to assign some, and I must have a list of the needed skills—"

Dena held out her hands. "There's a platoon of workers from a trucking company on *Esprit*. They're used to moving containers. I can have them unloading shortly."

"I did not—"

Ana crossed his arms. "And when can we expect the first platoon for field training? They need to dig shelters and get started on the field maneuvers."

"We cannot have everybody out of the ship," Isere said. "We must remain inside, for protection."

"I didn't want to bring this up." Ana waved his hands in front of him. "But you all stink. Like you've been dumped in a cesspool up to your armpits. Your life support is off badly. You need to get your troops out of that while you get it fixed.

And personally, I suggest a bath for you."

Isere sniffed himself and grimaced. "Yes, je comprend, but I must deal with—"

"We can take care of all this, Lieutenant," Ana said. "The loading and everything. But we need the people."

"The captain has not chosen who will take—"

"Scruggs has already assigned them," Dena said. "We talked about this before we landed. We know what needs to be done. If you ask her, she'll give you the names and you can send them out. Call her on the radio."

Isere coughed and looked at Dena. "Cadet Scruggs is in conference with the captain and cannot be reached."

"Ask Lee."

"Navigator Lee is also unavailable."

"Why?" Ana asked. "Radio's all down. Why is that?"

Isere looked at Dena. "You know why. What is going on here?"

Dena grinned. "I do. Now watch what happens. Centurion, we need those troops out here."

Ana nodded. "Understood. Isere, look up above you. Between the blue painted lines. You know what that is, along the bottom of the ship?"

Isere glanced up at *Heart's Desire*. After landing, Gavin had cranked open the heat shields. The truss mounted sensors and thrusters were exposed, as well as an oval-shaped sponson, with six metal rods supporting crystal lenses extending forward.

"A weapon?"

"Laser," Ana said.

The laser was pointed within a degree or two of the *Esprit*. "You won't dare shoot the ship with your people on it." Isere frowned. "Who are you, really?"

"We're the people who are going to fix up your

life support system, give you food and fuel, and pay your troops. You want that, or do you want to starve in some out of the way system while your captain gets rich? The same captain who Dena says won't even give you proper skinsuits for ship travel." Ana had raised his voice. The four crew standing next to Gavin were paying close attention.

Isere glanced at them. "You can ignore them. They don't speak Standard."

"Henri." Dena waved. "Come here for a moment."

The nearest man ran over. "Oui, Madame Dena?"

Isere did a double take, and his mouth dropped open. "We should—"

Ana grabbed his shoulder. "Nope. Look down." Isere did. Ana had a revolver pointing at his stomach. "It's one thing to die for the Empire in combat, Lieutenant. It's another to be shot in the stomach and left to die for a man who won't even give you your pay regularly. Daille and the others have been screwing you the whole time, you know that."

Isere shut his mouth. "That is so. But I made a promise. I am under orders."

Dena smiled at Henri. "Henri, go see Cadet Scruggs. Ask for Fireman Joe and his team."

"Fireman Joe?" Henri nodded. "Oui."

"Fireman Joe and his team. For the water. And Cargo Jenny's squad. For the food."

Henri nodded. "Food and water. Yes."

"Yes." Dena nodded. "Fireman Joe. Cargo Jenny. Understand?"

"Oui. Fireman Joe. Cargo Jenny." Henri ran off.

Isere looked back and forth between them. "I remember your Duke now. I do. He is a rebel, isn't he. I saw his picture."

"The Empire would like to talk to him, yes."

Ana nodded. "But they can't, because he's busy pointing a laser at a ship load of Rhone troopers who haven't been paid in forever."

"You will not get away with this. You don't dare shoot our ship. Not with your people in there."

"Lieutenant," Ana said. "This is a war. People die. Lee is a Praetorian, in the Empress's service. They swear to defend the Empire with their life. She's ready to die anytime. Scruggs boarded a battleship and shot the captain. By herself. They're not afraid of anything. We'll shoot you and your ship both, and they'll cheer us on."

"Your Duke will never allow it."

"Our Duke, the reason you recognize him, is because he was court-martialed for nearly starting a war by ramming an enemy landing boat. Hundreds dead. All his fault. He knew those people. But he did it. You think he'll care what happens to a couple dozen troopers from a planet he can't pronounce?"

Isere's mouth opened, then closed. His communicator beeped. He looked down. "It is the ship."

"Take it," Ana said. "Talk to them."

"And say what?"

"Whatever you think best. Tell them we need people. Tell them we're rebels and they should shoot Scruggs. Tell them to try to take off, if Lee will let them."

"What if I do that?"

"Then I'll shoot you." Ana smiled. "Whatever happens next, happens to you first. Your move."

"I don't know…"

"Join the Imperial Army. See the galaxy. Meet interesting people." Ana smiled. "Then kill them." He pointed to the beeping com unit. "Answer it."

Chapter 41

"And we'll break them into platoons of thirty-two." Scruggs pointed to the diagram she had displayed on Captain Daille's wall screen. "Each with four squads. And put the rest into a headquarters squad with all the specialists, communications, and so on. That's more Imperial standard. We'll have one squad doing wilderness training with Dena. She'll take them into the hills here and have them live off the land. The other three will be here for regular training. The centurion and I will handle that. Marksmanship, unarmed combat, all of that."

Scruggs waited for the translation unit to catch up. She, Lieutenant Fornet, Captain Daille, and Alain, one of Daille's guards, stood in front of the captain's desk in his office. She hadn't objected when, before the landing was complete, Alain had escorted her to Daille's office and made her wait, nor when he'd demanded her revolver. Things were happening, and she, Lee, and Dena had planned for happenings.

Flexibility is the key to Imperial Power, Centurion says. Scruggs stood at attention. Like always, Daille made her wait in front of his desk. After his meeting, the captain had returned in a foul mood, and issued instructions to his crew that Scruggs hadn't understood. The radio boosters were shut off before the landing—she wasn't getting a signal from outside the ship. And he'd put one of his bully-boys with Lee and her at all times. *He hasn't done that before. What did the others say to him?*

The lights dimmed. Captain Daille cursed and slapped his hand on his desk intercom unit. Hesitant Français voices answered his questions.

Daille spoke slowly. "Navigator has shut off main power unit?"

"Yes." Scruggs nodded. "It saves fuel to use the secondary unit on the ground." And the secondary unit isn't working, so we're on batteries now. Lee estimated ten minutes before the batteries die and all the systems fail. Looks like it's on.

"Your friend Dena has left the ship." The program translated that. "Why did she do that?"

Scruggs pushed her arm to the ceiling and stretched. "Sorry, Captain, too much practicing with the crew. Need to work out the kinks." Scruggs assessed the office. *Wooden chair behind the desk. Break off an arm and I have a weapon. If I can reach the pipes on the ceiling, I can pull myself out of the way.* "Dena? She's not needed here. I assume the Duke called. I haven't got any extra orders, except to continue with my training program. Did he mention any to you?"

Daille rubbed his chin and glared. Scruggs hadn't complained when told she had to stay in the ship, neither had Lee, and that bothered him. Daille pursed his lips, and asked more questions.

"Stay here?" Scruggs shrugged. "No problem for now. I can do what I need from here." She waved in front of her nose. "I would like to get out of the smell, though." Life support still hadn't cleaned the toilet stench of a hundred people in a metal box for three weeks.

The captain grimaced and nodded.

Scruggs stepped to the side and leaned on the wall, looking at Daille's desk. He'll have to stand up to pull a gun. And I can't get at him behind the desk—it's bolted in place.

The intercom buzzed. "Captain Daille? Navigator Lee here. We've secured from landing, and are on secondary power. Do you have any other instructions?"

Scruggs called out, "Lee, we're in conference right now. I'm sure he'll tell me. Any issues on your side?"

"None here," Lee said. "The first group is having a problem with the hoses. Second platoon is going out to help."

"Understood." Second platoon? Fireman Joe's platoon. Our best friends, and the least loyal to Daille, in other words. If Dena got them called out, then that means—"

"And first platoon is heading for Dena."

"Understood." First is Cargo Jenny. Dena's got them all off the ship. It's on. Now to give Lee the signal.

'The captain and I were talking about the smell. Is now a good time to vent the ship?"

"An excellent time," Lee agreed. "I'll need to go to engineering. Give me five minutes."

"Captain, Lee wants to remove the smell—" Scruggs explained slowly, letting the software catch up. "She needs to go to engineering to operate the vents, and get fresh air."

Isere yelled a question to the intercom, a torrent of Français came back, and he yelled more queries, until the voices quieted.

Lee's voice came up. "Looks like our friend Claude is going to accompany me to engineering. I'll let you know when I'm there."

"Let me know if you need any help," Scruggs said. "Now, Captain, I'd like to assign—"

The third bully boy—Bertrand—stuck his head back in. He and Daille exchanged rapid-fire remarks. The translator kicked in for several words before Daille silenced it.

"Isere orders, off ship, training platoon—"

Daille yelled. Fornet and Bertrand raced out. Alain and the captain exchanged words, then he left as well, heading for the bridge. Scruggs stood alone with the captain. She pushed the door shut.

Daille pulled a revolver from a drawer behind

his desk. "Qu'est-ce que vous faites?"

Scruggs raised her hands. "Whoa, Captain, what are you talking about? I'm—"

The lights went out. Scruggs dropped to the floor.

"Listen up," Ana yelled. "All you *Esprit* people, come here. School circle." Two complete platoons, almost half of the soldiers, had exited the *Esprit*, and stood waiting. At Ana's wave, they jogged over.

"Don't—" Isere said.

"Shut up," Ana said. "I still have this revolver." He addressed the crowd. "You've all been lied to. Tribune Devin is not revolting against the Emperor. He's taking a fleet into the Core to remove the Chancellor and restore his sister, the Empress, to her rightful place. There is no rebellion, but there was a coup. He dispatched one of his most trusted agents, Praetorian Lee, to seize your ship in his name. That's happening right now. And he's sent one of his most senior advisers, the Duke Friedel, to enroll you into one of his new brigades. The Rhone Brigade now works directly for the Empress. You'll serve under the Duke and his officers, be paid regularly, and we won't abandon you on some forgotten space station with no fuel."

Isere gaped. The entire speech had been in Français. "I didn't know you spoke Français."

"You never asked."

"But how, why—"

Ana raised his voice. "Isn't that just like these stupid officers. Never take an interest in their men, or know what they can do. He didn't know that I speak Français. Lieutenant Isere, how many of your men speak and understand Standard?"

"What? None, I—"

"Dena?" Ana asked.

Dena pointed. "Joe. Jenny. Sorry, Joseph, Jennifer, Jean-Pierre, Phillipe, Francois, Nicole…" She named off ten.

"Which we bothered to find out. And none of your officers did. So." Ana nodded at the group. "You have to make a choice. Those of you who only want out of this, we'll let you go. We'll drop you off at a nearby planet—a habitable planet—with supplies and money, and let you make your way. Those of you who want to join up with us can. We pay well."

"How do we know that you're telling the truth?" a man in back called.

Ana pointed to the *Esprit*. "Navigator Lee is a Jovian, you can all see that."

The man nodded.

"Not only a Jovian but a Praetorian, the Emperor's and Empress's most loyal troops. She went out of her way to get you here so the ship could be fixed. Could your crew have done that?"

"Non." One of the men laughed. "My cousin is on the crew. He'd never left cis-lunar space before. He was terrified every time he plotted the jumps."

"Do Praetorians ever betray the Imperial family?"

The man shook his head.

"Then you know you're on the side of the Emperor."

"Who will command us?" another asked.

"The Duke will be in overall command. Cadet Scruggs will have the first platoon. You've trained under her. She's good with training." Ana grinned. "Best you don't play poker with her, from what I hear."

The crowd laughed.

"What about the ship—" the first man asked.

An alarm rang. Vents all along the *Esprit* burst open, and a fine mist leaked out of the lower hatches.

Ana raised his voice more. "The Praetorian has seized the ship. She's venting all the bad air and running a washdown sequence. We've got both ships now, and your officers are our prisoners. They'll be tried for treason. So if you're leaving this planet, it's only if we let you leave. I'll give you sixty seconds to decide what you want to do. Starting now."

"We could rush you," the man said. "Take you prisoner and seize your ship."

Ana pulled his gun out and shot the man's hat off. The crowd murmured, then laughed. "You could try." Ana cocked it. "Waste of a good hat, though."

"You've only got five bullets left in that gun," the man said. "We could capture you."

"Thirty of you? You sure could." Ana pointed the gun at the man's face. "But after I shoot you, which four of your friends are going to take the bullets so the others can do the capturing?"

Chapter 42

"Imin! Where's my sword?" Devin scowled at the rack. His formal Tribune's sword, his gladius, rested next to his uniform, but his rack of wooden practice swords sat empty.

"Tribune," Imin called from the galley, where he was cleaning up the remains of breakfast. "Next to your toga."

"No, my practice sword," Devin clarified. "I'm going to the gym."

Imin appeared at the doorway of the Tribune's bedchamber. "Yes sir. As you recall, you destroyed your practice sword yesterday while exercising in the gym."

"I'm aware of that, Imin. We need stronger swords."

"Of course, Tribune."

Devin rounded on him. "Can you find me a stronger sword, Imin?"

"It's possible, Tribune," Imin said. "However, I would like to point out that regardless of how strong the wooden sword is, it's not designed to be smashed repeatedly against the metal walls and frames of the ship. They don't stand up to that sort of behavior."

"Jove." Devin rubbed his chin. "I was a little angry, and beating up the dummy wasn't doing it for me."

"As the Tribune says," Imin replied. "Your spare wooden sword—"

"Yes, yes, I get it. How many swords have I broken in the last week?"

"Five."

"Five? I've broken five swords in the gym?"

"Destroyed is a better term, Tribune."

"They weren't destroyed. Dented?"

"It doesn't catch the violence involved."

"Splintered? Shredded? Catastrophized?"

"I don't think 'catastrophized' is a word, Tribune."

"It is if I say it is."

"As the Tribune says." Imin nodded. "I'll look it up after breakfast."

"Perhaps I'll go to the gym and lift weights or something," Devin grumbled. "Something plebeian."

"As the Tribune wishes. If the Tribune desires to wear a sword, perhaps he could assume formal dress and attend the fleet maneuvers occurring as we arrive at the exercise area."

"I don't want to jog Lionel's elbow. He has things well in hand."

"The Prefect always has things well in hand, Tribune. However, I'm sure he, like most people, values your input and constructive thoughts on the upcoming Naval maneuvers."

"My constructive thoughts on Naval maneuvers? I'm more likely to sing the Imperial anthem out of my backside than to give useful orders for Naval execution."

"Yes sir. Shall I ready your sword? Or your backside?"

"I said I wasn't going up there."

"I have also laid out one of your uniforms. If you choose not to wear a sword, appearing in uniform would be a reasonable compromise."

"Why do I get the feeling you want me on the bridge?"

"Your presence is missed on the bridge, Tribune."

"I doubt that, Imin. A substantial portion of the crew might be trying to kill me."

"It's not a substantial portion sir. Perhaps a moderate portion, but not a substantial one. Further, the portion that is not trying to kill you is likely commenting on your absence, and the much larger portion in the middle—who hasn't decided either way—would welcome some direction on the matter."

Devin blinked, digesting that. "You know what! I'm the Lord Lyon. Commander of this task force. Imperial Duke and Tribune. Governor of the Verge sector."

"Indeed sir."

"They don't scare me. Give me my uniform."

Devin marched to the bridge hatch. The attending Marine braced to attention. His uniform was spotless. So was his sidearm.

"Marine, why are you armed?"

"Orders from the Prefect sir. We've been deployed at security level three."

"Very well," Devin said. He tapped his code into the bridge lock. "Why is that?"

"Security level three is mandated by the ship's commander," the Marine said. He recited the requirements, the number of Marines needed, their positions, and the relevant regulations, including Imperial Regulation 203.17, which required the captain to keep the ship secure at all times.

When the Marine finished, Devin asked, "Did you need to quote Imperial Regulations at me, Marine? Don't you think I know them?"

"I served with you on the *Pollux* sir."

"Yes, that's right," Devin replied. "I remember."

"On the *Pollux*, it would be unlikely for you to know the regulations."

"Don't know them?" Devin stared at him. "Impudent little twit, aren't you?"

"Yes sir," the Marine replied without hesitation.

"We're not on the *Pollux* now. You know that?"

"I do sir," the Marine said. "Were we on the

Pollux, you would not hesitate to ask for assistance interpreting regulations. Nor would you speak harshly to a crew member providing valuable information to aid your strategic decisions. Which is one of the crew's primary jobs sir."

Devin's mouth dropped open. "You're telling me what my job is?"

"Sir, I'm telling you what my job is—and what I need to do to support you in your job."

Devin shook his head. "Enough of this." He tapped his comm and glared at the Marine. "Imin, I want you to... I want you to..."

The Marine stared solidly at him.

"Yes, Tribune?" Imin's voice said.

"I want you to arrange for... Nothing. I will see you on the bridge." He turned off the comm. "Marine?"

"Sir?"

Devin gave the formal cross-chest salute. "Current ad Bellum." *I've still got people behind me. I have to remember that.*

"Curran ad Bellum sir."

Devin punched the door open, and marched in. "Tribune on the bridge!" No one moved. First I get them to abandon unnecessary formalities, and now I could use them, they were gone.

Devin sat. "Prefect."

Lionel didn't look up from his control board. "Tribune, it's good to see you." He typed a reply to a form, then switched to the next one.

"Thank you. You as well. Private channel, please."

Lionel blinked, but obligingly opened a secure line.

"You look like Hades," Devin said. "Your eyes are bloodshot, your face is sagging, and your hair's a mess."

Lionel patted his hair. "Sorry, I'll fix that at

once."

"Never mind. Not sleeping well?"

"No."

"Worried about the future?"

"Yes."

"Stressing over things you can't control?"

"Yes. Same as you. Otherwise, you wouldn't be here in full uniform."

Devin nodded. "Pretty astute observation. I'm worried."

Lionel grimaced. "I'm exactly the same way. That dinner you had wasn't reassuring. I'm still not sure you should have spread our plans that widely." Devin had organized another meeting of many of the more junior officers, and explained his and Lionel's, plan for taking New Malaya in ninety days.

"I wanted their input."

"Some of them are possible saboteurs."

"Maybe. But they deserve to know what I have planned for them."

"Word will get out."

Devin shrugged. "It always does. It's not like the Chancellor doesn't know we're out here somewhere."

"No need to tell him exactly what's going on."

"Well, it's done. What's our status?"

"More hedge-hopping."

Lionel had designed hedge-hopping, his improvised strategy, a week ago. Instead of taking a direct path into the enemy core, they'd started hopping into secondary systems to sweep for Imperial warships. The detours kept the fleet busy and training up, without risking a major engagement.

And gave them time to figure out what to do with a ship full of potential mutineers.

"What have we got?"

"*Collingwood* jumped in two hours ago to flush

out the locals. They're performing well."

"Perhaps they're responding to my dinner conversation."

Lionel grimaced. "Perhaps. We're sweeping behind her now. She scared up an enemy frigate exiting one of the inner planets and running for the far jump limit."

"Can we catch it?"

"Yes, or at least the light units can. We're trundling along behind."

"General chase?"

"Already done."

Devin watched the battle unfold. Lionel, despite his complaints about unworthiness and exhaustion, was an exceptional tactician. He'd adapted single-ship tactics into fleet maneuvers seamlessly.

His chasing units cut the pursued frigate off from the direct path to the jump limit, forcing it deeper into their engagement envelope. "How do you figure this out?" Devin asked. "You've never been trained in fleet maneuvering."

"I'm not maneuvering a fleet," Lionel said. "I'm maneuvering a single ship running away from a fleet."

"Explain."

Lionel brought up a screen and pointed. "One frigate, max acceleration, maybe 3Gs. If I were the captain of that frigate and this fleet appeared, I'd run fast and hard. I pretend to be him, and figure out the worst thing the pursuing fleet could do to stop me—and that's what I order the fleet to do."

"That's clever," Devin said. "A great idea."

"Yes," Lionel agreed, "until I encounter another fleet. Then I won't know what the Hades I'm supposed to do."

"That's my job," Devin said.

"Uh-huh. And do you know what the Hades you're supposed to do?"

"Nope."

"Supposed to talk a better game than that."

"We're past lying to each other. We're both in over our heads. We have to keep rolling forward, do our best, and hope for the best."

"I'm not sure hope is a strategy."

"It's all we've got. But I will try your thing – think about what worries the enemy, then do that. Carry on, Prefect."

The battle unwound at a leisurely pace. Target-1, now confirmed as a frigate, now angled along at only 2.1Gs, clearly overdue for maintenance. Pursuing it were two destroyers, *Rigorous* and *Rowena* and the corvette, *Collingwood*.

Target-1 needed fourteen more minutes to escape across the jump limit. Unfortunately for them, Lionel had correctly extrapolated their course. *Collingwood* had raced ahead into position blocking access to the jump limit. The destroyers *Rigorous* and *Rowena* closed in from behind. Between the destroyer's fire and the corvettes ahead, the target was doomed.

"Well done," Devin said. "Well done."

"Status change," the sensor operator announced. "Jump signature!"

Lionel sat upright. "Jump signature? Who?"

"*Collingwood* has jumped sir."

"What do you mean they've jumped? They don't need to pursue. Target-1's not past the jump limit yet!"

The sensor operator shook her head. "Target-1 is still there—but *Collingwood* jumped sir."

"She jumped? What messages did they send?"

"None sir."

Lionel frowned. "That's not good. Why would the commander... confirm who is the commander."

The sensor operator was already scanning the crew roster. "First Lieutenant Monti—she was in temporary command."

"Hold that thought," Lionel said. He turned to Devin. "She was at your briefing the other day."

"Yes." Devin nodded.

"She knows your plans."

"Most of them."

Lionel cursed. "Sensors! What's their fuel situation? Who has the latest report?"

Rudnar, at the helm, spoke up. "They tanked up before we left last system sir."

Devin leaned close. "Can we chase them?"

"Maybe," Lionel said. "Catching them is something else sir. But we'd have to choose right now—chase the Imperial corvette or *Collingwood*. We can't follow both. And I'm not sure we can follow either."

"How long to accelerate someone on their vector?"

"I can get you a number, Tribune, but I have to check with engineering—"

"Carry on," Devin growled. He sat, watching as the clock ticked down and Lionel snapped out commands. *She timed it well. We can't catch her.* Ten minutes later, the Imperial frigate disappeared into its own jump.

Rudnar looked back. "Sir, other ships are asking for instructions. They want a course."

Devin watched the screen. She's off to warn the Empire. About me or about the Pollux, or our plans. She'll find somebody to buy her story. He shook his head. I hope it's worth it for her.

Lionel gritted his teeth. "Do you think she's on her way to spill our plans to the Empire?"

"They know we're coming. Doesn't make any difference."

"Do you believe that?"

"I do." Devin nodded. "Comm, tell the others to stand down. Prefect, carry on with the system sweep. I'll be in my dining room. Tell Bosun Sanchez to rustle up a wooden practice sword for me. I'm going to need it."

Chapter 43

Scruggs dropped to the deck in the darkness of Daille's office and rolled sideways. She closed her eyes, and listened. Daille's breath hissed "Arrêtez!" His gunshot boomed off the walls, hurting her ears. The flash burned through her closed eyelids. *I can't hear now.. More of that and I won't be able to see.. But neither can he right now.*

She opened one eye and gathered her feet under her. *Hit hard. Hit fast. Get out. That's what Centurion always said.* Could she reach the ceiling? She jumped as high and as hard as she could. Her left hand slammed into a ceiling fixture, her right hand caught a plastic pipe. She grasped both, then pivoted at the waist and drove her feet forward.

Crunch. I'll bet that hurt. Are you still glad you made me report in full uniform, including boots, every time? Boots hurt more than feet. She bounced back as her heels struck Daille's chest, then dropped and rolled below the desk. Her ankle burned from the kick.

His gun fired again, blinding her open eye. The emergency lights flickered red, then died. Bad maintenance was on her side now.

Thunk. A curse. Must be loud to cut through the ringing. Daille must have hit the back wall. Another thunk, another curse. *Coming around the desk.* She rolled and crawled under the table, ignoring her pained ankle. *"Use all three dimensions,"* Centurion had said. *"Attack from above. Attack from below. Attack from the side—not only the front."*

Scruggs opened one eye, the one not dazzled by the gun flash. In the dimness, she spotted a pair of feet skittering away.

An alarm blared. Dim red light strobed behind her through the hallway door cracks. Scruggs watched the feet shuffle away to her left. She crawled forward, rolled, and grabbed the arm of the office chair. *Need a weapon.* She wrenched it left, then wrenched it right. It didn't move. *What about…* She yanked the whole chair up, and it lifted clear off its track.

She stood and swung—hard. The chair swept in an arc above the table.

THUD.

The chair bounced off Daille and crashed into the dark. Daille screamed. Scruggs ducked back and dropped behind the desk. She crawled to the right of the desk and listened. Where was he? She couldn't see him now, but…could she find him by sound? The fans weren't spinning, but an electric circuit hummed overhead. Or was that the ringing from the gunshots?

She closed her eyes and sniffed. Spearmint. This arrogant twit had hoarded the soap and toothpaste during the trip there. She turned her head left, then right. The scent was stronger to her right. She stepped forward and punched for the smell. A grunt, and searing pain. She'd cut her fist on his teeth, and it hurt. *But his body thumped to the floor. Bet that hurt even more.*

To her left, the red light brightened. The hallway door was opening. She jumped onto the desk and pulled herself up to the ceiling.

Dim red light illuminated the far wall. Somebody outside fired a weapon, killing her hearing again. It sparked off one wall, then another, then another. *The idiot is firing solid slugs. It's as likely to kill Daille or him, rather than me.*

But now both eyes were blinded and she couldn't hear. The shot had come through the open door. *She needed to get at the door—*

A cold mist sprayed over her head. Fire suppression. Lee had triggered the firefighting system. Foam everywhere would make the floor slick. She held on to the ceiling, waiting. The red light brightened as the door eased open another inch.

Surely he could hear her heartbeat and her breathing? She clamped her mouth shut and watched. What was he waiting for? He couldn't see any better than she could, and he couldn't risk getting ambushed. Centurion said the only way to decisively clear a room was grenades. If you didn't have grenades, then you had to go in fast— The door kicked open, and dim red light flooded the room. A uniformed figure charged past, leading hand holding a revolver. Soft hat, not a helmet. Not ship crew or regular soldier, then one of the bullyboys. Bertrand, the big one. The door spun farther open, hitting a moaning Daille, and rebounded, smacking into the arm holding the gun.

The revolver fell. Scruggs pivoted her feet and dropped down— and tripped to the side.

The damn chair had somehow rolled under her.

Now her elbow banged onto the ground, jetting pain through her. She lay still for a second, catching her breath. Fighting in the dark is so much more tiring. Now I understand why Centurion says shoot first, and don't bother to ask questions later. It's much less of a bother.

She scrambled free, and stumbled back, hitting his I-love-me wall, and banging her head on wood.

His shadowbox. She reached up and wrenched it off the wall, then threw it at the darkened figure.

Daille chose that moment to stand up. The box smashed into his head, smashing open and showering the room with medals. She swung again and something warm spurted onto her face, and Daille dropped.

Warm liquid. Smells like copper. She'd cut him badly.

The newcomer—Scruggs recognized Bertrand's

bulk—peered into the dimness.

Gotta get out. Scruggs measured his height. He's too big for close-quarters combat. If he gets hold of me, he'll just smash me against the wall.

She hopped over a prone Daille. No time to check him, and not necessary with his blood on her face. She dropped her shoulder and rammed into Bertrand. He flew back, slamming into the wall. Scruggs pivoted right—into the hallway.

And there, in front of her, rolled one of the guns. She scooped it up and bolted, hobbling a bit on her damaged ankle. What now? Where to? What would Centurion do? Poorly armed, in the face of superior forces, Centurion would counsel retreating to fight another day.

The air blowing on her face meant at least one of the crew hatches was open. She'd climb up to the dorsal surface and escape from there. The Rhone brigade wasn't used to ships. They wouldn't think to go up. She turned to the stern and jogged in the dark.

But Centurion never gave her instructions, only objectives. And operations was always in service of objectives, he'd said. What was her objective? Survive at all costs? No. Her objective was to seize the ship and neutralize the Imperial officers. How to do that?

Scruggs stopped. If they controlled the bridge and engineering, they controlled the ship. Lee held engineering, she hoped. Which meant she had to seize the bridge.

Scruggs continued to the bridge, but she keyed the radio. "Centurion," she gasped. "I'm on the way to secure the bridge. Stand by—"

"Scruggs—" Click. Ana's voice died. Somewhere a smarter than average crewman had turned the jamming back on. *Oh well.* She sprinted for the bow. The crew still hadn't leveled the landing legs, so she climbed the ladder like stairs. Her ankle pained every time she stepped down. Her foot slipped. She fell and slammed her elbow on the ladder. Luckily, her revolver didn't discharge. *Why not? She'd had her finger on the trigger. The gun hadn't fired, which meant...* She checked it. The trigger didn't move—the pistol was worthless. The alarm cut off.

Uh-oh. She hadn't checked it before scooping it up. *Centurion would be mad about that.*

Scruggs cursed and scrambled up. She could see no one through the mist and dim light. The crew would be regaining control of the ship. No time left. She raised the gun and sprinted through the two habitats, through the cylinders, up to past the lounge. Darkened figures stood in the lounge, talking by flashlight.

She charged past, jumped over the open ventral hatch, and ran onto the bridge. Fresh air blew in from all the hatches, cutting the stink. "Freeze! Everybody freeze!" she yelled.

The three bridge crew members raised their hands, babbling in Français. Scruggs brandished her gun. There—standing slack-jawed behind one of the boards—waited the other bully boy, Alain.

He must have convinced them to shut off the alarm, she thought.

She stepped closer, raised the gun, and leveled it at the middle of his forehead. Alain's jaw dropped even further. Slowly, he raised his hands. "Gun. Drop it." She pointed at the holster at his waist. "Drop it. Now. Fingers."

Alain babbled something. Scruggs made a sharp motion with her gun, as if tightening her grip.

He held up his left hand. "Non," he said. Then he inched his right hand down and dropped the revolver to the floor.

That was too easy. Why—oh. Scruggs rubbed her

face. Her hand was sticky. She must look like she had torn out somebody's throat with her teeth. *Rocky would be proud.*

"Good." Scruggs stepped back, keeping the gun trained on him, and waved him away, making sure to gesture with her free hand—not the one holding the gun. "Move. Move."

Alain's eyes flicked between her hand and the weapon, tracking them back and forth.

Scruggs glared. *If he comes at me now, all I can do is hit him. I still won't be able to stop him. He's too big.*

Alain raised both hands to shoulder height, palms forward, and walked down the corridor.

Scruggs followed, keeping a safe distance. When he reached the bridge hatch, he hesitated, shifting slightly to the side. Scruggs didn't wait. She stepped forward and kicked him hard behind his left knee.

His leg buckled. He fell forward, into the open hatch, yelling.

She reversed her grip on the gun, holding it by the barrel. Leaning in, she hammered down on his right hand, gripping the hatch's edge. Alain screamed and let go, his body tilting sideways. Only his left leg and hand kept him from falling.

Scruggs stomped on his left hand. He let go. Only the tip of his boot remained hooked onto the edge. She grasped his boot and shoved him. He tumbled out and hit the ground outside the ship with a wet thud.

Scruggs slammed the hatch shut, rotated the lock, and sealed it. The whole fight had taken twenty seconds. She marched back into the bridge.

One of the officers had picked up Alain's dropped gun. Scruggs didn't slow. "Give me that. You don't know how to use it. You're just going to hurt yourself."

She lunged forward, grabbed his hand, and

pushed it upward. The officer didn't resist. She pried the gun from his grip, tucked it into her belt, then stepped back and slammed the bridge hatch shut. She locked it, and walked back to the controls. She pointed at the board. "Turn off the alarms. Turn on the radio. Now."

Imperial Legionary

Chapter 44

"Centurion, Centurion, come in." Lee's voice crackled over the radio.

"I'm here, Navigator." Ana scanned the charred brush between the two ships. No visible threats. The troopers Dena talked to were smiling and laughing, and had no weapons. Dirk was locking up a now disarmed Lieutenant Isere. *Should I shoot him? No, we might need an officer later, keep him just in case.* Ana smiled to himself. *He could shoot Isere later if necessary.* "Where are you? What's your status?"

"They're onto us. I'm in engineering. I'm seizing the ship."

"Where's Scruggs?"

"Last report was Daille's office. Unsure now."

Poof. Dust blew off the *Esprit* as Lee fired the emergency evacuation sequence. Any hatch that wasn't already open unlocked and blew out. The anti-chemical weapons system venting internal air at speed. Three seconds later, she turned on the firefighting system. Sprays of liquid—water and foam—spat out of all the hatches.

Ana grunted. "You could have warned us, Navigator! Some time to plan would have been good. I've already had my bath today."

"I'm warning you now. They're onto us. I'm gonna get as many of the crew out as I can. I'll take care of engineering. You're in charge of the ground support units."

"Outstanding." Ana strode to the waiting Rhone Brigade soldiers. "Dena, I need to speak to you." Cargo Jenny and Fireman Joe waited there, chattering in Français.

"Is the ship on fire?" Jenny asked. "What is happening?"

"Freedom." Ana nodded. "Freedom is happening. Your freedom."

Two uniformed figures climbed down the mid-hold ladder, and lumbered from the ship.

Ana pointed. "Who are they?"

"That's Bertrand. He's one of the bully boys. The officer is Fornet."

"Problems for us?"

"Yes, he's one of the loyalists."

"Outstanding."

Fornet pulled up to Ana, glared at the soldiers, and raised his voice. "Ecoutez—"

BOOM. BOOM.

Ana shot each in the chest. Bertrand dropped at once. Fornet staggered, scrabbled for his pistol, then fell. Ana stepped over and fired twice more. The Rhone troops gasped. Ana took his revolver, spun out the cylinder, reloaded it, and replaced it in his holster.

"Listen up, Rhone Brigade. The Empire has placed you under the orders of Duke Friedel. The Duke has been appointed in charge by Tribune Devin—the rebel. Tribune Devin. Well, he's not. We are going to put the Empress back in charge. Your officers have chosen not to assist in the endeavor, so they have been eliminated."

The group gawked at him.

"I understand that you may be confused. We are going to stop stealing your pay, and make sure you get fed and get training, and stop sending you to backwater hellholes. Time to choose. What do you say?"

Jenny said, "I am with you." She walked past Ana and spat on Fornet. "Enough of these couchons. They have always been out for themselves. I'm done with sitting in my own crap for weeks while they steal my pay." She sketched a salute. "Your people have treated us well. We go with you."

Joe did the same. "What do we need to do?

How can we help?"

Ana lowered his voice. "Dena, can we trust them?"

"Yes," Dena said. "These are the ones most likely to be on our side. We set it up that way."

"Can we give them weapons?"

"Jenny and Joe, sure. And this group, at least."

"Will they shoot people if we tell them to? Their old friends?"

Dena looked at Ana. "Shoot their friends?"

Ana raised his voice. "Listen up. Cadet Scruggs and Praetorian Lee are being held hostage on that ship by anti-Imperial elements. We're going to arm eight of you with rifles, and you're going to help us re-take the ship."

Ana pointed. "Dena, get that box of hoses open. Rifles are in the bottom under the extensions. Hand them out." He frowned. "No, strike that. Jenny and Joe, pick four people each. Take the rifles in there. Go with Dena, take your rifles, load up, and follow me."

Dena and Ana helped hand out the rifles, gave a quick check, and then charged at the ship.

"Squad," Ana yelled, "forward! Save the cadet!"

Anyone departing the *Esprit* had to climb down a ladder or jump twenty feet and slide on the rocky ground. Dirty, wet, stinking crew were dropping from the hatches. There was no possibility of getting into the ship as people continued streaming out.

"First platoon, that's you, Joe. Collect those troops! Form them up by squads as they come out! Second Platoon—Jenny, you're second platoon leader. Get them together, get them over there! Move it, people, move it!"

A combination of command voice, the minor amount of military discipline that remained, and a complete unwillingness to go back into the stinking starship forced the troops to form up in lines.

"Dena," Ana said, "who's going to cause the most problems? Who are we going to have to shoot?"

"Two of the sergeants may be a problem. They're in the Headquarters platoon. I don't see them. In fact—" Dena stood on her toes and surveyed the growing number of soldiers. "I don't see the HQ platoon at all. That's all the main loyalists. The hard cases. The rest, they want to be paid and not yelled at."

Lee's voice came on the radio again. "Centurion, I've secured engineering. I had to shoot Claude. We're locked in here, and the engineers are going to wait it out. Have you heard from Scruggs?"

"No, not yet."

Scruggs came up on the radio. "Centurion, I'm on the way to secure the bridge. Stand by—"

"Scruggs," Ana said, "we don't need—"
Click.

"Scruggs." Nothing. Ana cursed. "Channel's down. Lee, you there?" Only static answered him. "Counter-attack's happening," Ana said. "All right, what's going on with these people, Dena? How many still in the ship?"

"Maybe sixty. But more coming out all the time."

"How many will fight us?"

"Half a platoon of loyalists who will stand up for Daille and his crew, the other two officers could fight, and the bully boys. Could be as many as thirty? Forty?"

"Where's Daille?"

"Daille—I don't know where he is. Scruggs was in his office."

"And the bully boys?"

"That was one you shot, Bertrand. We need to

find Alain and Claude."

"Lee shot Claude. I shot Bertrand." The forward hatch swung open, and a figure tumbled down, banging its head on the rail. He landed with a thunk.

Dena shaded her eyes. "Well, we found Alain."

The radios came back up. "Centurion, Scruggs here. I've secured the bridge."

"Very well. Casualties?"

"None on my part. Daille is dead, or at least incapacitated. And so is Alain."

Dena grabbed the radio. "You got Daille? Good job, Baby Marine. We got Fornet. Isere is out of it, Gavin's covering him. Was that Alain who fell out of the front hatch?"

"Yes."

"Centurion shot Bertrand. Lee got Claude. How many still on the ship?"

"Don't know."

"Outstanding." Ana grinned. "Lee, how long can you keep the water going?"

"Not much longer. Minutes."

"Get our idiot pilot and that punk engineer on the circuit."

Lee got the crew on a common circuit. Ana gave curt instructions on what he wanted. Dirk returned from the *Heart's Desire*, doing his best languid aristocratic pose. Dena harangued the soldiers streaming out of the ship into some sort of formation.

Gavin collected his tool box and jogged over. "What do you need? Are Lee and Scruggs okay?"

"Engineer." Ana pointed to the ship. "Get over there and get Lee to let you in. Get the radios back on, not only bridge and engineering, get the internal repeaters on as well. You armed?"

Gavin held up his ever present wrench, and gestured at a revolver on his belt.

"Right. You're the anvil. Get in there, open up as many hatches as you can remotely, but keep engineering isolated. Drop all internal communications except for what we control. Kill the lights everywhere. Don't let them get organized, don't let them get behind a barrier. And keep anybody from harming the ship."

"What about the armed crazies in there?"

"Keep them out of engineering, and keep them from getting out of the ship. Except open up that mid-hatch—" Ana pointed. "Right there. Nothing else external open unless I say so. Tell them anyone who comes out of that hatch won't be shot if they're unarmed."

Gavin ran to the nearest landing leg, snapped open a panel, and connected a radio.

Ana turned. "You're Jenny, right?"

Cargo Jenny stood next to them with her four chosen rifle recipients. "Oui. They call me Cargo Jenny."

"Welcome to the Empire's auxiliary corps. I'm First Centurion Anastasios, you'll follow my instructions. All these people here—" Ana gestured to the approximately sixty or so soldiers who were standing in lines— "We'll assume they're volunteers. The folks still on the ship are confused. Praetorian Lee and Engineer Gavin, here, are going to get in touch with them on the intercom and have them come out here with their hands up. You and your squad are going to be next to that hatch, pointing rifles at them, to stop confusion. Understood?"

"Sure." Jenny nodded. "What if they don't come out?"

"Any of your friends back in there? Still inside the ship?"

Jenny looked over the assembled troops. "Not sure." She hefted the rifle. "Only those maudit headquarters platoon people."

"If they come out with their hands up, we don't kill them. If they won't surrender, then Scruggs, sorry, Cadet Scruggs and I will shoot them. You want to help with that?"

Jenny looked from Ana to Dena. "You'll let the others go?"

"Yes." Ana nodded. "Not right away. We'll have to arrange transport, but we won't kill them out of hand."

Jenny jerked her hand behind her. "These ones out here, they have no love for Daille and his people, but they don't all want to fight for a rebel."

"They can go too. Only people who believe that Tribune Devin is part of the true Empire are wanted. If they're not sufficiently patriotic, they can go too."

Dirk arrived then. "Centurion?"

"My lord Duke." Ana grinned, turned so that Jenny couldn't see him, and winked. "The Empire's newest troops stand ready. Will you address them on behalf of Tribune Devin?"

Dirk nodded. "I will, I will. Ummm..." He gestured at the *Esprit*, still draining water, and the confused mass of troops standing nearby. "Have any promises been made?"

"Join us and fight for the Empress. Not join us but don't fight us, and you can go home."

"What if they want to fight us?"

Ana held up his revolver. "I'll take care of that." He turned to Jenny and her friends. "Now, who of you wants to shoot some suck-ups?"

Chapter 45

"They're just kids, Centurion." Scruggs unbolted the lateral hatch behind the bridge and prepared to swing it open. "We need to go easy on them."

Ana pulled out his revolver. "Armed kids who've been offered a chance to give up, and who made the wrong choice." Lee had broadcast several demands for surrender after taking control of the intercoms. Ana checked his loads, then turned to Jenny and the others behind him. "You five, show me your cylinders." He spun the cylinder of his revolver and flipped it out. "Like this. Check your ammunition."

Jenny and her four squad mates fumbled with their revolvers. Ana had borrowed a pry bar from Gavin and smashed open the ship's locker, trading their rifles for handguns. Their rifles had gone to the rest of the squad outside.

"Like so," Ana said, flicking his cylinder open again. "Spin one, push here. Spin one, push here." He took a lungful of air and retched. "Jove's knees. Didn't you even try to clean this ship? We'll be weeks getting the smell out." He controlled his breathing, fumbled into his pocket, and dry swallowed a pill. He stood bent over until his breathing settled. "Stink always affects me like this. Everyone ready?"

Jenny flipped her cylinder open. When she shook the revolver, three of the cartridges fell to the floor. She cursed. "Why do we have these stupid little guns?"

"Tactical flexibility," Ana said. "We're inside a ship and it's close quarters. Moving a rifle around while you're trying to duck into a room is difficult, but a revolver is easy to point and change direction quickly."

"But you gave rifles to those others." Jenny pointed at the rest of her squad, visible on the exterior cameras, clustered around the mid-ship hatch.

"They're outside," Ana said. "And they're standing under the ship pointing guns at a hatch. And if you stick your head out of a hatch, it's a lot scarier to see eight rifle barrels than eight pistols."

"And a killer space whippet," Scruggs added. Rocky waited with Dena. Anyone who suggested a threat had a snarling dog snap at them. Pet dogs weren't common on Rhone, the crew thought Rocky a barely tamed wild animal.

"And a killer space whippet," Ana agreed. He had suggested it. "Animals know people. Who's nervous, who's scared, who should have their face chewed off. Besides." He smiled. "When your friends start dropping out of the ship to surrender, they're less likely to do something stupid if a dog is snarling at them. That leaves just stupid people inside."

"All the stupid people are in there?"

"I hope so," Ana said. "I like to shoot stupid people, and I haven't shot anybody all day. I'm getting bored."

A ripple of unease ran through Jenny's squad.

"Listen up," Ana clapped his hands. "Écoutez."

He switched to Français. "Everyone's been given three chances. They had a chance when Cadet Scruggs and Cadet Dena signed them up—or tried to sign them up—for the Empress's forces. They had a chance during the crash when Lee broadcast that anyone who came outside wasn't going to get shot, whether they joined the Empress's troops or not. And they had a third chance when we let your friends call their buddies."

Lee had connected Dirk to the ship-wide circuit. He had given a reasoned, dispassionate discussion of reasons why the troops in the Rhone Brigade should sign up on the side of the Empress, the Tribune Devin, and—not incidentally—the Duke Dirk Friedel. This had fallen flat. Then Ana threatened to shoot anybody who didn't sign, and let Jenny and Joe talk to anyone with questions. That produced a flood of applicants, but there were still almost four dozen unaccounted for.

Some had run off into the woods before the chaos was contained. But according to Scruggs, at least half of the fifth platoon—the former headquarters platoon—was barricaded up with a rifle or a shotgun or a knife in a corner. They were waiting to take down one of the evil Imperial rebels.

"Bien sur," Ana said, "you've got plenty of firepower. The question is, are you going to use it? Shoot your former friends or not? Because if you're not, we need to talk about it."

"What if we don't want to kill anybody?" one of the troops said.

Ana said, "I don't care what you want. I want to kill somebody. And I'm going to kill somebody. Or somebodies. One way or another. The only choice left to you right now is which group you're going to be in. Group-shoot the suck-ups who turned down every chance they had, or group-shot by the incompetent thieves who've stolen from you and ruined your life?"

The man tilted his head in thought. Then he laughed. "Yes, I hate those couchons anyways. Let's go."

Ana hit his comm. "Navigator, what's your status back there?"

"Ship's locked down tight," Lee's voice came over the comm. "We've killed light, power, and life support to the entire rest of the ship. All the internal hatches are open, except mine. There's only three external hatches that are open—this one in engineering, that one next to you on the bridge, and the one in the middle, below cargo hold B. Dena says she has eyes on that. From here, we can bring lights and power to each space as you want."

"Outstanding," Ana said. "Here's what we're going to do." He jiggled his belt. He'd gone back to the ship to collect a case full of grenades.

"Scruggs, I've only got a dozen of these. How many compartments?"

"That's plenty, Centurion. Even with the temporary containers, there's only a half dozen places they could hole up. And they can't all be full."

Ana checked his guns. "Let's go."

They started from the bridge, and moved aft into the habitat rings. The first ring they searched was empty. That had been the officers' quarters, and the officers were now either all dead or captured.

The second ring was the lounge. Also empty. They continued through the cargo rings. Each time they came to a new ring, Ana called Lee and had the lights brought up, then they rushed each section.

Ana stopped at the hatch for ring two of the barracks containers. "Lee, lights on one, then we rush—three, two, one—lights."

Lights flashed ahead. "Go." Ana jumped in, revolvers in hand, Jenny's squad behind him. He stepped to the right, scanning the compartment. Scruggs stepped to the left. The others crowded in.

Scruggs tracked her revolver across the compartment. "Nothing. Clear."

"Check the closet," Ana ordered. "Behind the clothes, under the bed, look in the vents, everything."

By the time they made the rear third of the ship,

they'd found fourteen confused soldiers huddling with their hands up and no idea what was going on, six injured troopers and five corpses.

"Who shot them?" Scruggs asked.

"Who cares?" Ana answered. "Not our problem. You...and you," he pointed to two of the Rhone troopers, "give what first aid you can, and put them on a bunk somewhere. We're not doing anything more until we get the rest."

They stopped at the hatch adjacent to the next ring. "Lee, next compartment... three, two, one."

BANG. BANG-BANG.

As soon as the lights came up, whoever hid inside the compartment fired a rifle. Bullets ricocheted down the corridor. Ana cursed once, popped the pin in his grenade, and released the handle. He held it while he counted, "One, two, three, four," then lobbed it in. "Five, six."

BOOM. Somebody screamed from inside the room.

Scruggs furrowed her brow. "Aren't you supposed to throw it and then count to six?"

"If you throw it and then count to six," Ana said, "they have six seconds to throw it back out at you. If you count to four and then throw it, they have less than two seconds."

"What if your count's off?" Scruggs asked.

"You'll know right away," Ana said. "Don't mess it up."

"Shouldn't we ask them to surrender?"

"Again?" Ana grimaced. "Great idea, Cadet. Why don't we have one of our squad deliver it personally? You pick which one of your new friends here to push their head around the corner and ask for a surrender. See how that goes."

Scruggs's face darkened, but she didn't say anything.

The grenade scared another half dozen troops out of the next compartment, who arrived without weapons but with their hands already up. They'd been holed up with a pile of rifles, ready to shoot. Scruggs knew them as stalwart members of fifth platoon—Daille's favorite.

"I'll take care of these ones here," Ana said. "Bring them to the hatch. You keep moving with the squad."

Scruggs said, "Centurion, you won't—"

"I won't do anything hasty, Cadet."

"That's not what I meant," Scruggs said.

"I know what you meant," Ana said. "And I told you, I won't do anything hasty. Anything I do, I'll think about it first. Then I'll do any shooting that's necessary. Then I'll take a break after that." Ana tilted his head. "Pancakes would be great. Haven't had pancakes in forever."

"Will you promise me not to shoot them, Centurion?"

"No. Because they won't promise not to shoot me."

Scruggs gestured at the group of soldiers they were escorting. "I'll do it. Jenny and you two come with me. Wait for me, Centurion. You six. Move, move to the hatch."

They made it to one of the side hatches above cargo hold A. The first man swayed at the edge. The hatch gaped open on the side of the ship, twenty feet from the ground. If there had been a ladder, it was gone now.

"Out you go," Scruggs said. "Jump."

The first man looked out fearfully. "I cannot. You should not make us do this. It is cruel."

Scruggs kicked him in the back, knocking him out the hatch. He plummeted down. She spun on the others, revolver at the ready.

"If I leave you alone with the centurion, he's going to kill all of you. I'm saving your worthless lives. Now, get off this ship as fast as you can."

The others looked her in the eye and then ran for the hatch, hardly pausing as they swung out and dropped.

The two Rhone Brigade troopers with her stood slack-jawed.

"What?" Scruggs said.

"But... there—they might break their legs."

"Broken legs are a lot easier to recover from than a grenade, or a bullet in the head," Scruggs said. "Let's go."

She came back to the centurion. Ana kept a poker face but gestured to Scruggs. Now, she took the lead while they marched through the ship.

They found another compartment with two dead Rhone soldiers in it.

Jenny looked in. "Mon Dieu. It's... what? Why would they shoot them now? What who?"

Ana said nothing.

Jenny stepped back and retched in the corridor.

"That was a special friend of hers," Scruggs said.

Ana grimaced. "And 'was' is the operative word. You see now why we need to get the rest of them?"

"They weren't like this on the trip," Scruggs said.

"Nobody seems like anything until they are," Ana said. "We need to get these people off this ship. We've got limited supplies and limited time to fix things. There's only six of us we can trust trying to control a hundred people who may or may not want to be our friends. If we show any weakness, they'll swarm us. Let's go."

They cleared two more until they made it to the C ring of the containers, the final ring.

Lee came up on the radio. "Go carefully here.

I've only got limited sensors in there."

"I'm always careful," Ana said. "Bring the lights up in the top part of the ring, but not the bottom."

"No can do, Centurion," Lee said. "The wiring on this ship is sketchy. I can bring the whole torus up, or not at all."

"Bring it all up."

Lee brought it all up.

Yells echoed down the corridor. Gunshots clattered down the hall. Rapid gunshots.

"Outstanding." Ana leaned on the bulkhead next to the hatch. "That isn't a revolver or a rifle. That's an automatic weapon. Machine pistol. Didn't know they had that. Scruggs, know anything about that?"

Scruggs shook her head. "I never saw any, never heard any."

"Jenny?"

"One of the officers must have kept it hidden."

"Well, it's not hidden now," Ana said. "And it's an excellent weapon for close-quarter combat. Let's go. Do any of your friends want to go first?"

The Rhone company troopers looked sick. At least two more of them had puked on the way down, and Jenny was still wiping vomit off her collar. They all shook their heads.

"Not much fun when you have to do it yourself. I've had enough going first," Ana said. "Scruggs, you want to send some of your friends here?"

Scruggs shook her head. "I don't think they want to go."

"I don't think they want to go either. But that doesn't matter."

"Why aren't you going, Centurion?"

"Maybe I think I've done my share," Ana said.

"By hiding behind other people," Scruggs said.

Ana laughed. "If you think you can convince

me that I'm a coward or that I'm scared, you've got another think coming. You've known me that long. You know that."

"I do," Scruggs said. She ducked her head around the hatch. There were four doorways visible between her and the engineering airlock hatch. There could be men—armed men—hiding in any of those. "You're not scared of anything."

"Nope," Ana said. "It's not so much bravery, though, as resignation. But they're often mistaken for each other. What about you? Think you can do it?"

Scruggs counted. Four doors. She'd heard a submachine gun. The doors were directly across from each other. There's no way they could clear one room while keeping the other off. They don't have enough people, and somebody would get behind them and shoot them. Kill them. "I don't know."

Ana reached down on his belt, unclipped two grenades and held them out.

"Pull the pin. Count to four. Toss it in the room. If you pull the pins with your teeth while you're short of the first two doors," he gestured down the hallway, "you can have two of them, one in each hand. Then, when you count to four, you can do two doors at once. If you do the first two, the rest will either surrender or come out shooting. If it was me, come out shooting, but I'll bet they surrender. I suggest that once you throw them in, that you hit the deck. We'll be able to cover you at waist level and up." Ana shrugged. "We'll try, at least."

Scruggs stared down the hallway. She didn't move.

Ana didn't move either. He kept holding out the grenade. "You can ask them to surrender if you want, but then they'll know you're coming."

Scruggs nodded.

"Now it's my turn to ask. Are you scared?"

Scruggs shook her head, once. "I'm not scared. I don't feel scared. But... This is, I'm not sure," Scruggs said. "It doesn't feel like fear."

"Doesn't look like it." Ana said. "Looks like contemplation. There's a difference between fear and contemplation. You're contemplating doing something unpleasant."

"I've killed people before. You made me do it."

"If you toss in those grenades, they'll have no chance. If you call them to come out, they won't come out. If you give them the opportunity to surrender, they'll come out with guns blazing. What are you going to do?"

Scruggs stared at Ana for a long time. "Give me two," she said. "Two grenades."

"Very well." Ana held up two grenades. "Something they don't teach you in cadet school, grip one in each hand, then use opposed index finger to pull the other pin." Ana demonstrated but didn't pull. "The count doesn't start till the spoon releases."

She took them from Ana and then clipped them to her belt.

"Those two won't do you much good down there, Cadet Scruggs."

"Nope, they won't."

Scruggs held out her hand to Ana.

"Give me two more. There are four rooms there." She held out her hands. "I'm quick. I can do all four. If I don't give them a chance."

Chapter 46

"That course checks out, Lee," Dirk said. He set a countdown timer on his board. "When we reach the jump limit, we'll do the double jump, and we should be able to intercept the Tribune's fleet, or at the very least one of his patrol ships."

"Double jump?" Ana asked. He and Dirk sat next to each other in the *Esprit*'s control room. Lee and Gavin remained on the *Heart's Desire*, where Lee had used their superior computer software to calculate their return course back to the Tribune's fleet. Scruggs and Dena stayed on board, messing with 'their' troops.

"Yes," Lee said. "Gavin says there's enough fuel on both ships that we can make this jump then recalibrate our instruments in the next system. It doesn't even have a name, only a catalog number. Then if we're sure we're where we think we are, execute a second jump. It's the fastest way to get back to the Tribune, or at least get to where he's going to be."

"Can't we jump directly there?" Ana asked.

"Too far," Lee said. "*Esprit* can't do it in one go. The *Heart's Desire* could, but you can't. Speaking of limitations, how's your engineering staff?"

"Minimally competent, but good enough," Dirk said. "It's the bridge staff that worries me."

"Which is why we have your smiling face here," Ana said. "And as much as I would enjoy travelling on a different ship from you, I do want to get where I'm going. These yokels concern me."

"How do you know enough about jump mechanics to be scared?" Dirk said. "You keep telling us you don't know how to work a ship, and then a minute later, you're identifying destroyers in the warbook."

"I contain multitudes," Ana said.

"What does that mean?"

"It means bite me, is what it means," Dena said, coming onto the channel. "That's Ana-speak for bite me. Right, Old Man?"

"Bite me," Ana said.

"You only say that because you love me. Hey- can we have showers yet?"

"Yes," Dirk said. "Now that I've got the course locked in, I can release some water."

"Great. After that week in the woods, I smell like a Moose in rutting season."

Ana had insisted on more training for the remaining troops before they lifted. First he had them dig trenches and build berms for shooting practice. Then he'd had Scruggs repeating 'Breath-Relax-Aim-Slack-Squeeze' for another week to rifle squads. The second week he'd had them balance a steel washer on their rifle barrels, sight at a target and then pull the trigger. Anybody who could do it a hundred times without dropping the washer he turned over to Dena. She took them two days walk into the woods with only a tent, knife, and a spare pair of socks, then had them try to find water and food. Anybody who failed out early did a lot of cooking and painting.

After three weeks they had a group of soldiers who could possibly run across a field, hide in some trees, and possibly fire their rifles without dropping them. And none of the week three graduates ever complained about the food again.

Dena held up a spoon of orange goop in front of her camera. "Lee, what is this that I'm eating?"

Lee looked at her video pickup. "I don't know. Red, blue, number seven? Gavin?"

"Whatever was in the container we shipped over. Mixed trays. If you don't like it, I'm sure one of the troops will eat it."

"No, it tastes great," Dena said. "This is the

first tray I've eaten ever that is tasty. I love it. What do you think, Scruggs?"

Scruggs came up on the circuit. "I'm not fond of it."

"Come on, Baby Marine," Dena smiled. "You know you love all trays. All those wonderful tastes. Vinegar, mush. Too much salt. High living for you."

"No," Scruggs said. "It's fine, it'll do. What's our status?"

"Well, we're on track for jumping," Dirk said. "The courses are laid in. Lee and I agree that we're heading in the right direction, and Gavin says we all have enough fuel."

"I double-checked that," Dena said. "Gavin showed me how last time, so I ran his calculations again."

Everyone looked surprised. Dirk raised his eyebrows. "And they matched up? Your calculations and his?"

"No, they came out wrong," Dena said. "Mine said we were going to die in the middle of nowhere. I took them over and showed them to the Old Man here, and he helped me redo them and find my mistake, and they came up with the same number as Gavin. So we're good."

"And the centurion knows how to do fuel calculations as well. Fascinating," Dirk said. "You're going to have to explain this to me sometime."

"I don't owe you an explanation on anything, Navy," Ana said.

"I agree," Lee said.

"That's a first," Ana said. "Navigator's sticking up for me."

"No," Lee said. "You don't owe Dirk an explanation. I'm going to mention it to the Tribune, though. He might like to have a little chat with you."

"I'm not afraid of the Tribune," Ana said. "He can chat all he wants."

"Maybe he'll send his steward." Dirk said. "What's his name? Imin."

Lee nodded. "He might want to chat with you."

"Imin..." Ana bit his lip. "Steward Imin. He and I might have a few things in common. That could be an interesting conversation."

"Our money's on you, Old Man," Dena said.

Dirk sighed. "Let's move on. We know where we're going, we know how we're getting there. We have enough fuel. Do we have enough supplies?"

"Yes," Ana said. "We've got plenty of food. Those containers that Gavin had us shift over should give more than enough for sixty-eight people to get to the next system."

"Sixty-eight people?" Lee said. "Wait. There were five platoons when we landed, one hundred forty or thereabouts. How did you lose seventy people in a week?" Lee had left dealing with the troopers to Ana, Scruggs, Dena, and Dirk while she and Gavin had been busy repairing or upgrading software and ship systems.

"Losses during the revolt. Desertions. And there were some issues in training. We're down to two platoons now."

"A platoon was thirty, plus some headquarters people, plus some officers. And you went from five to two??"

"Got it right, Navigator."

"Where did the others go?" Lee asked.

Ana smiled. "You worried that I shot them all myself?"

"It's not beyond the realms of possibility," Lee said. "But it would be a poor way to recruit new soldiers. Inefficient. You wouldn't do it that way."

"Scruggs, you want to give us some numbers on

this?"

Scruggs blinked at her video pickup, then tapped the insignia on her shoulder.

"Sorry, my mistake," Ana said. "Cadet, you want to give us some numbers on this?" Ana said. "Taking some getting used to."

"Best to get used to it, Centurion," Scruggs said. "Something you should be able to get used to right now, okay?"

There was silence for a long time. "Right, Centurion," Scruggs said.

Ana nodded. "That's right, Cadet. So what's our status in terms of troopers?"

"We have sixty-two effectives," Scruggs announced. "Not counting the ship's crew and our people. We've put them in four understrength platoons. Jenny's leading one—Cargo Jenny, Fireman Joe another. We found two other NCOs, and we've appointed—well, Jenny and Joe appointed—a couple of their friends, squad leaders."

"I get that part," Lee broke in. "But what happened to the rest of them? What happened to the other people?"

"The officers—Daille, Fornet, and their bully boys—and one of their servants got shot in the fighting," Ana said. "Another twelve were either shot or wounded when we got to the ship—not by us, by somebody else. We found them that way when we went through the compartments. And between twenty or thirty ran off into the woods or disappeared."

"Still leaves twenty unaccounted for?" Lee said. "Any idea where they are?"

"Those. Scruggs killed them."

"Scruggs killed twenty people?"

"Closer to thirty," Ana said. "You want to update on that, Cadet?"

Scruggs didn't even blink. "They were in the compartments that I put the grenades in. They were armed and resisting. They didn't surrender. They had plenty of time. They're dead. I helped clean them out. We buried them on the other side of the ship."

The silence stretched again.

"Right," Lee said. "Other than the ones Scruggs and you shot—any idea?"

"No," Ana said. "And we weren't able to ask questions. There were a couple incidents after the crews got together, after the fight. The remaining troops—some of the people who disappeared into the woods—may have been encouraged to run. Some of the ones who supposedly disappeared are likely buried in shallow graves nearby. The Rhone Brigade has coalesced around its current leaders. And anybody who wasn't prepared to follow the party line, as it were, was dealt with by the troops themselves."

"Meaning you've got a ship full of murderers and liars there, Centurion," Lee said. "Is that what you're saying?"

"That's a good description of a mercenary brigade," Ana said. "Murderers, liars, cutthroats, all good things. At least if you want an effective military unit."

Lee looked to Dirk's channel. "Pilot, do you have any concerns about this?"

Dirk looked up from the board he was playing with. "We are in the Empress's service... Lee, it's much more convenient this way."

"Were you aware of what's going on?"

"I'm not aware of anything, Lee." Dirk tapped his board. "Centurion, Cadet Scruggs, and the Rhone Brigade dealt with things as they saw fit. I offered anybody who didn't want to come with us some supplies. Nobody stuck around to take me up on that offer, they ran off into the woods. We left a container load of food and equipment and a promise that we'll have a freighter call there in a month or two. No one's going to die of starvation in two months."

"Sounds to me," Lee said, "like you don't want to know what happened."

"Lee," Gavin broke into the connection. "We're in a situation here. There's a war going on. We're all here. We're all fine. But it was close. It's best to move on."

Lee sat for a long time, then sighed. "Fine. So you've got, what, two platoons of badly trained infantry?"

"Not extensively trained, no," Ana agreed, "but somewhat seasoned. They haven't been in a real fight, but they've been in situations with lots of noise and confusion and a certain amount of gunplay." Ana smiled. "Noise, confusion, and gunplay. That's what combat is. So the ones that came through that, they have some useful experience. It's better than nothing."

"It's not that much training," Lee said.

"I had an old centurion I worked for," Ana said. "He remembered a briefing he went to, where he was told that he'd be attacked by the enemy of inferior size, but they had a tank with them. The briefer proceeded to tell him that the tank wasn't very big, it didn't move very fast, and the armor wasn't very thick. They asked him if he had anything to say. He said, yeah. He said, 'Some tank beats no tank.'"

Everybody laughed.

Ana continued. "Some training beats no training. We've got troops that'll follow orders, shoot back when they're shot at, and they'll follow Scruggs."

Dena grinned. "Baby Marine, seems like you've

got a fan club. Bet you could get them to do some other things for you. That tall guy, Jenny's friend, he—"

"Shut up, Dena," Scruggs said. "They're not my fan club. They're my troops. And yes, they'll do what they're told."

"Wow," Dena said. "A bit harsh."

"We're in a harsh place now."

The silence stretched, again, until Dirk coughed. "Scruggs, why do you think they'll follow you? For my curiosity."

Scruggs looked up at him. "Now? They're afraid of me. I took on the officers. Word got around that I killed Daille. I throw grenades into packed compartments and kill people. If I tell them to do something now, they jump to do it."

Ana nodded. "Our young cadet here doesn't have any authority problems over her unit. They're going to do what she says. With this group as a core, she could go ahead and build an effective mercenary organization. A couple more fights, and she'll have a trained cadre. Then she'll be able to take in regular recruits. The cadre will train the recruits, she'll give orders to the cadre. Who knows where she'll go? Maybe she'll become an assistant to the 'Rebel Tribune' and his ground forces commander."

"Could be," Gavin said. "He needs one of those."

"Not true," Dirk said. "He already has a Marine Brigadier."

"For regular fights," Ana said. "But he doesn't have a special forces unit. I think I'm seeing that right here."

"Golly gee, Baby Marine," Dena said. "Isn't this really cool? Really keen?"

"Will you shut up, Dena? Just shut up. Centurion, I've given the briefing on the troops.

We're going into jump. That's not my concern. Do you need me for anything?"

Everyone was silent.

Scruggs said, "I thought so. I'm going back to my bunk. Call me if something important that I'm responsible for happens. But only if it's important."

Scruggs walked out of view of the camera. She didn't stomp, but everyone there got the impression that a stomp was only a few inches away.

"Wow," Dena said. "Who peed in her tray? Then again, how could we tell given what we've been eating."

"We're ready to go save the universe," Dirk said, "or at least the part we're in charge of, or at least the part that the Tribune has told us to be in charge of. Less than two weeks, we should be at the rendezvous. We'll meet the fleet units there, and then we'll see what the Tribune wants to do with his newly trained special forces platoon."

"It's more a company, not a platoon," Ana said. "Try to get it right, Navy."

"Sounds like a ground-pounder thing to me," Dirk said. "I don't bother myself with such details, either as a pilot or as a duke."

"Which is why half of the Empire is in rebellion against the other half right now—because you stupid officers and stupid nobles haven't been paying attention to details." Ana glared at Dirk.

Dirk shrugged. "I said I didn't pay attention. I didn't say it was the best strategy. And it's too late to fix it now. We're overtaken by events. Onward. Upward. Jove save the Empire."

Chapter 47

"It's a corvette ma'am. An Imperial corvette. ISS *Chilliwack*, according to the warbook." Silaski posted the relevant entry from the warbook on the screen.

"I can read a warbook as well as you can, Silaski. Are you sure in your identification?" Monti slumped at her seat and ducked her head to look at the display on the main screen. They'd crossed two systems since running away from the Tribune. *Two systems where the crew thought I was on a secret mission or pretended to believe that I was on a secret mission. Or whatever. It'll all be over soon.*

"Yes ma'am," Silaski said. "Their beacon is running, their dimensions match that of a *Collingwood* class corvette. Their acceleration is 1.5 G, which matches that of maximum cruising power for those. The visual from the telescope matches the visual in the warbook, and the beacon codes are current."

"Well done, Silaski," Monti said. "We've finally made at least a scan technician out of you."

"Yes ma'am. Shall I move to evade?"

"No, we'll continue on our present course."

"Um, at our present course—"

"Don't tell me that you've learned how to extrapolate courses now, Silaski."

"Bronwin— I mean Lieutenant Hooper— helped. We're going to pass close to them. Close enough to be in their weapons envelope."

"They're a corvette, Silaski. What sort of damage can they do to us?"

"Much as we can do to them ma'am."

"I've been informed. Carry on." Monti sat, silent, for the next hour.

"They're hailing us ma'am." Silaski broke into her thoughts.

"Very well." Monti reached for her screen.

"Ma'am—ma'am, you turned on the beacon ma'am. We're broadcasting."

"I know, Silaski. I've been in the Navy a lot longer than you. I know how to work a beacon."

"With respect, ma'am, I've been in the Navy longer than you."

"You have?"

"Yeah. I didn't do much."

"I got it."

"Ma'am, they can track us with the beacon."

"Understood. Carry on."

Silaski waited. Monti didn't say anything, only kept staring at the screen. Silaski inched a finger over her comm board. She looked to the captain, looked at the screen, and looked back at the captain again. Monti didn't move. Silaski tapped a button twice and leaned back.

One minute later, a disheveled Bronwin Hooper appeared, uniform barely on and mostly tucked in. She was missing her helmet, and she'd forgotten to put on her hard boots. She had remembered to bring her belt and sidearm.

"Franky?"

"Bron?"

"What's going on, Franky?"

"Just rendering passing honors to a warship."

"An Imperial warship?"

"The ISS *Chilliwack*. Corvette, just like us."

Bronwin looked to the main screen. "An Imperial corvette."

"Yes."

"You mean a rebel corvette, like us."

"I don't know. I don't think it's in the rebellion, Bron."

"Franky. What's your plan here? Why are you palling up to an Imperial warship?"

Monti shrugged. "The Tribune told us to scout.

I'm scouting."

"He did, did he?" Hooper's hand went to her belt. "I thought he told you to capture that other warship, which we screwed up."

"I told you that was a plan."

"I didn't believe you then, and I don't believe you now. But I have managed to keep the crew confused while I figure out what's wrong with you. They're not sure whether that was part of some deeper plan on your part or not. But even they're starting to realize that we ran away."

"So we ran away," Monti said. "You've got your sidearm with you."

"I do, Franky."

"I locked up all the weapons in the weapons locker. Did you keep a key?"

"I gave you my key when you asked."

"So how is it that you have a sidearm on my ship?"

"Do you remember counting the weapons in the weapons locker before you locked it?"

"Huh," Monti said. "Another reason why I'm a bad commander. Didn't ask. I should put you on charges for not following orders."

Hooper shrugged. "I did follow orders. I gave you my key. You didn't ask if I had any weapons. I didn't tell you."

"Why are you on the bridge with your sidearm?"

Hooper stepped close to Monti, and whispered so Silaski couldn't hear. "Why are you deep in Imperial space coming up to an Imperial Naval warship?"

"We're an Imperial Naval warship, Bron."

"Not anymore. What are you doing, Franky? I've kept quiet 'til now, but you have to tell me the truth."

"Bron, we serve the Empire. The whole

Empire. There's an enemy fleet on its way, and we're not doing anything to stop it."

"You didn't see a fleet. You saw some tankers—"

"Fleet tankers."

"Tankers. And we're doing a lot of things to stop the Chancellor from—"

"I don't care about the Chancellor. For that matter, I don't care about the Empress or the Emperor. I've never met any of them. I'm never going to meet any of them. I care about the Empire and what's going to happen to it, if a Nat fleet comes sailing in and attacks bases here and there, or lands troops and takes one over."

"Not much one little corvette can do about it, Franky."

"Which is why I'm palling up, as you say, to an Imperial warship. We tell them, they tell somebody else, word gets around. And even if they don't tell somebody, we head into New Malaya and tell them."

Monti unsnapped the cover on her holster. "You've done that already? Told them?"

"No, I haven't. You're going to shoot me before I can?"

"Can I talk you out of it?"

Monti shook her head. "Nope. This is what we've got to do."

"You realize that you're probably dooming the Tribune to an early death—him and a whole bunch of our shipmates. And us as well."

"They made their choices," Monti said. "I made my choices. Here we are. And either way, there's going to be a fight and a whole bunch of dead people. I'm doing what I think best."

"Well, go ahead then. Call them." Bronwin put her hand on her holster. "Call them now. Silaski?"

"Ma'am?"

"Open up a channel for the captain."

Monti shook her head. "No, Silaski, I'll do it myself." Monti reached for her board. She held her finger above it. Hooper pulled the revolver out of its holster but kept it pointing at the ground.

"Second thoughts, Captain?"

"All sorts, Bron, all sorts. This isn't why I joined the Navy."

"I don't think it's why anybody joined the Navy. I thought it would be simpler than this."

"I did too. I swore to defend the Empire."

"Lots of different ways to defend the Empire."

"Not in my mind. I should have stayed on Melbourne." Monti looked at the gun. "You gonna shoot me?"

"I've got my gun here to make sure you do the right thing."

"Which is what?"

"Well, only one way to find out." Bron's sidearm didn't point directly at the captain, but it wasn't pointing at the deck anymore.

Franceska Monti sighed. She tapped her screen, and said, "ISS *Chilliwack*, this is ISS *Collingwood*. Stand by for data stream." She clicked that button off and reached over to another. "Last chance to shoot me, Bron."

Bron's gun wavered. Her arm shook.

Franceska Monti leaned, tapped the button, typed in her personal authentication code, tapped another button, typed in the day's Imperial code—or at least the one she thought was in use in this quadrant—typed a few more message settings, and hit execute.

"Data stream outbound," Silaski said. "It's a big one."

"Records of the rebellion?" Hooper asked.

"Yep. Ships, status, the whole bit. Plus our entire scan log—the whole time we met those freighters and the indications or the intelligence briefing that I got from the Tribune. The intelligence briefing that said it was highly likely that there were Nat units inbound. It'll all be there in the *Collingwood* logs, which I just sent to the *Chilliwack*. Silaski?"

"Ma'am?"

"Make for the jump limit. You think you can set a course for New Malaya?"

"Uh, yes."

"Good. Do it. If the *Chilliwack* maneuvers to chase us, let me know." She turned back to Hooper.

"Well, Bron, you gonna shoot me? Get it over with. I'm ready for a nap."

"Nope," Bron said. She holstered her revolver and snapped it down. "I said I'd shoot you if you didn't do the right thing. That was the right thing."

"I didn't think you were with me. I didn't think you agreed."

"I didn't think I did either. But you're right. The Empire comes first. We come second."

"The Tribune?"

"Third."

Bronwin looked at the board showing the relative positions of the *Chilliwack*, the *Collingwood*, the Primary, and the Jump System. She walked over to the navigator's board and zoomed it out, showing New Malaya, the Tribune's fleet, and a projected course inbound from the Union of Nations.

"A very distant third. The Tribune—a very distant third."

Chapter 48

"Is it a mutiny, then." Tribune Devin adjusted his formal robes. The duty watch had forwarded a message to Lionel, and on to him. 'Problems in battery starboard-3 forward. Crew won't attend to duties. Come quickly.' He had put on his best toga, met Lionel, and went looking for trouble.

Lionel adjusted his own uniform. He was missing his hat, and uniform belt. "It hasn't happened yet. They're only talking."

"Nothing wrong with talking." Devin paused at a junction. "Do we go right here, or left?"

"Try right. Unless they're talking about mutiny. Which they aren't, yet. They're talking about stopping work, not fighting."

"More of a strike, then." Devin led the way.

"It's a mutiny if we call it a mutiny," Lionel said.

"Are you going to call it a mutiny?"

"No. I'm going to call it a strike. If I call it a mutiny, I have to throw them out the airlock. If I call it a strike, you can negotiate with them."

"Tribunes don't negotiate with mutineers." Devin stopped at the next set of stairs, which only went down. "Does Deck 3 go all the way to the bow?"

"No. Deck 4 does. And Tribunes can negotiate with strikers."

"We need to go up. Where do we—?" Devin pointed at the stairs.

"I'll have to check." Lionel brought up his comm and checked the plans.

"It's a poor ship's captain that doesn't know his way around his own ship."

"It's a poor fleet commander whose troops are mutinying because he can't find another fleet to attack."

"Touche."

Feet pounded up the stairs. Devin and Lionel spun to face them. Devin reached for his belt.

Nothing there. Oops. Forgot to bring a weapon. Lionel doesn't have his belt either. This mutiny might end before it starts. Killed by his own troops, how about chiseling that onto the family shrine. Expensive, longer than 'died in battle.'

Imin appeared at the top of the stairs, carting a bulky sack. "Sir."

Devin exhaled. "Don't scare me like that, Imin."

"Of course, Tribune. How would the Tribune like to be scared? Clowns? Mimes?"

"Never thought of mimes as particularly scary. Clowns, on the other hand..."

"Prefect?" Imin extended a holster belt with a pistol to Lionel. "I believe you forgot this in your quarters."

"I did. Thank you." Lionel paused. "How did you get into my quarters?"

"The door was unlocked sir."

"My door is never unlocked."

"It was unlocked when I got there sir. Tribune, your weapon." Imin extended another holstered sidearm.

Devin shook his head. "I'm an Imperial Tribune. Tribunes do not carry hand weapons."

"I thought you might say that sir." Imin strapped the pistol to his own belt and reached into the bag he was carrying. He produced a sword and sword belt. "If the Tribune will take his gladius—much more appropriate."

Devin buckled the sword on and struck a pose. "Thank you, Imin. How do I look?"

"Stern and unforgiving," Lionel said.

"Not good." Devin took a deep breath. "You have to look stern and unforgiving. I have to look relaxed and mellow. You're the bad person. I'm the good person. I want to understand what is going on. You, you…"

"Are planning on having them all executed for treason and murder?"

"Well, technically, we're the ones committing treason. And we've done more than a few murders. So perhaps something a little more refined."

"Cowardice in the face of the enemy?"

"Don't see any enemy."

Lionel shrugged. "I'll make something up."

"Brilliant idea. Imin."

"Tribune?"

"We're lost. How do we get to the forward turrets?"

Imin led them down the stairs and through a corridor. He didn't check their path with his comm.

Devin lengthened his stride to keep up. Good sense of direction? Or pure telepathy. With Imin, he wouldn't bet against it.

"How do we know where this gathering is being held?" Devin asked.

"Rudnar told me."

"She successfully infiltrated the mutineers?"

"They invited most of the bridge officers—her included. The guy leading it, Lieutenant Slusky, figured since they're disgruntled, she'd be disgruntled too."

Imin turned right at the next intersection. "Also, sirs, Lieutenant Slusky, he's sweet on Midshipman Rudnar."

Devin laughed. "Viva la revolution as a way to impress girls?"

"Lots of stupid things started out as a way to impress girls, Tribune."

They rounded the corner into the forward capacitor area. Set between all the turrets, it was where the turrets could be controlled in groups by master command staff.

They hadn't been noticed. Devin surveyed the crowd—approximately forty people were present—but a higher proportion of officers and chief petty officers than he expected. There were nearly a thousand crew aboard this battleship, but it only took a small group in the right places to seize control.

Devin raised his voice. "Good evening, everyone."

The crowd froze. Mouths gaped. Raised hands halted.

"What do we have here?" Devin asked.

"Looks like an illegal gathering," Lionel said.

"What makes you think it's illegal, Prefect?"

"My intuition."

"Can't hang a man for intuition," Devin said. "Yours or anybody else's. Let's ask them and see what they have to say." His face tracked down the line of crew. "You there. Slusky, isn't it?"

The officer nodded. "I'm Slusky."

Devin waited.

"I'm Slusky... sir."

"Excellent. But normally, we're braced to attention when speaking to the fleet commander."

Slusky frowned, but straightened and braced. "Lieutenant Slusky sir. What can we do for you?"

"I'm curious what this gathering is about."

"Board games sir. We run a board game league."

"Board games? You're meeting in the middle of third shift to talk about board games?"

Slusky nodded. "Yes. We're setting up the schedule for the next quarter. It's complicated, you know—with all the drills, people on shift, people off shift... They get disgruntled when their games get interrupted. It's hard to assign a winner if the game never finishes."

Imperial Legionary

"Would you like me to stop the fleet exercises so you can finish your board games?"

"Well, sir," Slusky said, "if the exercises are going to lead to something, we'd be happy to participate."

Devin raised his brows. "But we're exercising so we can fight our enemies."

"Yes sir. Wherever they may be. Wherever that is. And whenever. We're on your side sir..." Slusky looked around, made a quick count, and stood straighter. "And yet, sir..."

Devin tuned out and watched the room. Slusky droned on. He wasn't an orator, but the crowd listened, and some nodded.

Maybe coming down here with only three weapons wasn't the best idea. I can count on Rudnar to help us out, if she has a weapon. But that still only leaves four of us... Devin shook himself. Wait—one of those four is Imin. Oh. We're totally safe.

Devin did a headcount. A few more people had arrived. There were now almost sixty. Almost all of the non-*Pollux* division heads were there, but he didn't see any *Pollux* crew. Obviously, they'd decided anyone who came with him from the *Pollux* wasn't to be trusted in a mutiny—except for Rudnar. Devin gave her a once over. *She is strikingly attractive. Well, revolutions have been started over less. Not sure if she has the face to launch a thousand ships, but screwing up one old battleship? Well within her capabilities.*

Devin let Slusky drone on a little longer. He could see the others getting bored. *Yes, revolution is exciting—until you have to go through the details.*

"Wait," he said, holding up a hand. "Enough. You don't like the drills, and you want to fight. Is that it?"

"Yes."

"You have a mind to fight? Now?"

"Well, yes sir. Soon."

"And you don't know why we're doing the drills?"

"No sir. We think they're meaningless."

"They are meaningless. They're only to waste time."

Slusky exchanged a glance with the man to his right—Rebseman. Devin and Lionel had interviewed him before. Long-serving petty officer. Solid. Boring. Incompetent.

"I've been waiting until the time is right."

"Sir," Rebseman said, "the longer we wait, the stronger they get. Last report said we were already outnumbered by the fleets at New Malaya."

"We're outnumbered, right now, yes. I'm waiting for a fleet movement."

"The enemy will be leaving?"

"Oh no," Devin shook his head. "They're sending in more units. Should be twice as many ships by the time we get there."

"Twice as many ships?"

A murmur floated through the crowd. Faces clouded. Hands came out of pockets. People muttered to their neighbors.

"We're going to be attacking twice as many? Why didn't we attack already?" Slusky sputtered.

Devin held up a hand. "There'll be twice as many ships, of course, because the payroll needs an escort."

Every mutter stopped. Every eye focused on him.

"Isn't that right, Prefect?" Devin said. "Fleet payrolls get a big escort."

Lionel crossed his arms and nodded. "The biggest."

"Have you ever seen one? Ever picked one up?"

Lionel laughed. "Couldn't pick it up. It's tons

and tons. Tens of thousands of bureaucrats and soldiers and contractors and workers need to be paid. It's mostly electronic, sure—but you still need credit chips for operations. And the Empire operates on plenty of planets without Core banking systems. You need specie there—coins. Notes."

"And even for the electronic systems, you need some sort of security, right?"

Lionel nodded. "Actual Imperial credits. The minted type. Precious metals."

"Platinum, maybe?" Devin asked.

"Platinum's good."

Devin nodded. "Always lots of platinum. And, of course, if you've got lots of platinum, you need lots of escorts."

Lionel nodded again. "Even if you bring along a heavy cruiser or two, you split the cargo between them. Each cruiser might have a different destination once they pass through."

"But that's no matter," Devin said. "Seems like the troops here—" he waved a hand at the room, "—don't want to wait. They want to fight now. Attack ahead of this convoy. Is that right, Slusky?"

"We didn't know nothing about any payroll sir."

"Of course you didn't. That's why I'm the Tribune and you're not. You think I'd just charge into a station and take it over for no reason? Wait until the number of enemy ships doubles? For no reason?"

"Well, sir, we kind of thought—"

"Have I not made it this far, Slusky? Have I not slaughtered all my opponents?" Devin reached down and drew his sword. "Am I not the Mad Dog of the Verge? Have I not sworn to retake the Empire and rescue my sister? Have I not driven all my enemies ahead of me? Is there anything I've done that hasn't worked out?"

The crew was silent.

Devin reversed the blade and sheathed it again.

"The fleet will remain here for another two months. We will attack New Malaya when I have it scheduled." He named a date, then paused. "Check times. Check your calendars. We will have supplies. We will have escorts. Yes, there will be additional Imperial forces at New Malaya—but they'll be there to escort the sector payroll, which I want. So, we wait."

"Prefect," Devin turned to Lionel. "Can we lock communications down between the ships?"

"We can," Lionel said, "but—"

"No, no." Devin held up his hand. "I changed my mind." He looked back at the crowd.

"There's no reason not to spread the word in the fleet. Let everyone know we're holding position for ninety days—so we can not only seize New Malaya, but seize the payroll as well. Can you take care of that for me?"

"Of course, Tribune."

Devin looked back at the crew.

"Of course, if we do seize this base, as I intend to, the rewards will be substantial. Why, the prize money alone could be as much as a year's pay for each person in the fleet."

The murmuring was back.

"Now you know. Slusky, I'm going to go back to bed. Do you have any more questions?"

"Well, sir, no."

"That's good, because I wasn't going to answer them. Because I'm the Tribune, and I don't answer questions. What I do is tell you what to do, and you do it. And you do it because I know what I'm doing. Understood?"

"Understood sir."

"Do you need more time to deal with your board game situation?"

"No sir. I think it's been... resolved."

"Well, time for everyone to go to bed, then. Attention!"

The group reflexively snapped to attention.

Devin gave the full cross-chest salute. "The Empire!"

They all responded automatically. "The Empire."

"Dismissed."

The group broke up and wandered away. No one would meet Devin or Lionel's eye as they slipped out. Imin hovered in the back. Shortly, the entire turret was empty—except for Rudnar.

"Glad you got my message sir."

"Glad you sent it, Rudnar. What would you do with a year's pay?"

"No idea sir."

"Quit the fleet? Go live somewhere for a few months in riotous squalor?"

"No sir. I like being in space. Stay with you as long as you'll have me."

"You'll always have a place, then. Carry on, Rudnar."

"Sir." Rudnar walked out.

"Imin," Devin said, "take us back to our quarters."

"Sir, this way." He pointed to a set of dark stairs.

"Are you sure? We didn't come out this way."

"Yes sir. It's the quickest."

"Fine."

He followed Imin back toward their quarters. Lionel walked beside him. "What do you know about payrolls?"

"Nothing. How do they work?"

"All electronic. Some specie on the most primitive planet, but we use the Empire's credit to borrow it from locals, in local cash. They take care of all the details. We don't ship precious metals around. No need."

"I did not know that." Devin smiled. "I learned something. Today's not a wasted day. Imin, did you note the names of everyone who was there?"

Imin gritted his teeth. "Every single one sir. Every single stinking one."

"Do you know who the ringleaders are?"

"That's Slusky sir. And that Rebseman one has been germane in passing information."

"'Germane.' God help us all. Imin, you should be a university professor."

"I was for a little bit sir. But it didn't work out."

"Why? Did you kill someone in class? Torture one of your students to death for asking silly questions?"

There was a long pause.

"Never mind. Don't want to know that. Sorry I asked." Devin shook his head. "You have the names of all the actual ringleaders, and the followers?"

"Got them all sir. I know the people who started it, I know what they were talking about, and I know where to find them."

"That's good."

"Want me to throw them out an airlock sir?"

"No, no. I don't want you to throw them out an airlock. In fact, when we get to New Malaya, first thing we do after we win the battle—I want you to hand-deliver to each of them one year's salary. Imperial credits. Full amount. Negotiable, paper, whatever they want. Don't scrimp on anything."

"Sir."

"Make sure you deliver it to each of them. Yourself. Make sure they sign for it. Make sure there are witnesses. Can you do that for me?"

Imin nodded. "Sir, I'll do all that. You can count on me."

"Grand. Prefect, what time is it?"

Lionel checked his watch. "Mid first-shift, Tribune."

"Excellent." Devin stopped and stared down the corridor. "Imin, anybody nearby?"

Imin shook his head. "Not this time of night."

"Excellent. Excellent. Prefect, Steward, attention to orders."

Lionel blinked, but brought himself to attention. "Sir?"

"Prefect, you will allow travel between all the ships until the start of third shift tomorrow. Encourage it, in fact. Let the crews of the other ships hear about this incident. And the freighters, the escorts, everybody. I want word to spread."

"Sir, there is no payroll—"

"Quiet." Devin shut him up. "This is not about that. Third shift, you will conduct a drill involving all the combat units of the fleet, as well as the faster oilers and resupply ships. Load with maximum supplies and maneuver to sweep the outer system. Full ecom suppression. Understood?"

"Sir, we can do that, no problem."

"Excellent. I expect that we'll have much better performance now than we did before, don't you agree?"

"I do sir. But eventually, you'll have to tell—"

"No, I will not have to tell anyone anything, except what I'm telling you now." Devin paused. "Then, once we clear the jump limit, you will transmit new courses to all ships. I'm afraid you'll have a full day of calculations ahead of you, because this fleet will make all speed for the New Malaya system, and the base there. Best speed, understand?"

Lionel smiled. Then smiled wider. "Tribune, I'm looking forward to this work. You can count on me."

"I know I can." Devin climbed the ladder to the

next deck. "Oh, and Imin?"

"Sir?"

"After you get the receipts, in New Malaya, throw them all out the airlock. We're not going to stand for that kind of disloyalty."

Chapter 49

"Emergence in one minute. Jump clock is running," Midshipman Rudnar announced from the helm. "All drive systems reporting within mission parameters."

Devin, Lord Lyon, Fleet Commander and Emperor Designate, tried to watch every display screen on the *Canopus*'s bridge at the same time. *Too much information. Step back, Devin. Let the professionals do it.*

Prefect Lionel, next to him on the command platform, fiddled with his own screens. "Strapakova, confirm passive systems only."

"Confirmed." Strapakova, the senior sensor operator, pointed to the key turned to 'passive' on the master sensor board. "Active systems locked out."

"Very well."

Devin brought up a private channel. "Any last-minute comments, Prefect?"

"I want more fuel."

"Don't be greedy. We had to do it this way." Imperial doctrine dictated that a battle fleet never jumped into a system without enough reserve fuel for an immediate retreat. This stopped them from jumping into battle with superior forces and being unable to escape.

After suppressing the incipient mutiny, Lionel had hurried them directly to the system. Devin had ordered them jumped in from as far away as possible. Their arrival would be a surprise. They bypassed any picket ships in adjacent systems. But they couldn't jump again until they refueled.

"We've got *Hydrogen Queen* with us. When this is all over, we can fuel from her."

"She'll give us enough fuel to keep the drive going, but not jump. All we can do then is flee to the outer system." Lionel said. "If we don't capture the base and its fueling systems intact, we're stuck here, and we'll get pounded to pieces by the first capital ships that arrive."

"If we win, it will go down in history as the textbook way to have a glorious victory using unconventional tactics."

"Or a cautionary tale of what happens when you put foppish aristocrats in charge of a fleet," Lionel said.

"I am not foppish." Devin waved his hand.

Lionel nodded at the wave. "No? That's the most foppish wave I've ever seen."

"Enough blather from the lower classes." Devin waved his hand again.

Lionel laughed.

"Carry on, Prefect." Devin sniffed. "Rudnar? What's the count?"

Rudnar put her counter back on the screen. "Four, three, two, one. Emergence." The main board displayed an exterior view, washed green as the jump light dissipated. The third, or Charlie moon of the fifth planet of the Beta primary in the New Malaya binary system, properly called MalayaB-5C, filled the front screen.

The fleet's aiming point was a crater on the dark side. Devin bit his lip. *Big moon, Rudnar must have turned up the magnification.*

"Beacons. Many beacons," Strapakova said. "Imperial beacons."

"Locations?" Lionel asked. Only Devin could see his fingers drumming on his chair arm.

"Ten freighters, two runabouts—"

"Never mind the freighters. Where are the warships? Put them on the board."

Strapakova tapped on his board and frowned. "The warships aren't broadcasting. Passive sensors are having problems triangulating sir. They need more time."

Devin hooked his feet under the straps to keep from floating up. *Makes sense.* Lionel had diagrammed it for him— active sensors calculated bearing and range by bouncing a signal off a target checking the timing and direction of the return. Passive sensors gave you a bearing using the target's own emissions, but you couldn't tell range. A bright light far away looked the same as a dim light closer by.

Space was big and easy to hide in. Devin's lack of active emissions made his fleet invisible to his enemies. It also made them nearly blind to everything else until they could get enough passive data. *We need time to crunch the numbers. Just have to wait. Relax, and look Tribune-y.*

Lionel squirmed in his seat, but his voice was relaxed. "Navigation? Do you have our position yet?"

Kiernan, the navigator, shook her head. "Working on it sir." She had the same problem, without active sensors. She had to triangulate on known visible stars, and that took time.

"Status change," the backup sensor operator, Alleg, announced. "Multiple jump signatures behind us. Consistent with three Cleveland class light cruisers, a Suffren class heavy cruiser, and escorts."

"Very well," Lionel said. The first wave was *Canopus*, *Salt Lake City*, and *Pensacola*—the heaviest ships in the fleet. Second wave was *Fargo*, *Little Rock*, and *Santa Fe*, plus *Suffren* and her escorts. "The second wave is here. I need our position people. We have to give the fleet orders."

A bridge alarm blared. INCURSION.

Devin blinked. "Incursion? What's incurring?"

"Incuring isn't a word, Tribune." Lionel said. "And it's not important. One repetition only means a future possibility. A low-level possibility."

"It is so a word. If I say it is." Devin watched the board. He frowned. *That moon is much bigger than I remember from the briefing.*

"First opposing warship beacons coming in," Strapakova announced. "Putting them on the board."

"Shouldn't we call them 'enemy' beacons?" Devin asked.

"You've never been through a budget cycle, obviously," Lionel said.

"What's a budget have to do with enemies vs opponents?"

"The Nats and the Confeds are my opponents. But I'm in the Navy. I need funding. At budget time, my enemies are the Marines and the Ground Forces."

The entire bridge laughed.

Devin smiled. When you're tense, you laugh at stupid things.

A group of three beacons appeared on the main display board, centered over the large blue-white crater Lionel had specified as an aiming point.

"Strapakova, what's their course?"

"No listed course, but computer says that's their location sir."

"They have no lateral velocity." Lionel highlighted a setting. "They can't just be sitting there, not moving. They don't have any sideways drift. That must be an error."

The alarm blared again. INCURSION. COLLISION.

"Collision?" Lionel frowned. "That's new. Navigation?"

"Insufficient data from passive sensors sir," Kiernan said. "Working."

Devin continued to stare at the display screen. I wish I had the Pollux's crew here. I wish I never had to rebel. I wish the Chancellor had left my family alone. He grimaced internally. I wish it was time for lunch. Fish soup and a glass of wine. A dry white Rhone. Stop whining. You have a job to do. And right now, your job is to wait. The screen continued to display the opposing warships, but without course or speed.

Lionel's fingers drummed his chair arm. "Strapakova, fix those beacons. Navigation, get us a position. Alleg?"

Alleg looked up from the sensor board. He drifted upwards. "Sir?"

"Status of the follow-up wave? And strap yourself down."

Alleg pulled his belt tight. "Telescopic visual reports all ships present. *Valhalla* is launching shuttles." *Valhalla* was the Marine assault carrier. The heavy elements of the fleet, *Canopus* and her consorts would neutralize any Imperial warships in the sky above MalayaB-5C, and the Marines would land and capture the all-important fueling base, if things went according to plan.

"Very well."

INCURSION. INCURSION. COLLISION. COLLISION. TERRAIN. The automated alarm system generated a second level alarm.

"Terrain?" Devin said. *I've never heard that alarm before. Could it be...* "Prefect." He pointed at the main board. "That moon is too big. Fix it, please. Make it smaller."

Lionel glared at Devin. "We're in the middle of—" Lionel's face tightened. "Jove. Rudnar!"

Rudnar twisted at the helm, fighting against her harness. "Sir?"

"Turn down the magnification on the main screen for the Tribune."

Rudnar rolled her shoulder to see Lionel better. "Say again sir?"

"Turn down the magnification on the main helm screen."

"Aye aye sir." Rudnar tapped her screen. Her voice had said 'Of course.' But her face had said "Stupid useless commanders playing with screens in the middle of a battle." She tapped her board, then tapped it again. "No magnification sir."

"What?"

"No magnification sir."

Lionel's face blanched white, and he swallowed. "Jove's breath, Tribune—"

INCURSION. INCURSION. INCURSION. COLLISION. COLLISION. COLLISION. TERRAIN. TERRAIN. The alarms blasted.

Devin closed his eyes for moment, then spoke very softly so that the rest of the bridge crew couldn't hear.

"Lionel, never mind *Canopus*. We're done. Get the rest of the fleet out of here. I'll take care of the Marines."

Lionel nodded. "Active sensors, online now."

"Sir? Say again—"

"ALL ACTIVE SENSORS ON NOW."

Devin hailed the *Valhalla*. He didn't bother to wait for a secure connection. Time was critical. Their navigation was badly off. Devin looked at the range display. They weren't thousands of miles from their target moon. They were ten thousand miles, or less. And diving directly into it on a collision course.

Chapter 50

"We should see the tanker, Navy," Ana said. "You've screwed up yet again. Not unanticipated, of course. Anytime you put a Navy pilot in front of a nav board, you're bound to end up in the wrong place eventually."

"We are where we're supposed to be." Dirk checked his numbers again. "We emerged from jump at exactly the time specified, and as far as I can tell, at exactly the location specified."

He and Ana sat side by side on the bridge of the *Esprit*, the Rhone Company's transport freighter. Dirk had locked the ship down for the last shift before jump emergence. Officially, that allowed them to increase the safety factor in emergencies. Unofficially, it meant he didn't need to smell the sixty stinking troopers living in the habitation ring.

"Then how come we don't see a giant, great big tanker directly ahead of us—where it was when we came into jump, and where it's supposed to be when we come out of jump?" Ana pointed to the blank display screens. "Forgive a working-class army puke's poor knowledge of complicated things like stellar navigation, but isn't velocity conserved in jump space?"

"If we all came out at the same time, we should be at the same relative positions." Dirk tapped through his screens.

"And yet, they're not here."

"Well, that's assuming they're on the same course and stayed in jump for the same length of time."

"Exactly my point," Ana said. "Whatever course you followed, it was the wrong one." *Please let it be a wrong course. Otherwise, something has gone badly wrong.*

"Lee doesn't make that sort of mistake," Dirk

said. Lee and Gavin were back on the *Heart's Desire*. He called her on the radio and explained his problem. "I don't see the fleet, Lee."

Lee was running numbers across her boards. "I don't see the fleet either."

Ana crossed his arms as he listened. "She admits it? Your course was wrong?"

"No," Lee said. "I calculated it three times."

"You calculated it?" Dirk said. "Yourself? Didn't you take the parameters from the flagship?"

"I don't trust them," Lee said. "They told me where we were supposed to emerge. I knew where we were. I calculated the course myself. I didn't even look at theirs."

"Well," Dirk said, "we haven't run into anything yet, so no problem with that. But are you sure we're in the right place?"

"Everything checks out." Lee sent her findings to their screens. Their target—MalayaB-5C—was where it should be, and their nose was pointed dead at the middle of the crater they were supposed to be aiming for.

"No need to panic for now," Dirk said. "We're shielded from the base at LG1. But we need to find them."

The main fleet base at New Malaya was located between the planet—a large gas giant—and its largest moon, at Lagrange Point One: the point of gravitational balance between the two masses. By locating it there, they minimized the amount of energy spent on station-keeping. From this side, since they were on the ecliptic, they couldn't see the base—and the base couldn't see them.

Lee was checking numbers. "We are on course, and we emerged exactly at the position I calculated."

"And you know that how?" Ana asked. "Witchcraft? You're the one who says you need active sensors to calculate a position."

"I pre-calculated angles to prominent stars before we came out, with a time hack. One minute after emergence exactly, if I look thirty-two point five degrees off the bow, zero azimuth, I should see Arcturus. At two minutes, Rigel is fifteen degrees off base course, negative seventy-three point two azimuth. And at minute three, Aldebaran—"

"I get it. You have numbers." Ana shrugged. "But what do they mean?"

"The only way those three stars are at those three angles at those three times is if my course and velocity was exactly what I planned it to be—which it was."

Ana cocked his head. "That scans. Why doesn't the fleet do that every time?"

"It only tells you if you're exactly in a specific place, or not. If you're not exactly there, it doesn't tell you where you are. To find yourself if you don't know where you are takes longer."

"We're where we're supposed to be," Dirk said. "But where's everybody else?"

"Maybe they all died in jump," Ana said. "I would believe some of them—not all of them. Or maybe they all—"

BONG BONG BONG. The radar detector triggered.

"Somebody scanned us," Dirk said. "Hard. Either close by or they knew where we were and hit us with a directed beam."

Lee's face disappeared from the screen. "Let me backtrack it."

The radar detector kept alarming.

"It's the *Canopus*," Lee said. "They're way out of position. The rest of the fleet—Dirk, they're all way out of position. They're screaming into that moon."

Ana pointed to Dirk's board. "Turn our active sensors back on. We need more intel."

"No need," Lee said. "Two dozen radars just came on. I'm plotting them on the screen now." The screen filled with beacons and vectors. All three ran through screen plots.

"This is not good," Ana said a minute later. "They're gonna have to maneuver unless they want to smash into that moon. They came in way too close."

Dena's voice came over the intercom. "Hey, guys, I'm looking at the screen you're repeating here, and I'm kind of confused. Are we late to the party?"

"No," Ana said. "Everyone else was early. It looks like we—"

"Whoa," Dena said. "Sensor flash. Somebody hit something."

Dirk and Ana watched the flash on the screen. They watched *Canopus*'s beacon. If it died in the next few seconds, they'd know that whatever the collision was had destroyed the flagship as well.

"Look at those Marine shuttles," Dirk said. "They're coming in way too fast. They're going to plow big holes in the planet."

"The Marine pilots will get them out," Ana said. "They're tough. They have skills—not like you wussy-ass Navy guys."

"Even wussy-ass Navy guys can't beat gravity," Dirk said. "It's going to be tight. I wouldn't want to be them."

"Guys," Dena's voice came up again, "I don't get what I'm looking at. It's like things are going off the rails."

"Lee," Dirk said, "talk to us. What's going on?"

"The fleet's all over the place," Lee said. "I monitored data links going through some of the other escorts. Lionel has released everybody to scramble out of the way. The Marines are way, way too close. They'll land—I mean, they have to land—but I don't know if they'll be able to shed enough velocity to avoid a crash."

"Will the ones that survive be able to capture the fueling base?" Ana asked.

"The fueling base? All these Marines who might die?"

"Doesn't matter," Ana said. "Mission first, troops second. Besides, I can't do anything to help them, they'll have to help themselves. Answer the question." *In case we need to help ourselves.*

"No chance." Lee shook her head. "From these positions, they're not even going to be in the right hemisphere to see that fueling base. Forget an interception or an attack."

Ana drummed his fingers on his chair. "What's the conditions like? On the surface."

Lee brought up the sailing directions for the New Malaya System. "Cold. Very cold. Think high mountains. Low oxygen, high carbon dioxide. They'll need at least supplemental oxygen or a forced breather. Near freezing temperatures for water—well, near freezing at that pressure."

"Like being naked swimming in a freezing river," Dena said.

"More like being the last off a decommissioned station," Lee said. "Minimal life support and power draw. Cold. Not much air. However we describe it, I'm not sure I'd want to go there."

"They're going to land and try to go for it," Ana said. "That's what I'd do. That's what they'll all do."

"They're all going to asphyxiate or freeze before they get partway there."

"Doesn't matter." Ana shook his head. "They'll have to try." *Wouldn't be Marines otherwise.*

Dirk put up the main system plot. "Lee, I need

a course. Get us out of here."

"No, wait," Ana said. "Lee, can we reach the fueling base?"

"What?"

"Can Mr. Hot Shot Pilot here maneuver us far enough out and bring us down within assault distance? We've got Scruggs's—what did she call them? Scruggs's Slashers?"

"That's a stupid name," Dirk said.

"I've heard stupider," Ana replied. "They could have been called Friedel's Flowers, for example. But I remind you, lord high and mighty Duke, you work for the Tribune, and the Tribune's fleet is in a deep hole if they can't refuel."

Dirk rubbed his eyes. "Lee, can we do it? Land close enough to that fuel station to capture it."

"Easily," Lee said. "We're so far away, we barely have to change any vector at all. Our velocity's so low coming out, we'll have to speed up. But we can hit anywhere on the hemisphere that's rotating into view—which is where the fuel station is, according to the plans."

"And if we're close by the target," Dirk said. "We can handle the temperature and pressure for a few hours."

"Do it, Navy," Ana said. "Current ad Bellum."

"You remember, Centurion," Dirk said, "that I'm the one in command here as the ranking officer."

"You are the ranking Naval officer, yes. But this would be a ground campaign. So I say we do it."

"Interestingly enough," Dirk said, "you are not the ranking ground officer. Not anymore. That would be Cadet Sandra Caroline Ruger-Gascoigne. A.K.A. Scruggs."

Ana's mouth dropped open, then he grinned. "You enjoyed that tremendously, didn't you? Bet you've been saving that up for weeks?"

"I've been waiting for this for ages," Dirk said. "As soon as you all decided she was going to be an officer."

"Do your officer things, then." Ana tapped his board. "Cadet Scruggs, this is the bridge. Have you been monitoring our situation?"

"Yes," Scruggs said. She was back with the troops in one of the hab units. "It appears that the Marines will be... unable to arrive at their objectives. Never mind. Seize them."

"That's our analysis as well," Ana said. "Are your troops ready for ground operations?"

"As ready as they'll ever be," Scruggs said. "But what can we do from here? We're not an assault boat."

"No, but we have an assault boat pilot," Ana said, "and he says he can land us as close to that fueling base as you want."

"Won't they attack us on the way down?"

Lee broke into the conversation. "It's not as bad as it could be. They're all asleep over there right now. I haven't seen any surface-to-air firings. They don't know what's going on."

"See?" Ana said. "We have surprise, we have mobility, and we have initiative, we need to strike fast."

"Pilot," Scruggs said, "can you land us next to the base?"

"Yes, I can do that."

"Have we any orders from the flagship?" Scruggs asked.

"They're busy over there," Lee said. "There's lots of orders being transmitted, but they're mostly trying to stop ships from running into rocks."

"We have to make a decision soon," Dirk said.

"The Empire and glory?" Ana asked. "Or slink off?"

"Didn't you mean the Empire and glory and

violent death?" Dena asked.

"That goes without saying," Ana said. "No glory without potential violent death."

"Can we do that?" Dena said. "Capture the base, I mean, do we have enough people?"

"Well, they're not Marines," Scruggs said, "but we've got weapons. With the breathers and such in the locker, they can operate outside of the ship for a period of time. Even without them for a while. Engineer can probably scare up some oxygen. They won't expect an assault from this ship. We'll have surprise on our side."

"I like surprise," Dena said, "but I like not being blown up on the way down even more. Didn't you give a lecture saying how this was just a big, slow target?"

"It's only a big, slow target if someone shoots at us," Ana said. "Otherwise, it's a tactically flexible personnel delivery system."

"You made that up, didn't you?"

"Nah, I've had that one loaded for a while."

"Scruggs," Dirk said. "*Cadet* Scruggs, you're in charge of the ground element. I can get your people down there if you give the word. What will it be?"

The channel was silent. Dirk waited ten seconds, then opened his mouth to speak.

"We go in," Scruggs said. "The Tribune said that our number one priority was to seize the fueling base. The only people who have a chance of doing it are us. We have to do it."

"Understood," Dirk said. "Lee is laying in the course now."

"See?" Dena said. "There you go, Baby Marine. Death or glory."

"Or both," Scruggs answered.

"Or both."

Chapter 51

"I've got a headache," Dena said. "It's killing me. All I want to do is lie down and go to sleep."

"I'll bet a hundred credits that's the first time you've said that to a man anywhere, anytime." Ana adjusted his breathing unit, setting the filter mask firmly over his mouth and nose. He and Dena were in the captain's old office, using his display units.

"Bite me, Old Man. Why does my head hurt so much?"

"If you had been paying attention," Ana said, voice harsh through the mask, "you would have heard the pilot make ship atmo match that of the moon so we can acclimate."

"We're landing like now. How much acclimation are we going to do in ten minutes?"

"None," Ana said. "But we don't have enough breather units. We don't have enough spare oxygen—and that's madness to carry on a battlefield anyway. But what we need to find out is who's going to pass out before they do something important. Better to keel over in the ship before the shooting starts. Are you going to pass out, Nature Girl?"

"I said I wanted to have a nap, not that I was going to keel over." Dena wiped her forehead. "You're sweating and your face is red. Are you going to pass out, Old Man?"

"Better hope I don't. Otherwise, you're in charge of the backup troops." Ana was staying on the ship to co-ordinate military activities. Unofficially, Scruggs and the rest of the crew realized that he was sicker than he let on—his reaction to the low pressure and temperature showed it.

Dena sniffed. "Smells like oranges."

"Citric acid," Ana said. "Navy's upped the

carbon dioxide count to match the ground. And those crappy CO2 purifiers can't keep up. The algae in the filters are making citric acid rather than cleaning the air."

"So the whole moon smells like spoiled orange juice?"

"Better than you smell right now," Ana said. "You ready?"

"Don't I look ready?" Dena wore her nature girl outfit—leather pants, leather jacket—all tight-fitting. She'd added heavy, thick boots, gloves, and a knitted balaclava cap over her head.

"You gonna pull that down over your face and rob a liquor store somewhere?" Ana asked.

"It's cold down there, Old Man, and it's not gonna get warmer, even running around. We need to be ready. We don't get proper clothes for everyone, we're gonna have a—"

"Another problem I can't fix." They needed more cold-weather clothing for the troops. Snow flurries and near freezing winds blew across the moon's surface, and the air was as thin as the top of a tall mountain. "They're just going to have to be cold." He brought up the ship-wide broadcast system. "Heads up. Pay attention to orders."

The *Esprit* didn't have enough toilets, it stank of body sweat and feet, and sometimes the lights didn't work properly. But it did have an excellent internal communication system with display boards all over the ship. Ana suspected one of the previous Rhone Brigade officers had some sort of sweetheart kickback deal, taking a huge rake-off on imported electronics. "Listen up, everybody. Final briefing. Here's the map."

The screens displayed the south side of an oval lake with a stout peninsula sticking out from the bottom. Four clusters of buildings marked Red-1, Red-2, Red-3, and Red-4 marched from top to bottom, north to south.

"Fireman Joe," Ana said, putting Joe's face on screen. "Where do you go?"

Joe and his squad waited clustered at the bridge airlock. It had a belly hatch with a ladder. His squad would debouch from there.

"Red-1. We drop to the ground, run as fast as we can and take the pumping unit, the filter unit, and the distillation unit."

"What about people?" Ana asked. "And who are you?"

"We are the plumbers. Don't shoot anyone. Take prisoners only. Then turn off the water. If we have problems, call the engineer."

"On what channel?"

Joe held up a long-range radio. "Four-seven-seven." He had one of four orbital capable radios in the company. Since Gavin was on a different ship, he needed the range.

"When do you turn off the water?"

"As soon as we can."

"What if you can't find the controls?"

"Call the engineer."

"Outstanding. Carry on." Ana tapped the screen, cutting off Joe. Earlier, when he'd asked, he'd been as surprised as anyone by Gavin's answer to the question. "What's the safest way to take over the cracking plant?"

"Turn the water off first," Gavin had said. "At the feed pipes in the lake."

"That's it?"

"Yep," Gavin said. "Shut the water intake valves manually. No water, the pump sensors will detect a problem—they'll shut down. No water to the distillation plant means no distilled water for the cracker. No distilled water going to the cracking plant means the alarms trigger and they shut down. No cooling water to the nukes means auto-shutdown mode. That means no electricity. That means every single system that's electrically powered will shut off—all the sensors. All those containers are designed for hostile environments, and anytime they don't like some sensor setting, they cut to battery power and turn off to avoid damage. Turn the water off, the plant shuts itself down in five minutes."

"You sure of this?" Ana had asked.

"No," Gavin said. "Because I didn't build the freaking thing. And we don't have the plans. We don't even have good pictures. But that's how pump systems work in starships. Turn off the inputs and the outputs all shut themselves down."

Ana came back to the present. "Second squad. Babette, what's your job?"

Like Joe, her group had been given rifles. And like Joe, they had specific orders.

"Red-2. We drop out the airlock in the middle hab unit," she said. "We rush for the nuclear plant."

"What do you do there? Who are you?"

"We're the electricians. Don't break anything. Don't kill anyone, don't shoot anyone. If we have to, we turn the power panels off. We take prisoners, and we wait for Joe to shut the water down. We help protect Joe while he does this."

"And then what?"

"And we wait for him to shut the plant down," she repeated. "No, wait, we call in with our status."

"Channel?"

"Four nine nine. Then we wait for orders."

"Who do you ask for orders?"

"Cadet Dena, Cadet Scruggs, and then Duke Friedel."

"Right," Ana said. He had deliberately left himself out of that list. He grasped his stomach. *The pain is worse today. Don't be distracted. Just take*

another pill. "Very well. Group Number Three."
Group Three was Cargo Jenny and her squad. They also had rifles.

"We come out the engineering hatch," she said. "We're going to take over this spot here."

She highlighted Red-3—the administration building and the inclined railway.

The fueling plant followed a common Imperial arrangement. Electric tugs collected tanker-containers floating in the lake. The tugs shoved the containers across the lake and onto the railway track at the fuel plant. Once the containers plopped onto it, automatic systems hauled them up, inspected them for damage, and sent them to the cracking plant.

The cracking plant filled them—either with hydrogen, oxygen, or distilled water. At the end of the rail belt, when the angle was right, the mass driver fired them into orbit. Fleet ships intercepted them, sucked out the contents and dropped them back into the lake from orbit.

Cargo Jenny's squad had been assigned to the two buildings in the central portion: the inclined railway controls and the administration building.

"What do you do to the railway controls?"

"Nothing," Jenny said. "It'll stop by itself. As soon as the mass driver shuts down, it turns off."

"What do you do in the administration building?"

"We're the police. Don't shoot anything or anyone unless they shoot you first. Take prisoners. Make announcements, tell everyone to surrender. We can shoot up admin building, but not the railway."

"Yes," Ana said. "Outstanding. Finally, Cadet Scruggs, your plans, for our edification?"

"We will come out in three groups of three." The bridge crew showed in the background of

Scruggs's display. "Three from the bow hatch, three from the mid-one, and three from engineering. I'll be in the bow hatch. We'll have our weapons primed and loaded." Her group was armed with revolvers, not rifles. "We'll follow the other three squads. As soon as they've diverted to attack their targets, we'll attack the cracking building and seize it."

"What are your orders about the people there?"

"Kill them all and let Jove sort them out," Scruggs said.

"That's not exactly what I said."

"That's exactly what you meant."

Ana paused. What he had actually said was "Consider the tactical situation carefully, and take maximum effort to prevent sabotage or collateral damage." Even after it shut down, the cracking plant would be full of explosive hydrogen and oxygen. *She figured it out without being told. That's my girl.* "That is exactly what I meant, Cadet."

The cracking building would be full of hydrogen, free oxygen, and all manner of electrical systems. A saboteur would need only ten seconds to open a valve, fire a flare, or short an oxygen tank. The resulting explosion would level the complex—and everyone near it.

Ana didn't want to be leveled.

"All right, everyone understands. We'll be on the ground shortly. The Empire."

"The Empire," everyone replied.

Ana waited until the feed cut off. "Do you understand your part in this?" he asked Dena.

"Yes," Dena nodded. "I go with Jenny and the others and make sure they get to their objectives. I'm in charge of everyone except Scruggs's people."

"Outstanding."

"Why did you split up the squads? We've been working together, and now you've broken them into pieces."

"I didn't. Scruggs did," Ana said. "She picked who would go where."

"It seems like a complete cluster. People moved for no reason."

"Shows what you know. Joe and the people with him—they're older, quieter, mostly technical types. The kind of people who can be counted on to find a valve and shut it down. They won't shoot up everything they see. Scruggs set that up."

"She's a smart little woodchuck, isn't she. Ah-ha. That's why Babette is next door," Dena said. "Scruggs knew she's Joe's girlfriend, so she'd be looking at what he was doing anyway—or trying to keep track of him. Best to put her in a spot where her job is to protect him and talk to him."

"Sound observation. You know, it's theoretically possible that you're good for more than beating stray woodchucks to death with a rock."

"Thanks, Old Man."

"Theoretically. But practically, no."

"Bite me, Old Man," Dena said. "Okay. I get that part. And I get Jenny's in the middle for the same reason. She was a cargo master. She's understands warehouses and transport. If something goes wrong, she can shut off that railway before it explodes or vaporizes or whatever."

"And tactically speaking, her people didn't see much action last time. They're not as…aggressive, so they're more likely to threaten the admin staff first, not shoot them out of hand."

"Odd for you to be caring about enemy casualties in any sort of operation," Dena said.

"Not odd at all," Ana replied. "I don't care about enemy casualties, I care about the mission. The mission says we're to capture the plant intact and restart it. The more of the regular crew we have, the easier it's going to be to get the plant back online if there's a problem. I'm only meeting my operational objectives."

"I knew you didn't have a heart," Dena said.

"Never got issued one."

"Then what about Scruggs's squad? I mean, I understand why you didn't give them all rifles. Nobody in this ship can hit anything with a rifle, but surely something more than pistols."

"They can't hit anything with a pistol either. But I gave her all the killers, the ones who shoot first. We need to clear that cracking plant fast, and with pistols they know that you have to get close. They can't blaze away and blow things up." Ana smiled. "And they're behind the others."

"Behind the others?"

"Yep," Ana said. "If you tell Scruggs to run at something—attack it—and someone's shooting back, she'll keep going. Others might not."

"So?" Dena asked.

"This is the first real battle for everybody, except her. She tends to lead from the front. If she's going to command troops, she has to learn how to use them, to expose them. She needs more than personal courage."

"She's brave."

"Different type of bravery. Watching other people get killed is hard. Standing back and waiting to figure out a solution rather than running in is harder. She needs practice. Besides, we need her to follow up the rear and deal with any issues that occur."

"What type of issues?"

"People who don't push their attack hard enough. Stragglers."

"She's going to encourage the stragglers? How? By her great oratorical skills?"

"Maybe. She can talk to them. If that works, great."

"And if it doesn't?"

"Shooting a few usually works." Ana smiled. "That's my method. Less talking, more shooting." He smiled even wider. "Saves time, don't you know."

Chapter 52

"Urgent patch from *Valhalla*. Flagship wants to speak to you!" the voice in Brigadier Santana's ear screamed at him.

Not now!" Santana screamed back. "We're kind of busy." Landing boats were loud—the rocking and bouncing clattered everything not locked down—and the noise as gas was ionized was tremendous. The moon below had barely any atmosphere—like the top of a very, very, very exceptionally tall mountain back on Old Earth—but even trace atmosphere fought back when you went through it at 10,000 miles an hour.

"They say urgent relay from the flagship—"

"Scrap the flagship! Do not connect."

"Brigadier—" It was Tribune Devin's voice. *Valhalla* had cut him through despite Santana's denial. "Abort your landing now. Abort! Abort! Abort!"

"Tribune, we are deep in the gravity well—"

"Abort. Now."

"Tribune, I don't—"

"Status change." The pilot screamed in Santana's ear, cutting off Santana. "Stand by for new landing zone info."

"Stop breaking comm discipline without my permission," Santana screamed. "Your ass is mine when we land. What new zone?"

"Target on screen," the pilot said. "This is our new landing area."

"That's nowhere near the old one. That's not where we're supposed to be."

"Correct."

"Countermanded," Santana said. "Countermanded! Back to the original landing spot!"

"Not possible, Commander," the pilot replied.

"You've been overridden by Captain Newton."

"I'm a brigadier! Who in Jove's name is Captain Newton? We don't have a Captain Newton!"

"Captain Isaac Newton, Brigadier." He paused for a beat. "Our emergence was way off. We're too deep in the gravity field... we're too close to the planet... we're lucky if the *Valhalla* gets away."

"What?"

"Those stupid Navy pukes screwed up the navigation! Now, if we'd had Marines—"

"Com Link to *Valhalla*!" Santana yelled. "*Valhalla*—Sheer off. Climb."

Would Valhalla *hear him?* The line fizzed, and he heard the word "Understood."

The pilot came back on the channel. He'd kept talking—hadn't even noticed he'd been cut off. "—and all the others as well. We're going to come down. As soon as the gas pressure drops, we'll start retrofiring."

"Get us down to the planet. Get us down to the moon as soon as you can. Land fast."

"I can guarantee that," the pilot said. "Fast landing, no problem."

"What sort of shape are we going to be in when we land?" Santana asked.

"That's not something I'm going to guarantee."

Maneuvering lights flashed red inside the cabin. Santana dropped his arms and waited until the seat restraints locked him in. The ship pivoted forward. The pilot was attempting to reverse attitude so he could fire the main engines.

He didn't make it.

The ship pivoted up. It shook, bounced up, bounced down, bounced up again, and then settled back into a nose-first attitude.

"Status update," Santana yelled down the channel.

"Brigadier..." The pilot's voice was strained.

"Thrusters unable to overcome forward momentum at this time. We are attempting flaring and S-turns to dump velocity. We have insufficient aerodynamic lift to climb."

Santana cursed again. They were too high, moving too fast. Their engines weren't strong enough to pivot them fully, and the pilot was trying to slow them down by belly-flopping in the atmosphere.

"Will that work?"

"Past simulations have indicated that rapid S-turns followed by flaring convert kinetic energy into heat energy."

"How much heat energy?"

"A lot."

"Survivable?"

"Unsure."

"Options?"

"At this speed?" the pilot said. "Medium rare or well done. Pick."

"What if we keep our speed and try a hard landing?"

"Then we blow another huge crater in this moon."

Santana bounced against his restraints as the pilot slammed them into the atmosphere again. "Your discretion. Do your best."

"Already doing that." The landing boat banked hard left, and the internal temperature rose. "From your point of view, one good thing."

"What's that?"

"Either way, you'll be able to make fun of my flying without me having a decent comeback."

"Why's that?"

"The bow will burn up first," the pilot said. "After I melt, you'll have almost five seconds to say 'I told you so'."

Chapter 53

Lionel gave orders as fast as he could. *First, better sensor data.* "*Rowena*, pitch north and climb at full thrust. Repeat sensor links to *Fargo* and Pensacola. *Rigorous*, pitch south, same. *Little Rock* and escorts—"

INCURSION. INCURSION. INCURSION. COLLISION. COLLISION. COLLISION. TERRAIN. TERRAIN. TERRAIN.

Got to clear the moon. "*Little Rock* and escorts, yaw spinward ninety…spinward ninety…hold." Lionel paused. "Navigator, can they clear the moon to spinward."

"No data yet sir."

Lionel cursed. Spinward was safer—it was the opposite direction from the orbiting Naval base. The base defenses would chew up any light units that got in range. That was why the battleship *Canopus*, and the cruisers *Pensacola* and *Salt Lake City*, the heaviest units they had, were slated to pass close by and clear them out. But the planet and its associated moon were not only rotating spinward, but they were revolving around the star in the same direction. It would take longer to pass 'upstream' of the planetary rotation rather than 'downstream,' but it would be much safer.

Lionel didn't have time to run the full calculation. He rolled mental dice in his head. "*Little Rock* and escorts yaw spinward ninety. Max thrust 'til clear of battle. Comms, release—"

INCURSION. INCURSION. INCURSION. COLLISION. COLLISION. COLLISION. TERRAIN. TERRAIN. TERRAIN.

"Rudnar," Lionel said. "Make those alarms go away, understood?"

"Understood sir. Sensors are confused by the beacons in front of us…counters are not responding properly…"

Lionel stared at the screen. The three warships in front of him continued to have no lateral drift. "Focus Rudnar!" he yelled. "Don't tell me about those beacons. We're going to hit a moon. Comm, release—"

Rudnar slapped her board. The main display aspect rotated up ninety degrees, and filled with data from the now active sensors. Now the view was top down from the north. The gas giant clumped the right hand side. In a direct line to the left was the Naval base, its associated stations and storage units, then the moon, then *Canopus* lurking behind the moon.

Between the *Canopus* and the moon was the enemy's three-ship element, its course plotted from the moon's surface directly into the path of the *Canopus*. Rudnar had helpfully extended their course out-system, where it intersected the decelerating Marine units. A radar ranger counted down the distance to crashing into the moon.

INCURSION. INCURSION. INCURSION. COLLISION. COLLISION. COLLISION. TERRAIN. TERRAIN. TERRAIN.

Lionel swayed as the ship pivoted. "Rudnar. Stop those alarms. Comms, release all the logistics ships in convoy, best course to fuel source—"

Rudnar locked her board. She reached into a pocket and pulled a comm unit out, and stuck it on her console.

Lionel grunted. The sensor display had been right from the start. No lateral movement because they were coming right at us. Great days. Not only are we going to crash and burn on this Jove-damned moon, but those warships will slaughter our freighters and Marine landing boats as they come down. We can't get away. He controlled his voice. "My apologies, Sensors, your display was correct. As were the alarms. I should have believed you. Now, we, whooah—"

Rudnar unlocked her board, typed in a code, and slapped the maneuvering warning button. Emergency lights flashed and another alarm blared. Lionel flipped forward in his seat as the ship rotated. *Rudnar was pitching the ship? Why bother? That stood them on their tail...*

The pitching continued, and Lionel hauled himself back upright. Then Rudnar yawed the ship, spinning the bow left and the stern right. The yaw combined with the pitch to produce a crazy tumble. He hadn't expected that, and his arms flopped back again.

"Rudnar, what in Hades' name are you—"

WHAM. Rudnar fired the main drives at emergency thrust. Lionel crushed back into his seat. Spit ran from the corners of his flattened open mouth, and he couldn't breathe. *Must be six Gs. What's she doing? We can't operate at this thrust level. And we're still too close. We'll die nauseous.* Darkness closed his vision from the side. *Don't pass out, Lionel. You'll miss all the fun.*

FLASH.

Canopus shook.

What was that? Did the lasers fire? Did we hit something? We're too far from the moon. Was that the main armament?

Lionel couldn't move, couldn't breathe, couldn't move his head or close his eyes. His vision was nearly gone. He couldn't see the main board. He saw Rudnar pushed into her chair. *She probably can't breathe either. She should have put a timer on that thrust command. I'll mention that to her next time. Next time? Hah, there—*

Rudnar's finger twitched. A little. Enough to tap her screen.

The thrust died. Lionel pulled in a big breath,

then another. And another. His vision cleared. The darkness receded

"Rudnar, I think you'll..." Lionel looked at the main screen. The enemy beacons were gone. Only the icon for a debris field appeared. Had the enemy ships hit the *Canopus*? But even a battleship was too small a target in space. Had they passed through his drive plume? Or collided? He looked to the displays. Damage control was lit up red. So was the weapons board. Every capacitor on the ship had discharged at once. A pulsing red line showed that *Canopus*'s automatic defense systems had engaged.

He brought the tactical display up on his screen. The enemy ships had disappeared. And the crazy yawing had given them enough side velocity that they weren't headed for a crash landing. How had that happened—oh, the distance timer had changed—it was higher than before? They had enough velocity to clear the moon anti-spinward.

"On course," Rudnar said. "Automatic systems engaged and destroyed enemy."

Devin, next to Lionel, controlled his breathing. "Are we dead?"

"Not yet."

"Why not? Shouldn't we have hit that moon?"

Lionel looked at the screen. "Sensor ghost. When they came on, the passive systems confused that battle squadron with the moon, gave us false reports. Rudnar closed with them, then shot them out of the sky." He turned to Rudnar. "Why did you do that?"

Rudnar shrugged. "You told me to make the alarms go away." She pointed at the screen, at the debris field. "The alarms are gone."

Imperial Legionary

Chapter 54

"One minute," Dirk's voice said. "Green light on."

"Green light on," Ana's voice replied.

"Threats?"

"Radar is clear."

The thrusters fired. Scruggs jerked sideways against her restraints. She was locked into a spare seat on the bridge, unable to see Dirk and Ana directly, but with a clear view of the camera feeds Dirk had routed to the in-system monitors.

The front airlock was crowded with Fireman Joe's crew. The middle lock held Babette's group, and engineering was full of Cargo Jenny's squad—with Dena posted there to keep a further eye on things. Scruggs's own crew was scattered throughout the ship wherever they could fit.

Scruggs checked her holstered revolver. Gotta keep focused. Can't lock up. Watch the troops. Give orders. She checked her revolver again. I can do this. I can.

A clear, ice-blue lake passed underneath them, followed by a smoking volcano. Scruggs pulled the breather off her nose and sniffed. The high CO_2 levels still smelled like orange juice.

"One thousand meters," Dirk said. "First red."

"Understand 3,000 feet. First red. Radar still clear." The first red drop light flashed on the screen.

The blue line of the lake ended, and a white line with gray towers appeared at the top of the screen, dropping to the center as Dirk angled toward it.

"Checking radar," Ana said.

Scruggs's display flashed through the radio bands as Ana checked them. *He really is good at this.* They didn't have proper software to scan for missile targeting systems, so Ana was manually flipping through multiple frequencies on the radio system. Any sudden noise or static meant a targeting radar had gone live.

"Thirty seconds," Dirk said. "Second red."

"Copy second red," Ana said.

Wish he was in charge. I'm not ready. No. He won't be here forever. I have to learn what I can now.

The cracking plant grew on the monitor. They would overfly the plant from the east before hitting their landing zone—something about insertion orbits. Dirk had explained, Scruggs had ignored. Not her circus, not her tap-dancing tabbos.

A tug pushing a line of containers across the lake. The containers were different colors: blue, green, and black. Water, hydrogen, oxygen.

The railway opened up ahead, the buildings just beyond it.

The ship tipped suddenly to the right. A yellow streak flashed to their left, rocking them down. Scruggs slammed back into her seat, then bounced as Dirk changed aspect and slowed. The mass driver had launched a container, he'd ducked the ship under it. They crossed over the buildings at walking speed.

"Ten seconds," Dirk said. "Third red. Unlocking hatches."

"Negative. Negative on the hatches," Scruggs said.

Too late. A scream cut through the ship, followed by shouting voices.

On the rear camera, Scruggs saw someone plummeting from the ship. Those idiots. We told them—don't open the hatches until we're on the ground. How did they manage to fall out? Were they sitting on them? She shrugged mentally. Better that happens now than in the middle of the assault.

Scruggs tilted right as Dirk banked and

dropped. Thump. The ship hit and bounced. The thrusters fired again, and the entire ship lifted.

A bounce landing? That's not like him.

The bow pivoted. The main drive burped. *Esprit* rotated 90 degrees. The bow, now pointing north, bounced another fifty meters and settled with a solid thud.

"Down," Dirk said. "All green."

Cold air flooded into the bridge. The spoiled orange juice smell intensified.

All the ship's internal screens flashed green: GO, GO, GO.

Hatches clanked. People yelled. Scruggs unbuckled and stood. No space at the airlock. She'd have to wait. On the bow cameras, Fireman Joe's crew climbed down the ladder. In the middle, Babette's slid down. In the back, Jenny's people dropped down. *Engineering airlock is a good ten feet closer to the ground. Looks like an easy jump.* Someone screamed as they hit, then rolled to the side clutching their ankle. *Or maybe not.*

"Nice landing, Navy," Ana said. "Except, of course, for that stupid bump at the end. Can't you at least set us down where we're supposed to be set down?"

"The pad crosshairs are directly below the engineering hatch," Dirk said. "And because of that turn, everybody's now thirty meters closer to their targets."

Scruggs checked her revolver again. *Gotta hand it to him. He might be a foppish, overbearing twit sometimes—he's not exactly the greatest navigator either—but for hand-flying a ship, Pilot is one of the best.*

Scruggs waited until the last of Fireman Joe's crew dropped out, and counted them clear. "One-thousand one. One-thousand two. One-thousand three."

Her squad—three of the most experienced, armed with revolvers, waited. Waited to shoot somebody.

"Follow me." She grabbed the overhead bar, swung, and dropped through the open hatch. Her feet didn't touch the ladder. She landed and snap rolled, and jogged toward the cracking plant. The battle space spread out in front of her. From the left, the pump house and the filter plants, then the nuke plant, the admin building, and in front of her, the cracking plant. All surrounded by spoiled orange-flavored mist and wisps of steam.

Jove, save us. It's a massacre. Half the troops were down, sliding and rolling. They must have seen us coming. And started firing as soon as the troops debouched. Automatic weapons? Mortars? But why can't I hear them? They're hitting us—

Scruggs's feet slipped out from under her. She glimpsed grey clouds. WHOMP. Only the heavy pack she wore saved her from cracking her skull.

What just happened? What — She rolled over and climbed to her feet—bump. Down again.

What—ice? Ice everywhere. Of course. This was a water cracking plant, at the edge of an ocean.

Cracking plants produced hydrogen and oxygen, but they also dealt with surplus water—either high-salinity waste from the desalinator or cooling water from the reactors. All of it created fog, haze, rain, slush, and general moistness. On a planet this cold—Scruggs shivered as the wind cut into her soaked jacket—the moisture converted to ice. Ice everywhere. Ice coated the ground, the buildings, the paths, everything.

This time, she rolled onto all fours before climbing to her feet. The other buildings stretched off several hundred ice-covered meters to her left. No one was going to be running anywhere.

"Having fun, Baby Marine!" Dena slid past her,

carefully keeping both feet flat as she edged over the ice-covered surface. "Everybody's down. I'll get them moving."

"There's got to be a walkway," Scruggs said. "Put them on that."

"If nothing else," Dena said, "we can get to the shore. As long as they don't go—ah, crap. They're falling through the ice already."

Half of Fireman Joe's squad had slid their way out of the ship and charged onto the ice in the small bay. The sea ice wasn't thick enough. One by one, they were crashing through.

"I'll go rescue my skaters," Dena said. "I'll get them out of there. But we'll need a distraction. That's your job."

"Right," Scruggs said. "Can you take the water intake with only Joe's people?"

"I'm going to have to."

Dena skated off, pausing to slap people on the shoulders. "Stand up. Walk slow. Keep two feet on the ground. You, on the ice—get up. Wade in. Get up and wade into the water. Go until you're right on the shore."

Babette was using her rifle to lever herself upright and cursing. Half her squad was scrambling within earshot.

"Babette!" Scruggs yelled. "Squad Two! Stay down. Aimed fire. Shoot out the windows of that building." She pointed at the administrative building.

"Which windows?" Babette yelled

"Any window. Don't bother getting up," Scruggs said. "Shoot from prone."

The troopers lay flat and fired. Smashing windows would cause noise and confusion, without exploding anything dangerous.

No way she was getting this squad to sprint across that ice.

Dena had gathered her group. They were slogging along the beach, splashing through the icy shallows. Sometimes they sank to their knees, but the motion of the waves had kept that water from freezing solid. As long as they stayed in that narrow band—close to shore, but not too far out—they could slog through.

As long as they didn't get hypothermia. "Gonna be cold," Scruggs muttered. "That's gonna be cold."

Cargo Jenny was skating up, arms wide for balance. "We're stuck. We can't move."

"There's got to be a path somewhere. They get supplies, it can't all be ice. Spread out. Find a path. It will be salted or sanded or shoveled."

Scruggs slid three feet. The landing had melted a clear area below the ship. She could stand there and survey what was happening. *Centurion said not to lead from the front. Keep an overview of what was happening. Assign the troops as appropriate. He'll be marshaling the reserves now and getting them ready if we need them. But without weapons.* They didn't have enough rifles for all the troops.

Fourth squad formed up beside her. "Walk. Slowly. Toward the cracking plant. Keep moving. Don't stop. Don't run. Falling is okay. The important thing is not to stop. Got it?"

They muttered assent and started gingerly picking their way across the snow. They got ten feet before the first one fell—but he caught himself with one hand, stood, and kept going.

One of the lead members dropped to all fours and started skittering across the surface. The others quickly copied him. It was easier to crawl on the ice, and four contact points were better than two. But they couldn't shoot their weapons.

The big picture window at the front of the administration finally shattered into pieces and fell out. Everyone erupted in cheers like they'd won the lottery.

Sixteen people firing full tilt at a building and they've only managed to knock out one window. Jove help us if there are any real troops in there. Scruggs grabbed the radio. "Joe, report."

Dena's voice came back over the channel. "Joe's freezing and he can't talk. Halfway there. We're on the beach—sort of. Another couple minutes and we'll be at the valves."

"Any opposition?"

"Nothing," Dena said. "One person stared at us, but as soon as we pointed at them, they ran. I don't see anybody else."

"Copy that," Scruggs said. "Jenny! Hold fire! Hold fire!"

One of Jenny's troops, positioned to her left, kept firing. Scruggs slid over, braced herself, and kicked him in the side of the head.

"Hey!" the man yelled.

"Hey yourself! Pay attention. Stop shooting."

She raised her voice. "Listen up! Squads Two and Three. Second window, to the right. Aimed fire, one at a time. Squad Two, then Squad Three. By the numbers. Who's number ten?" A hand raised. "Ten, then eleven, then twelve and so on. Aimed fire—go."

The chaotic fusillade died, replaced by a steady crack... crack... crack as rifle after rifle fired single rounds into the administrative building.

Is that window armored? Scruggs squinted through sensor binocs. *It's hardly taking any damage.*

Ting! A crack appeared in the upper left corner. *No, not armored. They're just all horrible shots.* Another ting! A spark lit off a smokestack ten meters behind and above behind the building. *These are the worst shooters ever. Centurion was right. They're too nervous to be in real combat.*

"Cadet Scruggs." Jenny came slithering back. "We can't find a path between us and the buildings. Should we keep searching?"

"No. Cease fire. Bring your squad up there, across the snow. You go with them. Once the building's secured, call Second Squad up. I have to go with Fourth Squad."

Jenny slid away. Chances of that happening the way she ordered it? One in three. Maybe one in five. Didn't matter. The shooting would have unnerved anyone inside. Squad Three moved at the admin building. They fell down every second step. With that to watch, no one would notice Fourth Squad sliding up to the cracking complex.

Her radio burped. "Scruggs, it's Dena. Joe is in the filtration building. They're looking for the valves now."

"Understood." Fourth Squad was one-third of the way to the cracking plant.

She stepped forward, slipped, and her palm hit the freezing ice. She came up with a handful of snow, shook it off. Her fingers throbbed as the snow melted and chilled her further.

Anyone without gloves is going to be useless. They won't even be able to work their triggers. We won't be able to fire back.

She shoved her right hand into her pocket and used her left for balance.

A high-pitched alarm sounded in the nuke plant. Another started in the cracking plant. Steam flowed from a pressure release valve on the roof of the pumping building.

"Dena to everybody," her radio crackled. "We found the valves. Joe and his people are shutting them off. There's a lot of valves. This is gonna take longer than a minute. Joe says that those plumes are water, so don't panic."

Jenny's squad now did more falling than jogging. Fourth Squad was nearer to the cracking plant. One of them dropped—another slip. Another whistle. Another plume. Warm mist settled on her shoulders. *Great. It's warm now—but it's going to soak everybody. They're going to start freezing any second.*

Another one of her group went down. The first one still hadn't moved.

Was that a flash? She squinted up at the third story of the cracking building. It looked like— bam—this time, she saw it and heard it. Someone is firing from up there. And we can't fire back—no way I'm hitting anything from here. And if I miss, I could blow the whole building.

Another one of Fourth Squad was down. This is going sideways. Fast. They can see all of us from up there.

BANG.

Another of Fourth Squad dropped. The rest went to ground. Second and Third stopped moving and milled around. She had thirty people spread out on a wide-open, snowy plain, hiding behind drifts, lying flat on frozen ground. A few were trying to fire back. *A handful of decent soldiers, dug in and armed with rifles, could pick them off one by one from a safe distance.*

The wind picked up suddenly from the north, slicing through her like a blade. The chill settled deep into her bones as the mist on her clothes froze. If she didn't do something—and soon—she was going to lose the whole group. The attack was stalled, the enemy was winning.

Chapter 55

"So you're saying you took it upon yourself to override the captain's instructions?" Lionel glared at Rudnar's face on the screen. Even though she was only ten feet away, the current acceleration kept them pressed into their seats. The heavy element was sweeping anti-spinward, heading for the moons terminator. The moon shielded them from the New Malaya fleet base, its ships and sensors, but the recently destroyed ships must have given some sort of report. The base knew something was going on, but not what.

"Sir, if I could—" Rudnar started.

"If you could what?"

"If I could give some more details."

"Details? Is that going to help with overriding the captain's authority?"

Tribune Devin ignored the byplay and tapped through his screens. With every ship in his fleet blasting out active emissions, he now had full battlespace intelligence. Hundreds of beacons crowded his displays. Radar bounced off everything—his own ships, enemy ships, each other—and the screens were cluttered beyond usability. He displayed a list of identified beacons in the system and worked his way through them. *This will take me too long. Get the professionals on it.*

"Prefect?" Devin asked.

"Yes, Tribune?"

"Can you stop yelling at the helmsman? I need some assistance here."

"She usurped the captain's authority by giving helm orders to the ship. And by engaging the automatic defense systems and overriding their controls."

"Sir, I did not do that," Rudnar said.

"Didn't we blow up some ships and zoom all

over trying to avoid hitting a planet... or a moon. She saved us, correct?"

"Yes, but there are lines of authority to consider."

"It would've been better if we crashed into the moon? More authoritative?"

"There are certain niceties to be observed if you choose to disobey orders. You can't just disobey. You have to sneak around, deceive, equivocate."

"Deceive, equivocate, aren't they the same thing?"

"One requires the statement of actual false information, the other refuses to take a position."

Devin glared. "The difference between, say, refusing to follow my orders as opposed to mocking them?"

Lionel nodded. "Wouldn't be a problem if your orders weren't so mock-worthy."

"Mock-worthy? Now you're the one making up words."

"Sirs, concerning my maneuver," Rudnar cut in. "I did not override the flag captain's authority on the helm."

"Yet you maneuvered the ship," Lionel said. "And you used a command code to have the others follow us. How did you manage that?"

"Sir, I used the fleet commander's discretion code and recommended the assigned ships follow me. That code also allows me to change the rules of engagement, thus arming the automatic defense systems."

"Very well," Lionel folded his hands. "That's all right, then. As long as you're not telling me what to do with my ship."

"Sir, no sir." She smiled. "That's the Tribune's job."

Everyone on the bridge laughed, including Lionel.

Devin frowned. The tension level had dropped again. "Prefect, a private channel, please?"

Lionel complied. "Tribune?"

"What just happened? A second ago, you were mad at her."

"That's because I thought she was a junior officer trying to tell the captain what to do. That's not allowed."

"Isn't that what she did?"

"No, no, no. She used the fleet commander codes to issue instructions. Completely different issue."

"How so?"

"She overrode your instructions, not mine. That's your problem, not mine. For the maneuvering, she was just following duly composed orders from the fleet commander—bypassing the captain in a time of emergency. Perfectly acceptable."

"But... it's the same thing."

"Completely different. If one, she overrode my authority. If the other, she misinterpreted a garbled communication during a stressful situation. Her orders were relayed to her under the fleet commander's code, and thus superseded mine. She acted appropriately."

"But she made up those orders."

"Legally, Rudnar your fleet aide who made up your orders is different than Rudnar my helmsman who followed them."

"You care more about your crew following your orders than mine?"

"Of course. Why wouldn't I?" Lionel said. "My orders always make much more sense than yours."

"I don't think I'll ever understand the Navy."

"No. Probably not."

"What's our status?"

"We're safe for..." Lionel checked his display.

"Seven minutes. After that, no idea. And everything's gone to Hades—and beyond."

"Could you be a little more specific?"

"The fleet is dispersed. We do not have tactical control of our component units. Communications are—" Lionel paused. "Well, the laser links are spotty. And in any event, we'll pass behind the moon's shadow shortly and lose comms with the other elements."

"And the Marines? What did they do after I released them?"

"Nobody knows," Lionel said. "Not even the Marines, I'm sure. They've landed at random locations and are standing at their shuttles. Looking for cows to shoot, I imagine. The ones that are still functioning anyway. The shuttles that is, not the cows. Hopefully, they'll get back on board and fly somewhere safe." Lionel brought up a display on the board. "But we've got bigger problems."

"I suppose. Summarize them for me, please," Devin ordered.

"The fleet is split. We are currently converging on a heavily armed enemy base, surrounded by an unknown number of warships. We lack fuel. We have no tactical intelligence. We cannot combine our forces."

Devin nodded. "Good. Good. What happens next?"

"The technical term is 'defeat in detail.'" Lionel played with his screen. "The only thing that would make it worse would be extensive damage, and I expect we'll be seeing that shortly."

"Aren't you supposed to be positive about these things?"

"I am—I'm positive that we'll be extensively damaged shortly."

"Any chance still of us crashing into that moon?"

"Nope. We're not. Rudnar fixed that part. Good response time from the officers, if I do say so myself, including me. Why, I think some sort of award, perhaps monetary in nature, for the captain to show—"

Devin smiled. "Back to our status, Prefect. How's our plan working?"

"I have a better..." Lionel paused. "Well, we met the enemy—and they're not ours. And, as usual, the battle plan didn't survive contact with them."

Devin brought up a list of ships on his screen. "Recommendations?"

"We've split into two main groups, with dozens of outliers. I suggest releasing all the escorts to independently run away, if they can. I'd already started that by freeing them to evade the moon. They can head in whatever direction they choose. *Little Rock* and her escorts—"

Lionel brought up a map and showed a curved trajectory.

"—should take this course. It passes well clear of the station, but intersects the gas giant. They'll be able to use a gravity assist and escape to the outer system. Might even have time to pick up some fuel."

"And we, ourselves?"

"Us and the heavy cruisers should do something similar. Truthfully, it's good that Rudnar recalled them using the fleet commander's codes."

Devin snapped his fingers. "Right. What should I do about that? She saved us."

"As I mentioned, technically, as helmsman of the fleet flagship, she can't be faulted for following movement orders. Disobeying orders from the fleet commander's code link is a major offense."

"But you said she gave them?"

"There is an argument to be made that by

giving her the codes you delegated authority to her."

"Even if I don't remember giving her the codes?"

"Correct. She can be faulted for giving the orders, but not for following them. But only if you intervene."

Devin rubbed his forehead. "What should I do—put her in the brig?"

"Marvelous idea, Tribune," Lionel said. "In the middle of a battle, let's lock up your most experienced helmsman. Why not stab her with your sword, and be done with it?"

"I don't want to stab her. I like her. She does a good job. She did a good job. She saved our butts, wiped out those other ships, and pulled enough fleet elements together that we're a fighting force now. But I didn't order her to do it."

Lionel shrugged. "Rules are rules. Stab her, don't stab her—make up your mind. I'll say this: stabbing people who go out of their way to save your sorry butt at great personal risk to themselves is not a winning strategy long-term. But some sort of chastisement is in order."

"Chastise it is," Devin agreed. "Public channel. Put the whole bridge up." Devin waited until the comm lights flashed green. "Midshipman Rudnar, Do you recall what I said before your operation?"

Rudnar put herself on the main screen. "No, Tribune, I do not. Would you like me to check the logs?"

"I'm not sure the logs recorded it properly, but I'm sure it was 'Execute. Execute.'"

Rudnar blinked. "Sir, could there have been another 'Execute' or two in there?"

"I'm sure that's what I said, and you heard. A bunch of 'Executes.' Carry on, Rudnar. Good job."

"Sir."

Devin stretched. "Right, that's solved. Tell me again—what are we doing now?"

"We're running for our lives," Lionel said. "We've got two big groups. We'll put them together, then send them in opposite directions. Look here—simple explanation."

Devin's display changed to a top-down view of the system. Lionel highlighted two groups on either side of the moon.

"They're going spinward. We're going anti-spinward. That's about ninety percent of our combat power. They'll shift course here, slingshot behind the gas giant, and head into the outer system. We'll do the same, but on the opposite vector."

"There's a chance we meet up again?"

"Unlikely. Theoretically possible."

"And if we do... what then? Die gloriously?"

"No, no, not a chance of that," Lionel said.

"Oh good. I was worried."

"We'll die. Only not gloriously. We'll either starve to death or freeze to death. We don't have enough fuel to get out of the system. They're not going to leave us alone long enough to scoop any from the gas giants. Our tankers don't have nearly enough."

"So we just... degenerate?"

"Slowly, yes. Run out of fuel, food, air. At some point, the remaining crew shoots the officers and surrenders. That's what I'd suggest were I one of them."

"Shoot the officers? You'd recommend that?"

"If I were one of the crew, I'd shoot the officers sooner rather than later. And frankly, as an officer—I deserve it. We brought the fleet in like amateurs and botched the attack. We deserve to be shot. Or eaten, if we're out in the black long enough."

"Eaten," Devin said. "How truly good. Eaten by our own crew. Not the glorious death you anticipated, was it, Prefect?"

"Not at all."

"Very well. New plan." Devin manipulated the course display. "Have *Little Rock* and her escorts occupy this course—" he dragged the path backwards on the display, "—they'll still be going anti-spinward, still circling around, but passing between the moon and the gas giant."

"Tribune," Lionel said, "they'll be passing very close to the mooring field."

"The fleet mooring?"

"The fleet mooring we don't have good intel on yet. The fleet mooring that's probably full of ships. Ships with lots and lots of weapons."

"You just told me we'll have intelligence in a few minutes, as we come around the moon."

"As we move around the moon, we'll see the station at Lagrange-one. And we'll also lose communications with the *Little Rock* Element—because they'll be on the far side of the moon from us. As we find out what's there to shoot at, it'll be too late to tell *them* what to shoot at."

"Understood. Have them close the anchorage."

"Tribune—" Lionel lowered his voice so the bridge crew wouldn't hear, "—Devin, if there's any sort of organized defensive response there, they'll get chewed up. Maybe not *Salt Lake City* or *Pensacola*, they're big ships. But the others? They'll be meat."

"They're the anvil. They don't have to do much—except be there. Likely they won't be doing any shooting at all."

"They're the anvil. And the hammer?"

"Want to guess?"

"I have a horrible feeling that I know who it is."

"That's the spirit, Prefect. I knew I could count

on you. Rudnar."

"Sir?"

"Use the fleet commander's code. You know how?"

"Yes sir."

"Issue helm orders to every ship capable of following us. Pass between the station and the planet."

Devin dragged a new set of vectors onto the display. "And issue this set as another batch. Anyone who can follow them. Have them close the moon—low. As low as they can go."

"Sir." Rudnar paused. "Sir, I believe we did an extremely large amount of work to avoid coming closer to the moon."

"Yes, well, that's the Navy for you," Devin said. "First they want something, and then they don't. First stay away, next close the moon as low as we can go. Signal any ship that can follow us to tuck in behind. Low, slow—we're coming around so we get a nice view of all the massed fleet units above us."

"We'll be outnumbered and outgunned," Lionel said.

"I know." Devin smiled. "I've got them right where I want them."

Chapter 56

"Scruggs, east of you, third floor, south corner." Ana's voice cut through from the radio embedded in Scruggs' skinsuit.

Scruggs pulled the breather from her mouth to speak, and gagged on the spoiled orange juice taste. "Say again, Centurion?"

"Due east of you. Third floor—Up top. Somebody's trying to blow up the plant. You see them?"

Scruggs shaded her eyes. A technician in a red and blue snowsuit hammered at a valve on the third floor. A padlock held it in place, but the wrench he was swinging would make an effective key. Narrow stairs lead up to the first level, then ladders from there. Only a single trooper could fit up those at a time, anyone firing from the next floor would have a killing advantage. The hammering technician was protected from all her people's efforts—the third floor might as well have been one of the Lagrange points above the moon."

"I see him, but we can't shoot him from here."

"You need to neutralize him."

"I'm open to suggestions, Centurion."

"You're in command. It's your decision." Ana didn't say anything else. Another soldier dropped as she watched. Would he let his troops die while he waited for her to decide?

A puff of snow jumped next to another troop. She jumped and dropped, trying to roll behind

Of course he would. What should she do?

Scruggs cast her view around. She had no idea. The attack was stalled, they were under fire, they couldn't return the fire without destroying the plant. That would kill even more of her own troops and some innocent Imperial civilians who had gone to work this morning to do their jobs. Nothing was going right.

"I'll have the others retreat. They can get out of the shooting at least."

"There's other guards somewhere, hiding right now. If you retreat, they'll get organized and your casualties will rise. You'll kill more of your own troops."

Scruggs's throat tightened, and she gulped. She couldn't get the troops to go forward, the weather and the terrain was against her. If they retreated, they'd be captured or killed.

"Advance," he said. "Seize your objective."

"You do see the rifle poking out on the second floor? Fourth Squad is pinned down, when they show their face, they get shot. And my objective is surrounded by impassable ice fields."

"They're not impassable. The locals get there somehow. Find the paths. Change the axis of attack. Assault from another direction."

"The troops in front, they're exposed. Do we leave them there?"

Ana's silence was eloquent.

I have to sacrifice some of them. She knew all their names, and had joked with them. One, Parlo, she'd won the last poker game against. If she left them there, exposed, they'd be killed, once at a time.

She couldn't do that.

"I don't think—right." Scruggs took a breath. "Understood. Find the paths. Change the axis of assault." Scruggs clicked off. They land supplies here at the landing pad. There had to be a way. Not just a way to reach the cracking plant—but a way to move heavy items. Fuel. Supplies. Gear. There had to be a road.

She scanned the landscape again. There wasn't a path east from the landing pad. But maybe it wasn't to the east. She turned south.

Yes. There it was.

Imperial Legionary

A snow-covered path ran north-south in front of the cracking plant extending to the water intakes at the point. The snow looked smooth and undisturbed—but flat. Too flat to be natural in this terrain. It was a road. Or a service path. And it ran south…

"Centurion."

"Yes, Cadet?"

"I need a half squad at the engineering hatch. Rifles and bayonets."

"Copy half squad, rifles and bayonets, engineering hatch."

"Roger."

"We don't have ammunition." The troops on the ground had it all.

"They don't need ammunition, only bayonets. Send them. I'm going there now."

Scruggs ran toward the stern of the ship. Troopers shouted at her as she passed—confused to see her running away from the battle. She pounded up to the engineering hatch as four portly troopers shuffled down the ladder. *At least they'd figured out it was freezing outside. Jackets, hats, gloves, towels—improvised but better than nothing.*

"Gimme your rifle," she said to the first one, grabbing it. The bayonet was already fixed.

"It's not loaded—"

"Outstanding. Follow me!" She took off due south, away from the fighting. "Move it. Move it."

The troops followed, the one without a rifle trailing behind. "Ma'am, we—"

"Shut up. Close your mouth. Stop gaping like a drunken ballet teacher. Look for a road—look for a road. There!"

Now that she knew what to look for, she spotted a flat, level rectangle edging away from the rear of the landing pad. Twenty meters farther south, it turned left and ran east. She crunched through the snow at full speed, and this time, she didn't slip. Instead of the icy mess she'd dealt with before, her boots landed on scraped concrete.

Somebody's been maintaining this. After every storm—cleaned it. It's clear. Is it clear the whole way?

Rifle in hand, she ran parallel and away from the main fight—outside the firing lanes. She was invisible to whoever was in the cracking plant. A left turn and she was heading east.

Perfect. We should be able to get close to them, under their field of fire.

"Follow me! Come on! Go, go, go!" Her four troopers sprinted behind her.

At the junction, she turned north. They ran until they were in front of the cracking plant. She could touch the concrete foundation and the metal walkway. Now she was invisible to the upper levels. A rifle poked out from above a pipe above.

"There! The rifle!" She pointed upward. "Second floor. Shoot at it."

"Ma'am," the trooper said, "we don't have any ammunition. I don't even have a rifle."

Scruggs bent down, scooped up a handful of snow, mashed it into a tight ball, and hurled it as hard as she could. Ting. It thumped into the rifle, which disappeared.

"Keep throwing snowballs! Snowballs, rocks, chunks of ice—anything! See where that rifle came from? Just keep flailing around there."

"Ma'am," one of the troopers said, "we won't hurt anyone with snowballs."

"They don't know they're snowballs. They could be grenades. They could be bullets. Just go! Keep throwing—go, go!"

Some of Fourth Squad had gone to ground only meters away.

"Fourth Squad!" she yelled. "Everybody, over

here! There's a road! Let's go!"

With a destination in view, and Scruggs in front beckoning, Fourth Squad surged forward, slipping and falling. Two of them hit the road behind her and ran along it. The original four she'd come with were still throwing snowballs and ice chunks, creating a steady rhythm of thud, thud, thud. Whoever was up there hadn't stuck their head out again.

"Come on! Come on! Let's go, let's go!" She dashed along the front of the cracking plant. She puked a little in her mouth as the orange juice smell became too strong. *When did I lose my breather? I don't remember. Can't take too much more exertion in this air.* "There's a right turn up here—there!" Now she was running on the road that passed between the cracking plant and the administration building.

Her sprint—and the cascade of snowballs—had galvanized the battlefield. Troops were up and moving now. The troops to the north had found the central roadway and were moving along it.

"Jenny! Admin building! Train controls! Go, go! Clear it out!"

Jenny waved and yelled at her troops, sending them east into the train controls and the admin building.

Three gasping Fourth Squad members caught up with her.

"You, you, you—with me. We're going into that cracking plant. Come on!"

Scruggs scrambled up the first stairs. The first-floor catwalk ran along the top of the concrete foundation. Metal-floored catwalks ran between masses of pipes—green for hydrogen, blue for water, black for oxygen. Pumps and valves jutted everywhere.

"You, you—" she pointed to the first two, "—clear the first floor. Stay close together. Run down this walkway. Find anybody, arrest them. Don't shoot unless you have to. You—with me."

Scruggs searched for the stairs to the second floor. Nothing.

Where's the—? There. A ladder. "Come on, let's go!"

She jumped on the ladder and started hauling herself up.

Got to get to the top. The shooter's on the second floor. That guy on the third is the one hammering at the valves. Got to get them both.

"Follow me."

Scruggs climbed up the ladder, the rifle over her right shoulder. "Stay close. They'll take care of the first floor. We'll get to the second and clean out the shooter." Her hands shook with cold and burned on the metal. *Much more of this and I won't be able to fire anything.* Her head rose above the second floor, partially screened by a pipe. She grabbed another pipe, hauled herself upward, and reached with her right hand to swing off the ladder.

BANG

A bullet creased her arm. She swung left and dropped down a step, losing control of her right arm. Her rifle clattered away. Uh-oh. Centurion would make me run a hundred miles for dropping a weapon. But I don't have any ammunition. It was unloaded. But they didn't know that.

She hung grimly by her left hand and legs, swinging. The shooter couldn't get an angle on her. More bullets cracked through the air.

BANG. BANG. BANG.

Scruggs stuffed her head between two pipes and twisted. Ahead, she saw a red and blue snow-suited figure kneeling on the ground, fiddling with a rifle. A white snowball arced in from the side and banged into him—stunned? *Hurt? Too much to hope for. But distracted. I can take him!*

She set her feet and shoved herself up, grabbed the rail with her left hand, and swung awkwardly onto the walkway. *You've got this.* She started along the catwalk. Her right hand hung useless. It didn't hurt—all the muscles in her arm had been stunned.

THUMP. Her forehead smashed into an overhead pipe. The pipes were much lower than she thought. She cursed, rolled over, half stood and shuffled forward.

Another pipe crossed the walkway. Too high to jump over. She set her butt on it, and swung her legs over. The shooter was still fiddling with the rifle.

I can take him. I can take him.

Click. The shooter's magazine seated. The shooter rolled onto their side and tried to bring the rifle down. It tangled in the pipes above them. They cursed, tried again—tangled in a different set of pipes.

Scruggs half jogged, bent over. Another pipe crossed at chest level.

The shooter cursed a third time—and abandoned bringing the rifle down. They stood.

The pipe was eye level to her face. If they got that rifle up, they'd have her. She dove forward, hitting the floor and sliding. *Stay low. Keep focused.* Gunshots sparked overhead. *Please don't hit the oxygen. Please don't hit the oxygen.*

She slid under the pipe and crashed into the shooter's legs. The rifle went flying over the edge, but stuck on the rail. Scruggs rolled, but the shooter collapsed on top of her.

Rather than fighting her, the shooter stood and hopped onto one leg. They stretched over the rail, scrabbling for the rifle.

Scruggs stepped in, grabbed a fistful of belt with one hand and a leg with the other, and heaved. Overbalanced, the shooter tumbled headfirst over the pipe—now clutching the rifle—fell twenty feet, and hit the ground with a thud.

Squad out front will get him. One down. Now, where's the other?

Scruggs yelled at the trooper behind her. "Clear this level. Make sure there's no one else here. Arrest them if there is. Don't shoot."

"I don't have any bullets—"

"They don't know that. All they'll know is that their friend with the rifle is gone. Go."

Scruggs glanced over the rail. Stunned or incapacitated, the shooter was at the bottom. Some of her squad had arrived and were searching for weapons and administering first aid.

Scruggs lusted after that snowsuit. She was freezing. Her face was burning cold. The extra CO_2 made her gag on spoiled orange juice taste. Her whole right side appeared to be useless—either shock from the graze on her shoulder or bruises from slamming into pipes.

"Right," she said. "Get a move on, Sandra. I'll go upstairs and get the saboteur. They're not armed, so it shouldn't be a problem."

She wobbled down the catwalk. She'd have to go all the way to the far end and climb up again.

The climb was painful, but this time, she remembered to look first, from under the pipe. From the gap between the pipe and the floor, she saw a set of toes pointing away from her. The pipes clanged as the saboteur hammered away at the lock.

She shoved herself up the ladder, grasping every second or third rung until she was high enough to step from the ladder onto the catwalk floor. She wobbled toward the shooter's perch. "Stop or I'll shoot." *Better draw the revolver, just in case.*

Her right hand still felt useless, so she scrabbled at her holster with her left, managing to unsnap it and draw the revolver. "I said stop."

Imperial Legionary

The figure turned. Blonde hair. Black eyes. Freckled complexion. A girl, like her.

"Stupid rebel. I'm not stopping for you."

"Stop," Scruggs said. "Or I'll shoot you."

The woman turned and hammered at the lock again. The wrench was heavy. She took a long time to get the swing up. "I don't care." The woman swung again. "You're not going to shoot me in the middle of a bunch of liquid oxygen. One spark and you won't be around to celebrate your victory, you stupid rebel."

"We're not stupid rebels. We've got a Tribune. Listen—"

CRACK

The lock snapped open. The woman transferred the wrench from her left hand to her right and scrabbled at the padlock. She was able to unhook it and yank the chain free. "Stupid rebel. We'll deal with the likes of you."

"Look, I don't know what you're doing—"

The woman lobbed the wrench at her—an easy underhand toss that went spinning through the air. Scruggs had plenty of time to step away and watch it land. She shook her head. "That doesn't help you much, just makes me angry—" *Uh-oh.* The woman wound up her left hand. *She's not right-handed. That was a decoy.*

The woman pitched the lock forward—

CRACK

Scruggs felt the bones in her wrist give, and her revolver fell from nerveless fingers. *Jove, that hurt.*

The woman gave a war yell and charged. Scruggs got her hands in front of her before the woman plowed into her, knocking her down. She blocked the fists with her arms and grunted in pain. *Well, at least it was a woman.* She was tired of having her head smashed in by guys twice her size. She wasn't twice Scruggs's size, but she was twice as fast. And she didn't have a busted shoulder or a broken wrist.

The woman pummeled Scruggs—punching her in the chest, in the head, in the chest again. She smacked Scruggs in the nose. Blood spurted. She hit her again, all the while screaming, "Traitor!"

Jove. She's just going to pound me to death right here on the ground, with her bare hands.

She struggled to get an arm in the way. Every time the woman hit her, pain lanced up either her arm or her shoulder.

What would Centurion do?

Scruggs arched her back, kicked her feet up, and got a foot over the woman's head and shoulders. Then she kicked down. Scruggs rolled, cursed as her hurt wrist hit the floor, and staggered to her feet. She kicked the woman in the ribs—once, twice, and again.

"Listen," she said, "you don't have to do this. We're going to—"

The woman yelled again, grabbed her around the waist, stepped forward, and slammed her into the back wall. The air drove out of her chest. Her vision dimmed. The woman got a better seat under her, then slammed her into the wall again. If it had been a solid pipe or a metal wall, it would've snapped her backbone. Instead, it smacked her pack. *Thank Jove for the pack.*

The woman stepped up and lifted up. Scruggs's arms dangled down her back and her hands scrabbled. She needed something. She needed to get her—

Oof!

She hit the wall again. Needed to—oof!—hit the wall again.

The blood was rushing to her head. Her arm was screaming. She was going to pass out if this kept up. Scruggs shifted her balance and leaned in.

Her right arm dropped. Her hand was still numb, but she felt something very cold.

The wrench. It was ice cold. Her skin froze on contact.

This is going to hurt.

"Stupid traitor! Stupid—"

Scruggs grasped the wrench firmly in her hand, took the roll as the woman lifted her, and swung.

The wrench hurt as she moved it. She missed the woman's leg—but snapped into her other ankle.

Crack.

The woman screamed, and the two of them dropped down.

Scruggs rolled over, blood gushing from her nose. *My turn now!* She dropped both knees on the woman's chest. The woman grabbed Scruggs's hand, and squeezed. Scruggs's vision dimmed. She swung back with the wrench—

Slam. Slam.

Darkness. Tunnel vision.

Aim higher. Slam.

More darkness. More tunnel vision.

She was going.

She'd hit the shoulder. Aim up. Above the shoulder.

Aim. Slam.

The hands loosened.

The figure relaxed underneath her.

Scruggs breathed heavily and watched her own blood mix with the woman's as the light ran out of her eyes.

Scruggs rolled off and breathed hard. *Don't puke. Don't puke. It will ruin my reputation. This stupid orange juice smell.* She wasn't upset about beating the woman, but the squad would never believe it.

Scruggs spat blood and wiped a hand across her bloody nose. Two new figures from Fourth Squad climbed up the ladder and raced toward her.

"Ms. Scruggs! Are you okay?"

"Don't I look okay?" Scruggs asked.

The two looked her over. She was limping, her right arm hung awkwardly, her hand was scraped raw where the skin had frozen on the metal. Her nose continued to leak blood. The whole area was smeared with red snow.

The first one swallowed. "Sure. Of course. Did you shoot her?"

"No." Scruggs shook her head. "No shooting in the plant, remember."

"Sure. Sure." He looked back at his friend, his eyes wide. "How did you, what, I mean…"

There was blood everywhere. The woman's head was half mashed, and blood and gore covered everywhere, much of it on Scruggs. Given the blood on the ground, and her face, it almost looked like she'd bitten the woman's head off.

What would the centurion do? Make a legend.

Scruggs spat blood again. "Clear the floor. Make sure there isn't anybody hiding in the pipes. Secure the building. Go."

The two men rushed to obey. "Wait!"

They both stopped. "Ma'am?"

"Who has a radio?"

"Uh, Jenny does ma'am. Cargo Jenny."

"Once you clear this floor, run down there and have her call the ship, talk to the navigator. Tell her that we've secured the fueling station and to inform the Tribune. And ask her a question and bring me back the answer."

The two men exchanged glances. "Ma'am? What's the question?"

"Ask the navigator if it's a full moon here today." Scruggs regarded her hand, her bloody, scraped, bleeding hand. "I'm not sure, but I think it is. I'd like to know." Scruggs sucked the blood off her hand. "I always like a good scrap on a full moon."

Chapter 57

"Fleet anchorage in view," Strapakova, the sensor operator, said, as *Canopus* and the other heavy cruisers raced past the moon. "Naval station and shipyards coming over the horizon. Processing telemetry."

"Very well." Lionel stretched in his seat aboard the *Canopus*. "Sensors, catalog the ships." Dozens of Imperial ships littered the area of Lagrange-1. Here, the balanced gravity between planet and moon allowed them to float co-orbitally with the stations and other ships. Only irregular bursts of station keeping thrusters were required to keep them there.

Tribune Devin looked up from his screen, where he'd been examining his messages. "Brigadier Santana messaged. He says the Marines were unable to execute their mission. He blames the Navy."

"Even if he is a Marine, for once, I have to agree with him," Lionel said. "We've been seducing canines since we got here."

"What?"

"Military term," Lionel translated. "Means screwed the pooch."

"Look at all those ships," Strapakova said, then flushed red.

Devin peered at the screen. "Are we outnumbered?"

Lionel gestured toward the sea of beacons filling the screen. "The appropriate question, Tribune, is not if we're outnumbered—but how badly. Strapakova, give us the cruisers and up."

"Sir, nine ships of cruiser mass or larger. Still calculating classes."

"And each one of those cruisers will be flagships of a division, with a couple light cruisers, and a half dozen escorts. There's at least a hundred ships out there."

"Very well," Devin said. "How long until we know what classes they are?"

"How long until we really care?" Lionel countered. "If I told you there were three Pensacola-class cruisers and four Colony-class cruisers. What would that mean to you?"

"Well, one starts with 'C' and the other starts with 'P'... but they're both cruisers. Do they have different weapons?"

"Are you sure you're really in the Navy?"

"I've got a uniform and everything. But I'm a Tribune. I have staff for that sort of thing."

"Well, I'm your staff, so I'll explain it to you. That's what class usually means," Lionel said. "Might even be different sizes. And we only have one heavy cruiser with this element."

Devin gestured at the bridge. "We have a battleship."

"We have an old battleship," Lionel agreed. "That's us—a battleship, two cruisers, and a gaggle of escorts. And we're approaching a fleet anchorage stuffed to the gills with near-capital ships and their attached units. We don't need to get an exact number."

"Good point," Devin said. His board flashed. "Incoming from... the good ship *Esprit*. Our special operations crew with Ms. Ruger-Gascoigne."

"Aren't we shadowed from them?"

"Repeated from the *Heart's Desire*, it says. Let me read... excellent. They've captured the main fueling plant intact. No fuel for our friends, fuel for us."

Lionel grimaced. "If we're not destroyed before we can get it."

"How long until we're in range of New Malaya's

guns?"

"Minutes."

"Excellent. Strapakova?"

Strapakova put her face on the main screen—she was strapped tight and couldn't move. "Sir?"

"Never mind all the electronic blather," Devin said. "I'm sending you two names. Locate me these ships. I don't need details, I only need to know if they're here. At least one might not have its beacon on, so you might need to do a visual search."

Strapakova's screen eyes widened. "You want me to visually scan for a specific ship? With all these ships tied up? In the middle of a battle?"

"Oh good," Devin said. "I was worried I wasn't being clear. Yes, that's exactly what I want. Thank you." He leaned back and tapped his fingers on the console. Strapakova nodded and attended to her scan. Lionel exchanged a few quiet words with the weapons and targeting operators. They focused all weapon locks on two of the larger cruisers.

Devin watched the targeting display on the main board. "Only targeting two ships?" he asked.

"Doctrine," Lionel replied. "Start with the heaviest and knock them out of the fight."

"Interesting." Devin tilted his head. "Any of those ships maneuvering? The big ones, that is?"

"No." Lionel checked his board. "In fact, almost nobody is. Everyone's tied up at the station or the anchorage. Lots of shuttles moving, that's all."

"Interesting."

"Sir," the sensor operator said. "I've located the first ship. The ISS *Collingwood*."

"Outstanding," Devin said. "Our treasonous escapees are here."

Lionel frowned. "So they're here. That means... what?"

"It means whoever's in fleet command here

knew we were coming." Devin grinned.

Lionel rubbed his forehead. "You know that's a bad thing, right? The enemy's not supposed to know you're coming to attack them."

"They would've figured it out eventually," Devin said. "This helps them confirm it."

"I don't really see how that's a good thing."

"Sir," Tapani said, "Target-1 is going to be shielded by its escorts. Shall we change aspect?"

"Negative," Devin said. He highlighted an orbit lower and to one side on the anchorage. "Rudnar, position the fleet here. Ensure we have clear shots from this angle."

Rudnar hesitated. Her console camera was pointed at both Lionel and Devin. Devin had been perfectly clear, but she was still looking to Lionel.

Lionel shook his head. "Tribune, I don't understand what's going on."

"Well," Devin said, "you once told me that when you commanded a fleet chasing a single ship, you'd think as the person with the single ship—figure out the worst thing the fleet could do to you—and then start doing it immediately."

"I don't think that's applicable here."

"Let's have some fun," Devin said. "Say you're a fleet commander. And some rebel deserters show up, giving you details of an attack coming in—" Devin checked the timestamp. "—twenty-seven days from now. What's the worst thing that could happen?"

"The worst thing that could happen is that it would be true, but I wouldn't believe them," Lionel said. "Obvious plant. Agent provocateurs. Designed to mislead."

"And yet they'll pass every test you give them," Devin said. "Lie detectors. Brain scans. All the same story: how they were with the rebel fleet, how they ran, how they couldn't take another day under the evil Tribune Devin's command."

"Well-trained agent provocateurs. Still wouldn't believe them."

"What if they said they'd detected evidence of a Union of Nations probing attack into Imperial space—and that the Tribune wasn't reacting?"

"Still wouldn't believe them. Nats aren't that stupid."

"You'd be surprised, but what if you start seeing rebel scout ships appear—on different approach vectors to your station?"

"Still wouldn't—" Lionel paused. "If I got all three indications, it would be harder to ignore. I'd be worried about the scouts—real ships mean real problems. I might deploy my own scouts to check for that attack. They could still be a diversion, but they're spending strength to find a path."

"Good. Very good. What if I started getting other intelligence—political intelligence—indicating your opponent had to attack you?"

"And what would have forced them to?" Lionel asked.

"Sir," Strapakova said. "I've found the second ship. The fast freighter, the *Anna Mazaraki.*"

"Outstanding. Where is it?"

"Tied up at the main station sir."

"Put it on the screen."

The main Naval station had risen over the horizon. A set of stacked rings, spun for gravity. Docking trusses extended hundreds of meters from the station, allowing ships to come alongside and fuel, and take on supplies and personnel. Strapakova highlighted a generic fast freighter at a remote docking part.

Lionel frowned. "I've heard that name before. Somebody visited you from that ship. Who was it?"

"Raka Flintheart."

"Your banker?"

"More my loan shark."

"What's she doing here?"

"Explaining to the local commanders why I have to attack the Empire a month from now. Giving them exact time and dates. And telling them why."

"What?"

"Money," Devin said. "I'm out. And the only way to get more is to attack. That's what she's telling them. Or told them."

"She's telling them, but she made you…I'm confused."

"If I win, she gets all those tax concessions. But if I don't, she can get forgiveness by giving them detailed intelligence."

"She sold you out!"

"That's what she does. Now, Prefect. What would you think of that? If you got that intelligence? What's the worst thing you could imagine?" Devin studied the screen. "Weapons, shift targets. Off the capital ships. Off any ships in the anchorage, unless they're underway. Switch to the base. Take out anything that's docked. System defense ships if you can. Take them first. Then the escorts, the smaller ships. Only target the cruisers if they're moving."

"Sir?" the weapons officer said.

"Divvy them up. Make sure every boat gets a shot from the main battery."

"Sir, our guns are capital ship guns. I mean, they'll—"

"They'll obliterate them. Yes, I know. And I know they're tied up at the trusses. Keep your focus on them." He turned to Lionel. "You starting to see?"

Lionel stared at Devin. "You lied to the bankers. You told them you were going to attack in a month."

"Yes."

"You lied to the *Collingwood*. Told them you were going to attack in a month."

"Yes."

"The scouts you sent out—they were designed to map paths that would take you a month longer to get here."

"Yes."

"And that's why you jumped out from so far. Nobody does that. They'll have picket ships scattered through all the systems you would've had to pass through... in a month."

"Bang on."

Lionel shook his head. "I never thought… but is the Union of Nations making an attack? "

"That one bothers me, I'm still not sure." Devin shrugged. "It's possibly been arranged by someone from the Core. That person is out here." Devin gestured at the station onscreen. "So tell me, Prefect. If I told you that you had to defend a major base from an attack arriving in thirty days—what would you do?"

"I'd gather up every ship I could find." Lionel ticked numbers off on his fingers. "I'd bring them into the base for a conference and repairs. I'd rotate them through the station, get the maintenance and repair crews onboard. I'd make sure they were stocked with provisions. I'd give them plenty of time to drill. And I'd move people from smaller ships to larger ones—get the jump-capable ships ready to chase or intercept. I'd prep the jump-capable ships for combat."

"Would you fuel them all?"

Lionel shook his head. "I can't. Not with everything going on."

"And while you're waiting…"

"I'd park them in the anchorage. Skeleton crew, minimal fuel. Work my way through them one squadron at a time. And I'd delay the fueling. Once I released them to patrol, the later I fueled them, the longer I could keep them on station."

"Exactly." Devin leaned back and cracked his knuckles. "The enemy knew we were going to attack. They knew how we were going to attack. They even knew what ships we were going to attack with." He smiled. "They got one thing wrong. When. Prefect Lionel?"

"Tribune?"

"There you go, Prefect," Devin pointed. "The biggest collection of Imperial ships in this sector. At anchor. Caught by surprise. Minimal crews. Fueling not complete. Anyone with enough fuel will flee the system when they're attacked. Anyone without fuel is helpless now that we control the fueling infrastructure."

Lionel nodded. "Targeting. The people who can cause us the most trouble are the system defense units. They could hide in the outer system, or the gas giants. As the Tribune says. Target them first."

Devin nodded. "They're the threat. They can hammer at us or hide in the gas giants, deny us control of the system."

"You knew," Lionel said quietly. "You knew this from the beginning."

"Of course. I'm the fleet commander." A pause. "Do you have any more questions?"

"None."

"Very well." Devin raised his voice. "Put me on the ship-wide intercom."

Lionel leaned forward and clicked it open.

"All stations, this is the Tribune..." He paused. "Execute. Execute. Execute. Execute. Execute."

Chapter 58

"All ships at Malaya Station," Devin said into the comm. "This is Tribune Devin, the Lord Lyon. Under authority of my sister, the Empress, I have taken command of all Imperial forces in this sector. All ships freeze in place, and stand by for inspection from Imperial Marines and attendant units. Any ship making way will assumed to be a rebel and destroyed. This is your final warning." He sat back on his seat and wiped his brow. He'd practiced the surrender demand twice before getting it right. "Are you sure 'making way' is a real Naval term? I've never heard it before."

"Message sent," Lionel confirmed. "And Tribune, the number of Naval terms you've never heard could fill an entire book. And that book would be called 'Directory of Naval Terms' because you never read anything we ask you to. Tapani, weapons status?"

"We're configured for single shots," Tapani confirmed. "Updating targeting on the station, and we're sharing information with *Pensacola* and *Salt Lake City*, splitting targets between us."

Strapakova cleared her throat. "Sir, *Salt Lake City* is requesting confirmation of your orders."

"Confirmed," Lionel said.

"Sir, I." She hesitated. "Sir."

"What? We're kind of busy right now, Strapakova."

"Sir, those are government troops, and this is a government station, the crew has questions…"

Lionel flushed. "This is not the time. You tell them—"

"No." Devin interrupted. "That's fine. You tell them to aim their shots, and wait for confirmation from me. I will personally order them. Tell them that. Tell the others as well."

Lionel looked at Devin and stabbed the button for a private channel.

"No." Devin shook his head. "No, no private channel. Their concerns are valid." Devin fumbled until he found the bridge intercom. "Attention on the bridge."

The bridge crew turned to Devin.

"I started this fight, I'm going to end it." Devin took a deep breath. "Those are government troops out there. Regular troops, doing their job, however incompetently. They're not evil, they're not insane, they're just in the wrong place at the wrong time. And I'm going to kill them for that. I take responsibility for it. The Empire is in trouble. The Empress is in trouble, and we're going to help her. To do that we need this system, and these ships. We'll do the minimal amount of damage, but we have to destroy them. I take full responsibility. Stand by for targeting orders. Let none survive." Devin killed the channel, then turned to Lionel. "Did I get that right?"

Lionel gave the cross-chest salute. "The Empire."

"On course sir," Rudnar announced two minutes later. "We are skimming—minimum viable altitude." Lionel had ordered the *Canopus* to screen the smaller ships, and moved everyone as far away from the warships as possible, while still keeping a course to sweep past the station.

"Understood," Lionel said. "Tribune, the fleet can't go any lower."

"Very well." Devin fussed with his seat harness. "I won't be needing this, but habits are hard to break."

Lionel looked up at the sensors. "Sensors. Status?"

"We will be in range of the enemy's weapons—

target's weapons from ships in the fleet anchorage in forty-two seconds. Our weapons will not range on the stations at least three minutes after that."

"Very well. And you were correct the first time. Use the word 'enemy,'" Lionel looked at Devin. "You still want us to hold fire for the station."

"Here's my targeting selection," Devin said, pulling up a listing on the screen. "These are clusters of system defense boats. I want to make sure they're all destroyed."

"Rudnar," Lionel said, "Take us low. Put us somewhere that will shield us from the heavy ship's weapons while we take out the lighter ships."

"Yes," Rudnar said, "but—"

"But what?"

"We'll be below the minimum acceptable altitude."

"Well?"

"We might run into the moon sir."

"It's a war. We need to take chances. Maneuver us so that we're shielded." He looked at the screen and bit his lip. "We won't get them all on the first pass."

"We'll come back again," Devin said.

Lionel laughed. "Of course we will. Of course we will. Rudnar," Lionel ordered, "bring us down as close to the surface as you possibly can. Hand-fly us, if necessary. Keep us in some sort of vector that has the station and the small ships blocking the big ones."

"And release the escorts," Devin said. "Let them go where they want. They can shoot at anybody they want."

"Understood. Any target in reach?"

"Every target in reach. I want a sea of lasers and missiles going out there. The more confusion, the better."

Rudnar's screen flared. "Enemy's heavy

elements are firing sir. Clean miss. And most of their batteries are masked."

"Understood. Rudnar, do you have some sort of random walk?"

"Already calculated sir."

"Very well."

The *Canopus*, her consorts, and dispersed escorts could maneuver in three dimensions relative to the anchored fleet. They could hide behind enemy ships. They could hide behind friendly ships. They could slow down or speed up, which would throw off targeting solutions.

The range was so short that normally this wouldn't help—lasers were lightspeed weapons, after all. But if you're only six thousand kilometers away, you only had one hundredth of a second to dodge. But all the heavy ships were still tied up. Fuel hoses were attached. Hulls were open. Repairs were underway. Supply shuttles were landing. Personnel were streaming aboard across gantries.

It would be minutes—possibly hours—before the ships were free to maneuver. In the meantime, they were sitting ducks.

"Range in one minute," the sensor operator announced.

"Very well," Lionel said, leaning back in his seat. "Let the games begin."

WHAM. *Canopus* shook. WHAM. Second time, the shook was a jump.

"Colony class cruiser," Tapani reported. "Fired port batteries, then rolled and fired starboard. Heavy damage to port turret-3."

"Make sure the others are shielding behind us. Target—no." Lionel looked at the board. "Tapani, is she moving?"

"Nope. Just sitting there, waiting for her capacitors to recharge."

"Ignore her," Devin said. "But make a note.

That's a smart captain. Suckered us right in. Why aren't the other ships firing like that?"

"Not enough officers on board," Lionel said. "Worrying about hitting the moon facilities. Dithering."

"Dithering. That's a great word," Devin said. "I hope they dither more."

Lionel had nothing to do for the next sixty seconds. Devin had already picked out his targets—a line of defense ships tied up. Rudnar had coordinated with the weapons board. She'd plotted a course that kept the *Canopus* as close to the planet as possible, with minimal vector changes.

WHAM. WHAM. Wham. Wham. Other ships joined the shooting.

"Damage to port-turret-2," Tapani reported. "Damage to port-turret-4, more—"

WHAM. WHAM.

"All port turrets damaged. Loss of director control. Switching to local."

"Roll the ship, no. Strike that." Lionel wiped the sweat off his brow. "Retain aspect."

"Port broadside heavily degraded," Tapani said.

"Understood. Retain aspect."

Devin looked at Lionel and raised a questioning eyebrow.

Lionel grimaced. "Our worst crews are to port. And in local control, they can't hit anything anyway. Best let them soak up the damage."

"Hard knocks for the port crews," Devin said.

"Don't join the Navy if you can't take a joke," Lionel said. "Rudnar? Ready up there?"

"Firing in twenty seconds sir."

For large segments of the run, the ship simply coasted, dropping lower and lower into the atmosphere. At strategic points, Rudnar pivoted the ship and fired the main engines perpendicular to their course to lift them higher. All of this was fed into the targeting board so that the fire control teams could compensate.

"Want to make a bet on which turret is the most accurate?" Devin asked.

Lionel shook his head. "No bet. It'll be Four Forward. Slusky's turret."

"How do you know that?"

"Everybody else is fighting for duty. They're fighting for greed. Greed's a much stronger motivator."

"Status change," Strapakova said. "Beacons at the jump limit."

"We're busy, Strapakova," Lionel said. "Later."

"Sir, sorry, they're not Imperial Beacons. They're Union of Nation Beacons. Two of them."

Devin and Lionel exchanged glances. "Well," Devin said. "There's the invasion force. Two ships."

"But what are they doing this far in?" Lionel said. "And why not go through regular channels?"

"Must want to do something irregular, but what?"

"No time to find out what, right now, but we'll deal with it after this. Rudnar?"

"Maneuvering," Rudnar announced. "Stand by for main engines."

The *Canopus* pivoted. The main drive pointed straight at the planetary surface.

She fired a precise seven-second burst, lifting the ship, pivoting it, and commencing a slow roll. Only two of the port-side weapons even fired, never mind hitting anything, they were so damaged. The roll continued, bringing the starboard weapons into play.

Rudnar took over the main board. "*Salt Lake City* and *Pensacola* are unmasking. Tribune, they request orders."

Devin stared at the screen. "Never should have

let her marry that twit. All those people who died because I was too cowardly to say anything."

"And now, more are going to die because you're being brave," Lionel said.

Devin wiped his brow. "I hate being a Tribune."

"Nobody cares," Lionel said. "Time to do your job."

Devin sat up straight and cued his comm. "All units. Go. Shoot, let go—"

"Fire as you bear," Lionel hissed.

"All units," Devin said. "Fire as you bear."

Canopus's laser turrets locked onto a line of system defense boats at the station. Lasers chewed through the formation. Two beams missed entirely. The next six found targets—destroying dozens of the small boats. Even those not targeted directly suffered. One ship, tied up next to a vessel that suffered a reactor failure, vanished in the secondary explosion. If you're tied up next to something that blows up, chances are you disappear as well.

The *Canopus* edged along, firing—firing. Seconds later, *Pensacola* and *Salt Lake City* added their firepower. Dozens of ships at the station flashed into scrap. Chunks of ships flung off the station. One of the trusses broke free and sailed out into space, but not before banging into an adjacent ring and knocking a docking bay to pieces.

"Target only the—strike that." Lionel shook his head. "Continue." He glared at Devin. "We don't have control of the secondary effects. We might destroy the station."

"Carry on as ordered," Devin said. "Destroy anything that can move."

WHAM.

This time, the whole ship shook, and the overhead lights flashed red. Fans stopped, and a hot metallic smell seeped in from the vents.

"Damage?" Lionel asked.

"Main engineering took a hit," Rudnar said. "No response on comms. No internal power. I have helm control, but thrust is dropping, so they may have damaged the engines too."

On screen, *Salt Lake City* and *Pensacola* rolled. More lasers lashed out. Another dozen system defense boats exploded.

"Two more volleys, and there wouldn't be any system units left," Lionel said. "Rudnar, stop our roll, leave the remaining weapons pointing—"

WHAM. *Canopus* jerked.

"Helm inoperative. No response from engineering," Rudnar said. "Thrust at zero. No attitude control. No power. Weapons not responding." She looked up. "But sensors are functioning on internal backup. Our orbit is decaying. We're going down."

Lionel slapped a red button on his board. Only the captain had this button. "Abandon ship. Abandon ship. Hands to the boats. Pass the word. Pass the word," blared from the speaker.

"Rudnar, Strapakova, Tapani," Lionel said. "Abandon the bridge, pass the word on your way. I'll assist the Tribune."

The three officers, along with the rest of the bridge crew unbuckled, saluted and left. In moments, Lionel and Devin were alone on the bridge.

"You leaving?" Devin asked.

"Captain goes down with the ship." Lionel typed a code into his console. Console electronics smoked as burn charges destroyed codes and sensitive equipment.

"For a battleship, it was kind of a crappy ship," Devin said. "Mutinous crew."

"Near mutinous crew. And *Canopus* is a beautiful ship."

"Incompetent officers."

Lionel shrugged. "They could learn."

"Lazy crew."

"Just needed the proper motivation."

Devin pointed at the board. "They couldn't hit anything. Terrible shooting."

"I'll give you that," Lionel agreed. "But every Naval officer wants to command a ship. And once you command one, you want a bigger one, then another."

"Sounds like some sort of addiction. You should get that seen to. Well, it looks like we need to get a bigger fleet for you to command then, so come along. Hello, Imin."

Imin had appeared on the bridge. He carried the Tribune's sword and two small cases. Behind him, two ratings carried spare skinsuits and some cold weather gear. "Time to go, Tribune. Shuttle is standing by."

"Are we going to die in the cold dark wastes of space?" Devin asked. "A proper way for a noble to die, don't you think?"

"No sir. Going to land on the moon. It has atmosphere, so we'll be fine. A bit cold. Thin atmo and low gravity, so the landing won't be that bad, really. Just have to make sure *Canopus* doesn't crash on top of us."

"Oh." Devin blinked. "I see."

"You might get some frostbite, Tribune." Imin shrugged. "Cold ears, maybe. That's about it." Imin extended his hand. "I brought you a hat, Tribune."

Devin glared at the hat. "It's furry."

"Yes sir. Tabbo fur."

Devin sighed. "Can't even arrange to die in battle properly. What's in the cases, Imin? Imperial secrets? Codes?"

"These?" Imin hefted them. "Wine. And spices. Some maple syrup."

"Of course."

"I've already taken care of the sensitive systems. We need to move sir."

"Look." Lionel pointed to the main screen. Rudnar had left the sensor feed up. "*Little Rock* and escorts have come around the horizon. She's repeating your surrender demand. The station is all shot up, barely anything's moving. And those cruisers have stopped firing. Probably can't maneuver and need options."

"Tribune, Prefect," Imin said. "We need to go now. If you don't go yourselves, it might be necessary to… assist you."

"I got it, Imin, I got it." Devin unstrapped and strode to the bridge exit.

Imin followed. He glanced back at the board. "Did we win?"

"We lost," Devin said.

"We lost the battle?" Imin shook his head. "We've got the only remaining mobile force in the system. How did we lose?"

"Oh, we won the battle." Devin nodded. "I just killed more Imperial troops than any emperor in the last fifty years, probably the last hundred. By my orders. We may have won the battle, and we may be winning the rebellion, but we've lost the Empire. Imin?"

"Tribune?"

Devin strode through the door. "I'm lost. Show me where I need to go."

Chapter 59

Devin pushed his sword stand into the corner and draped his sword belt over it. He hoped that whoever had occupied this office before him had been killed in the fighting. Crimes against fashion and decorating weren't supposed to be terminal. "They should be," Devin said aloud. "They should be." He placed a picture of his sister and the Emperor on the wall to the left of his desk.

New Malaya station had given up without a fight. He'd been traipsing across the station arranging the surrender of fleet units and having long conversations with the nobles that were present. Dignity demanded they not surrender to Acting Lieutenant Rudnar, but the presence of the Mad Dog of the Verge mollified them. Devin had hoped for active support, but he'd only got a grudging acceptance. He had invited all the remaining admirals, who overlapped a hundred percent with all the nobles, for dinner in three shifts. Imin had brought him somewhere and dropped him off to sleep. Now that he was awake he puttered and moved the sword stand to the other corner. Maybe it looked better there?

Beep. A double knock on the door. "Enter," Devin said. The door slid open and a cacophony of noise swelled from outside. "Tribune. Lord Devin. A moment." Imin entered, carrying a tray. His face was fixed and white. "One moment, Tribune." He set the tray down. The yells continued. Devin heard the shouting of the Marine guard. Imin palmed the cutlery and stepped out into the hallway. The noise cut off abruptly as the door locked behind him.

Devin sat in his chair and took a sip of his wine. A rosé. Imin never served rosés. Quite good, though. And soup. Of course, Imin loved his soups—but without a spoon? The door hissed open and Imin returned. This time, the hall was deadly quiet. "An administrative matter to take care of." Imin laid the cutlery back on the table. Devin regarded it. Knife and a fork. "Where's the spoon, Imin?"

"I'm sorry sir. I had to make use of the spoon in another endeavor just a moment ago. I'm having one brought up—it'll be here shortly."

"Thank you, Imin. Imin, where are we?"

"We are at the main headquarters of the New Malaya system sir. Where the Tribune has defeated the combined fleets of the dastardly Chancellor."

"That's great. But I meant, where are my quarters?" He pointed to the room. "Where is this place? It's not the station commander's room."

"Second ring in sir. D-ring."

Devin lifted his knife and dropped it. It fell—but slowly. "We're not even in the full gravity section."

"No sir. I felt it best to have us at a more inner location. That way, any marauding ships would have farther to go if they decided to assault the Tribune's sleeping quarters."

"I see." Devin recovered his knife. "And the crowd outside?"

"They felt they had a reason to see you sir. I've arranged for them to be dealt with in another section of the corridor."

"I see."

"I also arranged for this section of the corridor to be locked down. There'll be more Marines here shortly."

"I can't hide from my people, Imin."

"You're not hiding sir. You're eating. Everyone deserves a quiet breakfast."

Imin looked at the sword stand and frowned. "With your permission, Tribune?" He walked over, picked up the stand, brought it behind the desk, and put it in the corner. Then he reached and unhooked the picture of the Emperor and Empress, and stuck it to the wall to the left of the main door. "Much better, sir, don't you think?"

"In this, as in many things," Devin said, "what I think doesn't matter. What happens next?"

"Sir, there's a number of administrative issues that have to be dealt with. Promotions, demotions, death warrants."

"Give them all to Lionel. He promotes and demotes as he decides. He assigns as he decides—up to and including ship captains. Have him review the capital ship crews with me, and I want to know any reassignment of the *Pollux*'s crew and where they are."

"Sir. And the death warrants?"

"He can decide."

Imin paused. "Can I speak freely sir?"

"You always do."

"He's not the right man for that job sir. He doesn't know what to do. He's had no experience there."

"Are you being disloyal to the flag captain, Imin?"

"No sir. I'm recognizing reality. He's in way over his head. He won't sign enough death warrants."

"Not enough death warrants?"

"Emperors, those that live, tend to sign more than those who don't."

"And you want me to live?"

"I do sir."

"Well, he's going to have to learn to swim, because I'm in way over my head. I've got my own problems. I imagine you have your own problems as well, Imin."

"I do sir."

"Right. Alright. The Prefect is busy getting the

base organized, getting the fleets running. What else is going on?"

"Sir, most of the fleet that came with us is docked and undergoing repairs. We suffered pretty heavily at the last."

"Canopus?"

"Destroyed on impact. Heavy casualties."

"Very well. And the newly acquired ships?"

"Most of them have been kept on station sir. There's a problem of crews."

"How many?"

"Of the crews who remain loyal to the previous commanders. Almost done sir. A few death warrants, and even most of those will go away."

"You're saying everyone is disloyal to the Empire?"

"I'm saying most everyone here is loyal to you sir—or going to be. Problem will be that some of them aren't really loyal to anything."

"They'll need to be dispersed."

"We can't really afford to disperse them. Again, speaking freely with the Tribune's permission—"

"Go ahead."

"A lot of the people, especially some of the NCOs—if you don't disperse them, their incompetence will collect together, form a giant black hole of incompetence, and suck the entire rest of the station and the fleet staff into it."

"Aptly put, Imin. What will we do with them?"

"The Prefect is organizing shipping them out to the periphery. They'll be found some useful but non-critical duties in the Verge or elsewhere."

"Was that the Prefect's idea?"

"Mostly sir. Try to act surprised when you hear it from him."

"I will. What about the Marines?"

"They're over at the Marine barracks sir. There's a whole Marine battalion there. They refuse to surrender."

"So there's fighting?"

"No sir. I believe they are drinking."

"Drinking?"

"Alcohol sir."

"I know what they're drinking, Imin. They're saying that... Who went over there?"

"The Brigadier went over with some of his staff. Commander Friedel went with them. The Duke Friedel."

"And as well some of his crew. And they think that's a good thing?"

"Well, sir, they're Marines. They're going to have some drinks and sort it out. We may have to kill them after this, but they'll all be good sports about it."

"I don't understand Marines," Devin said.

"No sir."

"I don't understand the Navy, for that matter."

"No sir."

"I don't think I understand anything at all, Imin."

"You understand the nobility and the Empire sir. That's your job. Leave the Marines and the Navy and everything else to us."

"All right. Did you find my banker friend?"

"Yes sir."

"Did she offer to bribe you?"

"No sir. She went one better."

"What's one better than offering to bribe you?"

"Offered to bribe you sir. She says she can access additional funding for the fleet, and it would be, and I quote, 'tactically short-sighted to have her executed at this time.'"

"I hate it when people are right. She in jail?"

"Ah, no sir. Hotel."

"What's to stop her running away?"

"I think you should read the interest rates she

proposes charging you sir. I think that's enough to keep her close by."

"Outstanding. Do we have any money?"

"Lots sir."

"That's good."

"Not enough to make payroll at the end of the month."

"That's not good. I thought you said lots?"

"In a relative sense, sir, we do."

"All right. Who's in charge of my schedule?"

"I am sir."

"Of course you are. After lunch, get the banker lady in here. We'll have a chat."

"She's already scheduled two hours into second shift sir."

"Of course she is. What about those two fleet officers from *Collingwood*?"

Imin stepped over to Devin's desk and shuffled the pile of death warrants. By tradition, they were on paper, and had to be physically signed. He extended two to Devin.

"They're to be executed?"

"They are in custody sir. Until the execution. Protective custody."

"Who put them there?"

"We didn't sir. They were when we came in."

"Should I kill them?"

"Your decision sir. They did betray you."

"That was the plan, that they'd do that."

"Yes, Tribune, but they didn't know that. From there point of view it was a real betrayal."

"They're my enemies, then?"

"When you make peace, you make peace with your enemies, not your friends.

"All right. Have them released and have them come see me."

"Fourth hour of second shift sir. I saved an hour for them."

"Since you're in a suggestive mood, Imin, any suggestions on what to do with them?"

"Well, I would assign them to Duke Friedel's other ship sir."

"Assign them to Duke Friedel's other ship?"

"Yes sir. The one with the mercenary unit. His mercenary unit."

"He has a mercenary unit? What are they called?"

"Scruggs's Slashers."

"A funny name. Goofy."

"I wouldn't say that if you met any of them sir. They're proud of it. Comes from their leader."

"Ah yes, that's Miss Ruger-Gascoigne's group. How is she doing?"

"We've made arrangements to start sparring on a regular basis sir. I was impressed when I reviewed the battle plan from the moon's fueling station. Improvise, adapt, overcome. Well done on her part."

"She's just a little thing. You'll smack her around. Don't hurt her."

"It's not the size of the dog in the fight sir."

"Yes, yes, fight in the dog. I get it. All right, let's get this whole thing sorted out. I've decided it was worth it."

"It's definitely worth it sir. Not for you, but for the rest of us."

"How do you figure that, Imin?"

"We're going to get an Empire that'll work again."

"What do I get?"

"Headaches sir. That's why you're in charge."

"Thank you so much."

Beep. The intercom on Devin's desk flashed. "Tribune?"

"Yes?"

"Uh, Lieutenant—I mean Acting Lieutenant

Rudnar here sir."

"Drop the acting, Rudnar. You're a lieutenant now. I say so. Anyone who complains, send them to me."

"Sir, I'm in the CIC helping co-ordinate the sweeps…"

Small ships had been coming and going for the last day. Some had been escorts that had managed to acquire enough fuel to flee the system. Others had been escorts returning to the system. They were easy to tell apart. The ones returning were forced to head for the station. At least thirty or forty small ships had headed for various gas giants to attempt to refuel, moons to hide, or asteroid belts to be silent. Lionel had coordinated small flotillas of escort ships to hunt them down and bring them back.

"Yes, Rudnar?"

"Sir, one signature matches a Union of Nations diplomatic ship."

"Does it? You sure?"

"I'm using a database from *Pollux* sir."

"Are we intercepting them?"

"I'm only a lieutenant sir. There's a full captain here in the command center. She doesn't believe what I'm saying to her."

"I see. How are you able to call me?"

"That's my fault sir," Imin said. "Given the circumstances in the past, I made sure certain key officers have codes to access you directly."

"Of course you did. Well done."

"Yes sir. Now that you've been informed, sir, I need to go."

"Right. Off you go, Rudnar," Devin tapped his fingers, staring off into space for a moment. Imin waited patiently.

"Will that be all sir?"

"Not yet, Imin. What's the code for CIC, or

fleet command, base command, whatever it's called?"

Imin tapped it out on the pad and helped Devin make the call.

"Captain DeWilliams, who's speaking?"

"This is Tribune Devin," Devin said. "Check your authorization link."

"Pardon, Tribune. We're not used to receiving commands directly from the base commander."

"Well, you'll be receiving them directly from me from now on. Do you have a contact at—" Devin read off the information from the screen. "At these co-ordinates?"

"Sir, I do. How do you know that?"

"I'm the base commander. I know everything. Get a flotilla of escorts. Fueled up with enough supplies to chase it to the border. Get them en route and then report back."

"Sir."

Devin closed the call. "What do you think, Imin?"

"Strange days ahead sir. Strange days."

"All right. I suppose when I've finished my meal, you have people lined up to see me?"

"Sir, I do. I'll bring them in."

Four hours later, Devin had more or less pardoned his banker and agreed to another meeting. Granted a giant loan with more tax cuts for her and her cronies. Given *Collingwood*'s commander a field promotion and sent her and her deputy off to work with Dirk. Ratified a surrender agreement with Santana that would take the Marines from the station here and ship them out to the periphery, where they could engage with smaller ships in pirate hunting operations.

He commed Santana. "How did you convince them to go out to the middle of nowhere and chase pirates?"

Imperial Legionary

"I didn't have to convince them at all," Santana said. "As soon as I told them they didn't have to bring any of them back alive, they had more volunteers that I could use. I wouldn't want to be a pirate in the Verge sector right now."

"Well, something good came out of this anyway. Do you have enough escort ships?"

"Same deal," Santana said. "We picked up some of the smaller ones. There's a number of fleet personnel who don't like you very much, don't like the Empire very much, but hate pirates more. They're perfectly willing to go on an extended pirate hunting tour, provided we give them the tools to finish the job."

"Give them all the tools they need. Is Duke Friedel with you?"

"He is."

"Send him back here. I need to talk to him, and as many of his crew as he wants to bring with him. Make sure that Miss Ruger-Gascoigne is included with that."

"Yes sir. I believe she's already back at the station. She had an appointment with your steward, Imin."

"He's teaching her how to cook?"

"They're cooking up something."

"Very well. I'm meeting most of the somewhat important folks who are left on the station tomorrow for lunch. I expect you to be there looking all Marine-y. Wear your decorations."

"Sir."

"Very well."

Devin's intercom buzzed again.

"We'll have more work for your people shortly, Santana. Don't let them get soft."

"Already scheduled the training sir."

Devin clicked off and clicked on a new line.

"Yes?"

It was Rudnar's voice.

"Sir, best you call the CIC about those escorts."

"Very well."

Devin clicked off, laboriously typed in the line for the main station CIC code.

"CIC. Yes, Tribune?"

"Captain, what is the status of the escorts dispatched after that bogey?"

"Sir, the escorts claim that it is a Union of Nations ship."

"I see. Does that match the warbook?"

"Sir, we haven't—"

"You need to scan it against the warbook. Make sure they have the latest one. They do have the latest one, don't they?"

"Sir, I'm not up to date on—"

"Same with their scans. They won't be able to tell. Have them repeat their scans here and have our people look at it."

"Sir, the bogey has left the system. The captain has been requesting permission to follow."

"Get the commander of that escort on the line."

That took a long time. The escort was far away, so the light-speed delay was considerable, but eventually, Devin got his report, delivered laboriously in back and forth questions.

"Visuals seem to indicate a Union of Nations scout ship and a diplomatic courier. Scans are inconclusive. However, we have good telemetry on where they're going, and I'm concerned about the presence of Union of Nations warships this close to our main base and this far away from the periphery. Request permission to pursue, and jump in pursuit."

Devin listened for a moment. Wonderful. An empire in revolt. Rebellion. Broken ships. Disloyal crews. Partially loyal crews. Loyal crews that were burned out. And now this—one more thing.

"Permission granted," Devin said. "Jump."

Want to find out what happens next? Follow the further adventures of Dirk and Company in *the next in the series*. Want a free prequel in the Jump Space Universe? *Get your free ebook*. Liked the book and want to tell your friends? *Leave a review here.*

Books by Andrew Moriarty

Adventures of a Jump Space Accountant

1. Trans Galactic Insurance
2. Orbital Claims Adjustor
3. Third Moon Chemicals
4. A Corporate Coup
5. The Jump Ship
6. The Military Advisors
7. Revolt in the Palace

Decline and Fall of the Galactic Empire

1. Imperial Deserter
2. Imperial Smuggler
3. Imperial Mercenary
4. Imperial Hijacker
5. Imperial Privateer
6. Imperial Raider

Join my mailing list and get a free ebook

Thanks for reading. I hope you enjoyed it. Word-of-mouth reviews are critical to independent authors. Please consider leaving a review on Amazon or Goodreads or wherever you purchased this book.

If you'd like to be notified of future releases, please join my mailing list. I send a few updates a year, and if you subscribe you get a free ebook copy of *Sigma Draconis IV*, a short novella in the Jake Stewart universe. You can also follow me on Amazon, or follow me on BookBub, or even follow me on Goodreads or Facebook!

Andrew Moriarty

ABOUT THE AUTHOR

Andrew Moriarty has been reading science fiction his whole life, and he always wondered about the stories he read. How did they ever pay the mortgage for that spaceship? Why doesn't it ever need to be refueled? What would happen if it broke, but the parts were backordered for weeks? And why doesn't anybody ever have to charge sales tax? Despairing on finding the answers to these questions, he decided to write a book about how spaceships would function in the real world. Ships need fuel, fuel costs money, and the accountants run everything.

He was born in Canada, and has lived in Toronto, Vancouver, Los Angeles, Germany, Park City, and Maastricht. Previously he worked as a telephone newspaper subscriptions salesman, a pizza delivery driver, a wedding disc jockey, and a technology trainer. Unfortunately, he also spent a great deal of time in the IT industry, designing networks and configuring routers and switches. Along the way, he picked up an ex-spy with a predilection for French Champagne, and a whippet with a murderous possessiveness for tennis balls. They live together in Brooklyn.

Please buy his books. Tennis balls are expensive.